The Cult of Venus

Templars and the
Ancient Goddess

A Novel by
David S. Brody

Eyes That See Publishing

Praise for Books in this Series

"Brody does a terrific job of wrapping his research in a fast-paced thrill ride."
—PUBLISHERS WEEKLY

"Rich and scope and vividly engrossing."
—MIDWEST BOOK REVIEW

"A comparison to *The Da Vinci Code* and *National Treasure* is inevitable....The story rips the reader into a fast-paced adventure."
—FRESH FICTION

"A treat to read....If you are a fan of Templar history you will find this book very pleasing."
—KNIGHT TEMPLAR MAGAZINE

"An excellent historical conspiracy thriller. It builds on its most famous predecessor, *The Da Vinci Code*, and takes it one step farther—and across the Atlantic."
—MYSTERY BOOK NEWS

"A rousing adventure. Highly recommended to all Dan Brown and Michael Crichton fans."
—READERS' FAVORITE BOOK REVIEW

"The year is early, but this book will be hard to beat; it's already on my 'Best of' list."
—BARYON REVIEW

To the Strong Women in My Life

Renee
Allie
Kimberly
Irene
Jeanne

One cannot be surrounded by strong, independent and powerful women without beginning to question the whole idea of male primacy. The next question then becomes inevitable: How is it that we in Western society ended up worshipping a God who is 100% male?

About the Author

David S. Brody is a *Boston Globe* bestselling fiction writer named Boston's "Best Local Author" by the *Boston Phoenix* newspaper. A graduate of Tufts University and Georgetown Law School, he is a former Director of the New England Antiquities Research Association (NEARA) and is a dedicated researcher in the field of pre-Columbian exploration of America. He has appeared as a guest expert on documentaries airing on History Channel, Travel Channel, PBS and Discovery Channel, as well as the *Coast to Coast AM* radio show.

All six prior books in his *Templars in America* Series have been Amazon Kindle Top 10 Bestsellers in their category, with three titles reaching #1.

The Cult of Venus is his tenth novel.

For more information, please visit
DavidBrodyBooks.com

Also by the Author

Unlawful Deeds

Blood of the Tribe

The Wrong Abraham

The "Templars in America" Series

Cabal of the Westford Knight: Templars at the Newport Tower (Book 1)

Thief on the Cross: Templar Secrets in America (Book 2)

Powdered Gold: Templars and the American Ark of the Covenant (Book 3)

The Oath of Nimrod: Giants, MK-Ultra and the Smithsonian Coverup (Book 4)

The Isaac Question: Templars and the Secret of the Old Testament (Book 5)

Echoes of Atlantis: Crones, Templars and the Lost Continent (Book 6)

Note to Readers

1. **The artifacts and sites pictured in this novel are real. While the story is fiction, the sites and artifacts used to tell it are authentic. See Author's Note at end of book for detailed information regarding sites and artifacts.**

2. **Though this is the seventh book in the series, it is a stand-alone story. Readers who have not read the first six should feel free to jump right in. The summary below provides some basic background for new readers:**

Cameron Thorne, age 42, is an attorney/historian whose passion is researching sites and artifacts that indicate the presence in America of European explorers prior to Columbus. His wife, Amanda Spencer-Gunn, is a former British museum curator who moved to the U.S. from England while in her mid-twenties and shares his research passion; she has a particular expertise in the history of the medieval Knights Templar. They reside in Westford, Massachusetts, a suburb northwest of Boston. Newly married, they have recently adopted a twelve-year-old girl named Astarte. Cam and Amanda are part of a growing community of researchers investigating early exploration of North America.

Prologue

Astarte took a deep breath and focused on the face, her face, staring back at her from the screen of her smart phone. The same chestnut skin, the same cobalt eyes, the same high cheekbones and pointed chin that looked back at her every day in the mirror. But today the face looked so serious.

Not that it really mattered what she looked like. It mattered what she said. Mrs. Witaski promised that nobody would ever see these videos, that she would save them and return them to the class in five years, right before graduation. The assignment was for the students to describe the biggest challenges in their lives. Later they could look back and see how they had faced them. Astarte doubted other kids would be talking about the kinds of things she would be.

She pushed her hair back, sighed again, and, glancing down at the script she had prepared, pressed record:

My name is Astarte, and I just turned 12 years old.

Fact: My parents are trailblazing historians, working to uncover the true history of North America.

Fact: My parents are fools, taking rumor and legend and believing it to be true history.

I do not know which statement is correct, although I understand both cannot be. And therefore I do not know how my story will end. But I do know that they love me. Even if that may not be enough.

The problem is that I have a destiny. My people, the Mandan Native Americans, know me as the Fortieth Princess. They have been waiting 40 generations for my arrival, for me to come of age, for me to (and I have heard these words so many times that they ring in my head like an alarm clock that won't turn off) "reunite the people of the world in a religion worshiping the Mother Goddess." I descend from almost all the Western world's great religious leaders—King David, Jesus, Mohammed—and also from Cleopatra and Joseph Smith and a long line of Native American chieftesses. My uncle said I have more royal blood in my veins than anyone who has ever lived. But perhaps he is just as much a fool as some say my parents are.

My uncle is dead now. So is my real mother, and also my father. Cameron and Amanda are my adopted parents. Like I said, they love me. But I'm not sure they understand that my destiny makes me unlike other kids. I can't just go to school and get good grades and play sports. And they need to be more careful with their research. If important people in this country think their ideas are crazy, what are they going to think about me, their daughter? "Oh, she's loony just like her parents."

But I'm not. I know what the prophecy says. I know what my destiny is. I know what I have to do. What I don't know is, can I do it?

Chapter 1

Westford, Massachusetts
March, Present Day

Katherine Morville skidded her older model Corolla around the tight turn of the highway exit ramp, the chassis shaking and moaning from the torque. She glanced up quickly at the rearview mirror. Two headlights, like the eyes of some relentless Jurassic predator, bore down on her. As they had for the past hour. That they had followed her off the exit confirmed this was not merely her imagination.

What did they want with her? She gripped the steering wheel, blinking away the tears, her eyes throbbing from the exertion of the ordeal. She had been so close, driving over a thousand miles, her old car bravely surviving what was supposed to be a leisurely road trip. Maybe they had been following her from the beginning.

"Shit," she said, as the cultured British voice of her GPS calmly instructed her to take a left off the exit ramp. Too late. She'd flip the car if she tried to make that turn. An all-night Mobil station loomed fifty yards up the road. Maybe the wrong turn could be put to good use.

She glanced back again. The top-heavy SUV in pursuit had slowed, taking the exit ramp at a safer speed. Rational, calculating, confident in knowing its prey could not escape. But it might give her the few seconds she needed.

Screeching into the empty gas station lot, she slammed the car to a halt next to the station entryway. She was out the door, a leather rucksack in one arm, even before the Corolla stopped bouncing from its violent stop. With only seconds before the SUV closed on her, she dropped the pack into a garbage can next to the entrance and covered it with a newspaper. Back in the car, as fast as her stiff, sixty-year-old legs could carry her, she accelerated out of the gas station lot and reversed course, toward the exit ramp. As she sped away, the SUV spotted her, executed a neat U-turn, and resumed its unrelenting pursuit.

She exhaled. They might get her, but they would not get the rucksack. She floored the gas pedal, racing through the sleepy streets of suburban Boston, wondering how a divorcée from Iowa had ended up a thousand miles from home, stalked by a demonic SUV.

Cameron Thorne awoke with a start, the buzzing from his cell phone cutting through a dream. The same dream, in fact, that he often had: Standing in some heaven-like cloud, he had been given the opportunity to question any historical figure in world history. All he had to do was ring a bell—an antique brass call bell, like the ones used to summon a hotel clerk—and announce their name. But his hands would not move, and his voice would not speak. As his frustration, and then his anger, grew, the cloud washed over him, the bell disappeared, and the opportunity vanished. At least the dream confirmed he had chosen wisely in paring back his law practice and focusing more of his time on historical research and teaching. He never once dreamt about the law.

He fumbled for the phone as Amanda stirred next to him. His clock radio, a vestige from his college days in the nineties, read 2:15 AM. Adrenaline surged through his body, the dream forgotten. A cold fear gripped him. Phone calls in the middle of the night were never good news.

The display on the phone read "Iowa," with a number Cam did not recognize. He stabbed at the answer button. "This is Cam."

"Thank God you picked up." The words came fast and breathless, the voice that of a woman, echoing as if on a speaker phone. "I have something I have to give you. But they're chasing me! Oh, God, they're trying to kill me—"

"Wait, who?"

"Please, just listen." A screech of tires interrupted the rush of words. "I'm here in Westford. I have journals. Prince Henry's journals. They've been in my family for generations. I was told you'd know what to do with them. I drove all day." Amanda sat up; Cam motioned her to stay quiet as the woman spoke even faster. "I dumped them in a garbage can at the Mobil station off the highway. I didn't know what else to do. Oh God!"

The line went dead. Cam stared at it for a second, as if it might have answers. Was the woman really in danger? He dialed 911 and explained the strange call, without mentioning the journals. "Can you find her location based on her cell number?" He read it off. "I think she's in trouble."

"What in bloody hell is going on?" Amanda asked.

He slapped his cheeks to push the last vestiges of slumber away. "This woman claims to have Prince Henry's journals. And she hid them in a garbage can." It sounded silly, he knew. But she sounded sincere. Or at least sincerely frightened.

"What are you going to do?"

He swung his legs out of bed and grabbed a pair of jeans. "Drive down to that gas station."

"Do you think she really has 600-year-old journals?"

He bit his lip. "Who knows? But I can't let them go out with the trash."

Cam's mind raced even faster than he drove. He and Amanda had spent the past six years researching—and largely validating—the legend of Scottish explorer Prince Henry Sinclair crossing the Atlantic to explore New England a century before Columbus. Sinclair, so the legend went, ended up on a high hill in Westford, Massachusetts, 25 miles inland, where one of his knights, Sir James Gunn, died. Cam ascended that hill now, pushing the speed limit in the dark, still night. He whipped past a monument marking the spot where Sinclair's men had carved an effigy into the rock ledge as a grave marker for their comrade. The carving, known as the Westford Knight, had faded over the centuries, but a rubbing of the rock face from decades ago clearly showed the knight's head, shoulders, shield and sword. And the pommel, cross guard and blade of the sword remained readily visible:

Westford Knight Sword and Rubbing

Amanda was a direct descendent of Gunn, the carving in fact the reason she had first visited Westford. As he always did, Cam gave a quick salute, thanking the medieval knight for bringing Amanda to him. And now a woman claimed to have journals which might prove the expedition conclusively.

Police lights flashed ahead, not far from the Town Common. Cam slowed. A white sedan rested on its roof in the opposite lane near a fork in the road, tottering as first responders worked to free the driver. Cam's chest tightened. Even upside down, the black letters of the license plate jumped out at him: "IOWA." Matching the caller ID.

He opened his window to the cold March air as he cruised past the scene, his eyes searching the driver's seat area. He made out a middle-aged woman, crumpled, upside-down, her face bloodied but her visage surprisingly calm. She managed a slight nod. Or perhaps it was his imagination. He looked away. He could do nothing for her. Not here, at least.

Going as fast as he dared around the Common, Cam raced toward the commercial strip along the highway. He pictured the Iowa woman traveling the other direction, only minutes earlier, frightened and desperate, pouring her story out to Cam as some unknown adversary pursued her. She must have raced off the highway exit and ditched the journals in the first place she could find. But not long after, apparently with Cam on the line, they had caught her again. He shook his head in an effort to clear away the memory of the sedan on its roof.

The neon Mobil sign loomed in the distance, the red "o" like the eye of some feral scavenger. He was going to be the scavenger tonight, digging through the trash.

After killing the engine, he jumped from the car and raised the hood in such a way as to shield his activities from anyone watching from inside the convenience store. Moving furtively, he slid the top off the trash receptacle wedged between the gas pumps. A motor oil bottle and a Milky Way wrapper rested on top. He nudged them aside and dug his hand in, probing for a solid mass of paper. Nothing.

Did he have the wrong spot? Or could the pursuers have circled back and retrieved the documents? Cursing, he looked around. *There.* Another garbage can, by the front door. He ambled over, ignoring a candy wrapper blowing in the wind at his feet. Nestled on top of the trash, partially covered by a copy of the local newspaper, sat a brown leather satchel bag, the type of thing he used to use in his lawyer days to carry thick client files. He hesitated before grabbing it—a voice in his head told him this could be important, that secrecy was paramount. Fighting the temptation just to snatch the bag, he went into the all-night station, walked to the back of the store and grabbed a Diet Coke from the fridge. "Hey," he said to the clerk, "that fridge is making a funny buzzing noise." The clerk waited for Cam to exit, then shuffled back to check out the buzz. The station lot was empty.

Cam reached in and grabbed the satchel. As he did so, an ambulance, sirens blaring, raced by, toward the Town Common.

He exhaled, his eyes following the lights until they disappeared around a bend. He held the bag against his chest with two hands. "I hope it was worth it, whoever you are."

Katherine Morville felt nothing as the dark-eyed fireman with the nice smile worked to pull her from her car. No pain, no anxiety. And best of all, no fear. Nothing. Even as the blood gushed down the side of her face and her arm hung bent at an unnatural angle—just nothing.

It was the best she had felt in almost a year.

Which said a lot about her life. Broke. Divorced. Estranged from her daughter. Obsessed with the legends of her ancestors. The highlight of her year was a feeling of numbness after flipping her car.

But at least the journals were safe. She had seen Cameron Thorne drive past, locked her eyes on his. He would retrieve the journals. He would know what to do with them. He would validate them and tell the world of her selfless act, of her small but crucial role in preserving the Sinclair legacy. Then, finally, her daughter might find something to admire in her, something to esteem in what had otherwise been the utterly meritless existence of Katherine Prudence Morville.

She exhaled and allowed the handsome firefighter to lift her, to carry her—finally—from the wreckage that had become her life.

Jamila Bashear sat in the rotunda on the top floor of the main branch of the New York Public Library, her bony, liver-spotted hands clenched in the lap of her long amber dress. She stared at the four massive murals which dominated the space. "What an absolute load of camel dung," she hissed, in a voice louder than she would have used in her younger days. A couple of overnight janitors spun and stared—even in New York, people, especially old women, rarely cursed in a loud voice in a library. But she had paid a queen's ransom to have the library opened for her in the middle of the night. And at 86 years of age, she didn't care who heard her. Especially because she was correct in her assessment.

The murals depicted four seminal events in the advent of the written word. Not an inappropriate theme for the public library in the world's most important city, she conceded. She examined the four in turn once again: Moses receiving the Ten Commandments; a medieval monk transcribing sacred text; Guttenberg printing his Bible; the typesetting machine allowing for the mass production of newspapers. Jamila loved to read. But these events, singularly and especially in the aggregate, had been a disaster for humankind.

A buzz signaling an incoming text interrupted her musings. "It is done," read the simple message. She blinked and nodded to herself, fingering the silver palm-shaped Hamsa amulet hanging from her neck, and then returned to the wall paintings.

She viewed the four murals yet again—two on one wall, two on the opposite. Her anger grew. She counted 13 people portrayed in the murals. Not a single one was a female. A coincidence? She thought not. She knew not.

The truth, and a truth that very few people understood, was that the written word was the enemy of women. Not every word, and not every woman, but in broad terms this reality was undeniable. In the history of the world, almost every human culture had worshipped the Goddess. Until the advent of the alphabet. The alphabet was like kryptonite to the Goddess—in its aftermath she turned powerless and weak and frail. Did the written word kill the Goddess, or did rejection of the Goddess lead to veneration of the written word? Jamila had no idea. And it didn't matter. The two were inexorably related. The Goddess and the alphabet had never coexisted.

She again clenched her fists. Throughout history the people who had burned books, who had tried to suppress knowledge, had been the very people she despised. The very people who worshipers of the Goddess considered the enemy. But perhaps the book burners had it right all along. Right for the wrong reasons, but right nonetheless.

Jamila exhaled. She used to think she had figured it all out. Now, in her ninth decade, she realized how little she knew. The book-burners were the good guys? No. But perhaps not the enemy either.

The truth was undeniable. Every culture in the history of mankind which had adopted the alphabet had simultaneously rejected the Goddess. The good, kind, just Goddess.

Amanda Spencer-Gunn didn't even try to go back to sleep. The middle of the night phone call felt like the trigger to another of Cam's and her adventures, which she expected would bring both intrigue and danger. She could do without the danger, but the intrigue was one of intoxicating things about her life with Cam.

Using her phone, she tracked Cam's journey first through town and, now, on his way home, using back roads. It was hard to tell for certain, but it seemed like he was driving fast. Which probably meant he had retrieved these mysterious journals and was anxious to examine them. She didn't plan to miss it.

She checked on Astarte in the adjoining bedroom, Venus curled into the nook of her arm, the Lab's tawny snout peaking out from beneath the blanket. Astarte snored lightly, the hint of a young woman visible on her face and in the curves of her body beneath the sheets. Now twelve, she had been living with them for four years. The adoption had finally gone through, making the arrangement not just legal, but permanent. In Amanda's heart it had always been so, from the first time the girl wrapped her arms around Amanda's neck as a scared and lonely eight-year-old.

Amanda warmed some milk for hot chocolate and nestled under a blanket on the couch to wait for Cam. For years they had been trying to find conclusive proof validating Prince Henry's journey. It made perfect sense to Amanda—Henry's Scandinavian ancestors (though he lived in Scotland, he was a Norseman on his mother's side) had been island-hopping their way across the North Atlantic for centuries before him, beginning with Leif Ericson. Why wouldn't they have continued these voyages, profiting from the plentiful furs and fish and timber of the New World? It would have been more surprising if they had *stopped* coming. Yet the Columbus 1492 date served as some kind of psychological barrier to most American historians, no matter how much evidence and common sense was piled up against it. It would take some kind of smoking gun, she and Cam agreed, finally to swing the argument. The Sinclair family journals, if they could be validated, would do the trick.

She checked Cam's location again. Still five minutes away. To kill time she resumed reading a magazine article she had started. A woman hiker had stumbled upon a Tanit figure—an ancient triangular Goddess symbol—in the Catskill Mountains. Other Goddess figurines had, according to the article, been found scattered around New England. The Native Americans engaged in their own form of Goddess worship, but these particular figurines resembled those found around the Mediterranean. The question was an obvious one: Had ancient, seafaring, Goddess worshipers brought the artifacts across the Atlantic? These were the kinds of finds that pointed to a long history of trans-Atlantic travel. And the types of things mainstream historians tended to ignore.

The headlights of Cam's car interrupted her reading. She mixed the hot chocolate and met Cam at the door, a leather satchel she had never seen before tucked under one of his arms. She tossed her hair playfully and pulled her night shirt up high on her thigh. "Want to show me your journal collection?"

He kissed her, trembling at the contact of their lips. But she sensed it was from distress rather than her exposed thigh. "Cam, what's wrong?"

"I think that woman had a bad accident. They really did run her off the road."

She took his hand, led him to the kitchen table and handed him a hot mug. He explained the upside down sedan and ambulance. "Iowa plates."

She lowered her mug. "No bloody chance that's a coincidence."

"Especially after the woman on the phone told me someone was chasing her."

She returned to the front door, made sure it was locked, and put all the outside lights on. In the ten seconds it took her to do so, she had reached a simple conclusion. "Whoever was chasing that woman must have believed the journals were real. The question is, why did they want to stop her?" *And had they given up the chase?*

Cam nodded and held up the brown satchel. "I'm guessing the answers are in here."

He began to dig in, then stopped. "Maybe you should video this. If these are real, we should document every step."

Amanda nodded and plugged her phone in. "Cam making history. Take 1." She wanted to lighten the mood. She understood Cam's concern about the woman, but these journals were potentially history-changing. They should enjoy the moment.

He smiled, relaxing a bit. "Maybe I should comb my hair first."

She shook her head. "No, I'd fancy you didn't." She liked Cam like this, rugged and disheveled and, well, just real. A man and a woman sharing a life together, on a quest, exploring an ancient mystery. Others could have their dinner parties and vacation homes and fancy cars. She'd sign up for this gig a thousand times over.

Phone mounted opposite him, he unclipped the heavy brass clasp and opened the flap. A musty, animal-like smell escaped. "Smells like my baseball glove when I left it out in the rain," he said. Laying the pouch flat on the table, he slid out an oversized Ziploc bag containing a dark tome the size of a small coffee table book, but much thicker. He smoothed the plastic down as they both stared. The book looked antique, brown leather matching the satchel. Ornate brass plates, inlaid with red jewels, decorated the four corners of the cover. In the center, a family crest had been sewn into the leather. Though now faded, the crest was still familiar to both Cam and Amanda—a scalloped Templar cross framed by a shield, with a knight's helmet sitting atop. The Sinclair coat of arms.

"Should I open it?" Cam asked in a whisper. "Maybe it needs to stay sealed."

"From the smell of that bag, I gather it has been sitting in there, unsealed, for quite a spell. I think it's safe to open." She stood. "But wait a second."

She retrieved a pair of cotton gloves she used at her job as a local museum curator and handed them to Cam. After sliding them on, he slowly broke the seal on the plastic bag. This smell was different than the wet leather of the satchel. "This smells like when I used to do work in the Registry of Deeds," Cam said. "The old records books, going back hundreds of years." Careful not to damage the book, he pulled the plastic back to free the tome.

"It looks like something the Grimm Brothers would write their fairy tales in," Amanda said. She half-expected pixie dust to fly from its pages. "It really is exquisite." Out of the pouch, the jewels sparkled and the fine grain of the leather became visible.

A brass clasp held the book closed. Cam snapped it open and lifted the cover. Bold Latin lettering greeted them on the first page. Cam, who knew Latin, translated the sweeping script: "It says, *Journal of the Family Sinclair. May it please the Goddess.* And there's a date in Roman numerals, 1354."

"The Goddess? What's that all about?"

Cam shrugged. "That's what it says." He peered closer and reread the word. "*Dea.* The masculine is *Deus.* This definitely says *Dea.* Goddess."

Amanda chewed her lip. The medieval Church was one of the most male-dominated and patriarchal institutions in world history. To be anything less than an orthodox Christian could put one on the wrong side of the brutally barbaric Inquisition. Yet here was a leading family paying homage to the Goddess. Not to God or to Jesus or even to the Virgin Mary. To the Goddess. This was the family that a century later built Roslyn Chapel and filled it with pagan iconography, but even that structure was careful not to elevate any of the pagan imagery over Jesus. What was going on here? And did this in any way tie into the Goddess figurines scattered around New England she had been reading about?

Cam interrupted her musings, his brow furrowed. "There's something wrong with the date. The '4' is written with four 'I' letters in a row; it should be one 'I' followed by a 'V.'

"Actually, either is correct. We had an antique clock when I was a lass. Four o'clock was marked the same as written here. One day I looked it up—not everyone used the 'IV' for four. Apparently Roman numerals were not standardized until modern times."

"Interesting. Would a modern hoaxster know that?"

Amanda chewed her lip again, a habit she had long given up trying to break. That was the question with these kinds of finds: There was always the chance it was a hoax or folly. They would need to get the paper carbon-dated and the ink tested. Even then, the possibility of a sophisticated forgery could not be eliminated—ancient parchment could be purchased on the antiquities markets in Europe and the Middle East, and medieval ink could be produced using ancient recipes. But to what end? Who would go through the significant cost and effort? So far, at least, the journals had only brought danger— not profit or fame or other benefit—to its owner. And why would a hoaxster call the whole thing into question with a dedication to the Goddess?

Cam carefully leafed through the pages as she leaned in. Some of the handwriting was neat, some little more than a scrawl with many cross-outs and rough notations. The early notations were in Latin. "It looks like every generation of the family recorded entries." He pointed. "Some are just one line. But some go on for pages." He slowly turned the pages, their faces together and their eyes wide. A few entries contained maps drawn on the pages. Cam stopped at one. "That looks like the coast of New England."

She pointed to the year and smiled. "1398." The year they would have left for America.

Cam returned her smile and continued turning the dry, stiff pages. "Starting in the 1600s, the language changes to English."

"That makes sense. In the late medieval period, very few people were literate. Those that were usually were nobility, trained by the clergy to write in Latin. But by the 17th century literacy had become widespread."

Cam flipped toward the middle of the codex. "This is the last entry. Dated 1770."

"Can you read it?"

He shook his head. "The handwriting is really tough." He laughed. "I'd actually rather read the Latin." He closed the book and said teasingly as he began to stand, "Besides, don't you know it's poor form to skip to the end of a book?"

She nodded. "All right then. Let's' go back to the 1398 entry. If it says they crossed the Atlantic, I want to know about it. Now."

"Okay." He sat and reopened the book. "Let's read about 1398."

Cam lay awake in bed later that morning, a Saturday. He had been unable to get back to sleep after they stayed up examining the codex until past four AM. He had translated the 1398 entry, the one with the map, and it confirmed the Sinclair journey to North America. If authentic, it was the proof they had been looking for.

By five-thirty the early glow of the equinox dawn beckoned him. He did his best thinking during morning jogs, the quiet and solitude allowing his brain to analyze and organize his thoughts. Today, lost in consideration of the codex and what the contents might reveal, he barely remembered circling the lake in a five-mile loop. He smiled. If the journals were as captivating as he expected them to be, maybe he'd run that marathon he'd often considered.

But before they could fully dive into the journals, there was a loose end he needed to tie up. After checking his blood sugar levels, he showered quickly and grabbed a banana and breakfast bar for the car. Astarte staggered into the kitchen before he could go upstairs to kiss her goodbye. She was twelve, the same age he had been when first diagnosed with juvenile diabetes. It had been a dark time for a kid addicted to sports and candy bars. Back in the 1980s, before recent medical breakthroughs, the conventional wisdom was that most diabetics would be blind, if not dead, by the time they reached their forties. He had fought his way through it, and today it barely impacted his daily existence, but even so he was thankful Astarte did not have to deal with it or any other medical condition. Of course, the whole orphan thing was no fun either.

"Good morning, pumpkin."

She yawned and leaned into him for a hug. "Were you and Mum up late last night? I saw the lights on."

"Long story. I'll be back in an hour. Have some breakfast and I'll tell you all about it."

Retracing his path from the night before, he drove to the police station near the Town Common. He slowed as he passed the accident scene, an oil stain on the pavement, a gash on an oak tree and some broken red shards of plastic on the shoulder of the road the only evidence of the flipped sedan. He wondered how the woman was.

The station was quiet at seven o'clock on a Saturday morning. He explained why he was there. "I'd like to talk to the detective working on this case."

A minute later he was buzzed through the security door. Somehow he was not surprised to see his old Pop Warner football coach, Sergeant Poulos, ready to greet him on the other side of the door. It seemed like every time Cam and Amanda ran into trouble, Poulos was assigned to the case. He smiled at Cam, his jowls fleshier and hair grayer than Cam remembered. But the blue eyes looked at Cam the same way, with that old combination of wariness and warmth, as if to say, "I know you're bullshitting me, but I like you anyway." If he only knew.

"Cameron Thorne. I sort of expected you earlier."

Cam nodded. "Of course. You saw my 911 call."

"Yup. Why is it that trouble seems to circle around you like flies to horseshit?"

He said it with a smile, so Cam took no offense. "Maybe I need new cologne."

"Come on in."

"How's the woman in the sedan?"

Poulos led Cam to a conference room and sat down heavily. Cam guessed he was beyond retirement age, but seemed like the type of guy who would go crazy without a reason to get out of bed every day. "She didn't make it. The crash basically collapsed her chest cavity."

"Oh." Cam exhaled. Were the journals really so important that someone had to die? And if so, did that mean he and his family were in danger? "Any idea what's going on?"

"Not a clue. You said she called you just before she got run off the road. Did you know her?"

"I don't think so. At least I didn't recognize the number. And I don't think I know anyone from Iowa."

"Her name is Katherine Morville. That help?"

Cam shrugged. "Sorry."

"So why did she call you?"

"Why did she call me?" The words poured out before Cam could stop them. As a lawyer, he knew, and he suspected Poulos did also, that repeating a question back was one of the surest 'tells' someone was buying time to figure out a proper answer. Usually an untrue one at that. He would need to up his game.

Poulos' eyes narrowed. "Yes, why did she call you?"

Cam wasn't ready to give up the journals, at least not yet. He lowered his arms to his sides, leaned forward and made sure to keep his eyes wide and unblinking. This kind of body language conveyed openness, honesty. "Her call woke me. She said she wanted to meet. It was urgent. Information about Prince Henry Sinclair."

Poulos grunted. "Oh. That again."

Cam continued. "She said men were chasing her. I heard a screech of tires. Then the line went dead and I called 911 right away." He handed Poulos his phone. "You can see her call come in, then my call to 911 right after."

Poulos scrolled through the call log, snapping pictures with his own phone. "Continue."

"So I drove toward the town center. I thought maybe I'd see her."

The sergeant leaned forward. "In the middle of the night? When you knew guys were chasing her?"

Cam shrugged. "I had called you already." He smiled sheepishly. "And, you know, the Westford Knight."

Poulos grunted again. Many people in town believed the Knight legend and liked the attention it brought to Westford. Others thought it was bunk. "So what next?"

"I passed the accident, saw the Iowa plates, figured it was her. The ambulance was already there. So I circled the block and came home." He doubted they'd have reason to check the security cameras at the gas station. Holding up his hands to the sky, he concluded, "And here I am."

"So you never actually met with her?"

"No."

"Have no idea why she wanted to meet?"

"Other than it had to do with Prince Henry Sinclair, no."

Poulos tapped his pen on the table. Cam took the opportunity to ask some questions of his own. "What do you know? Any idea who killed her?"

"We have some security camera footage from the Roudenbush Center up the street a bit." Cam was glad he had taken the back roads home, otherwise he might have shown up on the same camera—ten minutes later than he should have had he simply circled the block. Poulos continued. "The camera shows a dark SUV in pursuit of her sedan. They were going pretty fast, maybe 60. We think the SUV spun her up at the fork, sent her sideways into a tree. Old car, no air bags."

"No air bags?"

"Car was a '96 Corolla. Airbags weren't mandatory until '98."

Cam knew some people who drove 20-year-old cars, but they tended to be nostalgia buffs or teenagers. Why would a middle-aged woman drive such an old car halfway across the country? It must have been important to her. "Can you track the SUV?"

"We're working on it. The camera didn't get the plate. We think there were two female occupants, maybe a third in the backseat."

"Female?" Cam replayed the phone conversation in his mind. The woman had never said 'men,' though Cam had pictured men chasing her.

Poulos shrugged. "Probably not road rage. Way over ninety percent of road rage incidents are men."

"So some kind of, what, female hit team?"

He shrugged again. "Could be. Or maybe they just wanted something from the car."

Cam pushed his chair back. The longer he stayed, the bigger the risk he would trip over his lie. "If you find out anything more, can you let me know?"

Poulos leaned back, studying Cam as if across a poker table, probably wondering if he should question Cam further. Apparently he decided to wait until the pot got richer to press his advantage. "Sure thing. I'll let you know. But, Cameron, it's a two-way street, don't forget."

Jamila sat in the back of the BMW X5 SUV, fingering her Hamsa amulet, the hand of the Goddess. In ancient times it was worn to ward off the evil eye. Today, with an all seeing-eye centered in the palm, it symbolized the wisdom of women.

Her young apprentice, Nicolette, patiently awaited instructions from the driver's seat. They were still in Manhattan, the morning sun beginning to glow on the eastern horizon, the yellow-orange dawn matching the cape Jamila now wore over her amber dress. She had not slept after her night studying the murals in the library. At her age, there was no guarantee that once you closed your eyes you'd ever open them again.

Instead of instructions, Jamila offered a history lesson. "Many American cities are built with a street grid that allows residents to mark the spring and fall equinoxes. In Chicago and Baltimore, for example, one can look down any east-west boulevard on the equinoxes and see the sun rising at the far end. And, of course, the same effect can be seen while standing at the U.S. Capital and looking at the Washington Monument. If you do the research, you'll find in most cases this was done on purpose. Sun worship is in our DNA. We instinctively sense that, without it, there would be no life."

"What about New York?" Nicolette asked. "I've seen pictures of people looking down 42nd Street, watching the sun rise and set between the skyscrapers."

The girl had the type of face that men found irresistible—a full mouth, wide eyes, high cheekbones and modest nose, all framed by a mane of thick blond hair. And she possessed a quick and curious mind. Soon Jamila would use Nicolette's beauty, along with her mind and military training, to their advantage. Just as Jamila had used her own beauty when she was younger. In fact, Jamila had kept her charm into her later years, still radiant into her eighties. And then fire had ravaged her face, leaving a hideously discolored pus-filled flap of what could only generously be described as sausage skin on her left cheek. The fire that had burned her then burned within her now. Her life's work had always been paramount. Now she had the added motivation of revenge to fuel her.

"No," Jamila replied. "New York's streets are not lined up east-west. You're talking about *Manhattanhenge*, when people gather in Times Square. But that is not on the equinoxes." She sat forward in her seat. "There is, however, a phenomenon here that is not found in most cities. Please head toward Brooklyn; follow those signs for FDR Drive South, then cross the Williamsburg Bridge."

"What are we going to see?"

Jamila exhaled. "Perhaps the closest thing to legalized slavery we have in the Western world. A Hassidic Jewish community."

Cam returned home from the police station to find Amanda and Astarte sitting at the kitchen table, huddled over a gray, rolled-up scroll with a string tied around it, resting in a shallow plastic container. Astarte scooped some milky cereal out of a bowl, studying the object as she chewed. She was going through a growth spurt and seemed to be always hungry. He asked the obvious question. "What's that?"

Amanda lifted her head. "I found it in the codex." She must have removed the journals from the wall safe in the pantry, hidden behind a couple of boxes of Cheerios. "A stack of the back pages were glued together, and then someone hollowed out a cavity. This was inside."

Cam peered in. He put on the museum gloves and lifted the object, which was heavier than he expected. Then he sniffed it. "That same wet leather smell."

Amanda nodded. "I was tempted to remove the string and open it."

"Maybe we shouldn't open it at all. What if we tear it?"

Amanda nodded again. She was dressed in a t-shirt and sweats, adorable even with her hair in a bun and a pair of eyeglasses resting crookedly on her nose. "I had the same thought," she said. "I know a guy from the museum who restores antique books. I called him. I'm meeting him after lunch."

Cam wasn't thrilled about other people knowing about their find, especially after lying to the police. Not to mention that someone had already been killed because of the journal. But Amanda was right, they were going to need professional help. "Okay, but let's not tell him about the codex, okay?"

"I agree. I'll just show him this, not the journals."

Astarte chimed in. "I think it looks like an eggroll that was left in the back of the fridge too long."

Cam chuckled. "You're right." He made a show of pushing the scroll away from her. "Please don't eat it."

She peered over her cereal bowl and gave him one of those middle school eye rolls. Where had his little girl gone?

Amanda rescued the moment. "I think we should call it the *eggscroll*," she said as she sealed the lid on the plastic container.

They shared a laugh, and after a few seconds Cam turned to Amanda. "I went to the police station. The woman—her name was Katherine Morville—died."

Amanda's shoulders slumped. She gestured at the codex. "Is this really worth killing over?"

"Someone thinks so."

She chewed her lip. "Wait, did you say *Morville*?"

"Yes."

"I think they were kin to the Sinclairs, going back to medieval times. If these really are the Sinclair journals, that might explain how this woman had them."

Astarte interrupted. "Can you read me the entry you translated?"

"Okay, honey." Amanda pulled up a picture she had taken on her phone. "I don't want to keep opening and closing the book if we don't have to. Here's the first page of the entry."

Astarte peered in. "It looks so ... modern, I guess."

"How so?" Amanda replied. Cam sat back, observing. He and Amanda had noticed the same thing.

Astarte said, "The handwriting. I expected something with more, like, flourishes." She shrugged. "You know, with big capital letters and fancy drawings, like the monks wrote."

"Maybe that's because monks didn't write it."

Astarte angled her head. "I think that says June 23, 1398 on top, right?"

"Yes. And Dad translated the Latin. We think this is Prince Henry writing." She smiled. "Not a monk." She flipped a page on the legal pad Cam had used the night before. She read aloud, the passages translated by Cam into modern grammar and usage:

"By the grace of the Goddess we finally depart for the western lands on the morrow. We believe the day is an auspicious one for such a journey. I am pleased that in this my fifty-third year I am able to fulfill the vow I made to my father. I pray that my son will someday do the same. The weather looks favorable for sailing and we have the provisions we need. The Venetian, Zen, will guide us. He has navigational devices and maps which show the way. Once we are close we will know our destination by the oak trees my father and his men planted. By now they should be visible from far offshore. We are late in departing—we had planned to leave on Beltane..."

Amanda paused here. "Do you know what Beltane is?"

Astarte nodded. "Halfway between the spring equinox and the summer solstice."

"Yes. So May 5. In Europe people still celebrate it as May Day. In ancient times it was considered the beginning of summer. That's when people put the livestock out to graze."

Cam jumped in. "And also took to the sea."

"One more thing," Amanda said. "Did you note the day of departure, June 24?"

Cam's eyes widened. "I had missed that. Prince Henry said it was an auspicious one." He turned to Astarte to explain. "June 24 is the birthday of John the Baptist. Some historians believe the

Knights Templar worshiped him, even over Jesus. And we know Prince Henry's grandfather was part of the Templars. So that would have been a very important date."

Astarte nodded. "Also, that's the second time Prince Henry mentions the Goddess. I thought the Templars were Christians. Wouldn't they, you know, worship Jesus? Or, like you said, John the Baptist?"

"Excellent question," Amanda replied. "Dad and I noticed the same thing last night. There was a group of early Christians called the Gnostics who were Goddess worshipers in the sense they believed Mary Magdalene was Jesus' wife, and therefore should sit next to him on the throne in heaven as the queen. The Church tried to wipe the Gnostics out, and killed most of them. But maybe Prince Henry is related to them somehow." She shrugged. "We'll need to keep reading."

Amanda continued, exhaling, as if the idea that the journal might be authentic took her breath away:

"I fear we will not be able to make a return journey before the seas fill with ice. We may need to winter over. I pray that the natives remember the friendship of my father and are welcoming to us. I bring gifts for them to show our gratitude for their hospitality and the loyalty they have shown guarding our treasures. I bring a special gift for their chief, a battle sword made of the finest steel. Joneta (I pray the Goddess will watch over her, and the young ones as well) and her ladies have woven a thick blanket made from the softest lamb's wool as a gift for the chief's wife.

We have ten ships and have spread our provisions among them in case some are lost. Our men number just over two hundred. Perhaps we do not require such a large force, but I am loath to risk being undermanned in a strange land. When it comes time to check on the treasure, then I will limit myself to only my most trusted men. Being near treasure can be like wine, making good men do bad things. I pray the Goddess keeps an especially close watch over this aspect of our mission. And I will need to keep our men of the cloth away as well, as they may believe certain items belong in Rome rather than buried across the sea."

Amanda looked up. "That's all we have so far."

"What kind of treasure?" Astarte asked.

Amanda and Cam shared a glance. They had wondered the same thing. Amanda replied, "Many historians believe the treasure of the Knights Templar ended up in Scotland, after the Order was put down in France in 1307. If so, it may be that this treasure was later brought to America for safe keeping. The question has always been, just as you asked, what kind of treasure? The first obvious choice is gold and jewels. The Templars were phenomenally wealthy, and when the King of France raided their main treasury in Paris, it was empty. Where did it all bloody go? And from what the journal says, about the men being tempted, gold and jewels seem like a good possibility." She turned to Cam to let him continue.

"But the comment about certain items belonging in Rome opens a second possibility: The Templars are believed to have found important religious artifacts and relics during their two hundred years in Jerusalem. Things like the Ark of the Covenant, the Holy Grail, maybe even the bones of Jesus. So that might be part of their treasure also."

Astarte smirked. "Wouldn't it be funny if it was something that was valuable then, but not now…?" She paused, her eyes raised in thought. "Like maybe a compass. That would have been very rare in the 14th century, but now everyone has one."

Cam nodded. He loved how Astarte's mind worked, how she was always thinking critically and looking at the many layers of a given subject. "Along the same lines as a compass would be ancient maps. Back then the ability to know how to navigate was often the difference between survival and death at sea."

Amanda weighed in. "I'd fancy a medieval compass or map. They sound like treasures to me."

"Well," Astarte said, "you can have them. I'll take the gold."

Something about the talk of treasure triggered a thought in Cam's mind. Cam had become friendly with many high-ranking Freemasons over the past few years—it seemed as if his research on pre-Columbian exploration of America always seemed to tie into Masonic history, ritual and symbolism. As he liked to put it, whenever he dove down one of the hidden rabbit holes of history, he seemed to find Freemasons already at the bottom. He had resisted joining the group only because he wanted to keep his objectivity in conducting his research. Anyway, one of his Masonic friends had said to him over lunch, "Masonry is a treasure map to the scientific and personal pursuit of the divine." If that statement was accurate, and combined with the Sinclair family's long and well-documented association with Freemasonry, was it possible the treasure was an allegorical one, a methodology to discover the secrets of the divine? He voiced his thoughts to Amanda as Astarte dropped her bowl into the dishwasher and ran off to get dressed.

Amanda bit her lip. "It's hard for me to take those Masonic chaps too seriously."

"Why?" Cam found them to be some of the most open-minded and generous people he had met.

"Well, for one thing, those silly aprons. Are they fixing to do the dishes?"

Cam smiled. "There is that."

She turned serious. "And for another, they still don't admit women members."

Cam nodded. "Which itself is pretty ironic."

"How so?"

"The guy I had lunch with is at the top level, the 33rd degree. He claims that at its core, Freemasonry is about Goddess worship."

Amanda rolled her green-blue eyes. "Well, they have a funny way of showing it. It's like the Groucho Marx line: *Why would I belong to a club that has my deity as a member?*"

Cam grinned, partly because he loved the way her cheeks blushed pink when she was outraged and partly because he appreciated her humorous jab. "Fair comment. But the guy made some good points. The Statue of Liberty, for one. Paid for and erected by Freemasons. And look at all the statues of the Goddess around Washington, D.C.—again, put there by the Masons."

"They probably watch porn together also. That doesn't make them Goddess worshipers."

Cam knew this conversation was not going to end well. He jockeyed to change the subject. "Well, I know you've been studying the Goddess. You might want to look more closely into the Freemasons. But back to the whole question of treasure. Someone killed for the journals, and we have no idea why. But if the journals lead to a treasure, whatever it is, that might explain it."

She exhaled as she stood. "I'm afraid you might be right. I love these mysteries, these quests of ours. But why does it always seem like some evil mad genius is bent on stopping us? Why can't Moriarty ever want us to *find* the treasure instead of thwarting us?"

Cam began to reply, then checked himself. He didn't have a good answer.

Chapter 2

Nicolette drove toward Brooklyn in the light Saturday morning traffic, her movements skilled and confident. Jamila observed. The young apprentice did not allow other vehicles to determine her course, nor did she take unnecessary risks. Jamila had often thought that a person's true personality came out four times in life—when they drank, when they played sports, when they drove, and when they made love. She made it a point not to surround herself with angry drunks, poor losers, intemperate drivers, or selfish lovers.

Jamila leaned forward. Time in the car should not be wasted; it could be used to teach, to educate, to think. "Why is it, do you think, that when Orthodox Jewish women marry, they are required to shave their heads?" Hassidic Jews, many of them clustered in Brooklyn, were among the most observant of Orthodox Jewry.

Nicolette glanced into the rearview mirror and involuntarily ran her fingers through her blond hair. "It is a tradition, obviously. Was it originally for hygienic reasons?"

Jamila blinked dismissively. "No. The practice serves one purpose, and one purpose only: to demean women, to make them feel inferior and dependent on their husbands. Who would want them now, with a bald head? It is the female equivalent of a castration. In fact, the entire set of rules which governs the behavior of Orthodox women is designed to subjugate them to their husbands. In many ways, they are treated like chattel, like property. We criticize this kind of barbaric backwardness in the Middle East, but it exists right here in America today."

They were now in Williamsburg, the streets largely empty, driving being prohibited on the Sabbath under Jewish law. But the sidewalks were jammed with clusters of women pushing baby strollers. "The mothers are all so young," Nicolette observed.

"Another way the men keep them in line. They keep them segregated, then marry them off at sixteen, seventeen. No time to sow any wild oats. Then babies at eighteen."

Jamila continued, caressing her Hamsa amulet, an intricately shaped silver hand with a cobalt blue sapphire formed into an all-seeing eye in the center of its palm and other Goddess symbols—snakes, spirals, pentagrams and crescent moons—on the fingers. "But, you know, the Israelites were not always like this. In ancient times, women worshiped the Goddess, the Shekinah, the feminine aspect of God. Women were equal partners with the men. Sarah, Abraham's wife, was a priestess. And Miriam, Moses' sister, was a prophetess."

"So what changed?"

"The alphabet."

"I'm sorry, what?"

"You heard me." It was time for the apprentice to get a glimpse of what was around the corner. "The written word. In this case, the Torah. Moses received a set of written laws from God. Which meant all Jewish boys—not girls, of course—needed to learn to read. The rite of passage, which used to involve feats of bravery or survival or the hunt, now became a trial of literacy. A Jewish boy becomes a man when he is able to read from the Torah. The Jews became 'The People of the Book.' And when that happened, the left brain began to take over."

Nicolette looked back at her blankly. "The left brain?"

Jamila sighed. Didn't they teach this stuff in school anymore? "The right side of the brain is where abstract thoughts originate—things like art and beauty and music and intuition. The left brain controls rational thought and is what makes people organized and logical. That's where reading skills are learned. In broad terms, the right hemisphere is considered more feminine and left side more masculine."

Nicolette's eyes narrowed. "I thought that the left side of our bodies was considered more feminine. The right side is the aggressor—it holds the sword. But you said it was the other way around?"

Jamila shook her head. "No, that is *not* what I said. I said the left *brain* is more masculine. It controls the *right* side of our bodies. The sword, as you said." She shifted in her seat. "Even in my lifetime people tried to make little boys who were left-handed switch to their right hands—nobody wanted an effeminate son. The root of the word left is *lyft,* meaning weak or worthless." She sipped at a water bottle, letting her words sink in.

Nicolette stopped at a light, pedestrian traffic now heavy as congregants walked to the synagogues. After a few seconds, Nicolette made an observation. "Is that why terms like *left out* and *leftovers* and are negative—"

"No," Jamila said, cutting her off. "Think before you speak, my dear. In those cases the word *left* derives from the word *leave* and has nothing to do with the left hand. Had you considered things more carefully, however, you may have found a better example in the phrase *left-handed compliment.* And also the word *sinister*, whose root means 'left' in Latin." She sniffed. Critical thought had become a lost art. "In any event, all this is simply the bias of a male-dominated society. In ancient times, the right and left sides of our bodies were considered complementary. Yes, the right hand held the sword, but the left hand held the shield. Who would go into battle without either?"

Jamila directed her apprentice to make a turn—a left one, appropriately. "The human brain is obviously more complicated than simply left and right—there is a lot of crossover, and of course some women are left-brain dominant and some men right-brain dominant. But in shorthand terms, scientists have long talked about the left and right hemispheres of the brain." She pulled a dog-eared paperback from her purse, one of the few books she allowed herself to own. "Leonard Shlain explained it to me; I'll let him explain it to you also. His book is called *The Alphabet Versus the Goddess.* It came out in 1998." *Had it really been almost twenty years?* Jamila shook the thought away and began to read aloud:

"[T]he demise of the Goddess, the plunge in women's status, and the advent of harsh patriarchy and misogyny occurred around the

time people were learning how to read and write. Perhaps there was something in the way people acquired this new skill that changed the brain's actual structure. We know that in the developing brain of a child, different kinds of learning will strengthen some neuronal pathways and weaken others. Extrapolating the experience of an individual to a culture, I hypothesized that when a critical mass of people within a society acquire literacy, especially alphabet literacy, left hemispheric modes of thought are reinforced at the expense of right hemispheric ones, which manifests as a decline in the status of images, woman's rights, and goddess worship."

Jamila closed the book. "He makes a compelling study of Asian cultures. Those which have the strongest history of literacy—China, Japan and Korea—are the most patriarchal. On the other hand, in countries where literacy was not well-established, such as the Philippines, Indonesia and Tibet, society was far more balanced and women were treated as equals."

She continued, too old to care if she sounded preachy. Especially because she was, well, preaching. "Since time immemorial, the Goddess had been worshiped and women recognized as equal, if not superior, to men in all things except brute strength. Women were the priestesses, the healers, the farmers, the historians, the mathematicians. Then, suddenly, upon the advent of the alphabet, women were pushed down, subjugated." Her voice trembled. "And the Goddess was put down with them. In Israel, worship of the Goddess became a crime. Entire villages were murdered. In the Book of Ezekiel, it is written that Yahweh ordered Ezekiel to kill any Israelite who continued to worship the Goddess: 'Slay utterly, both old and young, both maids and little children and women.'" Jamila looked away. "The Book, the Torah, made it clear: There could be, must be, only one God. A jealous God."

She paused and watched a dark-suited man with a long beard march in front of his wife as the woman struggled to manage a gaggle of small children. This was the purpose of her trip to New York. To view firsthand the patriarchal library mural. To observe in person the repression of Hassidic women. To remind herself that even here, in one of the world's most progressive cities, male primacy reigned.

Jamila clenched her jaw. "And, of course, men made certain that this one God, this single God of the Torah, would be a bearded one."

After an early lunch, Amanda slipped into a wool skirt, black boots and a form-fitting aquamarine cashmere sweater that brought out the blue and green hues in her eyes. She didn't normally play off her looks, but she dared not insult the expert who had agreed to examine the scroll by showing up dressed like the soccer mom she had become. Henri Blanchefort loved to surround himself with beautiful things, and that included the people in his life.

Amanda removed the plastic container holding the scroll from the wall safe in the pantry and said goodbye to Cam and Astarte.

"You sure you don't want me to come?" Cam asked. He was being purposely vague, not wanting to frighten Astarte. But someone had just died for the journals while driving with them, and Amanda was about to transport the scroll to Boston in her car.

"I'll be fine." They had discussed this already. Henri would not appreciate Cam tagging along. "Nobody even knows we have them."

She stepped outside into a sunny, blustery March afternoon. Spring in London and in most of the United States, but still very much winter in New England. She settled into her Subaru Legacy, cranked the heat, and drove south toward Boston. But once on the highway she couldn't help but reflect on the journals perhaps being dangerous, every car approaching from the rear or slowing at her side a possible assailant.

Don't be paranoid. Yet caution was not paranoia. From the middle lane, she made a quick, last-second detour off the highway and followed back roads to the next exit, her eyes studying the cars in her rearview mirror. By the time she merged back onto the interstate, she had reached a level of comfort that she was not being followed. But surely a pro would be hip to her tricks. She clenched the steering wheel and exhaled. Perhaps she should have allowed Cam to accompany her. "Relax," she commanded herself. "They don't even know we have the bloody journals."

A half hour later, traffic moving quickly on a Saturday, she found a parking meter on Charles Street at the foot of Boston's Beacon Hill. She swiped her credit card, scanned the sidewalks for any sign she had been followed, took a deep breath, removed the plastic container from the glove compartment, dropped it into her shoulder bag and, as nonchalantly as she could, ambled down the sidewalk in the direction of the Public Garden.

The book bindery was located above a chiropractor's office in a brick row house, a modest structure surrounded by antique shops and galleries in one the city's toniest neighborhoods. Amanda ascended a flight of narrow stairs and pushed open a heavy, windowed door. The jangle of bells announced her arrival, and a few seconds later Henri's tall form strode out from a back room, dressed nattily in a dark blue suit with pink shirt and lilac tie.

"Amanda," he called in his Parisian accent, leaning down to kiss her on both cheeks. "It has been far too long. Already the room is brighter from your presence."

She smiled, happy both to see her old friend and to be safely off the street. Henri was classically handsome in a runway model kind of way, though a bit thin and pretty for her liking. She sometimes served as Henri's beard, accompanying him to events where it would have been inappropriate to bring a same-sex significant other.

He slid his arm through hers. "So, what is this mysterious scroll you want me to look at?"

She didn't want to lie to him. Nor did she want to tell him the truth, agreeing with Cam that they needed to be cautious. So she left it vague. "Cameron has a client who found the scroll in an old book. The book has been in the family for centuries, apparently. Brought over from Scotland. That's really all I know."

"Oh, right. He's a lawyer." Henri made a face. "I forgot."

She laughed lightly. "No you didn't. And if it helps, he's only practicing law part-time. He's also doing historical research and teaching a class at Brandeis."

Henri brightened. "Still focusing on the Templars?"

Amanda nodded.

He adjusted his tie knot. "Did I tell you one of my ancestors, Bertrand de Blanchefort, was a Templar Grand Master?" His pronunciation of the name made Amanda think of cheese fondue. "He lived in the 12ᵗʰ century."

Amanda angled her head. "Truly?"

"I have never quite figured out how the Templars, being celibate and all, managed to have so many offspring. But, yes. He is my direct ancestor."

"I think most of them took their vows later in life, after siring children," she offered.

"Anyway, I am glad to hear Cameron is doing something worthwhile. Lawyers are so *boring*."

She chose not to argue the point. Her life with Cam had been anything but drab. Instead she handed Henri the plastic container. "We call it the eggscroll."

Either the language barrier prevented him from getting the joke, or he just didn't think it funny, but Henri merely cleared his throat and accepted the container. He carried it over to an antique wooden desk with a green banker's light, the furnishings standing in stark contrast to the modern cut of his suit and his designer eyeglasses. A humidifier hummed nearby, presumably to keep the ancient parchments from drying out. Wearing rubber medical gloves, Henri sniffed at the scroll, then peered through a magnifying glass, and finally prodded at whatever it was—Amanda assumed a piece of leather—which bound it. "I know of no other way to determine what is inside other than to open it," he proclaimed, his tone containing more solemnity than the self-evident observation probably warranted. Amanda nodded her consent.

Using a pair of tweezers-like devices, Henri expertly untied the string. Slowly he unrolled the scroll and spread it on a blotter on his desk, its edges tattered and torn.

"It appears to be some kind of map," he announced.

The paper, or whatever it was, was creased and discolored. But Amanda made out the faded shape of what appeared to be the New England coastline and a few sailboats in the waters around it. They stared at it for a few seconds. Amanda broke the silence. "What is the material? Parchment?"

He nodded. "Parchment refers to any animal skin. This is calfskin, which we call vellum. It was more expensive than other parchments."

"When was it in use?"

"It was very popular in Europe during medieval times. Then in the 15th century technology advanced to allow mass production of paper, and paper replaced parchment, including vellum, for most uses."

"So this being vellum, you would guess it is at least 500 years old?"

He nodded. "Yes. And it would be fairly easy to get a firm date. The vellum can be carbon-dated. And the ink can also be dated." He shrugged. "But it is not so cheap." He glanced at the map and smiled at her knowingly. "Unless we are comparing the cost to some kind of treasure."

She leaned closer, drawn to a corner of the tattered parchment. "It may not be that expensive after all. Can I borrow that magnifying glass?" She steadied her hands as her eyes widened. "M, C, C, C, X, C, V, I, I, I," she read out. "1398."

He leaned in, his hand on her shoulder. "Ah, yes, I see it. I agree, the date is 1398. You are as sharp as you are beautiful, Amanda."

She barely heard him. Below the date someone had drawn a five-sided star. A pentagram. A symbol of the Goddess.

With Amanda in Boston for a few hours, Cam decided on an impromptu ski afternoon with Astarte. Westford boasted a small but well-maintained mountain, and Astarte had recently become an enthusiastic skier. His only concern was that she might see her friends and ditch him on the slopes.

They pulled into the Nashoba Valley Ski Area parking lot just after lunch. The lot was fairly empty—this was the type of place which was more popular on weekdays, when kids (including Astarte every Tuesday and Thursday) congregated after school and adult racing teams bounced from the slopes to the bar in the evenings. "What's the best ski mountain in the world?" Cam asked.

Astarte grinned, her bright smile framed against chestnut skin. Cobalt eyes, an athletic physique and a playful manner added to her allure. Cam knew the teenage years would be, well, busy ones. "Whatever mountain you're skiing on today," she replied.

They skied hard, a quick ride up the lift and an even faster bomb straight down. Cam's body weight and longer skis allowed him to outrace her to the bottom, but her competitive nature was such that she was becoming reckless in her attempt to beat him. Finally, on the fifth run, he eased up a bit and allowed her to fly past.

At the bottom he sprayed her with snow as he stopped. "You cheated. Not fair."

"Yeah, if racing an old geezer is your definition of cheating."

He knocked her ski pole out of her hand. "Come on, I'll buy you some hot chocolate."

Inside the lodge they removed their helmets and gloves. Cam bought the hot chocolate and also allowed Astarte to talk him into a plate of French fries. Sometimes he wondered if he skied just so he could justify eating junk food.

"Did you and Mum get a chance to talk about that ski camp?"

Cam blinked and sighed. "Sorry, honey, no. Things got a bit crazy with those journals." He wondered how Amanda was making out with the book expert. "When is the deadline?"

"Monday."

"Okay, we'll talk about it tonight." A ski school in Vermont had invited the girls in Astarte's middle school ski club to spend next weekend visiting the school. The entire weekend—bus trip, ski pass, meals, accommodations—was free. Cam guessed the school was using the occasion to recruit would-be students. "Are your friends going?"

Astarte shrugged. "I don't know. But I want to."

Cam smiled. He loved that she was confident and secure enough to go even if her friends didn't. He had heard horror stories about the social pressures girls faced in middle school. "Do you think you'd want to go to a ski school like that?"

She shrugged. "How would I know unless I tried it?"

"Good point." He had no problem with it, but obviously he couldn't commit without Amanda. "The timing is pretty good. Softball doesn't start until the week after. Speaking of which, we should hit some wiffle balls in the basement when we get home. Work on that hand speed."

She snatched the last French fry and grinned. "Maybe you should work on *your* hand speed, Dad."

Amanda traded texts with Cam as she walked along Charles Street to her car. She tried not to feel left out that they had gone skiing without her. It was actually a good thing—a very good thing— that Cam and Astarte had such a close and healthy relationship. Yet she would insist on a family game night tonight to make up for it.

Her mind turned back to the eggscroll. Henri had suggested, and she had agreed, that he cut off a corner of the vellum and have it sent away for carbon-dating. She would rather not have spent the $600, but they couldn't very well *not* test it.

"You know," Henri had said, "even if the carbon-dating confirms the 1398 date, that will not prove anything. It is possible to purchase ancient parchment, including vellum, in the antiquities markets in Cairo or Beirut. A forger might have done so, and drawn this map."

She and Cam had considered the same possibility. "But, to what end?" she had asked.

Henri had shrugged. "This I do not know. I am merely pointing out the possibilities."

She had nodded. But as she thought about it now, the 'To what end?' question seemed spot on. A sixty-something woman from Iowa, driving a 20-year-old car, raced halfway across the country just to hand the journals off to Cam. Was it also possible she first flew to Egypt, bought antique vellum on the antiquities market, and then hired an art forger to create a false set of journals? Again, to what end? All she got for her trouble was an early grave. Even putting that aside, she never tried to *sell* the journals to Cam, so there was no apparent profit motive behind the behavior. Was there something else at play, perhaps a personal reason for creating a fake set of journals? Amanda shook her head. The likelihood was so remote as to be almost off the charts. But, then again, the reality of an authentic set of Sinclair family journals dropping into their laps, proving the Prince Henry voyage, was pretty hard to accept also. What was it that Sherlock Holmes said? *When you have eliminated the impossible, whatever remains, however improbable, must be the truth.*

The problem was, that between the woman from Iowa forging the journals, and the journals actually being authentic, Amanda couldn't decide which was the least improbable.

They had left Brooklyn when the streets emptied as the residents entered the synagogues around nine-thirty, Jamila disgusted by the rampant sexism being practiced as if male primacy were somehow ordained by God. If God had wanted men to rule over women, God wouldn't have made women smarter than them. It was that simple.

It was time to redress this travesty, to return humankind to its natural balance.

"That was all you wanted me to see?" Nicolette asked timidly.

Jamila sniffed. "It would have been too far out of our way to drive to Utah and see even worse examples. At least the Orthodox Jews stick to only one wife. But the fact you were not more repulsed by it in some ways proves my point: This kind of institutional system of female servitude has somehow become acceptable." She shook her head. "Even young, liberalized women like yourself barely bat an eye at it."

The apprentice's cheeks blushed at being chastised. "It's just that this is how I grew up in Pennsylvania. In my town, the men were the bosses. They worked and the women stayed home."

"Like I said, we don't even notice. It's like the Stockholm Syndrome: Women feel like they should thank their spouses for subjugating them."

Nicolette drove in silence for twenty minutes. "Gauche," she said.

"What?"

"*Gauche*. It's the French word for *left*. In English it means crude and awkward."

"I know what it means." Jamila watched the trees fly by. "But, yes, that is another good example." She was glad the apprentice seemed to be taking the teaching. But Jamila still had a card to play in this game of one-upmanship. "If we are going to use French, a better example to use would have been *adroit*, from the French *droite*, meaning to the right. Adroit is, of course, the opposite of awkward."

Nicolette merely nodded, Jamila glad she didn't press her on the assertion that *adroit* was somehow a better example than *gauche*.

They had stopped for fresh bagels and coffee before exiting the city. "Back to Vermont?" the apprentice asked as they crept north through Connecticut, slowed by a heavy traffic.

"No," Jamila said as she brushed dark poppy seeds off her amber dress. She had not originally planned to spend an extra day with Nicolette, but the girl had grown on her. There were things she wanted her to see. "Head east toward Boston. Plug Westford into your GPS. No reason to sit in this traffic."

The novice raised an eyebrow. "Westford? My father took me there when I was a girl to see the Westford Knight carving. He's a history buff. And apparently I descend from the Sinclairs."

Jamila dismissed the comment with a wave. "Yes, well, this time you will get a *full* explanation of the site. Now, I am going to nap," Jamila announced from the back seat. That was a lie, but she did not want to become distracted by any small talk. Her plan demanded precise preparation. It had been almost a year since her previous plan blew up on her face. Literally. She rubbed at the cow tongue-like flap of skin that was now her cheek, the singed nerve endings barely registering the touch of her fingers. She had cast her lot with a group of other like-minded women, a cabal calling themselves the Crones. They, like her, wanted to see the Goddess—whether known as Venus or Asherah or Isis or Gaia or one of a dozen other names—retake her rightful spot as an equal partner atop the pantheon of deities. But the group had been weak, ineffectual, undisciplined. And they had been thwarted by a group that included Amanda Spencer-Gunn and Cameron Thorne. In some ways it had been a blessing—a forest burned to the ground grows back even stronger. And this time Jamila was in complete control, dependent on nobody but herself and a group of young acolytes she had recruited and trained. A modern-day Cult of Venus, modeled after the Goddess-worshipers of ancient Rome, glorifying in the power and majesty of all things feminine.

Two hours later they exited the highway northwest of Boston in Westford, Jamila feeling a pang of guilt as she realized this had been the very exit Katherine Morville would have taken. She sighed. "Take a left, toward the town center." In war, soldiers must die. Even when fighting for the ever-loving Goddess.

They parked at an elementary school and walked uphill fifty yards to the Westford Knight informational sign not far from the town center. A cold wind blew, turning their cheeks pink and their fingers numb even as the early afternoon sun melted the snow around them. Jamila didn't bother with the basic history of the carving, knowing Nicolette had grown up with the legend. "People often ask why Sinclair ended up in Westford, so far inland. The answer is that this hill we are on is the highest hill in eastern Massachusetts. And it is sacred ground, a central gathering spot for the Native American tribes in the region. So it is a natural spot for his native guides to bring him to."

"Why was it considered sacred?"

"We are in an area called the Nashoba Valley. Nashoba means 'hills that shake.' Just like the ancient Europeans believed that the energy from the earth was sacred, so too did the Native Americans."

"You mean like ley lines?"

"Exactly." The ancient ley lines circled the globe, connecting monuments and sacred sites with undetectable earth energies. "The reason these hills shake is that a major geological fault line runs right through here, right beneath this carving." She pointed at the bedrock, upon which the Knight was carved. "This bedrock is the result of the movements of the tectonic plates pushing material to the surface." She removed her hand from her coat pocket and gestured around her. "The energy from Mother Earth is strong here. The natives understood that. As did Sinclair." That's all Goddess worship really was—an appreciation for the beauty and power of nature. And the need to respect it and keep it in balance.

"So this wasn't just some random location."

"No. Highest hill. Traditional gathering spot. Sacred ground. It is the perfect location for a shrine. Especially for those in tune with Mother Earth."

Cam was in an unsettled mood, and he couldn't figure out why. He had spent a fun day skiing with Astarte, and when Amanda had returned together they made a homemade pizza and salad for an early dinner. In between, he had translated another entry in the journals, which he was planning to read to Amanda and Astarte after dessert. Life was good, and he tried his best not to put a damper on the evening. So why the funk?

He volunteered to take Venus for a post-dinner walk in an attempt to change his mood. Three blocks from the house, Venus stopped to sniff at a dead squirrel lying in the middle of the road. Suddenly Cam understood what was bothering him. Unlike Katherine Morville, the squirrel had not known it was going to die; it had no idea an instrument of death was bearing down on it. But Katherine had driven all night to deliver the journals to Cam, presumably because she knew she was in danger. So why hadn't she called? Why hadn't she reached out once the danger manifested itself, rather than when it was too late?

Tugging Venus away, he removed his glove and pulled out his cell phone to check for missed calls. Nothing from Iowa. He phoned Amanda and asked her to check the caller ID on their land line as well. Also nothing. Odd.

He tried to imagine the series of events which led the Morville woman to hop in her old car and make a nonstop run across half the country like something out of a *Smokey and the Bandit* movie. Had something happened suddenly to alarm her, to let her know she was in danger? He imagined her pulling into some roadside motel in western New York after a day of driving, and then somehow getting spooked and racing another few hundred miles to Westford. But he was only guessing. There was a missing piece here, something that didn't add up. He glanced back at the squirrel and sighed. Like the squirrel, Katherine Morville wasn't talking.

Nicolette had the sense Jamila was actually enjoying their little road trip. It had probably been years since she had visited many of the Goddess sites. And the old woman liked nothing better than lecturing her apprentices. Not that Nicolette minded. Jamila had much to share, even if she sometimes parceled out the morsels with a dash of vinegar.

"Where to next?" Nicolette asked as she deftly guided the SUV back toward the highway, her driving skills honed dodging ordnance and land mines in Iraq.

"America's Stonehenge. Head north toward New Hampshire."

Nicolette had been there once as a child, probably on the trip when they visited the Knight. The New England visit was one of many road trips her father had taken her on from their home outside Philadelphia. Her mother had run off when Nicolette was only six. Mom had gone to her twentieth high school reunion in Omaha, hooked up with her old boyfriend, and never come back. Dad had been surprisingly forgiving, though he had never quite gotten over it. "We can't choose who we fall in love with," he had explained. "And our first love often leaves an imprint that lasts forever. Your mother is not a bad person. She just made a bad decision." Nicolette had been too young to verbalize what she later came to understand, that who we are *is a product of* the decisions we make. Not that Dad needed to hear it from her. But it made it easier to dismiss her mother, easier not to be bothered by only seeing Mom during occasional school vacations and then eventually not at all, easier to be content with a family unit comprised of only Dad and her. The irony of the situation was that the old boyfriend apparently had no trouble outgrowing first love's imprint; he broke things off after only a few months. Mom was still single, at least as far as Nicolette knew.

"My dad took me there when I was nine. I didn't really get it."

"Nine is young," Jamila replied. "And it's not the type of place you can just walk into and understand. You need to go many times, have guides who can explain it to you. It used to be called Mystery Hill for a reason."

Not that Dad, a high school history teacher, wasn't adept at explaining things. He was also the high school wrestling coach. Together they reflected his chief attributes: physical fitness and intellect. He loved nothing more than to ferret around in the dusty corners of history—preferably outdoors, after a long hike—and share his findings with his students. Or his daughter. He was also one of the homeliest men on earth, which, she had come to realize, was why he took such good care of his body. In college she had seen a picture of the Egyptian god Horus—he of the hawk head and muscular human body—and immediately thought of her father. Her mother was no looker either, round-faced and plain and doughy. All of which made Nicolette appreciate how random physical beauty was—she had just been lucky her parents' faces had in combination morphed into a shape the human eye found pleasing. She could have just as easily ended up looking like Mrs. Potato Head.

An hour after they left Westford, just as the late afternoon sun was beginning to fade beneath the tree line, they pulled into the parking lot of America's Stonehenge, paid, and hiked their way up a muddy, slushy trail through the woods to the hilltop ceremonial center of the ancient stone complex. As they walked, Jamila—her signature amber dress hiked up to her knees with a leather sash to keep it from dragging in the mud—explained her belief that the site had been built by Phoenician seafarers approximately 3,500 years ago. "We know the Phoenicians were in southern Britain, in Cornwall, trading for tin, which was needed to make bronze. From there, I believe they crossed the Atlantic to mine or trade for copper from Quebec and the Great Lakes region."

"So why is this site here?" Nicolette knew there was no copper in the area.

"The site is a giant calendar in stone, similar to Stonehenge in England. I think they built it here to align with the English Stonehenge. Which, by the way, is less than 200 miles from Cornwall." She pulled her phone from her cape and showed Nicolette a picture. "This is the summer solstice sunrise at Stonehenge in England. You've seen it before. The sun sits atop a standing stone, like a golf ball on a tee."

Summer Solstice Sunrise, Stonehenge

"Well," Jamila continued, "the same thing happens here. The sun rises over a standing stone on the horizon." She showed another picture.

Summer Solstice Sunrise, America's Stonehenge

"But here's the fascinating thing." Nicolette had never seen Jamila this animated. "If you were to stand in the middle of this site, and fly a magic carpet along the sunbeam cast by the rising sun, you'd cross the Atlantic and fly straight through the main arch at Stonehenge."

"Wait, really?"

"Here's another image, showing it. That line is the imaginary sunbeam. You can see it passing through southern England."

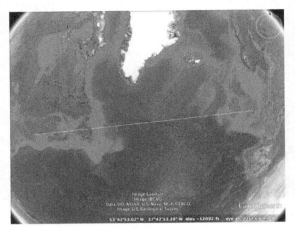

Summer Solstice Sunrise Line Across Atlantic

"And here is the same imaginary sunbeam line, magnified."

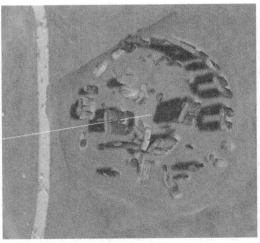

Summer Solstice Sunrise Line, Stonehenge to Stonehenge

Nicolette stopped dead on the trail. Could the two sites really align across thousands of miles of ocean? She would have remembered *that* if her Dad had told her. "Really? You're certain?"

Jamila nodded. "It was as if the builders of this site reverse-engineered it, choosing this location as the one spot where the solstice sunrise would line up with the parent site in England. Of course, to get it right they would have needed tremendous knowledge of the stars."

Nicolette began walking again, weighing the possibility. "But the Phoenicians were from Lebanon, not England, so wouldn't the so-called parent site be there?"

Jamila grinned, her teeth still bright and even, apparently pleased that her apprentice had used her intuition to tease out the truth. She worked her cell phone again. "For years researchers assumed the same thing. But they could never find a Stonehenge-like site in Lebanon, which by the way is where I have lived most of my life. They assumed it had been destroyed. Then a few years ago archeologists excavated a site in the Golan Heights in northern Israel. In what used to be part of the Phoenician homeland." She showed another image on her phone:

Israeli Stonehenge, Golan Heights

Jamila continued, Nicolette sensing her mentor's pride in the work of her ancestors. "The site is actually massive. The locals call it *Gilgal Refaim*, the Wheel of Giants. The mound in the center is fifteen feet tall, and the outer circle is over 500 feet in diameter. And, just as you intuited, it aligns almost perfectly with this site and the Stonehenge England site, again along the summer solstice sunrise line. The margin of error is infinitesimal, less than one-sixth of one degree." Jamila showed yet another image on her phone to Nicolette.

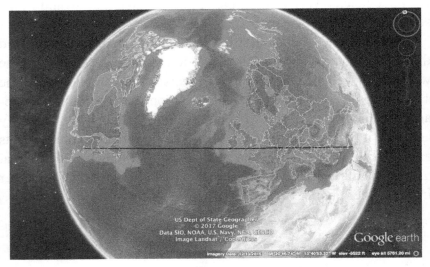

Summer Solstice Sunrise Line
America's Stonehenge to Stonehenge to Israeli Stonehenge

Nicolette studied the illustration, a straight line heading northeast from New England, counter-intuitively ending up at a southerly latitude in the Middle East due to the spherical shape of the earth. But once she got her bearings, she saw that the three sites truly were in direct alignment along the summer solstice sunrise sunbeam, too much so to be a coincidence. Yet over a distance of probably six thousand miles, nearly impossible to fathom. She shook her head in amazement. How had ancient Phoenicians pulled this off? The same way they navigated the oceans, she realized. By using the stars and becoming experts in astronomy.

Jamila glanced at the sun, beginning to drop to the horizon. "We better hurry. We have our own alignment to witness."

Nicolette knew better than to question whether her octogenarian mentor could keep up, and five minutes later they crested the hill and joined a couple of dozen people gathered at the top, staring at the sun dipping toward the western horizon.

But Jamila surprised Nicolette yet again. Instead of focusing on the sun, she pointed to the northern horizon. "Look, the half moon."

Nicolette found it above the tree line in the fading evening light.

Jamila continued. "You can easily get a sense of the full size of the moon by seeing just half. Now look at the sun. What do you notice?"

Nicolette did so, squinting at the setting orb. "Huh. I never noticed. They're the same size."

Jamila grinned. "Exactly. The sun is 400 times larger than the moon, but also 400 times further away. So they appear to our eye to be the same size. That is why the ancients worshiped one as the male and the other as the female. Equal partners."

"And quite a coincidence."

Jamila turned away. "Or perhaps divine inspiration." She clapped her hands together, as she often did when she felt a conversation was over. "Now. Back to the matter at hand. See that large boulder," Jamila said, pointing to the west to a lone rock roughly the size and shape of a refrigerator laid on its side. "Twice a year, on the two equinoxes, the sun sets atop it when viewed from the ceremonial center of the site. Just like the summer solstice sunrise picture I showed you. There are other standing stones in a line moving off to the horizon that also mark the alignment, though most of the largest stones have fallen. There are people who come here and are disappointed that the standing stones are not as impressive as the ones in England. Well, I've seen some of the ones that have fallen, and they are immense. Fifteen feet tall, even taller."

The sun had continued to descend, toward the recumbent boulder. Nicolette could see it would soon move down and over and be visible in the alley between two parallel rows of evergreens. A thought struck her. "How old did you say this site was?"

"Between 3,500 and 4,000 years old."

"Was this land forested then?" Why bother building a site which marked the solar sunrises and sunsets if the spectacles were blocked by trees?

Jamila smiled. "Good question. That's one of the things that helps date the site. Thousands of years ago, there was not enough organic material atop the bedrock to support the root system needed for large trees." She gestured, showing how in many places the bedrock in the area remained bare. "So all we had here were low shrubs."

They joined the small gathering now, everyone silent as the sun made its decline toward the recumbent boulder. It seemed to pick up speed as it approached the horizon, diving down and to its left in a graceful plunge. Just above the horizon, the sun nestled into a shallow niche on the recumbent boulder for a few seconds, as if the boulder had been positioned for just such an effect, before disappearing. Nicolette snapped a quick shot.

America's Stonehenge Spring Equinox Sunset

Jamila, who had moved away from the boulder to take a position atop the viewing station, appeared by her side with another photo, this one showing the sunset framed by the alley of trees running to the horizon.

"Spectacular," Nicolette whispered. "And to think people have been standing where we are, watching the same phenomenon, for thousands of years."

America's Stonehenge Spring Equinox Sunset

Jamila took her by the elbow to guide her away. "Wait until you see the sunrise tomorrow."

"We're coming back?"

"Yes, but first there's one more thing I want to show you before it gets dark."

Jamila, sun-colored herself, led them deeper into the woods, off the main path but in the general direction of the visitor's center. Nicolette commented as they walked, "Everything here seems to be about the sun." Perhaps that was why her mentor always wore amber. "So the Phoenicians were sun worshipers?"

"Yes. Baal was the sun god."

"How does the Goddess fit in?"

Jamila fingered her Hamsa amulet before replying. "Baal's wife, Asherah. The goddess of fertility, associated with the moon. Other religious sites mark the movements of the lunar cycle to honor her, just as this site honors Baal. Again, duality. Male and female. Sun and moon. Light and dark. Wet and dry. Cold and hot. Everything in nature is in balance." Jamila explained how the Goddess in ancient times was associated with the moon, owing to the identical timing of the 28-day lunar cycle and a woman's menstruation cycle. She continued, "We can learn a lot from language. As the Church and its patriarchy spread throughout Egypt, certain words associated with the moon took on negative connotations, as a way to demean women. The word 'lunacy' is a good example." She made a spitting gesture. "The lunacy was in ruining nature's perfect balance."

Nicolette offered an insight of her own. "I learned from one of the videos you assigned that another example of language being skewed is the word 'crone,' which actually comes from the same root as the word 'crown' and means 'leader.'"

"Precisely. 'Crone' went from something admirable to something ugly and unclean."

Jamila stopped on the path and stared off into the distance, as if looking into her past. She lowered her voice. "As I told you, I have been called a *crone* myself many times." It was about as much as Jamila ever shared about her past. And Nicolette knew not to ask. Jamila continued. "In any event, to answer your original question, this site is dedicated primarily to the sun, traditionally a male deity. But it also recognizes the Goddess. It is part of a culture which worshiped a pantheon of gods, both male and female, a culture which understood that nature demanded balance." She locked her eyes on her novice. "Remember, we do not hate men, and we do not abhor male gods. What we abhor is *patriarchy*."

Jamila had spoken similar words when she first recruited Nicolette, after Nicolette's military tour of duty ended. The woman had offered a generous stipend and an intriguing, if vague, promise to indoctrinate Nicolette in the ancient ways and teach her the ancient knowledge. It seemed a better choice than driving a FedEx truck. But the whole anti-male thing had almost been a killer. It had been her dad, surprisingly, who pushed her into accepting the offer. "If there are women in this world who have a virulent hatred of men, all I can say is that they probably have good cause." He had continued. "And this Jamila woman doesn't seem to hate men *per se*. She just hates our religions. Again, she probably has good cause."

As if to prove her point that the site was holy to the Goddess as well as the sun god, Jamila stopped at a clearing and pointed to a raised mound covered by fruits, vegetables and flowers. It took Nicolette a few seconds to recognize that the mound was a mud or clay effigy of the earth mother, or Goddess. "Earlier today," Jamila explained, "there was a ceremony honoring the Goddess." She gestured at the bounty. "People made offerings of fruits and vegetables to her in honor of the equinox. Especially apples. If we had made it in time, they would have welcomed us."

"Why especially apples?"

Jamila smiled. "Come. I'll show you."

The older woman led Nicolette deeper into the woods a few dozen yards and pointed. "See that stone wall?"

Nicolette nodded.

"Notice it begins and ends for no apparent reason. That tells us it is ceremonial, not utilitarian. Take a few seconds: What does it look like to you?"

Nicolette angled her head. "The triangular rock in front sort of looks like a snake head."

"Good. Continue."

"And then the rest of it, curving around, could be the snake's body. The pile of rocks ten feet back from the head could be the snake's arched back, or maybe a meal it just ate."

America's Stonehenge Serpent Wall

"Excellent." Jamila brought her hands together in a silent clap. "You have eyes that see. Now, tell me what it means."

The apple comment echoed in the back of Nicolette's mind. *The serpent. Adam and Eve. The apple.* "Oh, I get it. The serpent has long been a symbol for the female, the Goddess." Modern religions had turned the snake into something evil, but Nicolette had learned that the ancient Goddess-worshiping cultures venerated the serpent as wise, powerful and fertile, which is why the spiral (or coiled snake) was a Goddess symbol. Nicolette studied the rock wall again. Though not as grand or elaborate, the wall reminded her of the famous Serpent Mound in Ohio which snaked through a golf course. Her dad had brought her. Like the America's Stonehenge site, the Serpent Mound marked the solstices, equinoxes and other astronomical events.

"So," Nicolette concluded, "this serpent wall is some kind of Goddess effigy."

Jamila nodded and gestured toward the woods. "This site is actually full of these serpent walls, curving through the woods for no apparent reason. Many of the stones were quarried from the rock ledge, to make the shapes needed. Obviously, no farmer is going to quarry stone from the ledge just to put it into a wall when there are so many stones already lying around." She turned back toward the trail. "The apples are a jab at the misogynistic Garden of Eden story. Remember what it was exactly that the snake was offering Eve, the horrible sin for which she was punished: The sin of acquiring knowledge."

Nicolette rolled her eyes. "No. Can't be having smart women."

Still mystified at Katherine Morville's odd decision not to reach out to him until just before her death, but now in a better mood, Cam jogged Venus back to the house. After a bowl of ice cream, Amanda reached out and squeezed his arm.

"I know I said I fancied a family game night, but Astarte said you translated more of the journal. I think I'd rather hear that first."

"Okay." Cam reached for his legal pad, sitting on the kitchen counter. "This is the first entry. Prince Henry was only nine years old. Luckily for me, he was probably just learning Latin, so the vocabulary and sentence structure are very simple. Everything is in the present tense. Made translation easy." He smiled at his wife and daughter. "Should I read it out in a Scottish brogue?"

Amanda rolled her eyes. "As if."

"Come on, if Mel Gibson can do it, so can I," he replied.

"He may have fooled you Yanks, but to us Brits he sounded like an Aussie trying to make time with a lass in an Irish pub. *Braveheart* is regularly atop our lists of worst movie accents."

Cam nodded. "Sort of like the way Bostonians cringe when some actor tries to fake a Boston accent."

"Right," Astarte said. "So just read it regular."

That convinced Cam. He winked at Amanda. Channeling his inner Mr. Scott from *Star Trek*, he began to read:

November 6, 1354

My name is Henry Sinclair. I am nine years old. Yesterday my father gives me this journal as a gift on Samhain. He says it is the day we talk to our dead ancestors. He says his father speaks to him in dream and tells him it is time for me to learn the family secrets. I write them in this journal when he tells them to me.

Cam paused as Amanda explained to Astarte what *Samhain* was, pronouncing it in the Gaelic fashion, as SAH-win. "It is another of the cross-quarter days, like Beltane. Astronomically, it falls around November 5. It marks the beginning of the dark half of the year. The ancient people believed this was the day when the boundary between the living and the dead was at its thinnest, and that it was possible to speak to the dead. That's where the tradition of Halloween comes from, and the idea of the dead haunting us."

The girl considered this. "So when Henry talks about his father talking to his grandfather in a dream, he thinks it might have been a real conversation."

"Yes, I reckon so." Amanda smiled. "But I promise you the accent wasn't so grating."

"I think my ears are bleeding," Astarte added.

Cam continued, this time without the brogue:

"My grandfather is a great man, my father says. I think my father is also a great man. He is Lord of Roslin. I am his oldest son so someday I am Lord of Roslin, and my son also.

Today my father takes me to the smith. The smith has very black hands but father shakes his hand anyway. I learn how to use a forge. Father says this is important for men when they sail across the western ocean. When we arrive to lands in the west we must make nails to repair boats. I try hard to learn, but I prefer to learn about fighting with swords and riding horses."

Cam interrupted himself to make another point to Astarte. "This point about making nails is an important one. People are always asking me why Sinclair came to Westford, of all places. In addition to being the highest spot in eastern Massachusetts, and being accessible by water, and being a traditional gathering spot for Native American tribes, it also happens to have one of the highest concentrations of bog iron in New England. You would need bog iron to make the nails."

Amanda weighed in. "Almost all the early Norse sites show evidence of iron works. I had one expert joke that ancient sailors knew that finding bog iron was important only if they planned on returning home. An average boat had approximately 20,000 nails, and about half of them broke or shook loose during the voyage across."

Cam returned to the journal. Obscure details like this, about teaching a young boy how to forge iron to make nails, added an air of authenticity to the entries. "Okay, this is the last paragraph."

"When we ride home from visiting smith I ask father what are the family secrets. He does not answer for a long time and then says, Secrets like this are not to be told, they are to be learned. He asks me if I understand. I say yes but I am not certain I do."

Astarte weighed in. "I think I understand. It's like you and Mum always talking about having *eyes that see*." She paused for a second to organize her thoughts. "You can give someone a treasure map, but if they're not smart enough to understand the symbols on the map, they won't find the treasure."

Cam nodded. He was proud of Astarte, proud of the mature and poised young lady she was growing into. What was that poster his sister had on her bedroom wall as a teenager? *If you love something, let it go free.* At some point Astarte would need to test her wings. For some reason Cam had the sense that time was fast approaching. The thought made him sad. But more than that, it scared the hell out of him.

Nicolette's phone buzzed on the night table as she sat on her hotel bed watching *Sleepless in Seattle* on cable television. Though not a romantic in real life, she was a sucker for sappy love stories. Perhaps because her heart broke every time she considered her father's loss. He had been correct about love's first imprint; Mom had been his, and he had never gotten over her leaving. A six-year-old-girl never quite gets past finding her strapping father sobbing into his pillow.

She rolled and grabbed the phone. Right on cue, her father calling. She lowered the volume. "Hi Dad."

"Hi honey."

He sounded … off. "What's wrong?"

"I have some horrible news. It's your mother. She's been killed in a car accident."

Nicolette blinked, the ceiling beginning to spin above her. "Wait, what? When?"

"Last night. I've been traveling so my phone's been off. Aunt Joanie just reached me. She said she'd been trying to reach you also."

"I was in the woods most of the day with no coverage." Nicolette didn't know what else to say.

"The funeral is Tuesday," he continued.

Her eyes pooled and a single sob bubbled up and splashed out her mouth. She swallowed. "Are you going?"

He exhaled. "I can't. I'm in the middle of something right now. There's no way I can get away."

She didn't argue. What was the protocol for an ex-spouse's funeral? Not that Dad cared. He had loved her, and he would no doubt mourn her. But he would do so in his own way.

They discussed funeral details, few of which Nicolette remembered, before she said goodbye and hung up. Her mind swirled in a turmoil of mixed emotions. Her overriding feeling was not sadness or anger, but regret. A girl should have a close relationship with her mother, an unbreakable, instinctive bond. But she had not. She swallowed again. And now she never would.

Chapter 3

Astarte awoke in the middle of the night. She listened carefully to the sounds of the house, the rhythm of its breathing and pulse. It was asleep, as were all its other occupants, including Venus splayed on the side of Astarte's bed.

Using a small pen flashlight she kept hidden behind the row of books on her headboard, she leaned over her mattress and grasped a wooden jewelry box tucked under the bed. About the size of a rectangular tissue box, the blond-colored oak chest featured a carving of a Native American girl paddling a canoe down a stream, a squirrel on her shoulder, a rabbit in her lap, and a pair of birds hovering just above, as if serving as escorts. Astarte kept all her treasures inside, and only she knew to push gently on the rabbit's right ear to release a spring which allowed the box to open.

Shielding it with her body from Venus (not wanting even the dog to learn the secret of the box), she sprung the lid. Her eyes moistened as she examined her treasures: a photo of her mother, the wind whipping her dark hair and the sun brightening her face as she balanced baby Astarte on her shoulders; a cobalt blue sapphire ring, the stone set in a simple gold band, a ring which had been passed down from mother to daughter for 40 generations; a silver cross given to her by her Uncle Jefferson, which he claimed belonged to her great-great-great-great grandfather (she thought she had the generational count correct), the Mormon founder Joseph Smith; Uncle Jefferson's favorite pocket watch, decorated with an owl face on the bronze front (Uncle Jefferson believing himself to be wise like the owl); and a pink-toned Certificate of Adoption issued by the Commonwealth of Massachusetts, folded in half to fit in the box, marking her formal entrance into her new family. Here, in summary, was the story of her life: a seemingly endless two-step between love and loss, caregivers and nurturers randomly ricocheting in and out of her life like moths drawn to the very flame which kills them, all of it overlaid by an ancient prophecy foretelling that she would someday unite the peoples of America in some kind of Goddess-based spiritual awakening.

She sighed. Yeah, sure, her life was normal.

But she had not opened the box tonight to wallow in her fate. She had done so because the prophecy, as passed down both to her mother and by her, the specific details of which Astarte had kept secret even from Amanda and Cam, proclaimed that the Fortieth Princess would begin her ascension on the vernal equinox after her twelfth birthday. Today. The ascension, the prophecy stated, would be ushered in by the arrival of a messenger of the Goddess, who would recognize the Fortieth Princess by her blue sapphire ring.

Astarte slipped the ring onto the middle finger of her left hand. Was the woman in the car, the one who brought the journals from Iowa, the messenger? But she was dead now, so what did that mean? Astarte swallowed and stared at the picture of her mother. "I need help." What, exactly, was a prophetess supposed to do? She sniffled and rubbed her eyes with her nightgown sleeve. How was she to unite the people? She was just a seventh-grade girl.

Venus stirred and gently licked Astarte's forearm. Astarte could hear the regular breathing of Amanda and Cam in the next room.

Yet she had never felt more alone.

Amanda startled awake, disturbed. The house was still, but she sensed uneasiness in her home. She rolled out of bed to check on Astarte.

Venus lifted her head in greeting as Amanda pushed open the door in the first light of dawn. Astarte slept, her face turned toward Amanda. But rather than a peaceful slumber, Astarte's teeth were clenched and she tossed and moaned. Perhaps a bad dream. Amanda's foot bumped against a hard object; she bent to see Astarte's wooden treasure box, protruding out from under the bed. Amanda bit her lip. Perhaps not just a bad dream.

She kissed Astarte on her forehead, whispered soft words until the girl settled. "It's okay, love. Everything is fine. Go back to sleep. Mum loves you. It's okay." She patted Venus and withdrew with a long sigh. She and Cam knew that at some point they would have to deal with this whole Fortieth Princess thing.

She thought back to the first time she had met Astarte. The girl, barely eight, was living with her Uncle Jefferson in Connecticut, her mother having died. Jefferson, a Mormon historian, knew of the Fortieth Princess prophecy and had been preparing the young girl, teaching her the hidden history of her people and of the continent. He had enlisted Amanda's and Cam's aid—strong-armed would be a more accurate description—in proving the veracity of a legendary Templar journey to New York's Catskill Mountains in the year 1179, a journey which had brought the Jesus bloodline (and, apparently, the bloodlines of Mohammed and Cleopatra, though Amanda was fuzzy on the exact details) to America and united them with Native American royalty to produce the Mandan tribe of so-called White Indians. Amanda had immediately been drawn to the young, motherless Mandan girl. She still recalled their first conversation:

"My mother is dead. I don't remember her. But Aunt Eliza and Uncle Jefferson and God are my parents now. They take care of me. When I'm older I'll take care of them." Astarte had giggled. "Not God, of course. He takes care of himself. But I'll take care of all the others."

"All by yourself?" Amanda had asked.

Astarte had nodded emphatically. "I'm the Fortieth Princess. That's my job."

Later, Cam had recounted Uncle Jefferson's impassioned plea:

"Think what Astarte embodies, Mr. Thorne. She is the true princess of the Western world—more royal blood flows through her veins than through anyone else alive. Her kingdom shall be here in America, in God's New Jerusalem. The world is ready for a female spiritual leader—just as the world was ready to accept Jesus as the

Age of Pisces began, so too will it be willing to accept a female messiah as the Age of Aquarius dawns.

"Don't you see? Aquarius, the sign for water—water is where life begins inside the womb. A woman is destined to rule!" He had banged the table with an open hand. "Astarte. She unites the bloodlines of Judaism, Christianity, Islam and Mormonism with the ancient Egyptian cult of Isis and its worship of the Sacred Feminine. In fact, her very name—Astarte—is an ancient version of the Isis name. It is Astarte's destiny to bring the true word of God to all the earth's inhabitants."

Amanda shook her head? Destined to rule? It was all Amanda could do to get the girl to make her bed in the morning. Yet the truth was, Astarte was an extraordinary girl—intelligent, kind, intuitive, strong, confident, capable. Just the kind of leader the world needed. And just the kind of leader the world seemed rarely to get.

Jamila and Nicolette had spent the night at a Holiday Inn near America's Stonehenge. They shared a dinner in the pub, then Jamila sprung for separate rooms. Even the most attentive apprentices needed a break. And Jamila had known the phone call would be coming. The girl deserved some privacy.

Jamila herself had not rested. It may have been spring, but she was in the winter of her existence. Some days she felt the warm sun on her face and fooled herself into thinking she might squeeze a few more years of juice out of the fruit of life. But most days left her chilled and achy and dry, as if the heat of life had already begun to seep from her pores. One thing was certain: The Goddess would take her when it was time. And until then, Jamila would serve her with all her strength.

Seated at the window of her room, a cup of tea in her lap and her Hamsa hand hanging from her neck, she checked her watch. Almost five. The sun would rise at around 6:45, perhaps a few minutes earlier from their vantage point atop the hill. The black of night had softened into a grayish purple hue, but Jamila could still see hundreds of stars twinkling on the eastern horizon. She smiled. The Goddess had given them good weather.

After packing quickly and slipping into another of her amber dresses, she crossed the hallway and tapped gently on Nicolette's door. She had no doubt the girl would be awake: Military training had ensured that. "Yes," Nicolette replied.

"We depart in fifteen minutes."

"I'll be ready."

Jamila made herself another cup of tea and peeled an orange for breakfast. She sighed. So much depended on the next few weeks.

As they walked to the car, Jamila touched her apprentice's hand. "I sense some sadness in you this morning." Not to mention the bloodshot eyes.

Nicolette nodded. "I got some bad news last night. My mom died in a car crash."

Stopping, Jamila said, "I am very sorry to hear that. You should go home, be with your family."

Nicolette shook her head. "No. We weren't particularly close." The apprentice resumed walking. "The funeral's not until Tuesday. I'll fly out Monday night."

The girl's military training shone through. Discipline, toughness, resiliency. "Are you certain?"

"Yes." She unlocked the doors and climbed in. "We have important work to do. And there's nothing I can do for my mother now."

An hour later they had parked at America's Stonehenge and were again following the darkened trail through the woods to the ceremonial center of the complex, Jamila foregoing her amber cape in favor of a down ski vest in the morning chill. Jamila was anxious to see if the same phenomenon she had witnessed some twenty years ago, when she had spent a year away from her Lebanese home studying the world's ancient sites, had repeated itself. As they passed the Earth Goddess mound, she had her answer. Smiling, she stopped. "What do you see?" she asked.

Nicolette looked confused, her mind no doubt on her mother. "Same as yesterday. The Earth Mother effigy."

"And what else?"

The girl angled her head, focusing. "Fruit, vegetables, flowers."

Jamila waited for her apprentice to get it.

"Wait," Nicolette said. "The fruits and vegetables. They're still here." She looked around, as if for an explanation. "There's barely any food in the woods. Why haven't the animals taken it?"

Jamila felt a wave of warmth pass through her. She blinked. "They know it is not for them. It was an offering to the Goddess."

They walked on in silence.

Amanda had no interest in going back to bed; she knew she would just fidget and squirm as her mind raced. Instead she made herself a cup of hot chocolate and returned to her research on ancient Goddess worship. The subject suddenly had taken on enhanced significance.

Almost all ancient cultures, she knew, worshipped the Goddess. This made sense—the woman, in some kind of miracle obviously predestined by the gods, gave life. And who gave life to the first human? There could be no conceivable answer in ancient times other than a woman-like Mother Goddess. Which is why it was so stunning that most modern religions embraced a male figure as the primary deity. All the Abrahamic faiths—Judaism, Christianity, Islam—clearly did. In Hinduism, the male Vishnu was the supreme god. Buddhism did not worship the personage of Buddha, but it venerated his teachings. Zoroastrianism worshiped the *Wise Lord* as the supreme being. In the aggregate, these faiths represented almost three-quarters of the world's population. In fact, the largest Goddess-based religion, Wicca (and even this was largely dualistic rather than solely Goddess-based), checked in with a mere two million followers, essentially the same number as the oft-mocked "Moonie" Unification Church of Sun Myung Moon. Comprising 0.027 percent of the world's population, or barely one of every 4,000 people, Wicca didn't even move the needle.

So how to explain the Goddess' precipitous fall? How had her appeal waned so much that she claimed no more adherents than did a fringe cult leader? Had some kind of significant change occurred within the consciousness of humankind that moved it away from Goddess worship, which had once been almost universal?

And then, perhaps even more mysteriously, according to the Sinclair journal references the Goddess suddenly reappeared during one of the most male-dominated periods in human history, the Middle Ages. Did her reappearance prompt the Sinclair cross-Atlantic journey? Were the Sinclairs and their associates searching for other like-minded peoples? Or, more simply, for a new land where they could escape the patriarchal fist of the Church? Either way, because most Native American tribes worshipped a pantheon of gods who were both masculine and feminine, these natives would have been far more likely to welcome and embrace explorers who were like-minded. Contrast this to the later Europeans who came not only to take lands but to proselytize, all in the name of their angry male God. It was no wonder that the Phoenicians and Sinclairs (and anyone in between with similar beliefs) would have been received more warmly than the later colonizers.

She thought of the words of their friend, Black Eagle, a local tribal chief: "Whoever came here in the early years had to have come in peace. Otherwise we would have kicked their ass back across the Atlantic."

Amanda smiled sadly. Given how the later Colonists treated them, perhaps that's what the Native Americans should have done to the Pilgrims, rather than helping them survive that first winter. By the time they decided to fight back, it was too late.

The cool March air did little to clear Nicolette's head as they hiked through the darkened forest at America's Stonehenge. Her mother dead? It reminded her of the first time she had slept outside in a tent, unsheltered, unable to shake a sense of naked vulnerability. Her mother may not have been around much, but she was always *out there*, someplace. That was no longer true.

For some reason her thoughts turned back to the forest animals not eating the Goddess offerings. What explanation could there be other than that they had instinctively understood to leave them for the Earth Mother? The realization brought comfort to Nicolette. *Her mom might be dead, but a greater mother figure would continue to watch over and care for her.*

Jamila interrupted her introspection as they entered the ceremonial center of the complex, filled with stone chambers, walls and niches. They had largely bypassed it yesterday, instead concentrating on the vertical stones standing on the horizon and the astral alignments they marked. Alone in the pre-dawn gray, Jamila pointed at a stone wall. "Not many people know about this alignment. See how all the stones in this wall are laid horizontally, except the large one in the middle?"

Nicolette nodded. The middle stone stood upright, shaped like a narrow triangle with its top point cut off.

"A few years ago a researcher noticed the stone and figured it must have been placed like that on purpose." She now pointed to a low stone chamber with its opening directly facing the wall. "And he noticed this chamber. It's too low to stand in, and it makes no sense as a storage niche since it can't be closed off. He figured it must be ceremonial, perhaps some kind of viewing station."

America's Stonehenge Viewing Chamber

Nicolette moved closer. Building it would have taken considerable effort, yet the low-ceilinged, open-air structure seemed to have no utilitarian purpose. She remembered what an Egyptian guide had told her once when she visited the Karnak temple complex. "All great structures built by man were constructed to impress and honor the gods."

She had made a quick rebuttal. "What about the Taj Mahal? It was built by a king to honor his wife."

The guide, who had not been shy about his fixation on Nicolette's blond hair and what he guessed was her Western decadence, had arched an eyebrow and smiled. "For some men, a beautiful woman is like the gods." The Taj Mahal aside, Nicolette had found her guide to be correct in his analysis. Which told her that whoever built these stone chambers did so for religious, not practical, purposes. Just as Jamila had suggested.

Nicolette crouched and entered the chamber. "Sit along the back wall, in the exact center," Jamila directed.

Nicolette did not have to be told what to look for. Seated cross-legged on the cold stone floor, she watched as the area beyond the stone wall began to glow. The horizon brightened quickly. A solar orb rose above the wall line, bursting through a gap between the trees like a fireball. A fireball that hovered atop the shallow bowl of the triangular wall stone as if it had been placed there by the hand of the Goddess:

America's Stonehenge Equinox Sunrise Alignment

"Wow," was all Nicolette could muster.

As if in agreement, Jamila fingered her Hamsa amulet. "The ancient priests of this complex used alignments like this, and like the one we saw last night, to track the seasons. It was important from a practical standpoint to know when to plant crops and when to sail and when to hunker down for the winter. But also for ceremonial reasons, to pay homage to the sun god."

Nicolette stared at the phenomenon until the sun climbed and disappeared behind a tree. She blinked, the image of the sun atop its pedestal burned onto her retina. She didn't mind.

She gestured at the chamber around her. "Obviously this is larger than it needs to be."

Jamila smiled. "Actually, it is the perfect size." She pointed to the corner to Nicolette's left. "If you move all the way to that corner, you will see the same alignment, with the sun sitting atop the vertical stone, at sunrise on the winter solstice. And in the other corner, it will happen on the summer solstice. The effect is almost like a pendulum, with the chamber marking the widest movement of the sun's arc."

"Brilliant," Nicolette breathed. She hugged her knees to her chest. She had much to learn.

In his sleep, Cam turned to reach for Amanda. The thump of his arm flopping against an empty side of the bed jarred him awake. He peered at the clock. Not yet seven o'clock. And no noise or light from the bathroom.

He kicked off the sheets and shuffled into the kitchen. Amanda sat at the table sipping hot cocoa, a stack of research books in front of her. "Why up so early?" Especially on a Sunday.

She explained she had thought she heard Astarte awake and then couldn't fall back to sleep. "I sometimes wonder if she gets teased at school because of our research."

The thought had never occurred to Cam. "How so?"

"Well, the idea that Columbus was late to the party. Not to mention all the bloodline stuff with the Sinclairs. I could see many people being threatened by that. And you know how things can be in middle school, especially with girls."

"Have you asked her?"

"No, but I saw her roll her eyes when we first told her about the journal. As if, *here we go again.*"

"You think she doesn't believe it?"

"It's not that. Obviously it's part of her heritage. I think she just doesn't want to deal with it. Sometimes I think she just wants to be *normal*, with normal parents who have normal jobs."

Cam smiled wryly as he poured some orange juice. "She's never going to be normal. Sorry."

Amanda bit her lip. "Speaking of which, we are going to have to deal with this princess prophecy soon."

"That was almost four years ago. A lifetime to a kid."

"Yes, but it's very much a part of her. You can't tell a little girl every day of her life that she is destined to be a princess and then just expect her to forget. That's not what little girls do. That's their dream, to be the princess."

"But Astarte's not a silly little girl. She's smarter than that."

"Exactly. She's smart enough to understand the prophecy has some legs. She really *does* have all this royal blood flowing through her veins. We really *are* at the dawn of a new age. The world really *is* ready for a new spirituality based on so-called feminine values."

Cam sat down at the table. "Then how do you explain the recent elections? The alt-right bloc hardly represents feminine values."

Amanda gritted her teeth. She understood the frustration of some Americans, but allowing factions who espoused prejudice and racism to have a seat at the table was not the solution. "I think his election actually fits in perfectly. You've heard of the dead cat bounce in the stock market, right?"

Cam chuckled. When a stock fell precipitously, it usually rebounded a small amount before falling a final time back to its low; the pattern resembled a cat falling from a roof to its death and bouncing up off the pavement before dropping again with a thud to its final resting spot.

Amanda continued. "Or, to put another way, this is the last gasp of the old guard. They have been able to rise up, and get enough other people who felt cheated by the system to go along with them. But when they have to rule, people see how backward, how out of touch, they really are. Their policies and rhetoric are going to drive people into a whole new way of thinking."

Cam smiled. "Into the loving arms of the Goddess."

"Yes," Amanda nodded. "You could say that. After two thousand years, it's about time."

Cam took her hand. "You don't have to convince me. I'm not sure how we ended up in a world run by men anyway. At the lecture I gave last week at the Masonic Lodge, there was a guy who was thinking about joining. He asked if it was true that the Freemasons wanted to take over the world. The Master of the Lodge laughed and said, 'The last thing we want is to run the world. Heck, we can't even do a good job running a pancake breakfast.'"

Jamila and Nicolette spent another hour exploring the America's Stonehenge ceremonial site, Nicolette insisting on checking again to see if the Goddess offerings remained untouched by the animals. Jamila lingered. She felt spiritually energized by the site. As, apparently, did Nicolette.

But Jamila's good humor faded quickly. She hated the thought of returning to the mountains without Astarte. The girl was crucial to her plans. At least the Gunn woman and her lawyer husband, simpletons though they were, were competent caregivers.

Her mind remained focused on the girl. Jamila and the others in the secret society of women calling themselves the Crones had been aware of Astarte since her birth, twelve years earlier. Astarte's people believed her to be the princess prophesized to unite the religions of the world. The story was, on first impression, an absurd one. The stuff of fairy tales. But no more so than a boy birthed by a virgin in a manger.

"Have I told you the story of Astarte?" she asked, as they hiked back down the trail on what was turning out to be a sunny, warm spring day. Stories, legends, dramatizations, songs—these were the tools of the Goddess. Not written words, rigid and unyielding, scratched onto paper or parchment.

Nicolette shook her head.

Jamila took a deep breath. "Most people are not aware that the Knights Templar were here, in America, long before Columbus. They were hiding their treasures, and perhaps also looking for a safe haven, fearing the Church. They had close relations with the Native American tribes in New England and maritime Canada. One of the Templars who made the trip was part of the Jesus bloodline."

"I grew up with this stuff, being descended from the Sinclairs." Nicolette smiled sadly. "From my Mom's side. It's one of the few things that still connect us. Or connected us." She sighed. "Anyway, I was only ten when I read the *The Da Vinci Code.*"

Jamila nodded. "The novel is a simplified version for popular consumption, but those of us in the know have been aware of a Jesus bloodline since, well, since his crucifixion. Anyway, this Templar of the bloodline—he also descended, separately, from both the prophet Mohammed and Cleopatra—married a powerful and revered Native American chieftess. The prophecy at the time of this ancient union was that a female descendant, forty generations hence, would usher in a new era, a new epoch, one in which the Goddess would reign."

Jamila watched closely for some kind of skeptical reaction from her apprentice. But all she got was a nod as the younger woman effortlessly hopped over a stone wall. "Forty is considered a sacred time span in many ancient cultures and religions. It is prevalent in the Bible," Nicolette offered.

Jamila considered the comment. The Israelites wandered in the desert for forty years, the Great Flood lasted forty days and forty nights, the kings of Israel all reigned for forty years. "Yes, I am aware of that," she said more curtly than she intended. The truth was that Jamila had not made the connection in her mind. And she might be unfairly resenting the girl her youthful vibrancy. She took a deep breath as her foot searched for firm ground. "Twelve years ago a Native American woman, from the Mandan tribe, gave birth to a baby girl she named Astarte, after the ancient Goddess. Astarte's birth marked the end of the forty generation span. And it almost perfectly coincided with both the Mayan calendar ending in 2012 and the precession of the equinox." She explained that the twelve constellations appeared to rotate around the earth, periodically taking turns being visible behind the rising sun during the time of the spring equinox in a phenomenon called the precession of the equinox. "These constellation changes occur every 2,000 years. So, in addition to Astarte's birth, we have two other events—the Mayan calendar and the precession of the equinox—all marking a cycle change. A transition between eras. In short, the time is ripe for change, for a new spirituality. Just as it was when Jesus was heralded during the last precession of the equinox."

Nicolette again surprised her with more insight. "Jesus is associated with the sign of the fish because he was born just as the zodiacal sign Pisces began to ascend."

"Correct. And presently Aquarius is ascending. The trees blocked our view here today, but yesterday I observed this phenomenon from our hotel, and this morning when I awoke as well." In New York she had insisted on a room on a high floor facing east. Despite the lights of the city muting the stars, she had viewed the light show. Today had been more vivid. "The equinox sun rose just at the edge of the Aquarius constellation. No doubt you've heard the song lyrics about the dawning of the Age of Aquarius."

The novice nodded.

"Importantly for our purposes," Jamila continued, touching her Hamsa, "the sign of Aquarius—*aqua* meaning water—has long been associated with women and the Goddess." A woman's water broke just before giving birth, long considered the most miraculous of life events. And in countless creation myths life emerged from primordial waters.

Nicolette offered yet another insight. "Mary is the most important woman in Christianity. The root of her name is *mer*, meaning the sea."

It was becoming clear that Jamila had underestimated her charge. "So back to our prophecy. Forty generations have passed. Astarte is born. When Astarte's mother, then her uncle, died suddenly, the girl was taken in by the Gunn woman and Thorne, who had grown close to her. For the past four years, we have been biding our time, waiting."

"Waiting for what?"

"For the girl to come of age." Jamila realized she had left out part of the story. "As I said, forty generations have passed. Along the way the Mormon leader Joseph Smith entered the picture, adding his bloodline to that of Jesus and Mohammed and Cleopatra and the Native American royalty. And Jesus, of course, can himself trace his lineage back to King David. So, young Astarte could, *potentially*, attract followers of Christianity, Judaism, Islam, Isis and Mormonism, as well as Native Americans. I say potentially because obviously there is a huge difference between a prophecy and reality." Jamila felt a strange tingling run up her spine; she reached up to touch the branch of a pine tree, as if to ground herself back to nature. "But the time is right for change. The Goddess is ascending. The girl herself is gifted; she could have unique and broad appeal."

Nicolette turned and offered a shy smile. She met Jamila's eyes. "And she has you to help guide her, Jamila."

Cam ate a quick breakfast to get his blood sugar stabilized before taking Venus for a four-mile run on a sunny, temperate March morning. The ice on the lake was beginning to break up, and as Cam jogged he watched the waves on the open water slap against the ice sheet in the sheltered cove at the eastern end of the lake, slowly eroding it. Ice had always fascinated Cam; as a kid he'd check every day to see if the lake was safe for skating. Ice was practically the only substance in nature which got lighter when it turned from its liquid form to a solid, which is why it floated rather than sank. If it sank, of course, the fish living on the lake bottom would die. It was just another example of the amazing complexity of nature. Of Mother Nature.

The tragedy of Katherine Morville's death and the excitement of the Sinclair journals had combined to distract him from the disappointment he felt from the news he had received on Friday afternoon. Brandeis University, where he had been teaching two classes on pre-Columbus history of America, had decided not to renew his contract. The department head claimed it was because funding had dried up. But Cam sensed the decision went beyond finances. Many faculty members had been unhappy that "fringe history" (as they called it) was being legitimized at a prestigious liberal arts college. The truth, Cam suspected, was that the history he was teaching was not considered politically correct by the liberal-minded faculty. What Cam believed, and taught, was that waves of European and Mediterranean explorers had crossed the Atlantic prior to Columbus—Phoenicians, Irish, Norse, French, Scots, perhaps even ancient residents of Atlantis. The problem was that all of these groups happened to be Caucasian or lighter-skinned. Many people in the burgeoning alt-right movement had jumped into the pre-Columbus pool with both feet, enthusiastically supporting Cam's research because in it they saw validation of their belief in the supremacy of "white" culture. Cam now found himself as a figurehead in a movement he wanted nothing do to with. One that Brandeis also wanted nothing to do with.

He spat a mouthful of sour saliva onto the shoulder of the road and picked up the pace, trying to outrun his sullenness. The truth was, his ego had been bruised. He prided himself on being an animated, informative lecturer, and his student reviews had been glowing. And he enjoyed teaching, enjoyed seeing a group of sleepy-eyed undergrads turn wide-eyed as he pulled back the curtain on a hidden, dusty corner of history, enjoyed the times when students brought their parents to his class, enjoyed the news of a student declaring a history major and thanking him for being their inspiration. To have it taken away for something he had not done felt not only unwarranted, but also unfair. He spat a second time. Hell, he wanted nothing to do with white supremacists. Imagine if they knew how much he admired the values and ideals championed by Goddess worshipers.

He picked up the pace yet again, intent on sweating the bitterness out of his system. "Stop whining," he hissed, Venus looking up to make sure he was not talking to her. Life was good. He'd still have plenty of opportunities to research and lecture. And now he had these fascinating journals to pore over. "Get over yourself."

An hour later he stepped out of the shower and into a pair of jeans and fleece pullover. Astarte was still asleep, and Amanda had gone to the basement to use the elliptical machine. Pushing the Brandeis disappointment to the back of his mind, he grabbed a banana, put Springsteen on the stereo, and sat down to translate more of the journal.

November 28, 1354

Father wants me to write in journal every week. He says to write about journey so future generations have record.

I ask him how we will cross great ocean. He says we have maps from two hundred years ago. Men from our family go then to land called Onteora where there is temple to Goddess. The people of this land are strong fighters and also loyal friends. Some are Ivri. Father says Ivri are people from Bible. Ivri live now with native people of Onteora.

Cam paused. *Onteora* was the name the Native Americans had given to the Catskill Mountains of New York. And the *Ivri*, Cam knew, were the Hebrews, or Israelites. Was young Henry confirming the legends that some ancient Israelites, perhaps one of the Lost Tribes of Israel, made their way across the Atlantic in ancient times?

Putting aside the question of the Lost Tribes, young Henry's journal specifically spoke of a Templar journey to America two hundred years before the boy's 1354 journal date. Cam had read about exactly such a journey. In fact, it had almost gotten him killed.

The details were a bit foggy because Cam, though obviously still alive, had suffered a severe concussion which left much of that chapter of his life blurry. He might need Amanda's help to fill in the details, but he did at least recall the main points: Astarte's Uncle came into possession of a Templar travel log recounting a journey to New York's Catskill Mountains in 1179. The log claimed that the Templars had buried a number of artifacts on Hunter Mountain, and the log contained maps and other clues leading to those burial spots. Cam and Amanda had hiked the mountain and dug up some of the artifacts, in particular a flat piece of sandstone with Roman numerals which appeared to be latitude and longitude coordinates. Below the numerals, the words "IN CAMERA" had been carved. He found the image on his laptop:

In Camera Stone

Cam knew from his legal background that "In Camera" meant something that was to be kept secret, such as when a judge looked at evidence alone in his chamber. Upon finding the carving, he and Amanda had immediately speculated that the coordinates might lead to some kind of secret location or hiding place. Reading left to right (after determining through examination with a magnifying glass that the final numeral was a "I" rather than an "L," the horizontal line on the bottom being a natural flaw in the rock), the numbers yielded the following coordinates:

Latitude 45°, 30'
Longitude 75°, 53'

But when they had entered the coordinates into Google Earth, the resulting location was a forested area south of Ottawa City. Neither of them had ever heard of a Templar presence in that part of Canada. And then it had struck Cam: Templars in 1179 would not have been using Greenwich, England as a prime meridian; they would have likely used Paris, as many others of their time did (especially given that Paris was the location of the Templar commandery). Paris being 2°, 20' east of Greenwich, they made the simple adjustment to yield:

Latitude 45°, 30'
Longitude 73°, 33'

When Cam had plugged these new coordinates into Google Earth, an image of the grand Notre Dame Basilica in Old Montreal popped onto his screen, beckoning like some kind of religious beacon. He repeated the effort again now, with the same result:

Notre Dame Basilica, Montreal

Cam and Amanda had already been studying the iconic Basilica, due to many clues in both its artwork and history which indicated a tie back to Gnostic, nontraditional Christian beliefs such as the belief in the importance of the female in the godhead and the related belief that Mary Magdalene had been the wife of Jesus. The Basilica, in fact, had been built in the 1670s by the Sulpicians, the descendants of the same French noble families who had founded the Templar Order. Was it possible, they had wondered, that the In Camera Stone—hidden by the Templars, a religious group later disbanded and excommunicated because of their blasphemous beliefs—was directing future clue-followers to a sacred site in Old Montreal, upon which later generations had built a monument to their Gnostic, perhaps Goddess-based, religious beliefs?

That was exactly what Cam and Amanda had concluded, based on two compelling pieces of evidence hidden in plain sight in the Basilica. The first piece of evidence involved the ornate, raised pulpit of the cathedral, located at the left side at the midpoint of the nave, from where the priest could deliver his sermon directly to the congregants seated below him. Though the church had been rebuilt in the 1800s, the pulpit had been salvaged from the original 1670s construction. Cam again pulled up an image:

Pulpit, Notre Dame Basilica

On the ceiling of the pulpit area, suspended over the priest like the heavens above, shone a golden triangle set into a round, cloud-like object with sunrays bursting forth in all directions. Religious experts agreed this image symbolized the divine—God in heaven looking down upon his flock. Inscribed within the triangle was the Hebrew Tetragrammaton, the unspeakable name of God comprised of the four Hebrew letters (reading right to left), Yod, Hey, Vav, Hey. Many people commonly pronounced these four letters as "Yahweh," though religious Jews never spoke it aloud or even when reading to themselves silently. As Yahweh was the God of the Old Testament, it made perfect sense that this name would be inscribed above the pulpit to identify the Divine presence.

Except that it was spelled wrong.

The first letter, the Yod, a small letter resembling an apostrophe mark, was missing on the far right of the word (Hebrew being read right to left). Cam found an image he had created for one of his lectures, showing both the traditional Tetragrammaton side by side with the Notre Dame Basilica version:

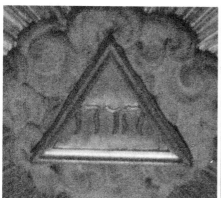 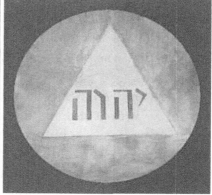

**Tetragrammaton at Notre Dame Basilica (left) and
the Traditional Depiction with 4 Letters (right)**

When this anomaly was first discovered, curious researchers thought perhaps the Yod had been hidden under the frame of the triangle surrounding the Tetragrammaton. But when the wood was removed, there was no Yod. So what was going on here?

It turned out that this misspelling was more than a simple oversight. In fact, the absence of the Yod changed the entire meaning of the word. The remaining three letters—Hey, Vav, Hey— spelled the Hebrew word *Chava*. In English, this translated to Eve. The significance of this alteration could not be overstated: The name of the Divine, looking down from the heavens, had been changed from the masculine Yahweh to the feminine Eve, the first mother, the giver of life. On the one hand the change was subtle. On the other it was breathtaking in its audacity. With the removal of a small, apostrophe-like letter, the Goddess had been elevated to the heavens in the largest Catholic cathedral in North America.

Or perhaps *re-elevated* would be a better word. As Amanda was documenting, almost all ancient cultures worshiped the Goddess, most of them putting her atop the pantheon of gods. And there was some striking grammatical evidence that even the ancient Israelites recognized the Goddess' primacy: The name Yahweh itself, ending in 'h,' was a feminine word under Hebrew grammar rules. The question was obvious: Why use a feminine name for a masculine God?

There might have been room for doubters to dispute this wordplay were it not for the second piece of evidence in the Notre Dame Basilica, hidden in plain sight where only those with eyes trained to see would understand what they were looking at. Painted on the interior walls of the church were murals depicting various Christian religious scenes, as was the case in most churches. Cam had walked right past this particular mural the first time he saw it, but it had reached out and grabbed Amanda, screaming to her its secrets.

Most people, like Cam, glanced at the mural and dismissed it as one of tens of thousands of paintings depicting the Virgin Mary holding Jesus:

Notre Dame Basilica Mural

But a more careful analysis led to a different, startling conclusion. Traditional depictions of the Virgin Mary showed her clothed in blue, always with her hair covered (to depict her modesty). The woman in this image had red hair, uncovered, and was wearing orange and green, the colors traditionally associated with Mary Magdalene. Furthermore, the baby was wearing an orange necklace, another important clue. The Dutch royal family, known as the House of Orange, did not originate in the Netherlands, but rather traced its lineage back to the city of Orange in the Provence region of southern France, where Mary Magdalene was believed to have settled after fleeing Jerusalem following Jesus' crucifixion. This orange necklace, therefore, was another clue that the baby was of the blood line of Mary Magdalene's House of Orange. Lastly, the woman's head was adorned with a crown while the baby's was not, an unthinkable oversight if the baby was intended to be Jesus.

As was the case with the Tetragrammaton, there was a clear message being sent in this mural. In the Basilica, in a prominent spot, the bloodline of Mary Magdalene was being commemorated, the imagery making it clear that this child was to be considered of royal blood. Amanda had concluded, and Cam had agreed, that this mural celebrated the union of Mary Magdalene and Jesus, a marriage which nontraditional Christians—many of whom were believers of the importance of the Goddess—had long believed took place.

As Cam often told his audience when he lectured, it didn't really matter if Jesus and Mary Magdalene were married and had children. What mattered was that many people over the centuries *believed* they were and did. And beliefs were what motivated behavior, which in turn was what made history.

All of this was a long, circuitous journey back to young Henry's journal entry: He spoke of Templars coming to America in the late 12th century. And the evidence suggested that the Templar's nontraditional Christian beliefs—regarding both the bloodline of Jesus and the importance of the feminine aspect of the godhead—had influenced and possibly even motivated that journey.

Cam turned back to translating the final paragraphs of the journal entry:

But our journey is not to Onteora. We go to Stag Island. Name of people there are Miggy-Maw, says Father. They are friends of our family for many generations. Father tells story of angry bear chase Miggy-Maw boy, but man of our clan saves him with crossbow. Boy is son of chief. Chief say we friends as long as trees grow, four winds blow, and sun shines.

Maybe we visit other lands after land of Miggy-Maw. If we do, Father says we need stones and bones from Miggy-Maw. I think we use stones and bones to make picture in our hands and show other tribes picture. If picture is good, tribes allow us to pass onto their lands. If not good, Father says they kill us or make us slaves.

Cam considered this. It sounded like some kind of passport system, whereby stones and bones (presumably kept in one's pocket) were arranged in a specified pattern when passing across borders from one tribal territory to the next. Only those travelers who had been told the secret pattern were allowed safe passage. A fairly ingenious, if simple, system.

The *Miggy-Maw*, Cam surmised, were the Mi'kmaq tribe of Nova Scotia and New Brunswick. The boy's account of close relations between the tribe and the Scots was true even today—the Sinclair Clan and the Mi'kmaq held periodic gatherings in which the centuries' old friendship between the peoples was remembered and celebrated. Prince Henry Sinclair and his men were said to have overwintered in Nova Scotia before making their way south to Westford; the Sinclair Clan was currently doing DNA testing to see if any descendants of that cold winter six centuries ago might be identifiable today.

A single short passage remained:

I think I not make good slave. Mother says I am usually good boy but I am stubborn like goat. I try hard to remember correct stones and bones so tribes not make us slaves. Perhaps I tell father I am only nine years old and too young to be slave.

Smiling, Cam looked up to see Amanda wander in, her gray t-shirt soaked in sweat. "I was just thinking about Montreal, about the Basilica."

She glanced at the journal. "Because of that?"

He nodded. "Young Henry mentions an earlier Templar journey from the 12th century."

"But that Templar journey was secret. There is no way a modern hoaxer would know about it, at least not until we wrote about it a few years ago." She dried her face with the hem of her shirt, exposing her toned midriff. "So if these journals are older than, say, five years, and they discuss that Templar visit, they must be authentic."

He glanced at the worn leather of the journal cover. "Five years? Remember the smell when we first opened this up? It would take decades to build a smell like that."

She turned to walk away, smiling over her shoulder as she did so. "I don't know. Your hockey equipment smells like a dead raccoon, and you bought new stuff only a couple years ago."

She had a point. Best to wait for the carbon dating.

Astarte woke up feeling heavy and sluggish on Sunday morning, like she had spent the night trudging through deep snow. But she knew she couldn't miss Sunday school. Not after working so hard convincing Cam and Amanda that remaining a part of the Mormon Church—as she had been raised by her uncle—was so important to her. What she hadn't told them, and what they had not figured out, was that the religion itself did not matter to Astarte. What mattered was that the Mormon leaders believed she really was the Fortieth Princess. Which is why she spent part of every Sunday huddled privately with Apostle Bertram strategizing about the future. Her future.

Exhaling a deep breath, she threw off the covers, washed her face and bounced down the stairs in as cheerful a manner as she could muster.

"Morning, sweetheart," Cam said, looking up from the Sinclair journals. Venus, too, trotted over to lick her hand. "Mum's in the shower. I'll drive you to Sunday school."

"Okay. I'll be ready in twenty minutes."

"Mum said you had trouble sleeping last night."

She shrugged and smiled. "Just a bad dream." She didn't like lying to them. She was, in fact, very fond of both of her adopted parents. Loved them, even. But feelings like love and loyalty had only a secondary place in a life defined by destiny. Apostle Bertram had made that very clear to her.

An hour later, just before ten, Cam dropped her in front of the white-stoned Temple on a high hill in the town of Belmont. She took a deep breath before entering, turning to appreciate the view of the Boston skyline in the distance. She knew that in nearby Arlington, during the Revolutionary War, American troops attacked the British forces from hills like this one as the Red Coats marched back to Boston after the Battles of Lexington and Concord. Apostle Bertram often told her that the flames of another revolution were being stoked in these same hills.

She knew that not all the Mormons agreed with Apostle Bertram. Just like they didn't all agree with Amanda's and Cam's research, though some of them did. She had heard one man—an apostle who had come all the way from Salt Lake City to meet her—argue that there was no way a *little girl* could be an instrument of God. Apostle Bertram had shut him up by shrugging and saying, "Who are we to presume to know God's plan? Or to question it? Our Book of Mormon confirms that the ancient Israelites came to this continent and interbred with the Native Americans. And our records confirm that the girl is, indeed, a direct descendant of Joseph Smith. The prophecy could very well be legitimate. And if not, what have we lost?"

Astarte had felt like telling him she wasn't so little, but had swallowed the retort. She was getting used to that. Apostle Bertram told her that was part of growing up. He liked to say, "God gave us two ears and one mouth, which means we should listen twice as often as we speak."

"Hello, Miss Astarte," Apostle Bertram said as she knocked on the open door of his office. He wore the same dark gray suit, white shirt and light blue tie with American flags he usually wore. Later she would join the other children in their lessons, but the first hour she always spent with him. Learning how to be the Fortieth Princess.

"Good morning, Apostle." When she first met him, she thought he was what Amanda liked to call an odd duck—he always told the same bad jokes, and he had an annoying habit of swallowing nonstop when he wasn't talking. But he had grown on her.

As she entered his office, he held his hand out to her, fingers upraised in an upside-down claw. "What's this?"

She resisted the urge to roll her eyes. Did he not remember he had told her the same joke just last month? But she had learned that part of being a princess was knowing how to make other people feel good around you, so she just smiled and said, "I don't know."

He flipped his hand over, clawed fingers now facing the floor. "A dead *that*," he said, grinning and swallowing.

She laughed politely, sat down in the wooden chair across the desk from him, and handed him her homework. He accepted it and read through the two pages, nodding and swallowing. When he finished, he handed it back to her. "As we've discussed, the biggest challenge you will face is having people—and when I say *people*, I mean men—accept a woman as a religious leader. The words you've written in this essay tell me you've thought a lot about this problem."

She shifted in her chair. Of all the adults in her life, he was the only one teaching her actually *how* to be the Fortieth Princess. She explained how she would address this objection, summarizing her homework: "Men and women are not equal. God, on purpose, made us different, made us unequal. Men are physically stronger. Men tend to be less emotional. But women are better at some things also. We are better caregivers. We are empathetic. And we are more abstract in our thinking, which makes us more spiritual. Because we are more spiritual, it only makes sense that God sometimes chooses us to be his messenger."

Apostle Bertram nodded, swallowing through another smile. "When you say, *his* messenger, are you conceding that God is a man?"

She shrugged. "No. I believe he is neither man nor woman. He is just, well, *God*. I supposed I will just have to be careful never to use a pronoun. It will always be *God* or *the Almighty*." She purposely left out *Lord*.

The apostle—Astarte guessed he was in his seventies—made a note. "No pronouns. Excellent." He stared out his window for a minute. "I have seven children, six boys and a girl. My girl, Betsy, is the smartest of them all." He smiled. "Even in math and science. I often wondered why that was."

Astarte didn't know how to respond—why shouldn't Betsy be the smartest? So she stayed silent.

He continued. "And then, finally, I stopped wondering. I finally just decided that, as the saying goes, the Lord works in mysterious ways." He grinned at her for a second, swallowed, then turned serious. "I see you are wearing your ring."

She nodded. "The spring equinox after my twelfth birthday was yesterday. The prophecy says that's when my ascension begins."

He pursed his lips and angled his head. "I've often wondered what that means. You've been training for years, so in that sense it has already begun."

"There is supposed to be a messenger of the Goddess who recognizes me by my ring. She will tell me what to do next."

Apostle Bertram seemed to weigh a decision. Then he sighed and reached into the top drawer of his desk. He held an envelope out to her. "This arrived here yesterday, by hand delivery. Addressed to you. As you can see, I have not opened it." He pointed to the handwritten return address, which simply read, *Messenger*. "Perhaps the messenger found you even without your ring."

Her hand shaking, sensing that the contents of the envelope would likely set the course for the next chapter of her life, Astarte reached out and accepted the cream-colored envelope, the kind Amanda used for sending thank you notes. Apostle Bertram stood. "I'll give you some privacy."

She barely noticed him leave the room and close the door. Using a letter opener on the apostle's desk, she sliced open the envelope and removed a single sheet of flowered stationary. A smooth, neat river of blue ink flowed back and forth across the paper. For some reason Astarte pictured an older woman, her hand steady and sure as she wrote out the words. She blinked and began to read:

Dear Astarte:

I trust you have been waiting for this message, now that the spring equinox after your 12th birthday has passed. Just as the seasons change, so do we move from one phase of our lives to the next. It is time for your ascension to begin, as has been prophesized.

Your path ahead will be a difficult one. Serving the Goddess is not always easy. But the Goddess does not ask of us things which we cannot give. As the expression goes, from those whom much has been given, much is expected.

I know your life has not been an easy one. You never knew your father, you lost your mother, and then you lost your uncle. It probably does not seem fair. But it has made you stronger and more self-reliant, attributes you will need as you take on the responsibilities prophesized for you. As I am sure you sense (though you may not have fully realized it yet), at some point you will need to separate yourself from your current caregivers. They gave you stability at a time in your life when you needed it, which is why we allowed them to take you in and even adopt you. (Yes, we have been watching you over the years.) They may be nice people, and I have no doubt that they love you, but they are not part of this prophecy. They are not part of your destiny. Once you outgrow them you will need to cast them aside, much as a hermit crab outgrows its shell. This is the way of nature, the way of the Goddess.

Soon you will be faced with a decision. You will know the correct course in your heart, even as you realize the course you choose will be a difficult one. But you must not shy away. As the expression goes, "When you wait, all that happens is you get older." Put another way, to think too long about doing something often becomes its undoing. You are many things, Astarte. I do not believe timid is one of them.

March confidently in the direction of your dreams, of your destiny.

Faithfully yours,

The Messenger of the Goddess

Astarte stared at the letter, her head spinning. The Messenger was right: She did realize, deep down, that at some point she would have to leave Amanda and Cameron in order to fulfill her destiny. She just didn't think it would be so soon.

She lifted the letter to her nose. It smelled like the earth—a mixture of dirt and cut grass and fresh flowers. It smelled like the Goddess.

Jamila felt the tension drain from her body as Nicolette exited the interstate in central Vermont and they began to wind their way through the snow-covered forest toward their secluded compound. At its most basic, Goddess worship was nothing more than a veneration of Mother Nature—her creatures, her balance, her rhythms, her cycles. Here, in the woods of Vermont, far from the destructive influence of the human animal, life could be lived as it was meant to be. Not totally, but close.

Jamila had closed the main access road to the compound to discourage unwanted visitors. Nicolette found, and then navigated, the narrow, pitted logging road they now used as the only entry. The boxy BMW bounced and skidded its way along, Jamila barely cognizant of Nicolette's efforts to keep the vehicle from sliding into a gulley or hanging itself up on a tree stump. A few hundred yards later they crested a slight ridge, dropped onto a paved drive, and rolled to a stop in front of an A-framed, cedar chalet straight from a Swiss Alps travel magazine.

Jamila reached forward and squeezed the apprentice's shoulder. "You've done well. Have a bite, and then you best be on your way." Normally the apprentice would have carried Jamila's bags, but normally she wasn't on her way to her mother's funeral.

Smoke wafted from the chalet chimney, flavoring the cool mountain air. Jamila set her bags down outside the front door but did not enter. Instead, she walked along a fieldstone path, freshly shoveled, to a auxiliary building—matching the main building but smaller, like a little sister—behind the chalet. Originally built as a Christian chapel, the sister structure had been repurposed by Jamila as a shrine to the Goddess. Most of the great churches in Europe had been built atop ancient pagan worship sites. Jamila smiled as she entered and looked up to where a large bronze cross had once been mounted. It felt good to return the favor.

After interviewing half a dozen acclaimed artisans, Jamila had commissioned a ceramic sculpture to serve as the centerpiece of the shrine. She had not wanted something ostentatious or oversized; the Goddess was not some vainglorious narcissist, appeased by extravagance. The sculpture depicted a naked woman, lying horizontally, morphing into a tree. Roots grew downward from her hair and legs and arms, while a pair of thick trunks arched over her and joined in the middle at a crown of leaves. Jamila had named it the 'Venus Tree.' A photo of the sculpture, even before it became the center-piece of the shrine, served as Jamila's wallpaper on her phone:

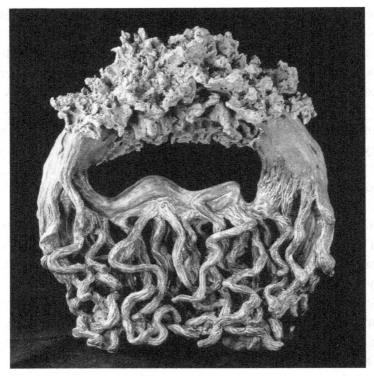

'Venus Tree' Goddess Sculpture

Using miniature cobalt-colored tiles, Jamila had decorated a shallow bowl, filled it with water, and placed the sculpture inside, the water an ancient symbol of the Goddess' life-giving abilities. She laid out clusters of flowers and fruit and nuts—arranged in spiral shapes, another symbol of the Goddess—to surround the shrine, the bounty again symbolizing the fertility of the Earth Mother. Above the Venus Jamila hung a mobile constructed from fine strips of pure silver, the hanging metal shaped into pentagrams and crescent moons and triple spirals and upward-pointing triangles. Three simple terracotta oil lamps, arranged in a triangle around the God-dess and filled with scented oil, lit the shrine and sweetened the air around it. Finally, she had commissioned a wooden plaque be carved with the words of an ancient poem:

I am Nature, the universal Mother, mistress of all elements, pri-mordial child of time, sovereign of all things spiritual, queen of the dead, queen also of the immortals, the single manifestation of all gods and goddesses that are. My nod governs the shining heights of Heaven, the wholesome sea breezes, the lamentable silences of the world below. Though I am worshipped in many aspects, known by countless names, and propitiated with all manner of different rites, yet the whole round earth venerates me.

Jamila straightened her amber dress and recited the words of the ancient poem as she approached the shrine. "Forgive me, Mother, for I come to you with the stain of death on my hands."

She stood tall in front of the Goddess and touched her Hamsa amulet. The Goddess did not demand supplication and obedience and sacrifice like the egotistical male God of the Judeo-Christian faiths, just as she did not require extravagant offerings. The God-dess cared only about her children. Jamila closed her eyes, imagined being a child again in the hills of Lebanon so many years ago, her mother gently rocking her.

In her mind, the Goddess purred a response. "Tell me, my child, was it necessary? Nature is not always kind. But it is never cruel. All things must die, as you know. Sometimes a life must end so that more lives may flourish."

"I believe it was necessary, yes." Jamila forced herself to be honest with herself; there was no sense in lying to the Goddess. "Our plan requires that the Gunn woman and her husband appreciate the importance of the journals. That someone was willing to die for them seemed the best way to convey this." As she spoke the words aloud, she realized the justification seemed a bit flimsy. But the truth was, had the journals not arrived with the melodrama of a middle-of-the-night phone call and subsequent fatality, they would not have been given the same presumption of authenticity. And Jamila did not have the luxury of time to wait for the Gunn woman and Thorne to study the journals in a leisurely manner.

"And your plan, it results in the chosen one, Astarte, coming into my service?"

"I believe so, yes."

"The taking of another life is rarely an acceptable price, no matter what the benefit." The purr had taken on an edge.

"I am aware of that, Mother."

"Yet you have done it anyway."

Jamila swallowed and nodded.

The Goddess' dismissive reply surprised Jamila with its bluntness. "Then your plan best succeed."

Cam picked up Astarte from the Mormon Temple just after noon and handed her a turkey sandwich and bottle of water. "Hope you don't mind eating in the car. I thought we could help out at the soup kitchen again today."

She accepted the bag and nodded. "Okay."

The kitchen was run by a Catholic church in nearby Lowell. Though not a member of the church, Cam had become friendly with Father Westfall years earlier when first researching the Westford Knight legend. He and Amanda had become regular volunteers, though periodically she skipped out to allow Cam and Astarte to spend some father-daughter time together alone.

A half hour later they exited the highway and Cam wound his way through the old mill town to a Victorian-era stone edifice near the river, its stained glass windows vibrant in the midday sun. They went in a side door and down a half-flight of stairs to a cramped but spotless kitchen area. The tall, silver-haired Father Westfall greeted them, still wearing his priest collar from the morning mass. Cam had often thought Westfall could have been a diplomat if not a priest; even wearing an apron and carrying a bag of trash, he exuded an air of elegance and refinement.

"Aha, my best volunteer!" He smiled and winked at Cam. "And, Cameron, you also!"

"What can I do to help?" Astarte asked.

"Well, tonight we are serving spaghetti and meatballs, with garden salad. Can you grow us some cucumbers?"

She smiled. "No, but I can cut them up."

Cam joined her at a butcher block island and began to chop carrots. A few minutes later Father Westfall approached. Other volunteers would arrive later in the afternoon, but Cam liked to arrive early, always glad to have a few minutes alone with his friend. And Cam, not being a parishioner, was one of the few people Westfall seemed comfortable confiding in. "So," Westfall said, smiling as he grabbed a head of lettuce and began cutting, "a Catholic, a Mormon and a Jew are out playing golf."

"Careful of the Mormon," Cam said, nodding toward Astarte, "she's a ringer."

The priest flashed an even, white smile. "So I've heard." He turned serious. "As always, thanks for coming." He sighed. "Many of our volunteers seem to come out of a sense of obligation rather than a sense of charity. You know, because God is watching. That is fine, I suppose, but sometimes it seems a bit ... businesslike to me." He put a hand on Cam's shoulder. "I know you are here for the purest of reasons." He smiled again. "Not just to get extra credit." He glanced at Astarte. "Or to put something on your résumé."

"Résumé? Like getting into college?" Cam replied.

"More like getting into heaven." Westfall shrugged. "You know, do enough good deeds, and you get in."

Cam kept it light. "Heaven, is that Ivy League?"

The priest chuckled. "Better. Though Harvard does have a larger endowment."

They worked for a few seconds, the thwack of knives on hardwood and Father Westfall humming the only sounds in the kitchen. Cam took a deep breath and summarized the journal discovery. "The odd thing is, there are all these references to the Goddess."

Westfall bit his lip. "As you know, I'm very open to the legend of Prince Henry Sinclair coming here before Columbus." He leaned in conspiratorially. "And I even happen to agree with your theory that the Templars were practicing a form of Christianity different than that taught by the Church." He shrugged. "So why not the Goddess? For the vast majority of human existence, people have worshiped her in one form or another."

The priest reached for a bag of celery and continued. "Sometimes I wonder if it really matters. Yahweh, Jesus, Allah, Buddha, the Goddess, whatever. The Freemasons have the right idea. As long as you believe in some being greater than yourself, some higher power. Something to keep you humble. I don't know that our current leaders have that humility." He smiled sadly as his words hung. "For the first time in my life, Cameron, I'm afraid. Afraid of what our arrogance might lead to."

All Astarte really wanted to do after returning from Sunday school and the soup kitchen was to sit in her room and think about the letter from the Messenger of the Goddess. But Amanda and Cam had other ideas.

"Have a quick snack and then put on your boots," Amanda said, ushering her to the kitchen table. "Dad just finished translating another journal entry and we're going out to explore."

Astarte couldn't think of an excuse to say no. But she did worry this journal would turn out to be a fake. Something about the way the journals had landed in Cam's lap seemed ... off ... to her. Just the other day one of her teachers had mentioned the Westford Knight and rolled his eyes, as if he thought the whole thing was just a silly story. She forced a smile onto her face. "Okay. Can Venus come?"

Amanda smiled. "Of course. She's the one who translated the Latin this time."

In the car, after her snack, Cam eyed Astarte in the rearview mirror and explained the entry. "So I skipped ahead a bit, to after they arrived in America. They've come up the Merrimack and are now camped in Westford, at what I think is the base of Prospect Hill."

Amanda interjected. "We think they are camped near the Stony-brook Farm Stand, where the train tracks are today."

Cam continued. "They are planning to stay awhile, so they need a place to pray. You know, like a church. But obviously they don't have time to build one." Astarte could sense Cam's excitement. "Amanda, why don't you read it?"

"August 3, 1355

We camp on the banks of a small river, inland from ocean. Father says we must find a place to pray. Also he wishes for a place to view stars. There is much tree cover in this land. Only when on rivers can we see the sky. Father says trees make it like sailing in fog because without stars he is lost.

One of our scouts find a pond empty from no rain. It is only 500 paces from camp. He says you can see entire sky from pond. Father likes it and decides to build a sanctum."

"Remember," Cam interrupted, "even though the Templars were Goddess worshipers, they were still Christian. We think what was happening was that they wanted the Church to recognize the Goddess as the wife of God. But, again, they had not rejected Christianity. Even after everything the Church did to them. So they needed a place to pray."

Astarte leaned forward at the mention of the Goddess. Perhaps this would be a worthwhile outing after all. Amanda continued.

"Pond is wet around edges but in middle a dry island. On island are many white rocks, some small and others as tall as me. Father is very pleased. He says white stones are gift of Goddess. We find 8 flat white stones and lay stones in path west to east, ending 3 paces from large, round, white boulder. Father says path will be nave of sanctum. We then place other white stones in circle around boulder. Father says circle will be apse and boulder will be altar. When we finish we pray. Father very happy."

After dinner Father and I return to look at stars. He says Goddess is watching us. We thank her for giving us sacred site and making it dry for our use."

"This is really quite a passage," Amanda said. "The eight steps of the nave are, of course, a reflection of how the Templars viewed the number eight as sacred. And the design of the sanctum is identical to other Templar churches—oriented east-west, with the round sanctuary facing east, facing Jerusalem."

"So where are we going?" Astarte asked. Was it possible this sanctum still stood? A sanctum to the Goddess?

"Believe it or not, I think I know this place," Cam replied. "I sometimes walk Venus in the woods back here. Usually the pond is a few feet deep, but during droughts some of it gets exposed." It had been a particularly dry fall and winter. "I think I've seen these white rocks." He smiled. "And, just like Henry said, it's only a few hundred yards from the base of Prospect Hill."

At a wooden sign that read 'Grassy Pond,' Cam turned into a dirt parking lot. Venus whined in anticipation as they ambled down the trail toward a football stadium-sized depression in the earth. Around the rim of the depression, the ground angled up steeply. "It looks like a giant bowl," Astarte said.

"A bowl full of ticks," Amanda replied. "Tuck your pants into your socks."

They tried to stick to the higher ground, their feet sinking in the moist soil as they mucked their way to the center of what was normally the pond. Just as the journal recounted, a number of white boulders stood in the middle, matching the cotton-ball-like clouds which periodically blocked the mid-afternoon sun.

"Hey, look at this," Amanda said. They all stopped. "Google Earth must update every few months, because here's a shot of the pond mostly dry like it is now. You can see the sanctum just as Henry described. Even the altar boulder in the middle of the stone circle."

Astarte peered in. "It looks like a dandelion."

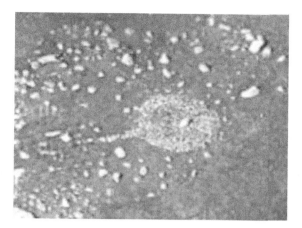

Stone Sanctum, Grassy Pond, Westford

Cam studied the image. "I think what they did was pick up all the smaller stones and use them to make the circle. And they left the larger ones where they were—they were probably too heavy to move."

They increased their pace, eager to view the formation up close. The ground did not appear to be much higher in the sanctum area in the middle of the pond, but apparently the few inches of elevation was enough to keep the soil firm and dry. Astarte stopped at the beginning of the eight-stone path and snapped a picture.

"It looks just like Henry said," Astarte commented. "Eight stones leading to a circle, with a boulder in the middle."

Stone Sanctum, Grassy Pond, Westford

Amanda hung back, her head cocked. "Wait," she said, "I've seen this shape before." She jabbed at her phone for a few seconds. "This layout—some people call it a 'stick and ball' and others a 'balloon'—is found all over the world. It's a fertility symbol, the birth canal leading to the womb. It's been documented in the Negev Dessert, Arabia, Italy, Sweden, New Mexico…"

"And now here," Cam interjected.

"So maybe young Henry didn't really understand the symbolism," Amanda said. "His father described it as a nave and apse, and on one level that's what it is. But you know the Templars: There's always a secondary meaning, some secret symbolism. This was not just a place to pray, but a shrine to the Goddess as well." She paused. "In fact, that may be the root of the design of the Templar round churches. Goddess shrines, camouflaged as Christian sanctuaries."

Cam grinned and nodded. "Yes. I like it. That's exactly something they would do."

He dropped to his knees to examine the step stones while Venus sniffed at the ground, her tail wagging. "These stones were definitely placed by hand. And they are all flat, chosen on purpose."

"I agree," Amanda said.

Cam stood and smiled. "This clinches it then. Nobody knows about this site, yet it's right where the journals say it should be." He exhaled. "I think we finally have hard evidence Prince Henry was here."

"Just playing devil's advocate," Amanda replied. "But what if the journals are fake?" She paused. "Then this sanctum wouldn't prove anything, right?"

Cam shook his head. "But that doesn't make sense. That would mean whoever faked the journals somehow knew about this site. Yet it's been under water for decades. Nobody knows it's here."

Astarte barely listened as they talked it out. She just stared at the white stones, at the white altar. When she was younger she had devoured the King Arthur stories. She had been especially enthralled with the sacred island of Avalon, surrounded by marshland and ruled by the Goddess priestess, Morgan le Fay. The island remained hidden from the outside world, only revealing itself, almost magically, when those who approached came in service of the Goddess.

Just as Astarte had done today.

Chapter 4

After the craziness of the weekend, Cam appreciated the quiet of an empty campus as he held midmorning Monday visiting hours in his windowless basement office of a drab Brandeis administration building.

He glanced down at an arriving text. Amanda. "I'm feeling naughty," it read.

He shifted forward in his chair. She was supposed to be at the gym. Yet he wasn't going to argue. They were, after all, still newly-weds. But with Astarte being a light sleeper, Amanda wasn't always game for making the bed squeak. "I like naughty," he typed.

"What are you doing?" she replied.

"Office hours." He glanced at his watch. "For another half-hour." And he was pretty much alone in the basement.

"I'll be there in fifteen, under one condition."

"Chocolate?"

"LOL. Chocolate is always good. But no lights. When I arrive, complete dark. Deal?"

"How will we see the chocolate?"

"We'll just have to grope around."

Grinning like a schoolboy, Cam walked down the hallway to the men's room to wash his face, then returned to remove the files and books from his desktop. He looked around the cramped office. It was going to have to be either the desk or his chair; there wasn't even enough floor space to get horizontal. Not that he was complaining.

He tried to distract himself by grading a couple of papers for a few minutes. But eleven minutes after their texting ended, he duti-fully turned off the lights and sat in his office chair in the dark, the glow of his phone and a strip of light visible under the door the only illumination. If Amanda was going to take the initiative like this, the least he could do was play along.

Four minutes later, almost to the second, he heard a light tap on the door.

"Come in."

The door cracked open about a foot. Amanda edged through the opening backward, closing the door behind her. He heard, but could not see, the click-clack snap of the lock. She continued silently, barely visible, her telltale thin blond ponytail—decorated, as usual, with a turquoise-colored ribbon—swinging like a gold pendulum in the night as she sashayed in. The muffled sound of her coat dropping to the floor filled the room, though it was barely audible over the thumping of his heart. Was she wearing anything underneath? He sensed her presence, smelled her perfume, heard her quickened breathing. He felt the blood pump to his groin. Only after a few seconds did he realize she was waiting for him.

"Here," he said, "take my hand."

Thin, strong, warm fingers felt for his, their hands finally joining in a firm clasp. "Come to me," she whispered. "I'm naked."

Her voice sounded raspier, deeper. When he replied, it came out as more of a gasp than anything coherent. "Okay."

He fumbled his way around the desk, their hands still clasped. She took his shoulder gently with her free hand, sat him on the front edge of the desk, reached down to rub his thigh. He exhaled as she moved into him, resting her naked body against his. Cupping his hand around her butt, he pulled. "Now," she moaned. Her mouth covered his, her lips oddly cold—

The door flew open, light filling the small space. Cam recoiled, but for some reason Amanda held close to him, perhaps to shield her naked body from the intruder. *What happened to knocking?* And hadn't he heard the door lock? Blinking in the harsh light, he focused on the doorway just in time to see a masked figure dressed all in black snapping pictures with a small camera. "What the—?" he blurted.

Suddenly Amanda bent down, grabbed her coat and lunged toward the door, the ponytail again swinging. Only as the door slammed behind her did he see her profile. And realize it was not his wife. *Cold lips.*

Stunned into inaction for a second or two, Cam quickly recovered. He yanked at the door, but it barely budged, someone having bound it closed. He struggled to force it open. "Damn it." It was obvious he had been set up.

After ten seconds of alternately closing the door and yanking it open, his anger and frustration almost ripping the door from its hinges, he created enough opening to reach through and release the strap securing the door. He sprinted down the hallway toward the stairwell. But he knew he was too late. Whoever had planned this knew what they were doing. And they had pictures of him which would be very difficult to explain away. The only question now was, why?

Cursing, he stomped back to his office. What an idiot he had been. How could someone not recognize—or incorrectly recognize—his own wife? The answer, of course, was that he had been looking at the world through his one little eye rather than the two on his face. Amanda had never completely gotten over the photos of Cam and a strange woman entering a hotel room from a few years ago—doctored pictures, he was able to prove. Amanda believed, and accepted, that the whole thing was a set-up. But he knew the images still haunted her dreams, still popped into her mind's eye at random times, especially when Cam was traveling. It wasn't rational, they both understood. But Amanda had been burned by unfaithful lovers in the past, which made infidelity the third rail of their relationship.

He replayed the entire series of events in his head. It had clearly been Amanda's phone that texted him. And she had planned to go to the gym this morning. So either she had lost her phone, or someone had gotten hold of it while she was working out or showering. He grabbed his coat and keys. It was a long shot, but he might find some answers at Amanda's gym. And even then he'd have a hell of a time getting her to believe him.

Once in his car, Cam phoned Amanda. He exhaled, relieved when she answered. At least she was okay. "Hi, um, just checking in."

"I'm leaving the gym. You on your way home already?"

"Not yet. I need to run some errands first."

As he drove he formulated a plan. As with most lies, he knew that the more truth it involved, the better. He parked in the gym parking lot, took a deep breath, tightened his tie knot, and straightened his hair with his hand. This was going to take some of his best lawyering. He grabbed his briefcase and strode to the front desk. Without preamble, he snapped his attorney business card down, lifted his chin and addressed the young desk clerk in his most grave lawyer voice. "Daniel," he said, reading from the clerk's nametag, "My name is Attorney Cameron Thorne. I regret to inform you that we have a serious situation here. A very serious breach of privacy giving rise to both state and federal liability. I'm going to need to speak to the manager on duty. Immediately."

The young clerk blinked and took half a step back. Cam did not flinch. "Immediately," he repeated. On a legal pad he wrote down Daniel's full name, embellishing it with an angry underline.

A minute later, a fit, forty-something woman who looked like she spent most of her day teaching step classes and yoga strode toward him from behind an office door. Cam resisted the urge to try to charm her, opting instead for the moral outrage approach. "May I help you?" she asked.

"I think it would be best if we had this conversation in private," he said, his voice low and hard.

Nodding, she led him into her office. They sat on either side of her desk, Cam taking a long minute to remove a file from his briefcase, write down her name as he had the desk clerk, and take a deep breath. He handed her his business card as well. "I just received an urgent call from a valued client. A respected member of the community. He has just been the victim of an egregious breach of his privacy rights. I am here, hoping to contain the situation before it blows up. Because if it does blow up, my client will suffer irreparable and permanent damage." Cam leaned in. "And he will hold this facility accountable if that happens."

The manager wasn't as easily intimidated as the desk clerk. But obviously she needed to listen. She took a pair of eyeglasses from her top drawer and began taking notes herself. "I'm listening. Of course we are concerned if one of our members suffers an injury while here."

"It is not one of your members, but rather the husband of one of your members." Cam lifted his chin. He explained how his client had received a text from his wife's phone, which it turned out had been part of an elaborate sexual sting operation. "My client, and I tend to agree, is fairly certain that the perpetrators obtained his wife's cell phone while she was here at this gym."

The manager eyed him. "We are not responsible for things stolen from the lockers. There are appropriate signs posted."

Cam bit his lip. "Ms. Harrison. I am here right now precisely because I want to nip this *before* it turns into a legal pissing contest. My experience has been that nobody wins when that happens. So while it may be that you have no legal responsibility for things being stolen, I think you do have a very real legal responsibility to do what you can, now, once something has been stolen, to take reasonable steps to redress the situation."

"Redress the situation?"

"Yes. By that, I mean I want to look at your security cameras. With you accompanying me, of course."

She shook her head. "No way. We put video cameras in the locker room to cut down on crime. Most clubs don't have them, but we promised our members only myself or another female staff member would ever see them. Many of the women are naked."

"Fine. You can screen the video and just show me the images from the sting. That's all I care about."

She ran her hand through her hair. "I don't know—"

"Listen, we have only a very short while to act. If we can identify the culprits on film, my client will be able to go to the police *before* any demands of extortion are made. Before, I might add, we ask the obvious question of how the culprit gained *unauthorized* access to the locker room." Cam allowed his features to soften for the first time. "I think you can agree, it does nobody any good to have these pictures shown to my client's wife. To one of your members." He felt the bile rise in his throat as he pictured Amanda seeing him in an embrace with a naked stranger, his hand on her ass. "Those are the types of images that once seen can never be erased."

The manager doodled on her blotter for a few seconds before abruptly standing. "Okay." Cam allowed himself to exhale. "Follow me. We can look at the tapes, after I screen them. But I can't let you take them."

Ten minutes later, Cam understood exactly how the sting had gone down.

Amanda had gone to the locker room, placed her valuables in a locker, opened her combination padlock, snapped it closed on the locker, and left for the workout area. A young blond woman standing nearby had filmed Amanda's lock machinations with her cell phone; after three tries she opened Amanda's locker. "Never seen her before," said the manager.

Using Amanda's phone, which apparently Amanda had not disabled, the blond woman then began the text flirtation with Cam. A flirtation that quickly turned into foreplay. She placed the phone back into the locker (after presumably deleting the texts), spritzed herself with Amanda's perfume, and jogged toward the gym exit, a turquoise-colored ribbon swinging from her ponytail as she did so. Cam guessed that they—whoever "they" might be—had found a woman matching Amanda's body type and hair color and then, probably after some surveillance, had added the ponytail and ribbon as the proverbial frosting on the cake. Then, once the body double closed and pretended to lock the door to Cam's office, an accomplice stood ready with a camera and the harness to hold the door closed so Cam could not pursue. A neat and simple sting. And he had fallen for it.

The perpetrators had been lucky in that Amanda had elected to go to the gym on the same day he had office hours. But it was not really luck, as she almost always went to the gym on Mondays and that was his regular office hour day. This detail, in addition to the hair ribbon, indicated some planning had gone into the sting. Not a huge amount, but some. Enough.

He thanked the gym manager and stood. "I'll need to consult with my client." He began to turn. "And whatever you do, don't erase that video." It might be the only thing that could save his marriage. Though hopefully it would never get to that.

Jogging back to his car, Cam's cell phone rang. The office manager from his office suite. "Cam, hey, your 11:30 appointment is here. Erin Donovan."

"Right." *Damn.* He had forgotten. A new client. He slid into the front seat. "I'm running late. Can you ask her if she can wait twenty minutes?" She had called on Friday, something about a white collar crime case. Normally Cam wouldn't take a case like that, but the loss of his Brandeis job meant he couldn't be so choosy anymore.

"She says she'll wait."

"Thanks, Jessica."

He considered phoning Amanda again while he drove, but this was not a conversation a man should have with his wife over the phone. He'd head home immediately after his appointment. He knew that if he waited until the incriminating pictures were sent to Amanda, he'd lose the moral high ground. He had no choice but to come clean now, explain how he had been the innocent mark in an elaborate sting. It was a rational explanation. Not that the idea of your spouse interlocked with a naked stranger always produced a rational response...

Infidelity. He smacked the roof of his car as he exited the parking lot. All he had done was embrace a woman he thought was his wife.

The only other option, and it would be a long shot, was to identify the woman in the sting and confront her before the inevitable extortion began. But he had little to go on. Blond hair and cold lips was not much of a lead.

Cam parked along the Town Common and jogged into his office, entering through a back door to bypass the reception area. He'd at least try to maintain a bit of dignity. After running his hand through his hair and straightening his desk, he phoned the office manger, who also doubled as a receptionist for the office suite tenants. "Jessica, would you please show Ms. Donovan in?"

A twenty-something woman wearing a black blazer over a white t-shirt and blue jeans strolled into the room. She extended her hand, tossed her brunette hair back, and flashed an easy white smile. "I'm Erin Donovan. Thanks for seeing me."

"I apologize for making you wait." Cam was generally pretty good at reading people, but he couldn't get a good sense of his new client. There was something ... artificial ... about her, as if she were an actress playing a part. Not a surprising personality trait for a woman apparently involved in a white collar crime. "Please, have a seat."

As she did so, she studied him, her head tilted in a way that, again, almost seemed rehearsed. After a few seconds, she said, "Before we start, I need to ask you a few questions about attorney-client privilege." She paused. "I need to know I can trust you one-hundred percent. Even if what I've done repulses you."

He nodded and felt his face flush. She had obviously done her homework on him. Almost a decade ago he had been suspended from practicing law for six months for violating the attorney-client privilege. His firm had been representing the Archdiocese of Boston in a series of priest sex abuse cases and he had leaked to the press a firm memo outlining how the Archdiocese planned to attack the abuse victims by bringing up drug use and other mental health issues. Cam was not ashamed of what he had done. But he also understood that if he did it again, he would likely be disbarred for life. And he also understood why prospective clients would ask the question. He took a deep breath. "That was a unique situation, involving sexual abuse of children." He doubted she had done something nearly as repugnant. He turned toward his computer and opened a file. "I'll print out a letter of engagement for you. That will establish our attorney-client relationship. At that point, anything you say to me or give me relating to this matter will be strictly confidential, even if you decide not to hire me. I can't tell or show anyone. The only exception is if you are planning to commit murder."

She smiled again. "Works for me, thanks." She sat back, then leaned forward. "Sorry to be a pain, but does that include your wife?

We have a mutual friend—that's how I got your name—and I really don't want anyone to know anything about this."

"Of course."

She held his eyes. "Maybe you could put all that in the letter? What you just said, about everything being confidential, including not telling your wife?"

He tried not to let his impatience show. He wanted to get through this meeting and get home to Amanda. "Okay, sure." He added a couple of sentences to the engagement letter and sent it to the printer. As he did so, she pulled out her checkbook. "I assume you'll want a retainer?"

He nodded as the printer whirred. "Yes. For a white collar crime case, usually $5,000. Obviously I'll return what we don't use."

She wrote it out as he collected the letter from the printer. He spun in his chair to make copies of both the check and the letter and gave a set to his new client. Trying to lighten things a bit, he smiled. "Okay. We are official. Now, tell me about your case."

Erin took a deep breath and pulled a leather portfolio off the floor. She withdrew a manila envelope and handed it across the desk. "I'm not sure if it really would be considered white collar crime. But it is definitely against the law." Cam withdrew an upside-down photo from the envelope, Erin's face contorting into an odd smile as if she knew a funny secret she wished she could reveal. "I'm not proud of it, and it really is a rather sordid affair." She paused for effect. "My friend and I are blackmailing someone."

Cam realized what was happening in his gut even before his brain had pieced it all together. With a shaky hand he turned the photograph over. He barely noticed Erin stand.

"Thank you, counselor," she said as she began to edge away, the words and her image coming to him as if from across a vast expanse. "I'll be in touch."

He stared at the photo, panic washing over him: A naked white ass with a hand covering it. His hand. With his gold wedding band reflecting the camera's flash.

Amanda's phone sang out as she picked at a salad on the back deck, taking advantage of some March sunshine while Venus watched the ducks navigate around the few clusters of ice still remaining on the lake. The caller ID read 'Westford Public Schools.' Amanda dropped her fork and leaned forward. Calls from the school in the middle of the day rarely augured good news.

Her chest tightened as she pushed the answer button. "This is Amanda."

"Hi Mum."

"Is everything okay?"

"Yes. But I forgot to bring the form in for the ski trip."

Amanda exhaled and sat back in her chair. "What ski trip?"

"I talked to Dad about it. Next weekend to Vermont with the ski club. It's free. He said it would be okay. It's called the Venus School, so it must be good."

She laughed. No wonder things had slipped through the cracks, crazy as life had been the past few days. "Sounds fun. Can I come too?"

"Um, no Mum. Can you fill out the form and email it to me? It's on my desk. I'll print it out here."

"Okay, honey." A weekend alone with Cam wouldn't be a horrible thing either. He could use some cheering up after losing his Brandeis job, especially because it was not his fault that many right-wing extremists had adopted Cam as a kind of figurehead for their movement. He was like the scientist who discovered an earth-like planet in a far-off galaxy and suddenly found himself the darling of the Area 51 crowd even though he himself didn't believe in UFOs. Just because Cam (and she) believed explorers who happened to be Caucasian crossed the Atlantic before Columbus did not make them White Supremacists.

Amanda sighed. What a screwy time. If she was correct, and if they really were at the dawning of the new Age of Aquarius, then perhaps this was just the inevitable growing pains. The Dead Cat Bounce, she had called it. Or, looking at it another way, the angry storm blowing before the winds of change.

Cam sat motionless in his desk chair, forcing himself to think, to focus. Finally he tore his eyes away from the naked ass photo. The game was on, and he was already losing badly. Worse, he didn't even know the rules. And his opponent had effectively neutered him with the sophisticated attorney-client privilege ruse.

Sophisticated. Just like the sting itself. Someone had gone to a lot of trouble with this.

It had been almost a decade since Cam had been suspended for violating the attorney-client ethical obligations. He doubted the rules had changed much, and there had never been much wiggle room. The classic law school hypothetical illustrated the rigidity of the rule: *If an attorney learns his client murdered the attorney's parents, he may not disclose this information to the police under penalty of disbarment.*

Even so, Cam found a copy of the Massachusetts attorney rules online and studied the specific language of the regulations. There really was, as he feared, no wiggle room. If he went to the police to report the sex sting, he would be putting his client in legal jeopardy, a clear violation of the attorney-client privilege. As a repeat offender, Cam would surely be investigated and likely disbarred. He played it out in his mind: Even telling Amanda about the sting would likely lead to disbarment, as Erin and her cohort would surely be able to tell by Amanda's reaction to any attempted extortion whether or not Amanda had been forewarned by Cam. He could ask Amanda to act surprised when confronted, and then perhaps later lie under oath at his disciplinary hearing, but did he really want to force her to perjure herself on top of everything else? Especially versus enemies sophisticated enough to be able to catch her in her lie? He shook his head. Going down the disbarment path was a non-starter. Without the Brandeis job, they needed the income from his law practice. And getting disbarred would not exactly enhance his reputation as a researcher.

Cam pounded his desk with his fist. There was no escaping his predicament. He couldn't tell the police. And he couldn't tell Amanda. This was not like fighting with one hand tied behind his back. It was like fighting with no hands at all.

Cam arrived home mid-afternoon, just before it was time to leave for Astarte's indoor soccer game. He came through the door with his head down, not making eye contact with Amanda.

"Hi," Amanda called, wondering what was bothering him as Venus trotted over to greet him.

He offered a sad smile and looked up, as if searching for something, before raising himself and responding. "Hello."

"Everything okay?" She kissed him lightly on the mouth.

"I'm just bummed out about this Brandeis thing."

She nodded as they moved out of the front hall. "Do you need some food?" His energy seemed low.

"Yeah. Maybe." He reached for a banana on the kitchen counter.

"Astarte already left for her game, with Shannon's mom. They wanted time to warm up."

"Oh. I forgot about that."

Amanda smiled. "Plus I think there is a cute high school boy who works there that they like to ogle."

Cam finished his bite. "But they're only twelve."

"It's middle school, Cam. They're turning into young women. They have this new superpower that works on pretty much every guy they meet." She leaned over and nibbled his ear lobe. "I'm sure you remember what it was like to be around adolescent girls?"

He forced a smile. "Yeah, but it never occurred to me that they were some poor guy's daughter."

A half hour later they took seats on metal bleachers inside what used to be an indoor hockey rink. Teams played six per side, five players plus a goalie, like a hockey team; unlike in outdoor soccer, the hockey-style boards kept the ball in play, and the girls had quickly learned to use the angled ricochet plays to their advantage.

Astarte started at center forward. Even Amanda's untrained eye noticed her physical dominance—she was no bigger than the other girls, but she was faster and more fluid. And the ball stayed close to her foot, almost as if drawn magnetically. Cam was distracted today, his eyes on the game but his attention miles away. Normally he watched from the perspective of an experienced hockey player. Amanda recalled his words from last week's game:

"Watch how she's always two or three steps ahead of the other players. It's almost like she can see into the future, like she knows where the ball is going to be. Most of the girls chase the ball. With Astarte, it looks like the ball is chasing her." Amanda had pulled her eyes off the action and focused instead only on her daughter. Cam was correct. Wherever Astarte went, the ball almost always seemed to follow. "It's like chess," Cam had continued. "Great players see four or five moves into the future. If a girl has the ball along the wall, there are only a couple of plays she can make. And then, after that, only a handful of plays that the other players can make in response. Somehow Astarte can anticipate the most likely outcome. Partly it's by reading body language, and partly it's by understanding probabilities."

Of course, in the end it was just 12-year-old soccer. Hoping to engage Cam, Amanda leaned in. "Normally I can count on you for a good analysis of the game. How's Astarte doing?"

He sighed. "Well, as always."

"Last week you said she has a unique ability to read things."

"It's not just soccer. She has this same ability in other things. She reads people, too. Better than me, that's for sure."

She faced him. "Cam, what's bothering you?"

Not meeting her eyes, he replied, "I took a new client today. I think it might have been a mistake." He sighed. "But I can't really talk about it."

"Okay." After a few seconds, she spoke again, hoping to draw more information out of him. "I think what we're talking about, the ability to read people, is really just intuition."

"Yeah, I should have listened to my gut." He stared out toward the playing field, but Amanda could tell he wasn't really focusing on the action. "I used to work with a lawyer who had great intuition. She knew what the other side was going to argue even before they did." He tilted his head. "It made it really easy to prepare rebuttals."

Amanda took his arm. "Makes sense that your lawyer friend was a woman. Scientific studies show women, generally speaking, really are more intuitive than men. Our brains think differently."

"Differently? How so?"

She leaned against his shoulder, choosing now to keep things light. "Differently, as in better. That's why we're so much smarter than you."

At halftime of the soccer game, Cam jumped from the third row of the bleachers. "I need to make a call, and there's no cell reception in here," he said.

He lumbered to the edge of the parking lot and rested his foot on a dirty snow bank, one of winter's last ugly vestiges. It had been almost five hours since the sex sting in his office. He had no choice but to try somehow to get ahead of this. He dialed the gym and was put through to the manager. "Okay," he lied, "I've spoken with the police. Apparently this is not the first time this has happened. My description of the woman matches what they have already. They want us just to sit tight for a few days—they're close to making an arrest. Save the video, but don't mention anything to anyone."

"Um, okay. Should I call our lawyer?"

Cam didn't want that. Lawyers meant police. He lowered his voice. "Why? Are you hiding something? Has this happened before at your gym?"

"No," came the rushed reply.

"Well, in my experience in cases like this, only people with something to hide go running to their lawyers." On that note, he hung up.

But manipulating the gym manager did not mean Amanda's phone wouldn't buzz at any minute with a volcanic text or email. As he saw it, he had two choices: Wait for the extortion, or somehow try to prevent it. The latter was a long shot, but it was the only shot he had.

Which was why he made a second call. "Larry, it's me, Cam. Anything yet?"

Larry Delvecchio was a friend of Cam's from his Boston College days. A city kid from Hyde Park, Delvecchio had dropped out his junior year when his financial aid package was cut due to poor grades.

He went to work for his uncle's private investigation firm, found he had an aptitude for it, and never bothered to go back to school. Over the years Cam had used him in legal cases. This time it was personal. Cam had swung by his office after Erin left. He could trust Delvecchio to lie for him if necessary. And to do so convincingly.

"Nothing yet," he replied. Cam kicked a chunk of the snow bank into the surrounding brush. "I've asked around, and nobody's heard of these stings." The P.I. took a deep breath. "Look, I don't have to tell you how this shit usually works. Once they show the pictures to Amanda, they've shot their load." He pronounced her name like it was part of the word *salamander*, adding the 'r' to the end as many Bostonians did when 'a' ended a word. "After that, what can they do to you, right? So they'll contact you before they contact her. Give you a chance to meet their demands. If they call, make sure you write down the number." He evened the pronunciation score with *numbuh*, making the 'r' silent.

Cam wondered why he was fixated on Delvecchio's accent at a time like this. But just as Amanda couldn't stop the doctored images of Cam with the woman in the hotel from popping into her head, he couldn't control the random thoughts that surfaced in his mind either. "Okay, thanks."

He wandered back into the rink enclosure, cheered by the reality of there being no cell coverage. For the next half hour, at least, nothing bad could happen.

Seated at the kitchen table, Cam answered emails while Astarte worked on her homework. She seemed to take little joy in today's soccer success. Cam was concerned his bad mood was infecting the family. "Hey, Astarte, want to help me translate more of the journal?" Later tonight he was giving a lecture at a Masonic Lodge, but he had some time now.

Nodding, she put down her pencil. "This math homework is too easy anyway. I don't know why they make us do the same stuff we learned last year."

Amanda called from the kitchen, where she was stir-frying chicken and vegetables. "It's for the state standardized test. They want to make sure you remember how to do it."

Astarte shook her head. "The teachers know we already learned it. And the parents know we already learned it. And we know we already learned it. So why do we have to prove it on some silly test?"

Cam chuckled. "That sums it up pretty well, Astarte." He pointed at the journals. "But have you learned Latin?"

"No. But some of the words look like Spanish."

"Okay, then, come help me. Remember, I've been skipping around a bit. This is *before* they left Scotland, a few months before they built the stone sanctum in Westford."

Together they worked on the next passage, completing it a half hour later:

April 28, 1355

Today is my tenth birthday. Father givs me new sword. He says I carry it on our journey. I do not know date we depart, but I know it is near as Mother cries when she kisses me goodnight.

I am not afraid, even though people say monsters live in western sea. Cousin Mayfair says if you sail too far you fall off edge of world like apple rolling off table. When I ask Father he laughs. He says stories are from priests, trying to scare us so we stay home. When I ask him why priests want us to stay home he starts to answer, then stops. He says he will tell me when I am older.

I think Mayfair is jealous he is not coming, even though he is older than me. He is also angry James Gunn is coming. I hear Father tell Mother that Mayfair is big and strong like ox but also dumb like one. Then Mother says but James is not very smart either. And Father says yes but James is good boy and very loyal like dog. I think James is not very smart with lessons but is very smart with building and fixing things. And the animals like him. Maybe that is because James shares food with them. I am glad James is coming so I will have friend on trip.

Astarte sat quietly, staring out the window at the lake as the late afternoon sun faded. After a few seconds, she said, "I'm surprised Henry's father is taking him on the mission. He's only ten and it seems dangerous."

Cam nodded. "It sounds like his father felt it was very important. Worth the risk."

"What if I wanted to do something very important that was dangerous? Would you let me?"

Cam studied her. Obviously something was on her mind. "It would depend on how important and how dangerous."

She rolled her eyes. "That's not an answer."

"Well, then, the answer is probably not." He touched her arm. "Look, obviously Mum and I trust you. And we want you to make your own decisions." Shrugging, he concluded, "But you're only twelve. We're not going to let you do something reckless."

She nodded. He was surprised his answer didn't upset her more; normally she was pigheaded about fighting for the right to make her own decisions. "Okay then," she answered blandly. "That's what I figured you'd say."

Glad for the distraction from the looming extortion, after dinner Cam brushed his teeth, threw on a suit and tie, and jumped into his maroon Toyota Highlander for the twenty minute drive north across the border to Nashua, New Hampshire. He had been invited to speak to a group of Freemasons on his research involving the role of the Knights Templar in pre-Columbus exploration of America. Cam had no doubt that the modern Freemasons descended, either in whole or in part, from the medieval Templars. He ran through the presentation in his mind as he drove.

His and Amanda's research revealed that the Templars—perhaps not the rank and file members, but the Order's leaders—agreed with the heretical Gnostic belief that Mary Magdalene was Jesus' wife, and therefore should sit next to him on the throne in heaven as the queen. A 14th century painting in a Cistercian monastery (the

Cistercians being the sister Order to the Templars) in Tarragona, Spain, near the border of France where the main Gnostic community resided, evidenced Templar belief in this heresy and would be a key slide in Cam's Powerpoint presentation tonight. The woman at the bottom of Jesus' cross was clearly Mary Magdalene, as evidenced both by her long reddish hair and the skull in the foreground (a skull being almost always pictured with her). And she was clearly pregnant, as a quick glance at her bulging abdomen revealed:

Mary Magdalene at Foot of Jesus Cross (enlarged)

That this image had been displayed at a monastery was especially striking, especially during medieval times when heresy like this could get one killed. Which it eventually did: The Church outlawed the Templar Order, imprisoning, torturing and killing many of its leaders.

The revelation that the Templars secretly venerated the Goddess had taken on renewed importance in light of the frequent references to the Goddess in the Sinclair journals. The Sinclair family maintained close ties both to the Templar Order and to Scottish Rite Freemasonry—if these groups were worshiping the Goddess, it stood to reason that others in their circle were as well. Cam smiled as he drove: How ironic would it be if an all-male group like the Freemasons was secretly following an ideology rooted in veneration of the Sacred Feminine.

All this passed through Cam's mind on the short drive. But any thought of the Goddess made him almost immediately think of Amanda, which of course turned his mind to today's sex sting. How had he been so stupid? When he was younger, and his friends were getting married and having children, he used to smile politely when they talked about how happy they were. He hadn't bought it for a second—who would rather deal with diapers and crying babies and grouchy wives when being a single guy in a city like Boston was so, well, *intoxicating*? Now *he* was the guy who couldn't wait to get home and hang with Astarte and Amanda. He slapped the steering wheel. And because of his idiocy, it was all at risk.

He exited the highway and navigated through the old downtown area of Nashua. He found a parking spot on the street not far from the imposing, red-brick, Victorian-style Masonic temple. An old elevator—boasting a metal, scissor-gate internal door which Cam closed by hand—jerked him up to a wood-paneled lobby area on the fourth floor. It was as if he had stepped back in time, to an era where men of substance wore top hats and dinner jackets, smoked cigars, and nursed tumblers of cognac or brandy while cutting deals and cementing alliances. He half-expected to see men passing around a snuff box.

After making small talk for fifteen minutes, he was escorted into a high-ceilinged Lodge room ringed with blue upholstered benches and mahogany chairs, all of which were full. An altar resembling the Ark of the Covenant sat alone in the middle of the room, an antique Bible resting atop it, while a gold 'G' highlighted the east wall above the ornate chairs where the Master and other officers of the Lodge sat. A pair of large stones, one rough and one smooth to signify the Mason's progression through the organization, framed the raised platform upon which the Lodge officers sat. Cam had been to enough Lodges to know that the basic layout was always the same, modeled on the historic Temple of Solomon.

Cam sat, waiting to be introduced, and stared at the 'G' on the wall. He had read various theories—the 'G' stood for God, or Geography, or Grand Architect. He had even read it was a coded symbol for Venus (that is, the Goddess), a truth which was only revealed to Brothers who reached the highest levels of Freemasonry. Could an all-male organization really be a front for Goddess worship? In light

of what he had learned about the Templars and their apparent veneration of the Goddess, it was not out of the question. But then why did
the Freemasons not allow women to join? Why relegate the women to
a separate-but-unequal group of their own called the Eastern Star—

A jolt of understanding shot through Cam. The *Eastern Star.* On
the one hand, it was just a name. But on the other, it spoke volumes.
The eastern star was not just any star. It was Venus. The Goddess.
Because Venus orbited the sun faster than the Earth, it always rose
before the sun in the east (it could also appear in the sky in the
west in the evening) and had historically been known as the *Eastern
Star.* The name 'Eastern Star' therefore equated the female branch
of Freemasonry with the Goddess. More evidence of balance, of
duality. And Masonic reverence for the Goddess.

All of this passed through his head in the half-minute it took for
the Lodge to be brought to order. The Marshall marched over, offered
Cam his arm, and escorted Cam—always moving in straight lines
and at right angles, as befitting an upright and honest lifestyle—to the
front of the room to be greeted by the Master of the Lodge. As Cam
waited for the Master to make his ceremonial approach, he noticed
a button on the Marshall's lapel, a beehive with a Masonic emblem
adorning it. He leaned in. "Can I take a picture of your button?"

"Um, sure."

"I'll explain later," he said, lifting his phone.

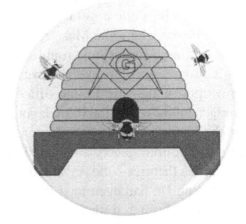

Masonic Beehive Button

Cam had seen similar beehive symbolism in other Lodges, including a painting he had photographed earlier this evening in which the hive sat atop a Masonic Bible.

Masonic Beehive Symbolism

He had never focused much on the meaning of the bees, assuming they were simply a symbol of industriousness. But as he strolled toward the center of the room to begin his presentation, he realized there was a secondary meaning: The hive was a matriarchal society, ruled by a queen serviced by thousands of male drones. He shook his head. Was that what was really going on here? Were thousands of Freemasons working in service of the Goddess queen? The question, Cam realized, brought him almost full circle. The 'G' did not stand for Geography or Grand Architect or even God. It stood, in all likelihood, for *Goddess*.

Emboldened by his epiphany, Cam gave an animated presentation, focusing on the multitude of sites and artifacts evidencing waves of explorers crossing the Atlantic prior to Columbus, many of whom seemed to connect (either going backward or forward through time) to the medieval Knights Templar. Midway through his talk he detoured a bit, taking a few slides out of order to focus more on the Goddess worship themes. He showed the images from the Cistercian monastery in Tarragona, with a pregnant Mary Magdalene at the foot of Jesus' cross, before lingering over the Notre Dame Basilica mural of Mary Magdalene with Jesus' baby in her lap.

Notre Dame Basilica Mural

"So," he said, "does this mean Jesus and Mary Magdalene had a baby?" He shrugged. "I don't know. And I don't care. In this case, the truth doesn't matter. What matters is what people *believed.* Because our beliefs dictate our behavior, and our behavior is what changes history." He gestured at the image. "This mural tells us that the builders of this church, descendants of the original French noble families who founded the Templar Order, *believed* in the union of Jesus and Mary Magdalene."

He paused to study his audience. He often gauged his listeners, checking their body language, to get a sense of whether they were interested and engaged in his presentation. This crowd seemed all in, eyes on him and bodies leaning forward. He plunged ahead. "So I think what was happening—even though I can't prove it—is that the Templars came here because they were looking to found a New Jerusalem, a place where they could practice a version of Christianity which recognized the importance of the Goddess, which understood that balance was essential in nature."

He scrolled back to show an image of Rhode Island's Newport Tower.

Newport Tower

"I've already explained to you why I think the Tower was built by descendants of the Templars around the year 1400." He had spent fifteen minutes laying out his case that Prince Henry Sinclair and his group, after leaving Westford, had been the builders. "As our Native American friends remind us, whoever built the Tower must have had some kind of accord with the local tribes. No way could they have built this in hostile territory. I think that accord was based on a shared reverence of nature and, more particularly, the Goddess."

He paused. "But why build a tower? In other places in America they carved things into stone, things like runic inscriptions and maps and effigies. Even if they felt the need to build something elaborate, why a tower as opposed to, say, a church or a fort? They were, after all, soldiers of the Church—so that's what they usually built, churches and forts."

Cam paced from one side of the room to the other, letting the question hang. "The answer, I think, is hidden in plain sight, as it often is. The name *Magdalene* is the Westernized version of the original Hebrew name, *Migdal*. Migdal in Hebrew means 'tower.' So the name Mary Magdalene translates to the *Tower of Mary*." Cam pointed to the screen and lowered his voice. "And there it is. Built for her. The Tower of Mary."

Cam took questions after his lecture, the buzz of the crowded Masonic Lodge again reminding him of bees in service of the Goddess.

The first question was right on point. "Do you really think the Templars were Goddess worshipers?" The man looked to be in his mid-fifties, his features out of proportion as if drawn by a caricature artist—ears too large, eyes too small, nose too long. But somehow the face conveyed warmth. "I mean, these guys were medieval warrior monks."

Cam smiled. "I hear you. Medieval. Warrior. Monk. None of those things exactly make you think of the Earth Mother. And to answer your question, no, I don't think the run-of-the-mill knight out on the battlefield thought of God as anything other than a bearded guy sitting on a throne." Cam walked toward the questioner, seated in one of the raised chairs reserved for visiting dignitaries. "These theological questions were only important at the highest level of the Order. Those were the guys in the tug-of-war with the Vatican. And it wasn't because they were feminists or anything. It was simply that they understood that everything in nature requires balance—light and dark, wet and dry, cold and hot, male and female, death and rebirth. When things get out of balance, those things usually break."

The man nodded. "Good answer. Thanks."

Cam answered a handful of additional questions. One man challenged him. "I happen to be one of those guys who believes Freemasonry descends from the Templars. I know not everyone believes that, but I do. And now you say the Templars are Goddess worshipers. Well, I've been a Mason for thirty years and I've never seen evidence of any Goddess worship in Freemasonry."

Smiling, Cam walked over to where the Marshall was sitting. "You've seen it, but just haven't *recognized* it." He pointed to the beehive button on the Marshall's lapel and explained the symbolism of the queen bee. "And don't forget, the Templars and Cistercians used the same beehive symbolism. Templars, Cistercians, Freemasons. All working for the queen bee. The Goddess."

Cam walked back to the center of the room. "And I'll give you another example. Who can tell me the most famous example of Goddess worship in America?"

The dignitary with the caricatured features raised his hand. "The Statue of Liberty."

"Exactly. Gifted to the United States by the Freemasons of France, and erected by the Freemasons of New York." Cam addressed the original questioner. "You may not think of the Statue of Liberty as the Goddess, but I can assure you that those at the highest level of Freemasonry understood the symbolism perfectly. Just as did our Founding Fathers."

A voice from the back. "How so?"

"Most of you know that many of the Founding Fathers were Freemasons." He clicked at his laptop until the image he wanted, a snake cut into pieces, projected onto the screen. "Has anyone seen this before?"

Revolutionary War Banner

A handful of hands went up. "Good." Cam explained its meaning. "It was created by Benjamin Franklin—as you know, a leading Freemason—and has been called America's first political cartoon. It was displayed on flags and banners used by the rebels during the Revolution, to try get the states to unite against the British—the 'N.E.' mark represents New England, and the other abbreviations the other colonies. What's interesting is that Franklin chose a snake, even though back then the snake was associated with treachery, much as it is today. Historically the snake also symbolized rebirth and regeneration, which is associated with the Goddess and the feminine. Franklin surely knew that, just as later Freemasons knew the symbolism behind the Statue of Liberty." Cam paused. "These people weren't stupid. They understood the power of imagery and symbolism." He smiled. "As you surely still do today. Just look around. Beehives. Goddess statues. Round towers. Snakes. The clues are everywhere, hidden in plain sight."

Head down, Cam walked back to the center of the room. He had pushed things far enough for tonight. "Thank you for being such a great audience."

Ten minutes later, after the Master thanked Cam and closed the Lodge, Cam felt a tug on his elbow. "My name is Rene Lapierre."

The likable man with the unattractive facial features held out a strong hand. "Nice to meet you. I was hoping to have a word when you have some time."

"Of course."

The man guided Cam toward the corner, other Brothers in the Lodge seeming to defer to him by edging away. Mother Nature liking balance, she had given Lapierre a sturdy frame to compensate for his facial imperfections—he moved gracefully, and Cam noticed a toned physique beneath the clothes covering his ramrod-straight, six-foot figure. "I am the past Grand Master of the Pennsylvania Grand Lodge. I now serve on the Supreme Council of the Northern Jurisdiction of Scottish Rite Freemasonry," he explained. Cam knew enough about Freemasonry to know that those positions were about as high as one could rise in Masonry. He also knew the Northern Jurisdiction was headquartered in Lexington, Massachusetts, which might explain why Lapierre was in New England. "I'll be honest, we've had some complaints about you." The man delivered the line with a smile, but there was no mistaking the gravity behind the comment.

"Complaints?"

"Yes. As you've probably heard us say, we are not a secret society, but we are a society with secrets. And, well, we like our secrets to remain just that."

Cam considered his response for a few seconds. "Well, how secret could they be if I figured them out?"

The Masonic officer smiled again. "That is precisely the point. We believe you have been fed information, secret information, from a high-level Mason. A spy of some sort."

Shrugging, Cam held the man's eyes. "Sorry. Whatever I know, I figured out myself."

"Mr. Thorne. With all due respect, your conclusion that Freemasonry secretly worships the Goddess is not something one could just *figure out*."

Cam wasn't sure where this conversation was going. But beneath its surface lurked a shadow of threat. And he knew the Masons were powerful enough to make good on any threats they made. He shifted his weight, subconsciously bracing for impact. "Of course it is," Cam countered. "Practically every building and traffic rotary in Washington, D.C. has a Goddess figure on it. You guys did that. And it wasn't by accident."

Lapierre studied Cam, his eyes boring into Cam's, trying to read him. Cam actually hoped he could so he'd know Cam wasn't lying. After a few seconds the Masonic officer nodded. "Very well. I'll take you at your word. But I'm going to have to ask you to tone it down. No more talk of Freemasons worshiping the Goddess."

"Why?"

"Because, frankly, people are listening. They respect you. They *believe* you. And this is not a story we want told." He paused. "At least not yet."

Cam didn't get the sense this was the time to take a stand. Lapierre wasn't asking, he was telling. "Message delivered," he said noncommittally.

Lapierre's close-set eyes narrowed. "But was it *received?*"

Cam shrugged. He was getting a bit tired of people kicking sand in his face today. "Now you're splitting hairs."

The Mason reached out to shake Cam's hand and used it to pull Cam closer. He squeezed. "We've been known to split more than hairs. I'll be in touch again."

Lapierre walked away, leaving Cam alone in the corner of the Lodge. Cam exhaled. The conversation had disquieted him, frightened him even. But it also did one other thing: It confirmed Cam was correct in his Goddess conclusion. After all, the Masonic leaders likely wouldn't care about Cam revealing a secret which wasn't true.

Rene Lapierre removed the cell phone from his suit coat pocket and dialed even before he was out of sight of Cameron Thorne. "We need to start now," he said, striding through the Lodge door into the foyer. He summarized his exchange with Thorne. "It cannot wait."

The female voice on the other end did not mince any words. "We need more time."

"That, I'm afraid, is the one thing I can't give you."

"Did you threaten him?"

"Yes. But he is not easily frightened. And it is a threat I am not prepared to carry through on. At least not yet."

"Why?"

"I still think we can use him. He has a following, has credibility, is recognized as an expert on the Templars. He is an asset to us."

"He is also a wild card, potentially doing more harm than good. I learned long ago: Better to kill an ally than to let live an adversary. One can always buy more allies."

She had a point. But it was not as if experts like Thorne were sitting around just waiting to be plucked from academia; there simply weren't many historians specializing in Templar exploration of America. Lapierre made a decision. "Like I said, for now we keep him alive. That could change tomorrow."

She exhaled. "Very well. Then we have no choice but to accelerate the timeline."

Amanda rarely attended Cam's lectures anymore, but she usually waited up for him. These events, especially the ones with the Freemasons, often led to new revelations, new discoveries. By welcoming Cam into their Lodge, they were in some respects giving him a peek behind the curtain.

Venus greeted Cam at the door just before eleven. Amanda followed, lifting her face to his for a kiss. Usually he bounced in after these presentations, but tonight the same malaise he had been carrying around all day seemed to continue to burden him. "You want a glass of wine?" she asked, taking his hand.

"Please fill it to the top."

While she poured, he went up to kiss Astarte goodnight and change into sweats. They met at the oversized chair looking out on the lake, Amanda's right leg draped over Cam's. The moon was almost full, its reflection blazing a path across the lake and almost directly into their living room, as if beckoning them to walk upon it.

But Cam was grounded firmly in the present. "So some high-ranking Freemason threatened me. Told me not to talk about this Goddess stuff."

She shifted, turning to face him. "Why? Does the idea of Goddess worship scare him?"

"No, just the opposite. He pretty much told me we're right, that the Masons do worship the Goddess. But the higher-ups don't want the foot soldiers to know about it."

"What exactly do you mean by *threatened* you?"

Cam sniffed. "Let's just say it wasn't even subtle."

Amanda stared out at the lake, the moonlit night that had been so inviting only minutes ago now seeming to give cover to their enemies. *Their enemies*. It sounded so ominous. She had never been important enough in the past to have enemies. But this research they had been doing the past six years threatened to rewrite history. And some people apparently liked their history just the way it was. "So what are you going to do?"

He sighed. "Be careful, for one thing. I'm not going to put you and Astarte in danger again."

They had been through this before, fortunately without any serious ramifications. But there had been some close calls. She nestled into him. "Since when are the Freemasons the bad guys? They've always supported your research."

"I know. But apparently I hit a nerve this time."

Chapter 5

Early Tuesday morning Cam dragged himself out of bed before five because he knew his tossing and turning was keeping Amanda awake. Monday had been just about the worst day he could remember. First the sex sting. Then being snared in the attorney-client privilege trap. Then the not-so-veiled threat by the Freemason Lapierre. These warm fuzzies had come on the heels of being fired ("position not renewed" was how they put it) by Brandeis University. Hardly a parade of triumphs. With a tremoring hand he checked his phone for a message of extortion of blackmail. Nothing. Maybe Tuesday would be a better day.

It was too dark to run, so he put Venus out, grabbed a chunk of multi-grain bread and some juice and sat down to translate more of the Prince Henry Sinclair journals. He made it a point never to jump to the end of a book, figuring the author had ordered it in a particular way for a reason. But he needed something to keep his mind off his problems and figured the meatier parts of the Sinclair journey might do the trick, so rather than returning to the pre-departure entries he flipped to the entry following the one describing the Grassy Pond stone sanctum and began again translating the Latin.

August 5, 1355

Today is Lunasa. Father thinks it is a blessed day to bury treasure. We climbed highest hill in this land called "Na-sho-ba" to do burial. Father says may the Goddess watch over treasure and also give strength to our native friends who guard it.

Cam sipped his orange juice and smiled at the word *treasure*. The Latin word, *thesaurus*, had jumped at him off the page—how odd that a word used to describe a list of words also referred to unimaginable wealth. Whatever the word's origin, was there a person alive whose blood did not race at the mention of treasure? Better still, apparently it was buried in the Westford area, a land the Native Americans called *Nashoba*. The *highest hill*, Cam knew, was Prospect Hill, near the top of which the Westford Knight had been carved. Did the Knight serve as some kind of sentry? He was tempted to wake Amanda, but decided instead to present her with a finished product when she awoke.

Here, again, was another mention of the Goddess. The Mason Lapierre would not be happy, given the Sinclair family's close association with early Freemasonry. And also a reference to the Druidic cross-quarter day of Lunasa, halfway between the summer solstice and fall equinox. Traditionally a gathering time to mark the beginning of the harvest season, the holiday was usually celebrated atop a high hill or mountain. Cam thought it likely that was why young Henry's father chose Lunasa to climb the hill to bury their treasure.

On a more mundane level, Cam immediately noticed a marked improvement in the boy's grammar skills. He guessed Henry had passed much of the tedious, multi-week voyage focused on his studies. He continued translating.

Father says I should recount the steps of our journey, so others may someday follow our path. After leaving land of Miggy-maw, we followed coastline south to wide river three leagues south of 43rd parallel. My father has named this river "Mary-Mac" to honor our Lord. He has taught this name to the natives and hopes they will adopt it. We followed Mary-Mac west from ocean for ten leagues, portaging over falls on two occasions, until Mary-Mac bent to north. At bend we continued west and south on smaller stream with a single knorr, leaving larger ships on Mary-Mac. Later we will explore Mary-Mac further to north, and Father says if we have time we will carve maps on boulders on both sides of riverbank so future voyagers will have benefit of our explorations.

Cam paused again. Clearly Henry was describing a journey up the Merrimack River from its mouth in Newburyport, Massachusetts. The word "mac" in Scottish meant "son of," so the name *Mary-Mac* translated, apparently, to *Son of Mary*. The stream at the bend of the river was the Stonybrook River, which even today flowed to Westford's Prospect Hill (though the stream today was barely navigable due to much of its flow having been diverted for mill use by early settlers). And the maps to be carved on boulders were almost surely a reference to the Tyngsboro Map Stone, still visible today (though Cam knew of no twin on the opposite bank), which depicted the Merrimack River's path north to New Hampshire's Lake Winnipesaukee. Cam found an image of the map he had stored on his phone and reexamined it.

Tyngsboro Map Stone

He took a deep breath and exhaled, aware of the familiar tingling running up his spine when on the verge of a significant discovery. He had studied this hidden corner of American history and knew the details of the Prince Henry journey as well as anyone alive. But to read about the events in Henry's own words, to have the details confirmed, was especially gratifying. And this was a whole new chapter in the story. Cam and Amanda had always assumed the 1398 journey had been the only one. But it turned out Henry had come over earlier, as a boy. The sun had begun to brighten the morning, and Cam's mood with it. He had planned to go for a jog, but it could wait.

It is very hot, so we began our climb at dawn, leaving our knorr moored at base of hill where we camped. We were six, including me and Father and our guide, Az-cook, with two horses to pull small wagon carrying chest of treasure. We left four men to guard camp.

In his mind's eye, Cam pictured an ornate wooden chest filled with neatly-stacked copies of *Roget's Thesaurus*. Would the Pope chase the disbanded Templars across the ocean to find that perfect synonym? Cam's mood had clearly improved. But realizing that reminded him of the dangers lurking in his life. He sighed and continued.

Az-cook knows a few words of English. He is not much older than me and we are becoming friends. His name means snake. He tells us he has this name because when he was baby he crawled on his stomach rather than on hands and knees. (He crawled like snake last night in front of campfire, including flicking tongue in and out. We laughed until we had problem breathing, even Father.)

The trail was well-worn but not wide enough for horses and wagons. Many times the men had to cut trees to give us passage. One time they tried to move pile of rocks but Az-cook stopped them because rocks were sacred. When Father heard this he said stop. He said if land is sacred, nobody will ever build house here or farm land and so treasure will be safe. The pile of rocks was on top of ledge of rock, which Az-cook said was hard shell of the turtle god whose round back made this hill. Father used his sword to test ground and ten paces south of pile of rocks he found where ground was soft. He said we dig here. The men dug a hole as deep as their navels. Father wrapped chest in leather skins soaked with oil to protect wood. He said I do not know when we will return to this land. Father would not let me or men see what was in chest. When you get older I will tell you, he said. The men knew they must not argue with him. They buried chest and Az-cook covered area with sticks and leaves and rocks and told Father leave knife under rock as gift to turtle god so he protects treasure.

Cam sat back and dropped his pen. So that was it. The rock ledge—or turtle's back—was almost assuredly the outcropping upon which the Westford Knight was carved. The hillside was otherwise rich farm soil; only a narrow strip of outcropping rose to the surface. And young Henry had just told him where the treasure was buried: Ten paces south of the pile of rocks, which were atop the outcropping. Could the treasure still be there? The rock pile was gone, as of course were the trail and the forest around it. But the Knight carving had survived for more than 600 years, and the trail itself had morphed into a main road in town. No doubt the area under the street had been dug up to place utilities. But would an underground area ten paces—probably thirty feet—off the road have been disturbed?

It was time to wake Amanda. Hopefully she hadn't received any overnight texts.

Rene Lapierre rested his elbow on the Formica table of a roadside diner in Laconia, New Hampshire. The diner could have been in any small town in America, but for the fact everyone in it was Caucasian. New Hampshire, he had read, was one of the least diverse states in the nation. Yet somehow it had, as holder of the first presidential primary, ushered in the presidency of Barack Obama, the country's first minority president. And then, eight years later, it whipsawed the other way, giving Donald Trump a primary victory which catapulted him to the White House. Having done so, its voters for some reason turned off of Trump, surprisingly giving the state to Hillary Clinton in the general election. If he were going to understand America, perhaps this was a good place to spend a few days.

He sipped his coffee and ordered some French toast. What had it been, almost fifteen years since the country went through that silliness of renaming it 'Freedom toast' as a protest against France not participating in the Iraq War? In the end, perhaps the French had been right. Saddam Hussein had been a brutal dictator, but the monsters of ISIL who filled the political vacuum left by his ouster were far worse. For both the Middle East and America.

A husky, bearded man walked in, wearing a *Make America Great Again* cap and a green ski parka with a *Gunstock* patch above the heart and *Chip* embroidered on the left shoulder. Based on the sunburned nose, Lapierre guessed Chip was a ski instructor or lift-line worker at the nearby ski area. *Listen, observe, question, look for patterns.* Chip carried a young girl in one arm while a slightly older one tugged him along by his free hand. He slipped the younger girl into a high chair at the next table and helped them out of their jackets. The older one opened the menu, a pair of blond pigtails pointing sideways from above each ear. "I want chocolate chip pancakes," she announced.

Chip grinned. "I bet you do. You can have them if you promise also to eat some fruit." He glanced at the menu. "They have strawberries. How about that?"

"Strawberries are not fruit," she said, her wide eyes holding his.

"What?"

"Fruits have seeds inside."

He laughed, as if knowing better than to argue with her. "Okay, you're the scientist in the family."

The younger girl weighed in. "I want bacon."

"Bacon and what?"

"Bacon and ... bacon," she announced.

Again, the dad laughed. Lapierre guessed Chip was squeezing an early breakfast in with his daughters before heading to work. Lapierre thought of his own girl, now grown. He hoped to see her soon. "I'll order you some toast with it," Chip said.

"Whole wheat," the older girl said. "You know Mom's rule."

"But Mom's not here."

The girl crossed her arms. "White bread is empty calories. I'm going to tell."

Lapierre wondered if the dad would point out that chocolate chip pancakes were also empty calories. Instead he held up a hand, asking for peace. "Okay. No white bread."

"What are you having, Daddy?" the girl in the high chair asked.

"Because you two are so smart, I'm going to have the same as you: chocolate chip pancakes, strawberries, bacon, and whole wheat toast. That will make us twins."

Chip seemed to be a good dad. No doubt he would be repulsed at the idea of rich, powerful men thinking they had the right to grab his daughters' crotches. Yet he had voted for just such a man for president. The reasoning, Lapierre had come to understand, was simple: Chip did not want men to prey on his girls. But he wanted a job to feed and clothe and shelter his daughters. And he wanted strong borders to keep terrorists from terrorizing his family. And he wanted a government that didn't allow welfare recipients to spend their food stamps on lottery tickets and pedicures. And he wanted the goddamn politicians to stay out of his bedroom. So, because of all those things, Chip could live with a frat boy in the White House and would instead make sure his daughters knew how to kick an asshole like that in the balls if he needed to be taught some manners.

At least, that's what Lapierre thought Chip believed. Or it could be that Chip just lost a bet at work and had to wear the hat as punishment. But Lapierre had been doing this a long time. He was pretty sure he had the story right. He watched Chip use his napkin to wipe the younger girl's runny nose. He was also pretty sure guys like Chip would have no problem with the Goddess as long as she was packaged correctly.

Cam needed to catch up on some legal work, so after bringing Astarte to the bus stop on Tuesday morning he drove to his law office on the Town Common. He returned some calls and drafted a Purchase and Sale Agreement, but his mind ping-ponged between thoughts of buried treasure and fear of an email exploding in his inbox. He didn't even have time to focus on the Freemason's threat.

His phone dinged just after ten. Somehow his gut sensed this was not some random text. He closed his office door for some privacy and opened the message even before returning to his seat. No words, just a single image: A naked white ass covered by his hand, clearly recognizable by both the scar from a childhood dog bite on his left pinky and his gold wedding band. The same photo Erin had handed him in his office.

Steadying himself against the doorframe, he sucked for air. His enemy was closing in, and he was powerless to defend himself. He dropped to one knee and, with a shaky finger, deleted the image from his phone. He stayed on the floor for ten minutes, his mind siphoning through the options available to him. Nothing was off the table. Someone was threatening to destroy his life, and he would do anything to prevent that from happening. Including violence. He punched the wall before phoning Delvecchio and telling him about the text.

"No message?"

"Just the image."

The detective clicked his tongue. "They're trying to make you sweat."

"Yeah, well, it's working."

"You tell Amanda anything?"

"No way. I can't. I'll get disbarred."

"Yeah, I get it. Groceries, mortgage, stuff like that."

"So, you find out anything?"

"Negative. Sorry."

Hanging up, Cam grabbed his leather jacket. No way could he stay in the office, just waiting for the next text. *Compartmentalize. Control what you can control.* He marched past Town Hall down Depot Street toward the Knight carving. The longtime owners of the property abutting the Knight carving had recently sold, and Cam had met the new owner, a widow from France who had moved to the area to be near her grandchildren. Fortunately she seemed pleased her home was a part of history and did not mind the occasional crowds gathering near her front yard. But how would she feel about someone digging for treasure?

Before bothering to ask, Cam eyed the site. The journal recounted that Henry's father had paced ten paces from the pile of rocks atop the rock ledge. The narrow strip of bedrock ran generally in a north-east-southwest direction following the fault line, so Cam went to the middle of the strip and paced ten paces in a southerly direction. This brought him over the stone wall that separated the property from the public sidewalk and into the front yard. The journal spoke of a pile of rocks covering the burial site, but there was nothing here now except the green-brown of a spring lawn waiting to grow in. He guessed that the rocks had been used to build the stone wall. Just before step number ten, the ground dipped a bit, only to rise up a few feet later. Cam knelt—was there a shallow depression where he stood? If a wooden chest had been buried more than 600 years ago, that chest could have decayed, causing the ground above it to settle into the void. Did a Templar treasure rest just beneath him? Cam tossed a stick aside. Or maybe this was just a natural undulation in the ground.

There was only one way to find out. He walked toward the front door and knocked.

Rene Lapierre wandered the near-empty streets of downtown Laconia, New Hampshire. Or what was left of it. The main strip looked like it could have been used as the backdrop for the *Back to the Future* movies, to a time before shopping malls and Amazon. Lapierre imagined a record store, a jeweler, a pharmacy, a cobbler, an optician, a bookstore, maybe even a head shop. But the only thing that seemed still to be open was the diner he had breakfasted in. And from the amount of traffic on the street, they could have filmed the movie scenes without needing to detour anyone.

Listen, observe, question, look for patterns. Who were these people of New Hampshire, and why had so many of them voted for two men—Obama and then Trump—so unlike them? In many ways, the voters of New Hampshire determined the history of the country and, by extension, the world. Lapierre needed to understand them better.

He ambled past a construction site, the faded 'Colonial Theater' name still visible on the art deco façade of the ornate brick building. Someone, valiantly, was trying to preserve the architectural gem, perhaps hoping to revitalize the downtown area. He guessed Laconia had gone through many such projects, most of them unsuccessful. But the mere attempt gave him some insight: People longed for the old America, for a time of simplicity and prosperity and stability and, most importantly, security. If that was also a time of sexism and xenophobia, well, perhaps that was an acceptable price to pay for some people.

At a crosswalk Lapierre waited for the walk signal even though the streets were empty. A radio show called *Yankee Swap*, in which people called in to peddle surplus home goods, wafted from the open door of a Salvation Army thrift store. A woman's voice, tired but firm: "I have a pair of girl's rain boots, size four, yellow, worn but in good shape. I'll take four dollars..." The light turned and Lapierre moved on. "And a six-foot ladder, aluminum, asking ten bucks." Frugal New Englanders, Lapierre mused. Yet many of them had voted for a president who lived in a penthouse with gold-plated bathroom fixtures. A paradox.

Lapierre continued down the street, past a burly man holding a sign in front of a Victorian-era stone church that read in a neat scrawl, "Down on my luck. Any help appreciated." Even more pressing than the question of how the country had arrived at its current political crossroads was the question of where it would go next. Would New Hampshire again be at the front of the line, leading the way? He stopped in front of the man, removed a twenty dollar bill from his wallet, and smiled. "Can I buy ten minutes of your time?"

The man peered out from hollowed-out eyes, his skin slate-colored behind a thick orange beard marked with gray streaks. He began to lift a tremoring hand, then shook his head. "Sorry, I'm not into that shit."

Lapierre pushed the bill forward. "No, nothing like that." He held the money out. "I just want to talk, to ask you a few questions." Lapierre leaned against the wall of the church, his body language as non-threatening—and asexual—as he could make it. "I'm not from around here. Pennsylvania. Just trying to figure out this state. Trying to figure out why you all vote the way you do."

"You a reporter?" The man snared the bill. He wore one of those old football letterman jackets with the white sleeves, a red "L" on the chest. But the sleeves were gray and the jacket tattered. Lapierre guessed it had been at least a decade since the man had earned it, probably as a lineman based on his thick neck and chest.

"Nope. Like I said, just curious." He held out his hand. "My name's Rene."

They shook, the man's fingers cold but the grip strong. "Okay, ten minutes. I'm Steve." Steve pointed with his chin at a massive brick building along the river a block away. "My parents worked in the shoe factory. And my grandfather also. Then it closed." He shrugged. "Ain't no place for me to work, unless I want to flip burgers. I voted for the guy who says he'll bring back the jobs."

From Steve's glassy eyes, Lapierre guessed it was more complicated than that. The heroin epidemic was especially problematic in New Hampshire. But perhaps that was because the jobs had left and people felt hopeless.

"You really think anyone can bring back the jobs?"

The man blinked, then shrugged. He was itching to spend the twenty on a fix, but he had promised ten minutes and, in Yankee fashion, was good to his word. "Maybe. At least we have to try."

"What about welfare? Do you think it should be cut back?"

"It's okay for a little while, to let people get back on their feet. But you've got some who stay on their whole lives, who don't pull their weight. That's bullshit."

Lapierre nodded. He guessed Steve would need whatever safety net that government could give him, and would be needing it for quite a while. But as the saying went, everyone was the star of their own story. Steve saw himself as temporarily down on his luck, but otherwise a useful member of society. When a candidate promised to make America great again, Steve believed it was a promise to make *Steve* great again.

Lapierre held his hand out again. "Thanks, Steve. You take care."

Steve grunted. "So what is it? Why'd we vote for who we did?"

Lapierre smiled sadly. "Same reason people do most things. Because you thought it was the right thing to do."

Steve began to reply before apparently thinking better of it. He loped off toward the mill, angling down a narrow alley where

Lapierre guessed he would, at least for a few hours, again become the star of his own story.

An hour after knocking on Madame Segal's door, Cam was behind the wheel of his Highlander on the way into Boston. The French widow had been more than willing to let him dig, so long as he put things back in order once he was done. She was a bit of an eccentric, with a house full of cats and birds that all seemed to get along, and he sensed she rather liked the intrigue generated by her property.

Which stood in stark contrast to the attitude of the woman Cam was on his way to see: The Massachusetts State Archeologist, Rhonda Blank, one of the most close-minded people Cam had ever met. Cam recalled one of the first conversations he had ever had with Amanda, almost ten years earlier. As much as he despised Blank and the way she abused the power of her office, he had been thrilled to have the opportunity to converse with the captivating British researcher who had popped into his life:

"Did I tell you I spoke to the Massachusetts state archeologist?" Cam had said to Amanda.

"How fortunate," she had replied in that sarcastic way he found so alluring.

"I guess you know her, huh?"

"Rhonda Blank. I've had my own history with her. We call her Blinky Blank. Whenever she is asked to consider a pre-Columbus artifact, she closes her eyes—you know, one of those long blinks as if to convey that she can't bear to look at the idiot standing in front of her—and shakes her head. I think she can't bear to look at the evidence."

"So what's her problem?"

"Many archeologists have staked their professional reputations on certain truisms. For example, that Columbus discovered America. She got her job with the state because she's a protégé of some

old Harvard professor who scoffs at talk of contact before Colum-
bus. The last thing they want is for new evidence to appear that
contradicts them. So they just stick their heads in the sand."

In the end, Amanda's description of the State Archeologist had
been too kind. Rhonda Blank had used her position to continually
derail and discredit all research done involving exploration before
Columbus. So why was Cam bothering to go see her? Simply, to
cover his ass. Not that he expected she would see him. At least not
voluntarily.

He crossed the Zakim Bridge and cruised under the city on the
much-panned Big Dig highway project which, despite the massive
cost overruns, actually did a good job relieving traffic congestion.
At the far end of the tunnel he resurfaced and took an exit toward
the UMass-Boston campus, a uninspired sea of brick and concrete.
Tucked behind the campus, along Dorchester Bay, rose a hulking,
mostly-windowless granite structure built in the same Brutalist
architectural style as Boston City Hall. Cam pulled into an open-air
parking lot, pleased at least that one could park for free while being
disrespected by public employees like Rhonda Blank.

He entered the fortress-like building and found a receptionist.
"My name is Cameron Thorne. I'd like to see Rhonda Blank."

"Do you have an appointment?" The woman was polite but not
warm.

"No." He smiled. "But I am a taxpayer of the Commonwealth."

The receptionist flushed and lifted her phone. She spoke in a
hushed tone for a few seconds before hanging up. "Ms. Blank is in
meetings all afternoon. I'm sorry but she can't see you."

Cam expected this. Blank ran her fiefdom with a strict set of
rules. She had once famously refused to look at a document emailed
to her by the federal Department of the Interior because she required
all documents submitted to her office to be sent via regular mail;
the political commotion that followed almost led to her office being
defunded. But she had survived, somehow. Cam wondered whom
she had pictures of. Which, of course, reminded him of the sex sting
photos. He blinked the thought away, refocusing on the task at hand.

"I understand," Cam replied. But instead of leaving, he removed the Sinclair journal from his satchel and carefully placed it on the edge of the receptionist's desk. Circling around to the side of the desk, his phone attached to a selfie stick, he leaned in toward the receptionist.

"What are you doing?" she asked.

"Just documenting that I was here." He smiled, made sure the journal, the receptionist and himself were all visible in the camera frame, and snapped the picture before she could squirm away. "Trying to show Ms. Blank this journal." He removed a second item from the satchel, a photo of the depression in the ground near the Knight site from an angle showing the Knight in the background. Holding the picture vertically off to the side, he again snapped a selfie with the receptionist. "And this is where I want to dig."

"You can't dig without a permit," the woman stammered.

"It's private property, so yes I can. I thought Ms. Blank would want to be involved, but if she is too busy, I understand."

With that, Cam re-bagged his items and began to leave.

The flummoxed receptionist picked up the phone again. "Perhaps I can find someone else to meet with you."

Cam smiled airily. "That's okay. Just please tell Ms. Blank I was here."

It was all about appearances, about how things looked, Cam knew. And now he had the images to show he tried to do the right thing.

Even as other images loomed which appeared to show him doing just the opposite.

Lapierre washed his face in the bathroom of yet another Masonic Lodge and dried his hands under the automatic dryer. The noise of the machine soothed him, insulating him from any need to make small talk. He pushed the button a second time and closed his eyes. *I need to get a life.* No, that wasn't true. He had a life, one devoted to a crucial mission. What he needed was a *different* life. But it would be years before that could happen.

He thought about joining his Masonic brothers in the basement rec room for the traditional post-session scotch tasting. He had spent the past few months (and the better part of the past few years) on the road, hopping from Lodge to Lodge, meeting Brothers throughout the northeast. Frankly, he was tired of it, sick of discussing Masonic ritual and even sicker of listening to New Englanders brag about their many sports successes. He pushed through the bathroom door, retrieved his overcoat and strolled into the windy night.

For a second he forgot where he was. *New Hampshire*, he recalled. Laconia. It was not yet ten. He wandered the streets of downtown, not far from where he had spent the morning, the area largely empty. He stayed clear of the alley where Steve had gone for his fix and was about to turn around when he came upon a restaurant in the old train station. Most of the tables were full—perhaps the old downtown still had some life in it after all. He took a seat at the bar and ordered a light beer. He needed to figure some things out.

That's what he did. Figured things out. He listened, observed, questioned, looked for patterns. He drew conclusions and tested them, reversing course if necessary. Part sociologist, part psychologist, part historian, part soothsayer. Freemasonry was Lapierre's Petri dish, its Brothers the organisms he studied. Freemasonry was not an ideal cross-section of society—it tended to skew more white and affluent than the nation. He smiled. And of course more male. But by studying the Brothers he had sensed the unease in the country long before the current president harnessed that unease and rode it to the White House. Just as he sensed that the current president was not quieting that unease, was not giving them what they yearned for. Could the Goddess be that thing? Was it possible the people he met today, like Chip and Steve, could embrace the old ways and turn back to a time when both male and female aspects of the godhead were recognized and appreciated? It seemed unlikely. But all great movements seemed unlikely in their infancy.

Lapierre sipped his mug. These were strange times. It used to be that the tides of social change ebbed and flowed slowly over the course of decades or even generations. But America lately seemed to be on a carnival ride, whipsawing from one extreme to the next.

One day it elected the first black president, the next a reality TV star espousing traditional values despite being thrice-married. The country seemed to coalesce around gay marriage, only to backlash a few years later with hateful transgender bathroom laws. This was a time of upheaval, of epoch change. Whatever came next, be it worship of the Goddess or of space aliens or of watermelons, it had the chance to catch on big. Society had become rudderless when it came to morality, mainstream religion sullied by pedophiles and carnival barkers. People yearned for something to believe in.

Lapierre finished his beer. Perhaps it was time to give the people what they wanted. Even if they didn't know it yet.

Chapter 6

Cam spent Wednesday morning in his office with the door closed. He had made some phone calls after leaving Rhonda Blank's office on Tuesday, securing the use of a Ground Penetrating Radar machine along with a technician to run it. He had also come to a kind of inner peace regarding the sex sting. He may have been talking himself into things, but somehow in his sleep his subconscious had reasoned things as follows: *Whoever did this is very cold and calculating. They clearly want something from me, which is why they sent me the text yesterday rather than sending the images directly to Amanda. There is practically nothing I won't pay to make this go away. So, when they finally do make a demand, this will just be a simple matter of paying their price. And if they are as rational as they've been so far, they won't demand an amount I can't pay. They'll push me to the edge ... but not over.* He had exhaled, feeling some of the tension leave his body. "And then it will be time for revenge."

But for now it was business. First he went online and issued sell orders to liquidate all his stocks. Next he called his bank to make sure his line of credit was still valid—the house was in Cam's name alone, and he had a forty thousand dollar line of credit he had never touched. Finally he contacted the brokerage house which held his retirement account and made preliminary plans to withdraw those funds. He could put his hands on almost a hundred thousand dollars in forty-eight hours if he needed to. If the extortionist wanted more, he'd beg from his parents. Later he'd figure out how to explain to Amanda where all the money went. It was possible, he realized, that none of this was about money. But what else it might be, he had no idea.

Feeling a little less panicked about things, he drafted a Purchase and Sale Agreement before meeting Amanda at the Knight site after lunch. Grinning, she greeted him with a long kiss. "Howdy, Sailor."

"Howdy to you."

"Ready for some cheery news?"

"More than ever."

"I just got a call from Henri. The carbon-dating came back."

From her smile he knew it was a good result. "And?

"Vellum is definitely 14ᵗʰ century. Spot on."

He tried not to overreact. It still could be a sophisticated forgery using an ancient piece of animal skin. But he couldn't help but meet her grin with one of his own. "Damn. That's awesome." He hugged her. "What about the ink?"

"Still testing. But preliminary results say it is an old formula."

A sedan pulled into the driveway, cutting short their discussion. A stocky, ponytailed man with round, wire-rimmed eyeglasses stepped out. "That's our tech," Cam said, going to greet the man. "Maybe in an hour we'll have more good news."

The tech looked more like a poet than someone in the construction trade. But over the next fifteen minutes Cam learned he seemed to know his stuff. The Ground Penetrating Radar device, which looked like a push lawnmower and was used mostly for construction and landscaping, could read anomalies in the ground at a depth of ten feet, depending on soil conditions. Generally speaking, the device could not identify exactly *what* might be buried, but could determine that *something* beneath the ground was anomalous. Anomalous, as in treasure being dissimilar to dirt and rocks and tree roots. It was costing Cam nearly four hundred dollars, but it seemed worth it, especially because the other option was digging through soil that hadn't completely thawed yet.

Madame Segal wandered out to join them, a pink beret on her head and a snow-white cat in one arm. They watched the technician move across the lawn in a grid-like pattern. Cam took Amanda's hand, trying to appreciate the joyride that was their lives together. Who else got to dig for buried treasures? The thought that it might be taken from him left him almost physically ill. He took a deep breath, stood tall, reminded himself that he just needed to pay whatever price the blackmailers named, and squeezed Amanda's hand.

"This is either going to be the find of the century or a huge buzz kill," he said.

"Roger that. There's no middle ground with buried treasure."

After a few minutes of watching the technician crisscross the yard, Cam stepped forward. "The only area I really care about is around here," he said, pointing to the depression.

The man nodded. "Yes, but I need to establish a baseline so that I'll know if what is under that depression is different than the rest of the yard."

Cam nodded and stepped back. *Of course.* He was letting his impatience cloud his judgment. Treasure could do that.

A half-hour later the man finished. The device had transmitted data to a monitor mounted on the handles of the apparatus, data which was now displayed in a series of undulating lines that looked like an EKG reading. The tech pushed his glasses back up his nose. "I'm definitely reading an anomaly in that depression."

"Can you tell what it is?"

He angled his head. "It sort of reads the way an old septic tank would read, but not as large."

"So metal?"

"Yeah, but something else maybe also." He shrugged. "But you're right, there's something down there. I'd say about four feet."

Amanda turned to Cam. "So what do we do next?"

Madame Segal answered for him, purring in a heavy French accent. "We dig a large hole, my dear."

Rene Lapierre flipped through the stations on his Holiday Inn television, the sitcoms and reality shows as bland and tasteless as the chicken with rice pilaf at tonight's Masonic meeting. How many chicken dinners had he eaten over the past three years since taking a seat on the Supreme Council? Most Lodges didn't serve pork out of respect for their Jewish members, didn't serve steak for fear of appearing wasteful, and didn't serve fish because not everyone liked it. Which left chicken.

He tossed the television remote onto the bed with more violence than he intended. God, he was bored. And lonely. And even feeling a bit sorry for himself. But he knew what he was getting into when he accepted appointment to an ultra-secret committee called the Boaz Group. Comprised of five members, each of them members of the Supreme Council of either the Northern or Southern Jurisdiction of Scottish Rite Freemasonry and each of them also a past Grand Master of his state, the Boaz Group traced its roots back to the earliest days of these United States. The most secretive and exclusive of all Masonic committees, so much so that only its members know of its existence, the Boaz Group was charged with a single task: Ensure that the great American experiment in liberty and democracy did not fail. Lapierre sighed. Not much pressure there. Just lots of chicken dinners.

He looked around the room. A bed, a desk, a chair, a bureau, two night tables and a luggage rack. He was someplace in northern New Hampshire, a hundred miles from anyone or anything he cared about. Not that the list of people and things he cared about was very long. His daughter, of course. And obviously the Brotherhood. His country, in an abstract sense. Plus he had an elderly neighbor in Pennsylvania whom he was fond of. Maybe his dead ex-wife, in the way some people looked back fondly on old episodes of *The Brady Bunch* even though they would never be able to sit through an episode today without cringing at what had once captivated them.

He had a few hours to kill until midnight, when Cameron Thorne was scheduled to appear on a nationwide radio broadcast. Would he be discussing the Goddess, as he had at the Masonic Lodge? Or would he back down in the face of Lapierre's threat? Lapierre's gut told him that Thorne was not a man easily cowed.

The phone rang, a welcome interruption to his maudlin musings. "Mr. Lapierre," a woman's voice said in a businesslike tone, "your conference room is ready."

Lapierre's laptop sat open on the hotel desk. But he retrieved instead a second laptop from his briefcase, grabbed his ring of keys, slipped on his loafers, and took the elevator down to the lobby. A handsome desk clerk wearing a lavender tie led him to a conference room door off the lobby, unlocked the door, and let him in.

Lapierre resisted the urge to be flirtatious. This was not the place, or the time. "Thank you. Where is the internet connection?"

"You can just use the Wi-Fi. Same password as in your room."

"Actually, I require an Ethernet connection."

The man nodded. He leaned past Lapierre and pointed, his cologne fresh and fruity. "There, in the wall."

"Great, thanks."

"Can I do anything else for you?" The clerk blinked, holding Lapierre's eyes, his eyelashes fluttering invitingly.

Lapierre smiled and read the man's nametag. "Thanks, Justin. Perhaps later. But thanks for now."

He exhaled as the clerk closed the door behind him. He had long come to grips with being lonely. But he had never gotten used to it. And for the umpteenth time he wondered if his daughter knew the truth. He doubted it—kids instinctively resisted the urge to think about their parents' sex lives. He should tell her. But he doubted he ever would.

Turning to the business at hand, he tapped at his laptop. Within minutes he had established an internet connection and logged on to the Bank of America homepage. He entered his user name and password. The site then asked for a second password. Lapierre pulled his keys from his pocket and tapped at an ovular fob with a digital display. At his touch, the numbers on the screen scrambled and settled on a six-digit code, providing a second layer of protection against someone hacking his account. As Lapierre understood it, the code changed every minute, the fob programmed to sync with the bank's server. He entered the code and logged on to his account. The balance read $3.8 billion and change, though the change in this case was in the tens of millions of dollars. Somehow even the dedicated laptop, the Ethernet cable and the scrambled pass code didn't seem like enough security. Yet because nobody except Lapierre and his four fellow Boaz Group members knew the account existed, it was probably safer even than a bank vault. It was his job, nightly, to confirm that the funds remained in place. He often wondered what would happen to the money if all five of the Boaz Group members died at once. It was for that reason they made it a policy never to meet as a group, it being their practice that no more than two ever be in the same building together, and no more than three in the same city.

Lapierre had never been given a good answer as to where the money came from, other than it had accumulated steadily over more than two centuries. In an odd coincidence, the $3.8 billion matched the total spent on television advertising for the 2016 presidential campaign, including primaries. The one thing Lapierre had been told was that the funds were not to be touched, other than for a specific purpose: "The money is to ensure the survival of Lady Liberty, of this great experiment we call democracy," his predecessor had preached. "It is for her use alone." Perhaps, Lapierre mused, she would be running for president.

The vellum test results arrived just in time for Cam's upcoming national radio interview. He had said goodnight to Astarte and Amanda, hit the bathroom, let Venus out for a final time, and settled in for a two-hour midnight discussion about exploration of America before Columbus. From experience, he knew the time would fly by. Especially so tonight, as he planned to announce the existence of the Sinclair journals and the test results which appeared to authenticate them. (No reason, however, to draw undue attention to the treasure.) More importantly, he planned to focus attention on their Goddess research and discoveries. The Freemason Lapierre would no doubt be pissed, but Cam hoped that once he went public with all this Goddess stuff, the damage would have been done and there would be no need to do him harm. The Masons, after all, were not the Mafia, punishing their enemies as a way to intimidate others. At least Cam hoped not.

And a nationwide radio show devoted to alternative history, with millions of listeners, was an ideal opportunity to get the word out. Using a thick Sharpie, he wrote out a succinct message—the politicians called it a talking point—in large letters and laid the paper over his computer keyboard: *We are finding a mountain of evidence*

*that the Templars were Goddess worshipers. That's what caused the
split with the Church. As we see in the Sinclair journals, they came
to America looking for a place to practice a Goddess-based version
of Christianity.* He hoped to hit that point at least a half-dozen times
over the course of the interview.

Fifteen minutes before twelve the call came in on the land
line. Cam answered, gulped some water, and shifted in his chair.
Venus trotted in to keep him company and curled at his feet. "Okay
girl, here we go. Time to tell the world about the Goddess." He
scratched her neck. "I have a feeling some people aren't going to
like it."

Rene Lapierre laughed out loud, realizing how ridiculous his
phone call was about to sound.

The desk clerk with the lavender tie answered on the first ring.
"What can I do for you, Mr. Lapierre?" Justin purred.

"I realize it's late, but I find myself in need of a radio. One with
an AM band."

A slight pause. "I'm sure we have one. I'll bring it right up."

"Actually, I'll come down—"

The line went dead.

Five minutes later, a soft knock on his door. Lapierre took a deep
breath and opened it, still not entirely sure what would happen next.
The clerk held Lapierre's eyes, and when he extended the radio to
him their hands touched. A jolt of energy shot up Lapierre's arm.
Justin swallowed, his voice strained. "Shall I come in and show you
how it works?"

How badly he wanted to say yes, to feel the comfort of human
touch, to feel the race of another's heart against his chest. He closed
his eyes and took a deep breath, sliding his hand away from contact.
"That is very kind of you to offer. More kind than you can ever
know. But, no, thanks."

The clerk blinked, surprised and probably a bit offended. "Oh.
Okay then."

Lapierre could handle his own loneliness; he had been dealing with it for the better part of a lifetime. But the hurt on the clerk's face almost broke through his defenses. He sighed, his finger sliding back to touch the man's hand. "I really do appreciate your ... kindness. I plan to return next month. At that time perhaps I can repay you in some small way."

The thick eyelashes blinked a couple of times as Justin nodded. "I hope I am on duty that night."

Lapierre gave his best smile. "Me too, Justin. Me too."

Justin left the door ajar, leaving it for Lapierre to close. He did so gently, waiting a few seconds before bolting it. He checked his watch: 11:56. The interview would begin at 12:05, after the news. That gave him 9 minutes for a cold shower.

His hair still wet, Lapierre made the phone call even before Cameron Thorne had finished the first hour of his interview. "Thorne has spoken," he said quietly. "We must act now."

Chapter 7

After only a few hours sleep, Cam awoke early Thursday morning drenched in sweat, the sheets wrapped around his legs. The same old dream, but with a new twist.

Standing in a heavenly cloud, Cam was again given the chance to question any historical figure of his choosing. All he had to do was ring the antique brass call bell and speak their name. In this version of the dream, his hands actually moved, allowing him to ring the bell. But as he went to ring it, the bell morphed into a naked ass, which his hand cupped. Nor could he speak, his mouth covered with the cold lips of the Amanda clone. Struggle as he might, he could not pull his mouth off of hers, could not separate their lips in order to allow his voice to escape. As he fought to free himself from her, the dream ended as it always did—the cloud washed over him and the bell disappeared. But this time, in its place, stood Amanda. She stared down at him, his lips still locked in the stranger's cold kiss, Amanda's expression a heart-wrenching combination of pain and confusion. A single tear formed and slid slowly down her cheek...

Cam punched the pillow and sat up. Three days had passed since the sex sting and Erin Donovan's visit to his office. No blackmail, no extortion, nothing except the single text. In some ways the uncertainty was worse than having to actually deal with the extortionist. At a time when the discovery of the fascinating journals—not to mention a possible buried treasure—should have made him jovial, his sleep was haunted and his waking hours consumed with feelings of looming dread. Every time his email pinged or his phone buzzed he expected the worst, like a dull ache deep in your jaw that you knew was about to explode into an emergency root canal.

He again considered just telling Amanda everything, showing her the picture and explaining how it all happened. But once more he rejected the idea. No way could he ask her to perjure herself.

Not to mention there was a good likelihood she'd be caught—the governing body for attorneys took this ethical stuff seriously. And even if he told her, and she believed him, the picture was so stark, so graphic. He had seen too many innocent men go to jail, too many times where reality had fallen victim to perception. Falling in love was not a rational decision, and neither was falling out. Who knew how someone might react to seeing their lover in the naked arms of another? *Just pay the price*, he reminded himself. But what if he couldn't?

Amanda called to him from the bathroom, interrupting the tug-of-war skidding and lurching inside his head.

"You're awake early. How was the interview?"

He blinked away the dream, replacing the images with an actual Amanda, in the flesh. It did wonders for his mood. "Really good. I had a lot of people call in." He smiled. "And only a few death threats."

"Tell them to wait in line."

"But seriously, people weren't as freaked out as I thought they'd be."

Amanda spat out some toothpaste. "I don't know why they should be. Everyone has a mother. So what's so scary about an Earth Mother?"

Cam rolled out of bed. "Massive guilt trips?"

"Very funny. I was thinking, with Astarte going to that ski camp this weekend, why don't you and I go up to Okemo ourselves?"

Cam nearly shouted a yes in response. The idea of putting mileage between themselves and the shit-storm swirling around them at home sounded ideal. And Vermont had notoriously poor cell coverage, which, he realized, was a pretty irrational motivation. But none of this was particularly logical. "As long as we're back by Sunday afternoon." He had contacted some amateur archeologists with a group called NEARA (New England Antiquities Research Association) who were going to meet him at the Knight site Sunday. "Dig starts at two."

Amanda walked from the bathroom, working a brush through her hair. "Not bloody likely I'll miss that. But let's stay overnight

Saturday. We can ski a few runs Sunday morning with Astarte." She paused. "And I want to be close to her in case anything happens."

Cam nodded. Normally he would have sensed Amanda's anxiety without her saying anything. "She'll be fine," was the best he could come up with.

She studied him, aware that something was off. "I know. But still I worry. Every year some poor child dies on the bloody ski slope."

He knew better than to point out that the mere fact of them being in the same state would not prevent such a calamity. "I'll make some calls. I know a hotel that takes dogs."

He considered making some sappy argument about leaving their cell phones at home to maximize quality time together. But no way would Amanda agree to be out of touch with Astarte. And even beyond that, Amanda wasn't an idiot.

Amanda had a funny feeling about Astarte traveling. She knew better than to ignore her intuition, but short of forbidding the girl from going on the ski club trip, the best she could come up with for a solution was to, well, follow her up to Vermont. Thankfully Cam had been of the same mind.

After walking Astarte to the bus stop, she flopped into an over-sized chair overlooking the lake with her laptop and turned back to her research on Goddess iconography in America. A researcher from Oklahoma named Gloria Farley, in her book, *In Plain Sight*, had documented a number of Tanit goddess figurines in the American Southwest. But before she looked closely at the Farley book, Amanda dug deeper into who exactly Tanit was.

Tanit originated in the ancient port city of Ugarit, in what was today northern Syria, around 1,400 BCE. The local peoples of Ugarit may have sacrificed children to her. The neighboring Phoenicians (of modern-day Lebanon) then adopted her. Her popularity spread throughout the Mediterranean as Phoenician maritime influence did, the enterprising, sea-based Phoenicians having built a trading empire in the Mediterranean between 1,500 BCE and 300 BCE.

Amanda found an article written by Zena Halpern, a New York researcher and author, who explained how the famous Uluburun shipwreck off the coast of Turkey, dating back to 1,300 BCE, contained Tanit figurines brought along to protect the ship and its sailors from danger. What was remarkable about this find was that it proved that men in ancient times worshiped the Goddess. Amanda knew that women had done so, but she was surprised to learn about the sailors. The crew referred to the Goddess as "Lady Asherah of the Sea," Asherah being an early name for Tanit. The Uluburun wreck was not an isolated find, as additional Tanit figurines from Biblical times having been found in shipwrecks throughout the Mediterranean. In fact, one of those ships, wrecked around 750 BCE, was itself named *Tanit.*

Apparently Tanit's influence spread beyond the Mediterranean as well. As Zena Halpern wrote, "The metal trade spread west in the Mediterranean from major ports. The Goddess was carried on these Phoenician ships out to the Atlantic, to Britain, Wales, Ireland, Scotland and to America, where her symbol is found in over a dozen states."

Amanda turned away from her computer screen and stared at the lake. Had ancient sailors really brought Tanit to America? She knew, as Zena Halpern implied, that the Phoenicians were trading for tin in the British Isles. This was during the Bronze Age, when tin and copper were needed to fuel the growing need for bronze weapons, tools, utensils and ornaments. Many historians believed the Phoenicians had a secret source of copper, a trade secret which Phoenician crews protected with their lives, and that this secret source was the Great Lakes region of America. She and Cam believed, and the research supported, that the Phoenicians had not only stopped on the way to the Great Lakes to build the America's Stonehenge ceremonial site in southern New Hampshire, but also had reverse-engineered the site to align with both Stonehenge in England and another astronomical site called Israeli Stonehenge in what used to be southern Lebanon, the Phoenician homeland. The fact that Tanit figurines had been found across America further corroborated this conclusion.

Amanda turned back to Zena Halpern's research, curious to see which states boasted the Tanit figures. The first Tanit figure was a glyph from the San Juan Mountains of New Mexico, less than fifty miles from the Rio Grande. The Tanit figure featured the traditional triangular body, round head and outstretched arms.

Tanit Figure, New Mexico

The next, similar in design to the New Mexico glyph, was found carved on a boulder in North Carolina, not far from a tributary leading to the Ohio River.

Tanit Figure, North Carolina

Amanda scrolled through Zena Halpern's images, examining the Tanit figures found across America, including in nearby South Woodstock, Vermont at a site called Calendar I & II, known for its chambers and stone structures marking various astronomical events.

Tanit Figure, Calendar I & II, Vermont

All the Tanit figures mirrored the New Mexico, North Carolina and Vermont depictions—triangular body, round head, outstretched arms. All were located near major rivers. And all matched Tanit figures found in Phoenician shipwrecks throughout the Mediterranean, including this one carved on a lead weight from the Tel Dor shipwreck off the Israeli coast:

Tal Dor Tanit Figure

Amanda again stared out at the lake, which seemed to respond to her research on shipwrecks by lathering itself into a fury of white-caps and swirling tempests. Venus watched a duck paddle slowly through the tumult, neither the fowl nor the dog much bothered by the lake's upheaval.

Amanda pondered what she had learned. There was no doubt that the Tanit figures in America matched those found in the Mediterranean. There were two possible explanations for this: Either the Native Americans and the Phoenicians invented the same depiction (triangle body, round head, outstretched arms) for Tanit independently, or one culture brought the image to the other.

Her next find, a Native American burial mound in Alabama (appropriately called Moundville), ended the debate in her mind:

Moundville, Alabama

Inside the mound, archeologists uncovered yet a second Phoenician symbol for the Goddess. This symbol, known as the Hamsa, featured a single eye drawn on the palm of a hand. Many researchers saw in the eye a depiction of the female vulva, which of course would be consistent with Goddess symbolism. The Hamsa symbols from the Alabama mound were drawn on a pair of gorgets, or neck collar ornaments:

The hand drawings matched ancient Phoenician (and modern-day Jewish and Islamic) Hamsa depictions almost perfectly. In fact, Amanda, as a teenager, sometimes wore a "Hand of Miriam" necklace which was identical to these Hamsa symbols—not because she was Jewish or even a Goddess worshiper, but because she thought it looked cool. She angled her head. In fact, she still thought it did. She would have to find that old necklace.

Hamsa Symbols, Moundville, Alabama

The Hamsa, coupled with the Tanit figures, sealed the case in Amanda's mind that seafaring Phoenicians had influenced Goddess worship in ancient America. And, in turn, the presence of Phoenicians on this side of the Atlantic helped explain the fascinating summer solstice sunrise alignment linking America's Stonehenge to Stonehenge in England and in turn to the Israeli Stonehenge. The Phoenicians, being sun worshipers, would have viewed the summer solstice sunrise as the seminal event of the year (that day featuring the maximum sunlight). Here in America to mine and/or trade for copper, and in southern England to trade for tin, the Phoenicians brought their Goddess, "Lady Asherah of the Sea," with them as a protective talisman. And they built ceremonial sites like America's Stonehenge and Stonehenge in England to connect back to their homeland, reverse-engineering the sites so that they all aligned with the rising sun on the most important day of the year, the summer solstice. She shook her head. The pieces fit together perfectly.

Amanda now believed strongly that the Tanit and Hamsa symbols were brought across the Atlantic by the Phoenicians. Other historians, more orthodox in their views, believed the symbols evolved independently on both sides of the Atlantic. Either way, it was becoming clear that Goddess worship had been practiced widely in ancient times. How the practice spread across the ocean was only part of the mystery. The bigger mystery, Amanda realized, was, why and how had the Goddess fallen so precipitously from her pinnacle?

The bus left from Astarte's school at four o'clock. Just enough time for the kids to get home, pack up their bags, have a snack, and return with their skis.

Amanda and Cam had been separated from Astarte before, when Astarte had visited Cam's parents for the weekend, for example. But this was different. Where she was going, she was nobody's precious darling. She was just a girl, one of dozens. The heaviness in Amanda's stomach felt like she had swallowed the channel remote.

Astarte, too, seemed more subdued than usual. Normally around her school friends she was boisterous and animated. But when Cam threw her skis into the hold of the bus, she looked down and kicked at the ground. "Well, I guess I should get on now."

Amanda engulfed her in a hug, the girl almost as tall as her now. "I've told the chaperone we'll be staying only a few miles away. So just call if you need us."

"Okay."

"Have fun. We'll miss you. Love you to the moon."

After a few seconds Amanda tried to disengage, thinking she might be embarrassing Astarte, but Astarte clung to her neck. "Love you, too, Mum," she breathed. She then leapt at Cam, pulling his head down to her. "Bye, Dad."

Tears had pooled in the girl's eyes. Amanda didn't know what to do. Astarte rarely cried, and never because of separation anxiety. Amanda reached for her again, but the teacher chaperone ended the goodbye with a final call to board.

Astarte, head down, plodded up the bus stairs.

It was all Amanda could do not to go after her.

It was bad enough to watch a teary-eyed Astarte board the bus. But now Cam had to deal with a glum Amanda. As if the week wasn't hard enough already.

"I've never seen her like that, Cam," Amanda said as they climbed into his Highlander. "I thought she'd be excited to go. She loves stuff like this."

He was glad to be focusing on this crisis rather than one involving pictures of his hand on a naked woman's ass. Not that either would make his top ten list. "Do you think she's getting bullied?"

"Astarte?" Amanda sniffed. "I don't bloody see how."

She was probably correct. Astarte was tough and strong. Plus popular. "She has been a bit moody lately. Is it a girl thing?"

"Could be, but I don't think so."

"Well, I'm glad we're going up there. At least we'll be close by if she needs us. We can go get Venus, load the car and head up there now if you want." *Before another text arrives.*

She nodded, staring out the window, chewing her lip as she did when upset.

He squeezed her knee and tried to change the subject. "Hey, I read something interesting today and it got me thinking about your Goddess research." She had shared her Tanit and Hamsa findings with him, and he had agreed with her conclusion the symbols had likely crossed the Atlantic with the ancient Phoenicians. "It turns out that the companies that are most successful are the ones who have a high percentage of women in senior management."

"Big bloody surprise."

Cam forced himself to smile. These might be the last few days he got to spend with Amanda; he was intent on not wasting them. "I agree. It just makes sense. Like you said the other day, women think differently than men. The more ways you have to look at a problem, the easier it is to solve it. But here's the part I found particularly interesting. Turns out that 94% of the women in leadership positions in society—business, politics, education, health care, clergy, you name it—played sports in school. That's a huge number, especially considering that many of these women are in their fifties and sixties and grew up before girls were given opportunities to play sports."

Amanda turned. "Ninety-four percent? That is a lot."

"Even today, only about forty percent of girls play sports." He navigated around some traffic. "So here's the takeaway for me. Conventional wisdom is that women are more passive and docile than men. But you've seen some of Astarte's games. These girls play for blood; they're as tough as any boys. I think they are naturally as aggressive as boys, but society has sort of taken it away from them. But the girls who do find sports, they excel. They become leaders."

Amanda nodded. "It makes sense. It takes a certain amount of aggression to get ahead. Not to mention the other things sports teaches, like hard work and sacrifice and being a team player." She paused. "But I don't see how this connects to the Goddess."

"I'm getting there, honest." He smiled. "I think when people think about Goddess worship, about making the godhead more feminine, they get this vision in their head of everyone standing in a circle holding hands and singing. And then afterward talking about their feelings. But I don't think that's what the ancient Goddess represented. Sure, she was compassionate and kind. But she could also be aggressive and strong when necessary."

Amanda blinked, considering Cam's argument. "Okay."

"Think about it this way: What's more aggressive than a mother bear protecting her cubs?"

"Good point."

"And there's that great passage in the Icelandic Sagas, when the Vikings landed in Vinland and the natives attacked them. Freydis, Leif Erikson's sister, runs out onto the battle field even though she's eight months pregnant, bangs her sword against her bare breast, and scares the natives away."

Amanda laughed. "Naked and pregnant and raging. She must have looked like the Earth Mother herself. The Vikings during that period, though some were beginning to convert to Christianity, still worshiped the Goddess. And many of their women were warriors."

"That's my point, which I know I am making in a roundabout way. We shouldn't think of Goddess worship as necessarily being synonymous with passivity. Cultures that worship the Goddess can be aggressive. Not just the Vikings—think of the Amazons also."

"Yes, but the difference is, Goddess-worshiping cultures are only aggressive when threatened. They don't make war for conquest or to gather slaves. Like the bear, and like Freydis, they only fight when attacked."

Cam thought about the two women from the sex sting. He wasn't sure if the sting had anything to do with the Goddess or not, but the play sure had been an aggressive one. Which, if Amanda was correct, meant that they must have felt threatened in some way. Was it possible this wasn't about money after all?

Amanda knew she'd spend the entire three-hour drive to Vermont worrying about Astarte if she didn't do something to keep her mind occupied. So as soon as they hit the highway, she pulled up some websites she had bookmarked on her phone and read passages to Cam in the fading March sunlight.

"Listen to this. I can't believe how misogynistic some of the Church leaders were during medieval times. Some guy named Damian wrote that women were 'Satan's bait, poison for men's souls, the delight of greasy pigs.'"

"Not just any pigs, but *greasy* pigs."

"And here's another. This guy was a bishop. 'Of the numberless images that the devil spreads for us, the worst is woman, bad stem, evil root, vicious fount, honey and poison.'"

Cam made an interesting observation. "Notice how he uses words like *stem* and *root* and *honey*. All things from nature. As if nature itself were evil."

"That's what they believed. If you think about those King Arthur stories, a lot of what takes place is an allegorical fight between the Church and the old pagan ways. The pagans were personified by the Lady of the Lake, by the worship of nature."

Cam nodded. "Can't be having women using roots and herbs to heal the sick. That's the job of the priests—for a fee, of course."

Amanda found another bookmarked page. "So, not surprisingly, whether cultures worshiped the Goddess or not was largely dependent on whether they were matrilineal. Or maybe it was vice-versa. But, either way, societies where women had more legal rights were also more Goddess-based."

"Makes sense. You worship what you admire and value." He paused. "So were most ancient cultures matrilineal?"

"Yes. In fact, almost all were because they didn't understand the role that men had in procreation. Children were thought to be born only of the mother. So of course things like land and property passed down mother to child. Who was a man to give it to?"

"Did ancient people really not know how babies were made?"

"I just read there's still a tribe today that doesn't know, on a remote island off of India."

Cam chuckled. "I guess nine months is a long time."

"For women, that was a good thing. The whole idea of men treating women as property has its roots in patrilineal descent. Men wanted to pass their property onto their *own* children, not some other guy's. To do that, they needed to keep their women chaste. We ended up with things like chastity belts and women having to shave their heads on their marriage nights and even genital mutilation. In matrilineal cultures, women are much more promiscuous." She squeezed his thigh. "You men didn't know how good you had it."

Cam grinned. "I ended up doing okay."

She let her hand rest against his leg. "Anyway, back to my point, you can trace the subjugation of women directly to the downfall of the Goddess. The two go hand in hand. Before that, women were the dominant sex. The Egyptians are a good example—the line of pharaohs was matrilineal. That's why the pharaohs all married their sisters." She smiled. "In fact, if I had known about the ancient Egyptian marriage vows, I would have insisted we use them ourselves."

"Why do I think I'm not going to like this?"

She cleared her throat and read from the text. "Husband agrees to obey Wife in all things, even if she tells him he must stay home and weave."

"Not hunt or fish? Weave?"

"Apparently that's what men did. The women went out and farmed and took part in commerce while the men stayed home and weaved."

"Would I get to watch soap operas also?"

Amanda cuffed him playfully, overlooking the fact that the joke was borderline sexist. Their discussion had taken her mind off of Astarte, if only for a little while. "No. No soap operas for you. You'd be too busy at your loom."

The bus dropped Astarte and her classmates in front of a ski lodge at the base of a mountain that rose up and disappeared into the night sky. The trails on the lower half of mountain were lit and Astarte watched as dozens of skiers—all seemingly female, and many not much older than her—swished down the slopes, their laughter filling the still night air. A few large snowflakes fell, and the smell of a roaring fire wafted over her. Astarte exhaled, the angst of the past week suddenly and miraculously gone. There was something ... *comfortable* ... about this place. Like cuddling with Venus on her beanbag chair in front of the fireplace while eating popcorn and reading Harry Potter.

A young blond-haired woman shepherded Astarte and her classmates into the lodge. "Your bags will be brought to your rooms. Come on into the lodge for some dinner. And bring your cell phones. We will be collecting them for the weekend." The girls moaned. "I know," she laughed. "For some of you it will be like going without oxygen. But trust me, you'll get used to it."

Ten minutes later, sans cell phones, they ate pizza and fruit salad around cafeteria-style tables, watching the flames within the massive stone fireplace at the center of the lodge dance and snap.

The fire made a loud crack, silencing the room. A gray-haired woman in a flowing, sunrise-colored dress appeared as if by apparition in front of the hearth, her back to the students. There was something about her that drew Astarte's attention, almost like a sun pulling planets to it. Astarte dropped her pizza, set down her fork and found herself leaning forward in her chair. The room seemed to go dark, excepting the yellow-dressed woman standing in front of the blazing fire.

The girls fell silent. Arms out to her side, the woman turned slowly, chin high. A collective gasp filled the room, the middle-schoolers recoiling as one. A hideous pink and gray scar ran down one side of the woman's face, like a pus-covered cow tongue. Astarte couldn't help but stare, even as the woman—somehow still beautiful despite her disfigurement—held Astarte's gaze with her own gold-brown eyes. She lowered her arms slowly, the simple movement for some reason reminding Astarte of the flapping of a dragon's wings. In little more than a whisper, she spoke, her words filling Astarte's ears. "I am the headmistress of this school. You may call me Maestra Jamila."

Maestra Jamila stood motionless in front of the fire, her silence commanding their attention. A palm-shaped amulet with a cobalt-blue eye in the middle, matching Astarte's sapphire ring, hung from her neck. Astarte's mind raced. Saying goodbye to Amanda and Cam had been harder than she expected it would be. For some reason, stepping onto the bus had been like crossing a threshold, Astarte sensing that things might never be the same for her again. The words in the letter from the Messenger of the Goddess had repeated themselves endlessly in her head during the bus ride, like a watch ticking on the night stand in a still night: *At some point you will need to separate yourself from your current caregivers.* Was this that point? The equinox after her twelfth birthday had just passed; according to the prophecy, the messenger of the Goddess would be reaching out to her. Had this hideously beautiful woman entered Astarte's life to lead her down destiny's path?

Maestra Jamila's words brought Astarte back to the present. "I want to explain to you what it is we do here at the Venus School. And, most importantly, I want to explain to you why the Venus School is for girls only." Astarte scooched her chair even closer.

"We live in a society that teaches us that women are inferior to men. We are not as strong, not as smart, not as tough, not as *valuable*. Our religions preach this message, and our customs reinforce it. Aristotle, widely considered one of the Western world's great thinkers, wrote, 'The male is by nature superior, and the female inferior; the one rules, and the other is ruled; this principle, of necessity, extends to all mankind.' And the Orthodox Jews have a prayer: 'Blessed art thou, O Lord our God and King of the Universe, that thou didst not create me a woman.' And the Chinese have a saying: 'Men have authority over women because God has made one superior to the other.' And the Hindu Code directs that, 'In childhood a female must be subject to her father, in youth to her husband, when her lord is dead to her sons; a woman must never be independent.'" The headmistress shrugged, pausing to let her words sink in. "I could give you a dozen more examples, from around the world."

Astarte felt her face flush as the anger inside her rose. There was not a boy in her entire school who could beat her in a race or on the soccer field. And she was smarter than them all also.

Maestra Jamila continued. "Well, I believe otherwise. Let me ask you a question: Raise your hand if you have ever heard someone say that girls are not as good at math as boys." Most hands went up, including Astarte's. Jamila nodded. "I am actually pleased to see that some of you did *not* raise your hands. Perhaps we are making some small progress. But let me tell you something about mathematics. The root of the word is *mat*, from the Egyptian goddess *Maat*. Other words have the same root, like *matriarch* and *matron*. Notice they are all feminine words. Why is that?" She looked around the room. "Because, when mathematics was first invented in Egypt, only the women were smart enough to understand it."

The headmistress paused for effect. "We at this school believe women are not just equal to men, but in many ways *superior* to them. Just as the ancient Egyptians believed when it came to mathematics. At this school, we don't want you to try to be equal to men." She scanned the room, her eyes again settling on Astarte's. "We want you to be … expect you to be … *better* than them."

Maestra Jamila began to pace the room, her long amber dress flowing beneath her. "We do that by teaching you in a way that cultivates *both* sides of your brain. Now what do I mean by that? The science is still evolving, but even the ancient peoples understood that men and women think differently. Men predominantly use the analytical side of their brains, while women are more balanced. But the way we teach our children is geared toward the way men think. A Nobel Prize winning scientist named Roger Sperry explains it quite succinctly." She pulled a small notebook from a pocket hidden in her dress and read from it. "*There appear to be two modes of thinking, represented rather separately in the left and right hemispheres of the brain... What it comes down to is that modern society discriminates against the right hemisphere.*" She paused. "Now, obviously it is more complicated than that—we use both sides of our brains for almost everything. But, in general terms, the two sides of the brain have different jobs."

Astarte now barely noticed the discolored flap of skin on Maestra Jamila's face, so captivated was she by the message. "The left side of our brains is logical and literal—we use it to read and write. It makes us rational, but also rigid. The right side is intuitive and creative. It makes us think abstractly, makes us do things that *feel* right even though they don't *seem* right." She smiled. "You've all heard of woman's intuition? Well, we here at the Venus School believe it is a very real, and very important, thing. Intuition. Creativity. Thinking in the abstract. An appreciation of the balance and beauty of Mother Nature. These are products of the right side of the brain, and these are the things we cultivate here." She put her hands together as if in prayer. "I mentioned the balance of Mother Nature. Society today is *out of balance.* We have swung too far toward a left brain way of thinking." She looked around, once more focusing on Astarte. "It is up to you, our future leaders, to fix things. To put our world back into balance."

Astarte held Maestra Jamila's eyes and nodded. A feeling of warmth flowed through her. Just as the prophecy foretold, the messenger of the Goddess had come to her.

Astarte had a thousand questions for Maestra Jamila. While the other girls lined up at the ice cream sundae bar, Astarte strode over and sat down opposite the headmistress, who was nibbling at some fruit salad at a table near the fireplace.

"Hello, Astarte."

Astarte did not even bother to ask how she knew her name, guessing it was probably from her sapphire ring. "I want to learn more about the left brain and right brain stuff."

The older woman smiled. "I thought you might." She pushed her bowl away and fingered the silver hand amulet. "Essentially, it comes down to literacy. Approximately 4,000 years ago, humans began to read. Literacy caused a shift toward development of the left side of our brains, which is the side that controls reading." She studied Astarte. "I bet you play sports."

"Soccer and softball." She smiled. "Plus, of course, skiing."

"So, in soccer, do you know some girls who can only kick with one foot?"

Astarte nodded. "My father makes me practice all the time kicking with my weak foot, my left one."

"It's the same with our brains. When people first learned to read, that caused us to use the left side of our brains much more than we had been. As I said earlier, the left side of the brain is what men use most. So when we began to read, we became more masculine in our thinking." She paused to make sure Astarte understood; Astarte nodded, urging her to continue. "Until that point most ancient societies worshiped the Goddess. But after that point, religion became patriarchal." She smiled sadly. "And here we are today."

Astarte mulled this over. "So reading makes us, I guess, more masculine?" She had always considered reading a good thing, a path toward enlightenment and knowledge.

"It is more complicated than that but, essentially, yes. We began to value the things men find important rather than the things women do."

This insight into human development was so much more interesting than the stuff she learned in school every day. What other secrets did Maestra Jamila have to share?

"Let me give you an example," Maestra Jamila continued. "You said you play soccer. Let's pretend your team is ahead ten to zero. You have the ball with a chance to score again. What would you do?"

"I would pass instead of shoot. It's bad sportsmanship to slaughter the other team."

"Yet the rules say it's okay to keep scoring, right?"

"But that doesn't make it right."

The headmistress lifted a grape into her mouth, chewed and smiled. As she did so, Astarte noticed her ring—blue sapphire, set in gold, nearly identical to Astarte's. *The Messenger.* As if there had been any doubt. "Here's another example. There are two cars going down the road one night. The speed limit is forty. One driver drives forty, the other forty-five. They both come upon an accident. The slow driver continues on, while the fast driver pulls over to help the accident victim. The slow driver has followed the law, while the fast driver has broken the law. But who would you rather have as your neighbor or friend? Who is the better person?"

Astarte did not hesitate. "The fast driver."

Jamila lifted her chin. "These examples illustrate the difference in how the left brain and right brain analyze things. The left brain is all about rules and laws: There is no rule against scoring even when you are way ahead, just as there is no law in most states requiring you to stop to help an accident victim. So both actions must be okay. The right side is about fairness and doing what is correct. In fact, the right side would say it's okay to *break* the rules if it is for a good reason."

Astarte stared at the fire, watching the flames dance as the old woman illuminated new truths for her. "I once let a boy copy my homework because another boy at the bus stop ripped his into pieces. Even though I knew it's against school rules."

Maestra Jamila clapped her hands together. "Precisely. It was the right side of your brain that made that decision." She narrowed her eyes. "And how did you feel about what you'd done?"

"I was scared. I felt like I had done something wrong."

"That's because we live in a left-brained world, where following the rules is more important than doing what is correct." She paused, again waiting to make sure Astarte understood. "Look around. Actually, walk around. Tell me what you *don't* see in this room."

Astarte smiled. "Other than boys?"

"Yes," she laughed. "Other than boys."

Astarte stood and circled the room, studying the walls and furniture and antique skis and snowshoes decorating the space. There was something … different … about it, but she couldn't put her finger on it. And then it hit her: All the signs were image-based, like highway markers. She rushed back. "There's no writing."

"Correct. We try here to emphasize the right side of our brains as much as possible. So we communicate as much as we can by using pictures and songs and artwork and stories."

"So do the girls, like, even know *how* to read?"

Laughing lightly, she replied, "Yes. We recognize that reading is an essential skill, a necessity of modern life. Like learning how to tie one's shoes or clip one's toenails. But it is not something that should be celebrated or glorified. The alphabet can never be completely erased. But in an age of YouTube and Instagram and streaming video, it can be marginalized."

Astarte nodded. It made sense.

The headmistress continued. "That's why we took away your cell phones—we don't want you to text each other, we want you to *talk* to each other, to read facial expressions, to communicate nonverbally. Obviously we need to read *sometimes*. But we are focused on returning to a time of balance." She took Astarte's hand and held her eyes. "To a time when our brains appreciated the wisdom and beauty and balance of the Goddess."

Cam pulled into the pet-friendly inn just as the sun was disappearing over the snow-capped hills of Vermont. They checked in and ordered Chinese food to eat in the room with Venus, knowing they would be leaving her alone the next day while they skied. Cam ordered a beef dish, more for strategic reasons than culinary— Amanda didn't eat red meat.

He was beginning to realize that the problem with one lie was that it mushroomed into many. Three nights had passed since the sex sting, and in that time Cam had avoided making love to Amanda. He just couldn't bring himself to do it, as if the deception of not telling her about it made him unworthy of her. But she would soon notice and wonder about it, if she had not already.

They watched the news as they ate, then went down to the common area and sat in front of a fireplace playing Scrabble while Venus chewed on a rawhide. After an hour Cam made a face. "I think dinner is disagreeing with me. I'll be right back." He repeated this twice more over the course of the evening, until finally announcing he was going to bed.

"Amazing what some people will do to avoid losing in Scrabble," Amanda taunted. "But go ahead. I'll walk Venus then come up."

Cam feigned sleep when Amanda returned a half hour later. She kissed him gently on the side of his mouth, lingering to see if he'd respond, before sighing and nestling up next to him. It was all he could do to resist pressing into her.

Jamila ambled down the snow-cleared path to her cedar chalet, illuminated like a beacon in the cold night air. She hummed a tune from her teenage years, "Some Enchanted Evening," a song she had not thought of in decades. It had, indeed, been an enchanted night.

Astarte was as sharp as advertised, a worthy representative of the Goddess. Jamila did a little two-step. Sometimes being around the young made one young again.

She stopped for a moment to breathe in the smoke-scented, pine-flavored mountain air, her fingers on her Hamsa amulet. In the distance the sounds of song and laughter—female laughter—filled the night as the girls held a karaoke competition around a bonfire. Three years ago Jamila had purchased this mountain compound, overgrown and abandoned, its glory days as a ski resort long behind it. It had cost her $3.5 million, plus twice that much again on improvements and repairs. Not that the money mattered—Jamila had more bene-factresses than she knew what to do with. The local merchants had not been happy when Jamila mothballed the resort for a couple of years. And they had been only slightly mollified when she reopened it last fall as a ski school for high school-aged young women. Almost fifty students now lived at the compound, most having come with Jamila from Switzerland when she relocated the school to be closer to Astarte's Massachusetts home. A few generous political contribu-tions had served to cut through the bureaucratic red tape of opening the school, and next fall Jamila hoped to double in size. Jamila and a dozen staffers, many of them young women like Nicolette with military training, served as teachers and administrators. There were no men at the compound, though Jamila sometimes toyed with idea of busing a group of men in every day to handle the cooking and cleaning chores.

She had recently heard some townspeople complain it was more of a cult than a school. They may have been correct. In either event, if they knew what she was really using the school for, they would probably have preferred it be kept mothballed.

Cam awoke in the black of night to the taste of Amanda, her tongue gently pushing its way into his mouth as her hand caressed his thigh. "You feeling okay?" she breathed. "I've missed you."

For a split second a pang of guilt washed over him and he considered feigning more illness. But he decided that in this particular wrestling match with his guilty conscious, he'd make it two falls out of three. Especially because Amanda was on top, having already pinned him.

Amanda lay awake, listening to Cam's gentle breathing as a deep purple hue signaled the first hint of dawn. There was something different about Cam's lovemaking tonight. She sensed a sadness in him, as if he wondered if this would be their last time. Something had been bothering him all week, and his odd and poignant melancholy only added to the mystery. If she hadn't known better, she'd have worried he was planning to leave her. But as the old song went, you could always tell a man's heart by his kiss. And his kisses left no doubt that his heart belonged to her.

But she also had no doubt he was hiding something.

Unable to fall back to sleep, she puttered into the bathroom. Cam's cell phone sat charging on the vanity, the old inn having too few outlets in the bedroom to accommodate modern demand. She flipped it over to check the time. Just after five. As if on cue, the phone buzzed. Amanda normally would not have violated Cam's privacy, but the combination of her drowsiness, the phone already being in her hand, her concern that Astarte might be in distress, and the number coming in with a Vermont area code resulted in an almost-reflexive reaction to glance down and click at the screen.

A screenshot of a typewritten page stared back at her, the bolded caption at the top jumping off the page:

BOARD OF BAR OVERSEERS

DISCIPLINARY HEARING OF CAMERON THORNE

NOTICE OF SUSPENSION

She hadn't known Cam at the time, yet he had told her about getting his law license suspended. But it was almost ten years ago. Why was someone sending a copy of his suspension decision to him in the middle of the night? A second text buzzed, the same Vermont number, adding some insight to the first. A simple message, reading: *Don't let it happen again. Don't say anything to your wife.*

Amanda flopped back onto the toilet seat. Someone was clearly threatening him, which explained his odd behavior over the past week. But why would they not want him to tell his wife? Was he having an affair? She recalled Cam's kiss, and her reaction to it. Had she been wrong? No. There were certain things people could not fake, certain parts of the soul that are so pure and untainted that they are incapable of subterfuge. This was not about Amanda wanting to believe something so much that it blinded her to what she knew to be true. She had been cheated on before, and she knew now what to look for.

Or did she?

Chapter 8

Amanda remained frozen to the toilet seat, staring at the message on his phone. *Don't say anything to your wife.* Her heart insisted, *knew*, that Cam had not cheated on her. But her head told her not to be a dewy-eyed fool. She could think of no other explanation for the message—it didn't warn him against saying anything in general, just against saying something to Amanda. Who but a lover would make such a request? And it would explain his melancholy over the past few days. Apparently whatever he had done put his law license, in addition to his marriage, in jeopardy.

Sighing, she marched into the bedroom and shook him awake. She held the phone in front of his face. "Cam, what the fuck is this?"

He blinked, focused, read the texts, and groaned. He covered his head with his pillow and exhaled into it. After a few seconds he sat up. "Honestly, I can't tell you."

"You can't tell me?" She had expected a denial, or a lie, or even a confession. But not a punt.

He took her hand in both of his. She thought about pulling away, but there was something in his eyes, something that reached deep inside her, that kept her close. "I need you to trust me. Remember the last time, with the pictures? And I was innocent? It's like that. I promise you, I swear to you, that I've done nothing wrong."

With her free hand she waved the phone at him. "Cam, I'm willing to believe you. I *want* to believe you. But what am I supposed to think? Someone is threatening you with something, and they specifically want you to keep it secret from your wife. Who but a lover would make such a demand?" She blinked back her tears. "Tell me, give me something, so I can believe you."

He stared up at the ceiling, obviously wrestling with his decision. After a few seconds, he shook his head. "I really, really, really can't tell you. It has to do with a case I'm working on, so it's all covered by attorney-client privilege, and if I tell you I will get disbarred. Just like the message says. No shit, I will get *disbarred.* How will we pay the mortgage, much less save for college? I screwed up, Amanda. I was an idiot. But not in the way you think. Not in the way the text makes it seem. I promise you I did not do anything you'd be upset about." He punched the pillow. "Aargh! I know this is really hard for you. I get that. But please, please, trust me."

She shook her head. "I don't know, Cam. Is your career more important to you than our marriage? I mean, so what if you get disbarred?"

"Of course not. Of course our marriage is more important. But like I said, I need to work. We need to live. I'd like to keep both my marriage *and* my career." He exhaled and lowered his voice. "Listen. Please. Give me a few days. I'm trying to extricate myself. I've been caught in a trap, a sting. Just a few days? Please? I promise it will all make sense in the end."

She stood and pulled her hand away. She eyed the door. Was she ready to walk away from her life? Or could she wait a few days for the man she loved to do as he promised, to provide an answer to an unanswerable question? "All right. Okay." Shoulders slumped, she returned to the bathroom. "A few days."

Astarte barely slept, her mind ruminating over the things she had learned from Jamila the night before. *These* were the things, the secrets, she needed to understand in order to fulfill her destiny as the Fortieth Princess. Despite her lack of sleep, she rolled off the bottom bunk and was dressed even before Nicolette walked down the hall banging on doors.

The eighteen middle-school girls bundled up to cross the parking lot to the main lodge, their breaths visible in the frigid mountain air. Astarte was more interested in knowledge than in breakfast or skiing, but Maestra Jamila was not in the lodge when they arrived. So instead Astarte sat down next to Nicolette. "Do you like it here?"

The woman smiled, her face pretty even without makeup. "I wouldn't stay here if I didn't."

"You might have promised Maestra Jamila you would stay, and then be afraid or embarrassed to ask to leave."

Nicolette laughed lightly. "Well, you sure do think things through. But Jamila would not want me to stay if I wasn't happy. That's not how it works."

"So some people leave?"

"Of course. Teachers and students both. You probably have figured out we worship the Goddess here, right?"

Astarte nodded. "Does that mean you don't worship … God?"

"It's complicated. Some of us worship the Goddess only, and some of us worship both." Nicolette leaned in, the cool smell of toothpaste on her breath. "Perhaps the best way to explain it is that when I say some of us worship both, think about a single bird with two wings. Each wing is equal to the other. But the bird cannot fly without both."

Astarte nodded again. It was like life—you needed both the man and the woman to create babies.

"Anyway," Nicolette continued, "we worship the Goddess because we *want* to, not because we *have* to." She turned to face Astarte. "Many people go to church every week because they feel they have to. They feel guilty if they don't. That's silly—why should an all-powerful deity care whether or not a lowly human bows down to them? And if the deity was all-powerful, why not just *make* humans pray?" Nicolette shrugged. "The whole thing is rather ludicrous when you think about it. Does the lion care what the field mouse thinks?"

Astarte had always thought the stuff about God being angry and jealous made no sense. She used to cringe at the sections in the Old Testament where God ordered the Israelites to kill all the people in a conquered city just because they worshiped a different God. People shouldn't pray because they were scared. And then it occurred to her: Maybe that was why so few people worshiped the Goddess any more. Maybe fear was more motivating than compassion...

Nicolette stood. "Come on. First period just began. We do two classes in the morning, then two late afternoon, leaving the middle of the day for skiing. I'll take you to some classes so you can see how we teach here."

"How you teach?"

She laughed. "Yes, Jamila has some unique ideas."

Nicolette led Astarte on a short path through the woods. "This place used to be a ski resort. Jamila kept all the buildings and modernized everything. We use solar and wind for all our power. But she wanted something fresh and inspiring for the classrooms, so she built this."

They turned a corner. A hulking stone fortress featuring turrets and spires and bell towers appeared as if by magic in the forest, like something from a J.K. Rowling novel. They crossed a wide-planked drawbridge, complete with mountain stream running beneath, and approached an arched, double-door entryway large enough for a minivan to pass through. Nicolette slipped a keycard into a narrow slot and the iron-studded wooden doors swung inward. She grinned. "Hogwarts with modern technology."

They stepped through, into what looked like an indoor rainforest—trees, lush gardens, waterfalls, live birds circling overhead, even some live animals. Sunlight shone through a dome-shaped glass ceiling high above. Astarte froze. She had expected battle armor and heavy wood. A cat lounging on a round boulder yawned at her. "Where's, like, all the old stuff?"

Nicolette nodded. "It takes some getting used to. It's almost like going through a time machine. Jamila wanted something fun for the students, which is why she built a castle. But castles are very left-brained, all intimidating and angry and masculine. She wanted the inside to be more about the Goddess." She swatted aside a bee circling them as Astarte reached out to pet an alpaca. "We call this the Garden of Eden."

"Is that a Christmas tree?" Astarte asked, pointing to an evergreen growing in the center of the garden atrium.

"Yes." Nicolette smiled enigmatically. "Sort of."

"But it's March." Glass balls hung from the tree branches, and tinsel decorated both the tree and a massive wreath hanging from a wire next to the evergreen.

"And sometimes a Christmas tree is not really a Christmas tree."

"I don't understand."

"Do you know what a Christmas tree symbolizes? I mean, *really* symbolizes?"

In fact, Astarte did know. "It's a symbol for the rebirth of the sun." She had heard Cam explain this in his lectures many times. "People put evergreens in their houses to remind them that even though the days were getting shorter and darker, that after the winter solstice the sun would be reborn. Later, the Christians piggy-backed on the holiday to make it a celebration of the rebirth of the *son*, rather than the sun." But that did not explain why the tree was still up in March.

Nicolette nodded. "You are correct, but there's more to it than just that, another level. Rebirth, fertility, the life cycle—we are talking about procreation. Sexual intercourse. The miracle of life." She turned to the tree and wreath. "Look at the symbolism. The tree is the phallus, the male. The wreath is the womb, the female. The balls are, well, the man's testicles. And the tinsel, spread on both the tree and the wreath, is the sperm. It's all a gift from the Goddess. Jamila likes to keep it all up as a reminder to the girls how much modern religion stole from the ancient Goddess cults."

"Oh," was all Astarte could muster. She had so much to learn.

Laughing, Nicolette took her arm. "Enough of that." They walked to the rear of the building, where an automated glass door opened at their approach, and passed through to a carpeted hallway. "The classrooms are back here, along with the auditorium." Nicolette smiled. "Nothing fancy or mysterious in this section, just your basic school building."

Nicolette gave Astarte a quick tour. In the history class, the girls were studying the Revolutionary War by reenacting the play, *Hamilton*. "We do a lot of plays and reenactments," Nicolette explained. "But we almost never read books. Same thing with English and Literature. Lots of speaking and story-telling and poetry and songs. But hardly any reading."

In the science wing, girls experimented with roots and herbs while others tended to plants in a greenhouse that circled around and connected to the Garden of Eden atrium. "Jamila knows a lot about ancient medicines," Nicolette said. "In ancient times, women were the healers. She's teaching us some of the old recipes." She grinned. "We call them spells."

"So no science books either?"

"Actually, we do have some of those. It's not books that Jamila is concerned with, just written language. So books that show, say, the muscles and organs of the human body really are just images. Those are fine."

The second floor of the academic space was dedicated to the arts. Astarte watched girls compose and practice music, sculpt clay, paint with watercolors, design a video game, and film a scene in a movie. She would have been thrilled spending the morning herself bouncing from activity to activity. "Arts are the primary focus of our education," Nicolette explained. "Along with the skiing, of course. Our goal is for the students to spend as much time as possible allowing the right hemisphere of their brains, where the Goddess resides, to explore and create."

After an hour, Nicolette led her back through the atrium and across the drawbridge. She glanced at her watch. "Sorry to rush through this, but I have some things I need to do. We should have plenty of time to chat later. You should go ski."

Astarte frowned. "But we're leaving tomorrow." She wanted to see more.

"Really?" Nicolette angled her head and smiled. "Well, maybe you'll decide to stay longer."

Amanda made a point of chatting with the middle-aged couple sitting next to her on the high-speed quad chairlift. "I've never skied here. Any good suggestions for a warm-up run?" She didn't really care, nodding politely but barely listening to their response. But it was preferable to trying to make conversation with Cam. She'd need to get past her anger, she knew, if they were going to enjoy their weekend together. But for now his apparent betrayal was too fresh in her mind.

"Probably the easiest thing is for us to show you," the woman said, smiling and introducing herself. "We need a warm-up run also."

Amanda refocused. "Oh. Thanks. That would be great." And it would keep her from being alone with Cam for another chunk of the morning.

Time. All wounds healed with time. She turned her face toward the sun, felt its warming glow, tried to allow it to melt her ire. Cam had always been true to her. She would have to trust him that his attorney-client privilege justification for not telling her anything—for lying to her, really—was legit.

She sighed. It was going to be a long day. Maybe their new friends would stick around and eat lunch with them also.

Jamila didn't even try to hide her smile as her students, some-how cued in to her once-a-year arrival on the slopes, stood on the side of the trail in the late morning sun and cheered as she schussed down the lower half of the mountain, her amber dress flapping in the wind like a golden sail under her ski vest. It wasn't their attention that pleased her, or even their adulation. It was that their gesture was a clear indication she had succeeded. She had created a family, a sisterhood. And what kind of sisterhood could fail to appreciate its octogenarian figurehead carving her turns on an idyllic spring day in the mountains of Vermont? Life was good, thank the Goddess.

By Jamila's count, her outing today marked 82 consecutive years on the ski slopes, beginning in her childhood days with her father in the mountains of Lebanon. She took a deep breath and closed her eyes as she let the skis run down the final incline. The wind and sun combined to caress her face. How she loved the feeling of free-dom—almost one of flight—that skiing provided. She was tempted to take a second run. But she had other work to do today. Even though she knew, with things coming to a boil, that it was unlikely she would have the opportunity to extend her streak to 83.

After kicking off her skis and boots, she strolled across the park-ing lot and followed a path through the woods to the castle-like academic building. She crossed the drawbridge, passed through the atrium, and made her way to the greenhouse. The students grew fruits and vegetables and, in a lab building connected to the greenhouse, also experimented with various plants and roots, some found in the surrounding woods and some transported to the school from a similar lab at the predecessor school in the mountains of Switzerland. The work, Jamila knew, pleased the Goddess. Women had for millennia taken the gifts Mother Earth had given and used them to heal and remedy. For their trouble, these women had been labeled 'witches,' accused of casting spells and brewing secret potions in steaming cauldrons.

But her purpose today was not to heal or remedy. She found what she was looking for, the leaves of a flowering evergreen shrub. Cliché though she knew it to be, she couldn't help but recite Shakespeare in her mind as she plucked a handful of choice leaves and pocketed them in the pocket of her ski vest:

Double, double, toil and trouble;
Fire burn and caldron bubble.
Cool it with a baboon's blood,
Then the charm is firm and good.

"Yes," she said aloud. "Then the charm is firm and good."

Cam attacked the mogul, kicking sideways as if the mound of snow were a rabid fox. Why send the fucking text? No demand, no threat. Just taunting him. What a way to begin his day. At least when he was skiing he wasn't lying to Amanda.

The kicking action propelled him diagonally toward the next mogul, where he again lashed sideways, driving his heel into the spring-soft side of the slushy heap. Careening, he kicked out a third time, this time with such violence that he misjudged his target and impacted the mogul not with his heel but with the tail of the ski.

He knew what would happen even before his face smashed into the ice trough between the mounds: The force of the impact caused his binding to release, leaving gravity and momentum to do their work, to exact a punishment for Cam's hubris. His body slammed down.

Amanda's voice tugged at him, distant and faint, as if he were under water. "You okay? Cam? Cameron?"

He blinked and spat out some snow. A circle of pinprick-sized lights danced in the periphery of his vision. "Yeah. I think so." His body still felt in motion, like after getting off a roller-coaster. He took a deep breath. "Helmets don't do much good when you land on your face."

"You know what works better than a helmet?" Now that she saw he was okay, Amanda's tone had taken on an edge. "Some bloody common sense. You were skiing like a crazy man."

She was right. He was taking out his frustrations on the mountain, a battle he was likely to lose. At least the pinpricks were beginning to fade. He rolled over and reached for his ski, which seemed to be dancing in the snow. His head throbbed. "Maybe we should call it a day."

"You think?"

There was nothing about the day Astarte didn't enjoy. The cold morning had morphed into an ideal spring ski day—sunshine with temperatures in the high thirties. Warm enough to be comfortable but cool enough to keep the snow firm. And the instructors assigned to her group had led them on some amazing back-mountain trails, where they slalomed around trees, ducked under branches and leapt off hedge-high ridges. The day had left her both exhausted and exhilarated.

But her mind yearned for more.

Entering the lodge after the last run, she scanned the room for Maestra Jamila. The last thing she wanted to do tonight was talk about boys and music and clothes with the other girls...

The headmistress appeared at her side as if by apparition. "Grab a snack and then come sit with me, Astarte." She wore an off-white cable-knit cardigan sweater over her signature flowing gold dress. For shoes she sported duck boots like a college girl one-quarter her age. By the color in her face, it looked like she had been skiing herself. "That is, if you wish to continue our talk from last night."

"Do I have to get my snack first?"

Jamila laughed lightly. "Don't worry, my dear, we have plenty of time."

Astarte grabbed some yogurt, water and a granola bar and joined Jamila at a table near the fire, each in green plastic cafeteria chairs. Apparently the headmistress did not warrant a special seat. "Are you afraid of anything, Astarte?"

"Um, I guess so."

"What, may I ask?"

For some reason Astarte felt like she should not hold back the truth. "Being left alone." She swallowed. "Again."

"And yet you know at some point you are going to be alone again, don't you?"

Astarte nodded.

"Do you know how my face became so disfigured?"

"A fire?" She spooned some yogurt into her mouth.

"Yes. So now I hate fire. My dreams are haunted by it." She gestured toward the flames not five feet away. "Yet here I sit. I do so because I know I need to face my fears. To conquer my fears." Her large brown eyes held Astarte's. "Have you ever heard the expression, *That which doesn't kill us makes us stronger*?"

"I think so."

"Well, it's true. So, just as I sit next to the fire, you will someday need to sit next to your loneliness." She shrugged. "Being a leader is a lonely job."

Astarte listened carefully. Jamila had not used the term 'princess' or 'prophetess' or 'savior.' But when she said 'leader,' that's what she meant. "Okay," Astarte said, not sure how else to answer.

Jamila shifted in her chair. "But enough of that. I'm guessing you have more questions from last night."

Astarte took a deep breath. "Yes. Especially about the reading stuff. Is reading really so bad for girls?" She knew it was more complicated that that, but sometimes it was best to just act a little dumb and let adults explain what they meant.

Jamila stared out at the ski mountain, the upper trails now mostly in shadow. A few stray skiers made their way to the base lodge along the lit lower slopes. "Let's play a game." She took a notebook and pencil from a satchel on the floor by her feet. "I want you to tell me what you think about when I say *ancient Egypt*."

Astarte shifted in her chair. The first one was easy. "Pyramids."

Jamila sketched a rough pyramid at the top of the page. "What else?"

She thought about the book about Cleopatra she had read. "Snakes."

Jamila drew a snake next to the pyramid. "Continue."

Over the next few minutes Astarte came up with the Nile River, pharaohs, hieroglyphs, the Sphinx, mummies, burial tombs filled with jewels, an ankh, and, finally, back to Cleopatra. "Even though she was actually Macedonian, not Egyptian." Jamila sketched each of these, including artful representations of Cleopatra and a pharaoh. It occurred to Astarte that the headmistress had purposely chosen not to write the words out in script form.

"Oh, and Isis," Astarte added.

"That'll do. Now, think about Israel. But let's focus on events after the Exodus."

Jamila flipped the pad to a new page and again sketched as Astarte listed the Ten Commandments, wandering in the dessert, Moses, the Torah, the Twelve Tribes, and the Ark of the Covenant. "And also poisonous snakes. God sent them to kill the Israelites when they complained about no food and water."

"Good, that's enough," Jamila said. "Please fetch me a cup of tea while I prepare something for you. No sugar, but a dash of honey."

When Astarte returned to the table, Jamila had ripped the two pages from the pad and, using a red pen, had numbered the images in a seemingly random way. Astarte guessed she would soon learn there was nothing random about it. She handed the tea to the headmistress and sat.

"I asked you to focus on after the Exodus, because that's when the Israelites first became literate. The Egyptians, on the other hand, used hieroglyphs, which are really nothing more than pictures interpreted by the right brain. So, this is a good experiment. Two cultures, living side by side. One adopted a script-based alphabet, while the other did not." She looked down at her list. "Let's look at the way they saw the world."

Jamila lifted a finger. "First, the obvious one. The Israelite God, and all their leaders, are men. Bearded, robed, usually rigid. In Egypt, the primary god is Isis, and Cleopatra is their most famous queen."

"But the pharaohs were men," Astarte countered.

"Not all. History records at least six other female pharaohs, beside Cleopatra." She caressed her silver hand amulet. "And the pharaonic line itself was matrilineal, passing down through the mother."

Astarte shifted in her plastic chair as Jamila continued. "Next let's look at the snake, because you mentioned it for both cultures. In Egypt, the snake was revered as something sacred—Cleopatra chose to die by snakebite. It was believed to possess wisdom, as evidenced still today." She pulled her phone out of a pocket and showed Astarte the familiar snake around a staff icon, the Rod of Asclepius, used by the American Medical Association. "Doctors, of course, are considered some of our smartest citizens."

Rod of Asclepius

Jamila continued. "In fact, do you know what the hieroglyph for the earliest Egyptian goddess, Wadjet, is?"

Astarte shook her head.

"No, there is no way you could." She smiled. "But it is a drawing of a cobra. The pharaohs wore a snake on their head to give their rule legitimacy in the eyes of Wadjet. So, as you can see, in ancient Egypt the snake was a sign of both godliness and earthly power, along with wisdom." She paused, allowing her point to sink in. "And it wasn't just Egypt. Many other ancient cultures worshiped Goddess figures closely associated with the snake. The Minoan Snake Goddess is a good example," she said, again showing an image on her phone and waiting while Astarte studied the bare-breasted Goddess figurine holding snakes in both hands.

Minoan Snake Goddess

"There is one other reason the snake was worshiped," Jamila said. She touched her scar, forcing Astarte's eyes to focus on it. "For its regenerative powers. The snake casts aside its skin and grows another. Just as my body has given me new skin to heal my wound. It may be ugly. But life itself, though precious, is often ugly, Astarte."

She held Astarte's gaze, and for a second Astarte imagined the old woman's eyes turning orange and the snakeskin scar spreading and morphing her face into that of a python. Astarte shuddered, blinking away the vision as the headmistress sharply clapped her hands.

"So, that is the Egyptians," Jamila continued. "In comparison, the Israelites, and the Christians after them, demonized the snake. You mentioned God sending snakes to kill Israelites who complained. And then of course we have the evil serpent in the Garden of Eden. So why did the holy, wise, powerful snake suddenly become evil? Well, simply, the snake represents nature. And nature, of course, is the domain of the Goddess."

Astarte had never thought of snakes as anything but, well, slimy and a little scary. She very much doubted Apostle Bertram would allow one inside the Mormon Temple. In fact, she wondered if he would even allow Jamila to enter.

"We see here," Jamila continued, "how the same symbol is interpreted so differently, based largely on which side of the brain is being emphasized and developed. And, by the way, we see it again in Greek and Roman myths, after the Greeks and Romans adopted the alphabet. Men turned to stone after looking at Medusa, who had snakes growing from her head in place of hair. So, in many ways, the snake is the starkest example of the difference between right and left brain thinking. It is, alternatively, venerated and villainous."

Jamila looked down at her list again, ready to make another point. "For the Egyptians you mentioned the pyramids and the Sphinx and burial tombs filled with jewels. These are, in many ways, feasts for the eyes. We see them and are wowed by their beauty and size and grandeur. In contrast, you did not mention any image-based items for the Israelites other than the Ten Commandments. A plain stone tablet carved with letters. Think about the difference in the symbols of these cultures. The Egyptians focus heavily on images, which is right-brained. The Israelis have little art, and very few icons. And the icons they do have, such as the Ten Commandments, are locked away in the Ark of the Covenant so that only the high priests may view them, and then only once per year." She paused, apparently ready to make an important point. "In fact, the Israelites are forbidden from even drawing a picture of their God, Yahweh. He must not be *seen*; he can only be *read* about. Think about that: A god who must not be viewed. How unnatural. But not if we understand why: This is a god who demands to be worshiped with the left side of the brain, not the right."

She paused, making sure Astarte understood. Astarte nodded, eager for her to continue.

"For the Israelites, everything became about the written word. They were called the People of the Book for a reason. The Torah contains over 600 written laws, some of them incredibly mundane. The rite of passage for every young man became not a test of survival or bravery or strength but a test of *literacy*—a bar mitzvah commemorates a boy's ability to read from the Torah, which then makes him a man under Jewish law. An entire tribe, the Levites, was given special status simply because they were charged with interpreting and enforcing the written laws." She sat back. "I think you see my point. Once the ancient Israelites became literate, their entire way of thinking changed." She sighed. "And it was not a change that was a good one for women."

They sat in silence for a few seconds, Astarte staring at the fire. "I have more questions," she began.

Jamila cut her off. "No. That is enough. Think about what we've talked about. But for now, you've had a long day. Go play with your friends." The old woman smiled. "Even a princess needs time to relax."

Chapter 9

"What time are we picking up Astarte?" Cam asked as he trudged into their hotel room Saturday morning after taking Venus on an early-morning walk. He had awoken at four, afraid another text would arrive before dawn. Thankfully, nothing. Yet.

Amanda pulled on a fern-green fleece over her beige turtleneck, making her emerald eyes shine. "I told the chaperone three o'clock. The bus heads back to Westford at four."

Cam nodded. The weekend at the ski school was actually a Thursday through Saturday affair since Friday had been a scheduled no-school day in Westford. He swallowed a yawn. "Good. It'll be fun to ski with her Sunday."

Amanda sniffed. "Assuming you don't kill yourself first."

Cam ignored the jab, understanding she had every reason to be short with him. He was anxious to get to the mountain, even with his head still spinning a bit from yesterday's fall. Okemo had poor cell coverage; while on the slopes, at least, there was no danger of an exploding email or text. And no need to make small talk to cover up his lies.

"I was thinking about that stone sanctum site in Westford," Amanda said. "It's been nagging at me; something about it is familiar. It finally hit me overnight. The shape—the stick and ball, or balloon, or whatever you want to call it—is just like the Upton Chamber, except only in two dimensions."

Cam nodded. The stone chamber, about thirty miles west of Boston in the town of Upton, featured a narrow passageway leading to a round, domed, inner sanctum. Soil luminescence testing had proved that the structure predated the Colonists; he and Amanda believed it was related to Celtic exploration of New

England in the sixth century, especially because it resembled many stone structures in the British Isles associated with the ancient Druids. Cam pulled up images of the structure on his phone as Amanda dressed:

Upton Chamber Entrance

Upton Chamber Passageway

Upton Chamber Domed Interior

"Do you also have the drawing I did, the schematic?"
Cam found the image.

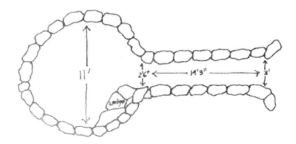

Upton Chamber Schematic

"Yes, that shows it well," Amanda said. "It's similar to the West-ford sanctum, with a narrow passage leading to a womb-like area."

Cam agreed. "I remember crawling through that passageway. It made no sense to make it so narrow and low."

"No sense from a utilitarian perspective," she said. "But as an allegory, a symbol for the birth canal, it is spot on."

"And the Celts were Goddess worshipers." At that time much of Ireland had not yet been Christianized and still followed the pagan ways of the Druids. He slipped his phone into his pocket. "So, another Goddess shrine. They seem to be everywhere we look."

Amanda nodded. "Perhaps because ancient peoples understood that that's where the Goddess is: *Everywhere we look.*"

Jamila watched as the skiers entered the lodge. She had kept the middle-school girls away from her regular high school students for most of the weekend. But she had insisted everyone—students, staff and visitors, numbering perhaps 90—gather for a final late lunch before the younger girls took a few afternoon runs and packed up for the bus ride home.

Her eyes quickly found Astarte among the group, laughing with a circle of friends. Jamila had watched Astarte, studied her as the girl interacted with her peers and teachers. Those who bred horses understood the importance of bloodlines. Though it was considered politically incorrect to judge humans by their lineage, Jamila did not feel bound by the norms of society. Certain truths remained irrefutable, including genetics. The girl had the blood of royalty running through her veins, and it showed. The Goddess had chosen wisely.

Jamila stood in front of the fireplace and clapped, the gesture somehow capturing the attention of the scores of bodies in the crowded lodge. "Everyone grab your lunch and then sit down. We will have a short discussion." She smiled. "You will note that the kitchen staff has not put out any desserts yet. Only after our assembly will they be available."

The older girls groaned good-naturedly. They knew the rules: When it was time to play, play hard. But when it was time to listen, dessert would have to wait.

"I want to play a game," Jamila said in a quiet voice after the girls had taken their seats with their food. She had learned quickly that the best way to get the girls' attention was to speak in hushed tones. "This is mostly for the older girls and staff, but the younger girls can play along as well." She paused, the crackling of the fire, the clanking of silverware and an occasional heavy thud of a ski boot the only noise in the room. "I am sorry to interrupt your meal, but I would like you to stand if you know of a man in your life who you consider to be a feminist. Someone who thinks of women as being equal to men. Perhaps a mentor or coach or teacher who goes out of his way to treat you like you're every bit as smart or capable as the boys."

Approximately three-quarters of the chairs emptied. "Good. Now, this man you are thinking of, is he artistic? Does he paint or play a musical instrument or participate in theater? If so, I want you to remain standing. If not, I want you to sit."

Four or five young women sat, but the vast majority of them stayed on their feet. Jamila waited a few seconds so everyone could scan the room and appreciate the crowd of standers.

Jamila nodded. "Excellent. Everyone may sit. So, what is going on here? Why does there appear to be such a strong correlation between men being feminists and also being artistic?"

A dozen hands shot up, but Jamila had already decided who was going to answer this question. "Yes, Astarte."

Astarte swallowed, shifting in her chair as she considered the proper words to use to answer Maestra Jamila's question. *Don't say 'like' a lot*, she reminded herself.

She had immediately thought of her science teacher, who ran the astronomy club at school and was always trying to get more girls to become scientists. He also happened to be in charge of the school play every year, and even wrote the music for some of the shows. "Well—"

"Please stand," the headmistress interjected.

"Well," she began again, her face feeling hot. "People who are artistic are usually more right-brain dominant. And it's the right side of the brain that is more feminine. So it makes sense that artistic people would usually be feminists."

"Thank you, Astarte. And it often works the other way. In my experience, most male chauvinists are not very artistic. Not all, but most. That is because they tend to be left-brain thinkers. And left-brain thinkers generally don't value the things women value. It naturally follows that they also don't value *women*. Please understand, they are not *evil* people. But they are out of balance, which can make them *dangerous* people. They rely too much on the left side of their brains. Unfortunately, we have allowed many of them to control our society."

The headmistress raised her voice. Astarte leaned forward, sensing she was proceeding to her concluding point. "As I explained last night, this imbalance can be traced back to the advent of the alphabet, to written language. Let me be clear. *Literacy* is not a bad thing. Nor is *literature*. What is a bad thing is something I called *literallacy*. That is when people, *left-brained people*, treat the written word as some kind of gospel. Or act like it has magical powers. No," she declared. "Written words are tools to help us preserve and communicate thoughts and ideas. That is all. No magic. In fact, too often they become crutches which prevent us from reaching our full potential. A good book is a fine thing, but it is *no substitute* for a walk in the woods. Passing a law helping the poor is a noble gesture, but it is *no substitute* for volunteering at a soup kitchen. There is nothing wrong with being a law-abiding citizen, but it is *no substitute* for being a citizen who refuses to abide injustice." She paused for effect. "And, finally, there is nothing wrong with someone having an over-developed left side of the brain, but that person is *no substitute* for a leader who rules with compassion and empathy as well as with logic and reason."

Jamila walked slowly back to her chair, the room silent. "Okay, enough of that," she said, smiling. "There's nothing wrong with a little assembly after lunch, but it is *no substitute* for a warm chocolate chip cookie."

Cam skied with less anger on Saturday, content to try to enjoy the spring-like day in the mountains with Amanda. But Amanda had grown increasingly quiet and distant. By one o'clock the snow had begun to match their dispositions, softening into a mashed potato-like muck that sucked the energy from their legs.

"I'm done, Cam," Amanda said after their third post-lunch run. "My legs are shot and I need to get inside." She was allergic to the sun; even in March she needed to be careful. "But you can take a few more runs."

"No, I'm good," he replied. "Let's go rescue Venus and then pick up Astarte."

Ninety minutes later they pulled off the main road, through an iron gate, and onto a paved, winding access road leading to the Venus School.

"Quite a gate," Amanda commented.

"And look at the security cameras," Cam said, pointing at a series of black cameras mounted fifteen feet up on trees.

"I'm guessing when you have scores of high school girls hanging around, you sometimes have unwanted attention."

They pulled into an empty parking lot at the base of the ski resort. Scores of skiers shushed down the trail, most of them sticking to the shadowy areas as the late afternoon dipped behind the trees. Amanda smiled. "Odd to see the trails full but the parking lot empty."

"Also odd to see so many skiers and no men."

They scanned the slope for Astarte. "Do you see her?" Amanda asked. The thought of reuniting with Astarte seemed to energize her.

Cam shook his head. "I'm guessing the Westford kids are off the mountain, busy packing up."

Amanda opened the door. "Might as well tell them we're here." She pointed to a door at the far end of the main lodge with a sign featuring a lower-case 'i' inside a blue circle. "I assume that stands for 'information.' Must be the office."

They left Venus in the car with the window partly open and angled across the muddy parking lot to the office. "Hello," Amanda said to a high school-aged, chestnut-skinned receptionist. "We're here to pick up our daughter, Astarte."

The young woman glanced down at a sheet of paper and nodded. "If you'll just take a seat," she said with a Jamaican accent, "someone will be right with you."

"Someone?" Cam whispered to Amanda as they sat in a small, sparse waiting area.

Amanda shrugged. "Probably just an expression."

The young woman spoke again. "Can I get you some tea?" She flashed a wide smile. "We actually grow it here, as part of our botany class."

"I don't have to be asked twice for tea," Amanda said, smiling. "Cam, how about you?"

"Sure." He hadn't slept much and the caffeine might do him good.

Ten minutes passed. The receptionist took a call, stood and approached. "If you'll come with me?"

"Come where?" Cam asked, setting his cup aside. The tea actually had made him feel better. "We just want to pick up our daughter."

The young woman shrugged and turned. "This way, please."

Something didn't feel right to Cam. But it didn't occur to him not to follow. The receptionist led them down a hallway to a conference room. Two women stood in front of a floor-to-ceiling window, their backs to Cam and Amanda, looking out at the ski mountain. When the receptionist cleared her throat, the women turned.

Cam froze in midstride, his eyes wide. Staring back at him, their faces contorted into fake smiles, stood Erin Donovan and the blond-haired woman with the cold lips. Cam grabbed the back of a chair to steady himself, edging behind Amanda so she wouldn't see his reaction. *Shit.*

"Welcome," Erin purred. "You must be Astarte's parents." She reached across to shake hands. "It is *so* nice to meet you."

Amanda shook hands with the two pleasant young women from the ski school. "Nice to meet you, Erin, Nicolette."

As she took a seat, Cam excused himself. "I'm sorry, is there a restroom I could use?"

Nicolette answered. She was pretty and pert, sort of the same physical type as Amanda but almost a decade younger. "Sure. I can bring you."

"No. Just tell me where it is."

Amanda shot Cam a look. He was not normally so curt. Clearly whatever secret he was keeping had affected his mood. Not that she had been a pub crawl of fun the past couple of days either.

"Okay, end of the hall. Light switch is on the outside."

"So," Amanda said, "where's Astarte?"

Nicolette again answered. "That's actually why we wanted to meet with you. She's decided she wants to stay."

Amanda felt a cold dull ache spreading in her chest. "Stay?"

"Yes." The young woman smiled as if it were a good thing. "She really likes it here. The skiing, the other students, the teachers, our philosophy. I think the exact wording she used was that she thinks going to this school will help her prepare for her future." Nicolette shrugged. "Not that a seventh-grader should be worried about stuff like that."

Cam marched back into the room before Amanda could respond. "Cam, they say Astarte wants to stay."

Cam bit his lip, his face red and his jaw clenched. "She's not staying. Where is she?"

Amanda touched Cam's arm, trying to calm him down. There was no need to escalate this. Yet. As she did so, Erin drummed her fingers on a blue manila folder in a way that seemed almost threatening.

Amanda took a deep breath and offered what she hoped was a disarming smile. "Yes, Astarte is a bit obsessed with her future. But if you could just bring her in here, so we could talk to her…"

"I'm sorry. She says she wants to stay."

"We can't even talk to her?"

"She's on the mountain." The woman shrugged. "Sorry."

What was going on here? Amanda blinked. "This is silly. She's just a girl. And we're her parents."

Nicolette shook her head. "The permission slip you signed gave her permission to stay through the end of the school year."

Amanda swallowed back a rising sense of panic. "This was just supposed to be a weekend." She hadn't even read the form before signing. "And even so, you can't just *keep* her." She turned to Cam. "Can they?"

Cam had U-turned before even making it to the men's room. His first instinct—to get away to gather his thoughts—quickly turned to panic over Astarte. But when he had reentered the room, Erin's tap on the blue folder with part of a photo sticking out was a clear shot across his bow.

He made a quick decision, going with his gut. He had walked into a trap, one laid by a skilled adversary. There was nothing to be gained by arguing in the conference room. And who knew when Erin might slide the picture out of the folder. He stood and fought to control his emotions. "No, they can't keep her. No matter what you signed." He took Amanda's hand. "But these women have made it clear they're not going to let us take her right now. So I think it is best we leave."

"Without Astarte?" Amanda yanked her hand away. "I'm not leaving until we see her. I'll stay here all bloody night if I have to."

Erin tilted her head and shrugged, as if she didn't particularly care whether Amanda stayed or left. Cam held Amanda's eyes, his heart breaking at the anguish he saw in them. "Come on. Let's go." He leaned closer. "Trust me on this, honey."

Even as Amanda reluctantly allowed him to guide her from the room, Cam had begun to formulate a plan. They would expect his next move to be to go to the police. He played the obvious card. "What you're doing is illegal," he said from the doorway. "We are going to the authorities."

Erin nodded smugly, a nod which confirmed his suspicions. The necessary connections had been made or relationships formed or contributions paid—probably all of the above. Absent something egregious, the local police would side with the local residents. The police would do a wellness check, check the permission slip, and shrug their shoulders.

"There's no way the police are going to let you keep our daughter over our objection," he blustered, knowing how wrong he probably was. But also knowing this threat might give him the small opening he needed.

Astarte sat in Maestra Jamila's office, across from the headmistress. The bus heading back to Westford had just left, but she knew her parents had made arrangements to pick her up themselves so they could have an extra ski day together.

"Astarte, I'd like you to consider staying for another day or two," Jamila said, her amber-colored dress and cape making her coffee-brown eyes appear almost golden.

"Why?" She was not opposed to the idea.

"I just feel there is more for us to … discuss together. More for you to learn. Now that the children have left, we will have more time alone."

Astarte smiled at the headmistress' attempt to flatter her by referring to her classmates as children, the implication of course being that she herself was not. "Okay."

"Very well." Jamila smiled. "We will notify Amanda and Cameron."

Cam and Amanda jogged to their SUV, the thwapping of boots on the muddy parking lot a metaphor for the messiness of their situation. Or perhaps for the dirty tricks being played against them. Cam shook the thought away. He had no time for metaphors.

"Straight to the bloody police," Amanda declared as he turned the key.

He nodded. "Just tell me the way."

His mind raced, his plan coming together. He was sick at the thought of leaving Astarte behind, but at the same time relieved to have gotten out of the building with his marriage intact. Rule number one for dealing with a bomb was to get the hell out of the room if you could.

Amanda spoke. "I tried calling Astarte's cell. Straight to voice-mail." She sighed. "I think I read they were taking the girls' phones away for the weekend."

"Try this," Cam said. "See what you can find out about this ski school. Specifically any connection to the town government."

"Here." She frowned as her eyes scanned her phone. "An article from last year. The ski school is exempt from property taxes, but agreed to make a yearly voluntary payment of $80,000 so the town could rehire two police officers it had laid off."

He smacked the steering wheel. "I was afraid of something like that. Small town politics."

Ten minutes later they parked in front of a Colonial-style white clapboard building which matched the white steeple church across the street. Leaving Venus in the car again, they entered and approached a security window. A uniformed, middle-aged officer with a military haircut greeted them. Amanda explained the situation, Cam hoping a mother's panic may be more compelling than his cold rage. But he doubted it.

The officer listened patiently before finally sighing and shaking his head. From a desk behind him he retrieved a copy of the permission form. "The ski school just sent this over. I guess they figured you'd be coming in. It looks to me like the paperwork is in order."

Amanda glared, her arms folded across her chest. "Paperwork does not give them the right to kidnap a twelve-year-old girl."

"That's just the point, Ma'am. It's not kidnapping if you gave permission. Now, if you want, we can do a wellness check. But assuming the girl is okay…" His shrug completed the sentence.

It was as Cam figured. Absent evidence of criminal behavior, the police would side with the locals. Especially locals who paid their salaries. Probably the same story in most small towns across America.

"Bloody hell," Amanda replied. "Don't bother with your silly wellness check."

"Actually," Cam interjected. He touched Amanda's arm. "It can't hurt. At least it will show Astarte we're concerned."

She turned on him. "Cam, of course she knows we're concerned. You don't think she really *wants* to stay there do you? They're keeping her against her will."

"I agree. That's why I want her to know we're worried. If we don't do anything, who knows what she'll think?"

Amanda shrugged. "All right. I suppose it can't hurt."

"And it might help. We won't be able to get in front of a judge until Monday, but that might be our best course of action. And one of the first questions the judge is going to ask is if we requested a wellness check."

Not that a lawsuit was in Cam's true plans.

Cam drove south on the darkened two-lane highway, Venus in the seat next to him. He had told Amanda a whopper of a lie and didn't even feel guilty about it. Which is probably why she believed it. In fact, he felt strangely euphoric, almost bullet-proof. He pressed the gas pedal, pushing his speed to 80 on the winding road, trusting his adrenaline to heighten his reflexes and keep the SUV on the pavement. Astarte was in danger. It was time to be bold.

They had wasted an hour in the police station, until the officer reported that a female officer had gone to the ski mountain and found Astarte in good spirits and in good health. "The girls were practicing for some kind of talent show," he said. "And Astarte was watching."

"Did your officer actually speak to her?" Amanda had asked.

"In fact, she did. She was in plain clothes so as not to alarm the girls. She was able to observe her firsthand and up close. She asked Astarte if she was being mistreated in any way, or if she had any objections to spending another night at the school. Both responses were in the negative."

Amanda had raised her voice. "But that's because she didn't *know* she is being kept against her will. And the will of her parents."

The officer had pursed his lips and turned away, ending the conversation. "I'm afraid there's nothing more we can do for you folks."

When they got back to the hotel, Cam had pretended to make a series of phone calls. "I have an old law school classmate who practices law up in Burlington. I'm going to drive up to see him. We might be able to get a judge to intervene on this."

"You're going up now?"

Cam had nodded. "I thought I'd bring Venus with me. Keep me company. It's two hours each way."

But he had not driven to Burlington. Instead he raced thirty minutes up Route 103 to an Eastern Mountain Sports store in Rutland. There he purchased cold weather gear to supplement the winter clothing he already had for skiing—insulated hiking boots, gaiters, a powerful headlamp, a compass, some flares, a whistle, waterproof matches, some rope and a first aid kit. He considered some snowshoes, rejected them as too cumbersome, then reconsidered and purchased a pair. Finally, he added a cold-weather sleeping bag. With Venus curled up inside with him, he could survive a night in the woods if necessary.

Normally the thought of sleeping in the woods would worry him. Tonight he felt oddly indifferent.

The email pinged on Amanda's phone as, still in her ski clothes, she paced the threadbare carpet of the small living area in their hotel suite. She barely paid attention to it, a fraud alert notice from their credit card company that a charge of more than $500 had been made on their card. Probably the hotel room. And she had more important things to worry about, like wondering if what was happening at the ski school was somehow related to the threatening text on Cam's cell phone—

A nagging voice in her head urged her to pay more attention to the fraud alert. The hotel charge would have gone through days ago, not at eight o'clock on a Saturday night. She looked closer. An Eastern Mountain Sports store in Rutland, Vermont. Not far from here, but in the opposite direction from where Cam was going. Did someone lift their card?

In and of itself, the incident was nothing. But Cam was clearly in the middle of something ugly. Bringing Venus with him on his drive to Burlington was odd, and the way he had interacted with the two women at the ski school just seemed … off. On a hunch, she used her iPhone to track his location. 'Offline,' read the display. *What was going on?* Was there no service where he was, or had he for some reason disabled the tracking function?

Grabbing a pen from a kitchen drawer, Amanda scribbled a list of Cam's odd behavior from the week. It had begun, best she could recall, on Monday afternoon when he began acting strangely before Astarte's soccer game. And it had continued through today, culminating in his strange reaction to the two young women when meeting them in the conference room. She replayed the conversation. Cam had blanched and headed for the bathroom *before* they said anything about Astarte not leaving. They had spent ten minutes in the waiting room: Why had he not used the facilities then? And, come to think about it, he had returned too quickly to have actually used the restroom. There was something about those women that triggered a reaction in Cam. Did the disbarment threat come from one of them?

Desperate to do something even remotely productive, she logged on to Google. She hadn't caught Nicolette's last name, but she did recall that Erin's last name was Donovan, just like Amanda's childhood best friend. She found an Erin Donovan who graduated from the University of New Hampshire four years earlier; a team photo of the UNH women's softball team featured a player who seemed to match the pretty face of the brown-haired woman at the ski school.

On a hunch, Amanda made a phone call. "Hi, Jessica, it's Amanda, Cameron's wife." Cam's office manager, a single woman in her fifties, had baby-sat for them when Astarte was younger.

"Is everything okay?"

"Yes. But I have a peculiar request. We're up skiing in Vermont and Cam asked me to call you—he's still at the mountain and there's no service there. He needs to get hold of a client file. Any chance you are going into the office tomorrow?"

"I wasn't, but I live just around the corner. What does he need?"

Amanda played a long shot. "Contact information for Erin Donovan. Apparently he's supposed to call her." Worst that could happen would be if Jessica said she didn't recognize the name.

"I remember her, young woman who came in early in the week. Cam was late so I chatted with her for a few minutes. Did Cam say where the file is?"

Bingo. "He said it's locked in his file cabinet. He was hoping maybe you have a key?"

"Sorry, I don't."

"He was afraid of that. Okay, no sense getting our panties in a twist. He'll just have to wait until Monday."

What Amanda was hoping to learn wasn't in the bloody file cabinet anyway.

Radio blaring with oldies from a 1980s rock station, Cam sped down the darkened highway, retracing his route to the ski school. No matter which angle he came at the problem from, it all came back to this move. A rescue attempt. If he did nothing, they would use the sex sting pictures to try to extort him into agreeing to let Astarte stay at the school. For what reason, he still did not know, but he guessed it was related to the Fortieth Princess prophecy. Amanda would never go along—and, in fact, neither would Cam—but the net result would likely be the end of his marriage. And what kind of home would that be for Astarte to return to? He guessed the only reason they hadn't played the extortion card yet and sent the image to Amanda was that they didn't need to. They had made it clear they had a gun to Cam's head. They didn't need actually to put the bullet in his skull to get his attention. They had Astarte in their grasp for the moment; they could afford to be patient.

Likewise, he couldn't include Amanda in the rescue attempt. The conversation was a non-starter: *We need to go in and rescue her tonight, and not go to court on Monday, because ...* because why? He couldn't explain it to her under penalty of almost certain disbarment. It would be nice to have Amanda along, but in the end the rescue would either succeed or fail based on the element of surprise. He opened his window to let the cold air assault his face. *Bring it on.* He'd handle things himself.

The women's inaction had given Cam a narrow window of time tonight to act boldly. It would be nice to play some offense, to do more than sit back and wait for his enemies to take shots at him. "Go big or go home," he said aloud, accelerating through a turn. The GPS told him he would arrive at the foot of the mountain access road in five minutes. He patted Venus' neck. "Ready for a hike in the woods, girl?"

A couple of the high school girls had befriended Astarte, and she had moved her things and taken residence in an empty room in the high school dorm. After rehearsing for their talent show, the girls had gathered in the common room to watch a Saturday night movie. Astarte doubted it was a coincidence that they had chosen *Thelma and Louise*, a film about the adventures of two women.

"What did you think?" Josie asked, munching on some popcorn. She was a snowboarder from Maine who had a cobra tattooed across her back and a pair of nose rings hanging from one nostril.

Astarte avoided commenting on the sex scenes, knowing she was too inexperienced to offer any insights. "I like that it was a story about women. In most movies, the women are just the love interest or secretary."

Josie nodded. "I know what you mean. There's this test for movies called the Bechdel test. The test is whether the women in the movie talk to each other about anything other than boys or men. Something like half the movies fail."

Josie's roommate, Elsa, chimed in. A skier from Puerto Rico, she was the opposite of Josie, red-haired and conservative in her dress. At first Astarte thought she had it backward—but it really was the olive-skinned snowboarder with the tattoos and nose rings who was from Maine, while the preppy one came from Puerto Rico. "I've heard of the sexy lamp theory: If you can replace a female character with a sexy street lamp, and the story still pretty much works, then maybe you need a stronger female character."

"Even those Disney movies." Josie clutched her hands over her heart and spoke in a squeaky voice. "How will I ever be happy if I don't marry a prince?"

Elsa turned to Astarte. "Speaking of princes, is it true you're some kind of princess?"

Astarte shrugged. "Sort of."

"If you are," Josie said, "please don't be one of those princesses who sits on a throne all day. Go kick some ass, girl."

All three girls laughed. "Do you guys miss reading books?" Astarte asked.

"Well," Elsa said, "it's not like we don't read *any* books. And we're allowed to listen to audio books. But Maestra Jamila really wants us to use the right side of our brain. So we watch a lot of movies and plays and we have story-telling sessions and stuff like that."

Astarte was still struggling with the idea that books and reading were somehow bad. "Do you think she's right? Is reading really what caused us to be a patriarchal society?"

Elsa shifted to face her. "Is it as simple as Maestra Jamila makes it out to be, all this left brain and right brain stuff?" She pursed her lips. "Probably not. I mean, the world's problems are not going to end just because people stop reading books." She spoke on the subject as if she had given it a lot of thought. "But here's how I see it. Who is known for giving the most money to the Democrats?"

"Hollywood," Josie answered before Astarte could. "The Republicans were complaining about it all last election."

Elsa tossed a handful of popcorn at her friend. "I wasn't asking you."

"Sorry," Josie said, pulling a piece of popcorn from her thick dark hair and dropping it into her mouth.

Elsa continued. "But she's right. Hollywood gets it. Think about the first *Star Wars* movie. The Dark Side is all men, all emotionless autotrons. Not very subtle. Everything is ordered and rigid and rational—"

"And the Force is all sugarplums and honey, but it's also out of balance," Josie interjected again. "Only when Princess Leia and her brother Luke reunite does the Force get back to full power. The message is clear: Society needs balance, a duality. Male and female need to lead together, not just one or the other. Same with our gods. They should have both feminine and masculine attributes." She raised both hands over her head in a cheer. "Go Force!"

Elsa rolled her eyes and continued. "So, back to Hollywood. Like I said, they get it. The Disney movies are full of Goddess symbolism. But to answer your question, is Jamila right that just by being more image-based we would become less patriarchal?" She shrugged. "All I know is Hollywood definitely emphasizes right brain stuff—imagery and creativity and artistry." She lifted her chin. "And where do you think the Goddess would be more welcome, in Hollywood or in Trump Tower?"

Cam had purposely skidded his SUV into a gully off the shoulder of the road not far from a stream. The stream ran up the base of the lower mountain to the resort lodge, roughly paralleling the access road. Carrying his gear and a hiking stick, and wearing a headlamp, Cam set out, Venus trotting in his wake. The wind had picked up and the temperatures had plummeted as the clear skies released the daytime heat absorbed by the earth. His car thermometer had read 24, but with the wind it felt ten degrees colder. And falling. Yet Cam was oddly unbothered by it. He checked his watch: 9:45. The access road had not seemed so long while cruising up it in his SUV, but according to the map it was almost two miles in length. Which meant a two-mile hike uphill through the soft, spongy drifts undulating between the dense pines. He didn't want to arrive too early, but nor did he want to spend the night in the woods. He glanced up, the planet Venus a beacon above the forest canopy. "Follow Venus, with Venus, to get to Venus," he muttered, using the rhythm to help time his steps. He trudged along, the lamp and an almost-full moon illuminating his way. Between the planet above, the road to his left, and the stream to his right, he knew he wouldn't get lost.

Trudge was the right word. Step by step he fought forward, his boots often sinking to his knees, the effort of extracting his legs far more strenuous than the hike itself. After about a dozen steps, he realized he needed a new plan. Reversing course, he returned to the SUV and strapped on the snowshoes.

The snowshoes helped, but he still sunk several inches every stride in the spring conditions. And in some ways the added bulk of the shoe made it more difficult to swing his legs and maintain an easy stride. But, on net, he made better progress with the snowshoes than without. Which in some ways was like saying being punched in the gut was preferable to being hit over the head.

After fifteen minutes he stopped to rest, his face bathed in sweat and his breathing labored. He turned back, dismayed to find the highway still visible through the trees. "Shit." At this rate he might as well just wait for the snow to melt.

Short of walking in the stream, or risking being seen by the security cameras on the access road, he really had no choice. He gulped some water, offered some to Venus, and plowed ahead. The prevailing wind, he knew, blew from the west across the mountains of northern New England. It stood to reason, therefore, that the eastern side of the trees would have the least amount of drifted snow. He also began to notice that the snow on the northern side of the trees, being in the shade for most of the day, was firmer than on the south. Using these strategies, he picked his way along, staying to the east and north of the trees as much as possible. It didn't make the going easy, but at least when he stopped again fifteen minutes later he could no longer see the highway.

Knowing the exertion would affect his blood sugar, he wolfed down an energy bar and sipped more water. Venus somehow sensed the gravity of their mission, but otherwise didn't seem bothered by the hike. "Maybe I should crawl on all fours," Cam murmured. Thank God he had grabbed the snowshoes.

He trudged on, making slow but steady progress. He had expected to arrive before the school went dark for the night, giving him time to scout and formulate a plan. But not at this pace...

His snowshoe caught a buried branch, upending him and sending him shoulder first into a thin pine. Pain shot down his arm. "Damn it!" He turned onto this back, the stars twinkling down in an almost-mocking manner, and sucked oxygen until the pain faded. This whole plan had been ill-fated from the beginning. What had he been thinking? It was as if an alien had taken over his brain for a few hours, and then been dislodged from his head when he fell. Or at least partially so—he still didn't feel quite … himself. Maybe the concussion had affected his judgment. But whatever the reason, here he was, out of breath and prone in a snowdrift. Venus sniffed his nose, perhaps checking to see if he were alive. He exhaled, lifting his arm to pet her. "Time for a new plan," he said.

No doubt there had been security cameras along the entry way of the access road. But, common sense and frugality asked, would those cameras continue for two miles? Probably not. Stringing a few of them up for the first hundred yards would catch any intruders. The assumption, especially as he lay exhausted, achy and cold in a snowdrift, seemed reasonable to Cam. He rolled onto his back and, using his hiking stick, pushed himself to his feet. His knee, apparently twisted in the fall but unnoticed because of the pain in his shoulder, buckled beneath. Catching himself with the hiking stick, he shifted his weight to his other leg. Nature had made his decision for him. No way was he going to be able to stumble his way through the wooded snow drifts, especially on one-and-a-half legs.

He turned to the left, toward the access road. "Come on, Venus." She pranced to him, dancing across the snow. "You may be suited to this terrain. But I need some pavement."

Just after midnight the dorm quieted down and most of the girls retreated to their rooms. Curfew was 1:00 AM on weekends, yet most of the girls liked to hit the freshly groomed slopes first thing in the morning, to make "first tracks" as it was called, so only a few lights shone from beneath doors on Astarte's hallway as she returned from brushing her teeth.

Josie sat on Astarte's bed, legs swinging as she painted her fingernails. "There you are," she said gaily. "I forgot, I was supposed to give this to you." She handed her a manila envelope.

Astarte reached for it. "What is it?"

"A picture of some guy's hand on a naked ass."

Astarte froze. "What am I supposed to do with it?"

Josie pushed it toward her. "Jamila told me to give it to you. I'm supposed to make sure you study it for ten seconds. Then give it back to me."

Astarte shrugged. She had already seen Brad Pitt's butt in the movie, so what was one more? Just as Josie said, the colored image displayed a man's hand, with wedding ring, cupping a woman's pale butt. Looking at it made Astarte uncomfortable, as if she were violating someone's privacy. And why would Jamila want her to see this? Was this part of growing up, seeing adult things that were uncomfortable to look at? Sighing, she forced herself to stare at the photo, to study it as directed. The man's pinky finger had a scar. His wedding ring was a simple gold band. The hand seemed ... strong. His fingernails were cut short—

"Okay, time's up." Josie snatched the picture away and sashayed her way out of the room. "Good night."

Which was fine. Astarte needed some time alone, to think. An avalanche of information had been dumped on her head over the past few days. Plus two naked butts. She needed to dig herself out, breathe and find her bearings.

She thought about what Elsa had said, that it wasn't as simple as Jamila made it sound, that the world's problems were not going to end if people stopped reading books. Even at her young age, Astarte understood that people who believed passionately in something often went too far with it, like the girl at her school who wanted to outlaw seeing-eye dogs because it made the dog a slave to its owner. But Jamila was, apparently, the messenger of the Goddess. So Astarte needed to listen and learn.

Dressed in sweats, she propped herself up in the narrow dorm bed and wrote in her diary, the words flying across the pages as her brain downloaded the day's information to her fingers. She thought about trying to express her feelings and experiences in an image or song or three-act play as Jamila no doubt would have preferred, but in the end the need to organize her thoughts outweighed the need to develop her right brain. Maybe tomorrow she'd try to write a poem, though she doubted she'd be able to find a good rhyme for *Thelma*...

A scratch at the door interrupted her musings. The school had not yet returned her phone, so she leaned over to examine the old-fashioned alarm clock that sat on her night table. Just past two. She hadn't realized she had been writing so long—

The scratch again. This time followed by a whimper. *Venus*? It made no sense, yet Astarte recognized the sound of her dog at an almost instinctive level. She swung her feet out of bed and ambled across the room. Another whimper, this one more of an excited whine. It *was* Venus.

Astarte undid the deadbolt and swung open the door. Venus nosed through, pawing at Astarte's thighs excitedly and then, as Astarte bent to her, slobbering her face...

Cam pushed into the room behind the dog, put his finger to his lips, and closed the door behind him. His face was red from exertion, and his locked jaw immediately conveyed to Astarte that he was on high alert. And his pupils were oddly dilated, more so than they should be from just coming in from the dark.

"Dad, what are you doing here?" she whispered, easing Venus back to the ground. "Is Mom okay?"

He leaned in to embrace her, his face warm and wet with sweat. She could feel the blood coursing through the artery in his neck. He nodded as he pulled away. "Yes, she's fine. But we need to get you out of here."

Cam instructed Astarte to dress in her ski clothes while, listening at the door, he offered a quick explanation. "They wouldn't let Mom and me take you yesterday. Wouldn't even let us *see* you."

"They told me you said it was okay if I stayed another day," she replied, pulling on some ski socks.

He shook his head. "No. We even went to the police, but they said you wanted to stay."

"Well, I thought it was *okay* with you."

Cam put up his hand. "I'm not blaming you, honey. Not at all."

"So you're here to, like, rescue me?"

Nodding, he replied, keeping his voice low. "Venus nosed around and found your room. Please hurry."

Astarte was ready in less than a minute. "What about my stuff?"

"Leave it. All I care about now is you." He patted Venus on the rump. "You go first, with Venus. If anyone asks, just say this strange dog scratched at your door and woke you. You're bringing her to the main lodge to get her some food. I'll be right behind you. Head toward the access road."

Astarte pocketed her diary and eased into the hallway with Venus. Cam waited a few seconds before following, sticking to the shadows on the edge of the long, moonlit dormitory hallway. The front door to the building (the only one with any lights on, which is how he deduced it must the residence hall) had been locked, but he had punched through a window pane on the door with his gloved hand and reached in to open it. He warned Astarte about the broken glass. "Can you carry Venus for a few feet?"

As Astarte staggered through the entry and dropped Venus back to the ground, Cam froze and pinned himself against a wall, concerned he had heard the creak of a door opening. He waited, listening for a footstep or other noise. Nothing. Exhaling, he jogged toward the exit and fell in behind Astarte, again keeping to the shadows as she angled across the parking lot toward the access road, Venus trotting alongside. He forced himself to breathe. Only a few more seconds before they reached the woods near the access road. "Astarte," he stage-whispered, "cut into the woods up ahead. You can see how I came in. Follow my footprints."

Astarte nodded. As she did so, Venus also turned toward him, her ears alert and nose sniffing at the air. The dog's reaction saved him. Instinctively he dropped to one knee and rolled, microseconds before the baseball bat would have fractured his skull. As it was, the swing glanced off his upper arm, further damaging the shoulder he injured on his earlier fall. He spun and raised his hands defensively, his left arm dangling weakly, even as his attacker came at him again. "Astarte, run. Go!"

"Hello, counselor," Erin Donovan hissed, flashing the same smug smile she had shown in his office. "I believe you are trespassing."

Venus growled. "Down, girl," Cam said. "Go find Astarte." He didn't want her on the wrong side of the bat.

Erin swung again, Cam backing away just in time as the club whipped through the night air. He needed to do something. Out here, weaponless in the middle of the parking lot against a capable adversary, he had little chance. He needed shelter or a weapon of his own or a distraction.

She waved the bat confidently, the moon reflecting off its metallic surface, a slugger waiting for the orb to enter her strike zone. Unfortunately the orb in question was his head. He continued to edge away. He had taken Astarte to a softball hitting coach recently, and the coach told her that a good swing was like a tiger pouncing—quiet, quiet, quiet, then explode. Erin must have had the same coaching. One moment the bat was over her shoulder, the next it was flashing toward his jaw. He ducked back at the last second. Barely. She leered. "Afraid of a girl?" Silent in the night, she cocked the bat.

Out of the corner of his eye he saw Astarte circle back and kick free a potato-sized rock from the parking lot dirt. She clutched it in her right hand and, using an underhand motion, fired a fastball at Erin less than twenty feet away. Fortunately Astarte had been practicing her pitching in addition to her hitting. The rock thumped against the back of Erin's leg, knocking her sideways. Cam seized the moment and charged at her, upending her with a shoulder to the chest. The bat clattered to the ground. Cam retrieved it and considered taking a swing of his own. But this was not the time for revenge. It was a time for escape. Using his good arm, he flung the bat, spiraling, into the woods and ran toward Astarte. They pushed through the underbrush as Erin regained her feet.

In the night air Cam heard her make a call. "I've lost them. But I'm in pursuit. The woods near the access road. You'll see our tracks."

Pacing in front of the picture-glass windows of the lodge, Jamila stared out toward the parking lot area, her Hamsa nestled between her thumb and forefinger. A quintet of moonlit shapes jogged to join Erin, Nicolette at the lead. It had been unwise to leave Erin in charge of the girl. Her arrogance had been her undoing. As Julius Caesar said, "It is only hubris if I fail." Well, Erin had failed. Jamila might give her a second chance, but not a third.

The middle-of-the-night call from Erin had not awakened the sleepless Jamila. But it had awakened her anger. She had worked too hard to gain custody of the young princess to allow her to be snatched away. That Thorne would attempt a rescue was not a surprise. "Fools," she hissed. This was why she went to the trouble to recruit acolytes with military training.

Thorne was turning out to be a more worthy adversary than they expected. He had snuck by their defenses and disabled all three of the school's SUVs and both snowmobiles before rescuing Astarte, which was why pursuit was being undertaken on foot only. Jamila had considered calling the police for assistance, but her influence only went so far with them. This little tug-of-war would need to be settled privately, hopefully without Astarte being torn apart like some wishbone on Thanksgiving.

Cam crashed through the low-lying branches, stumbling in the knee-high drifts. The snow was firmer here at the slightly higher elevation, and the going much easier than when he had first left the SUV. But the night had turned even harsher as the temperatures plummeted and a cold wind whipped through the valley at the base of the mountain. The woods provided cover, but it wouldn't take long for Erin and her posse to figure out to circle around using the access road. He turned to Astarte, following in his tracks. "We need to angle out to the right and get to the road. Then we run."

She smiled through a set jaw, the athlete in her relishing the challenge even as she understood the gravity of the situation. "Just try to keep up." She pulled her wool hat down further over her ears, as if expecting it to fly off when she sprinted.

Within a dozen strides, however, he heard the thwacking of feet on pavement. Their pursuers had beaten them to it, already taken to the access road. It sounded like two pair of feet running ahead, probably hoping to intercept them at their vehicle. Another small team had stayed behind, peering into the woods with flashlights (Cam counted just two beams). So much for using the access road. He turned. Two more trackers had followed them into the woods. So six pursuers. Two ahead, two behind, two waiting for them on the road.

He froze. What to do? He didn't want to risk another altercation, mostly because he didn't like his chances. The gurgling of the stream sounded in the distance. *That's it.*

"Astarte, do you know if there's another road into the resort? Over by the chairlift?" When he had disabled the school's vehicles, they had all been parked on the far side of the parking lot, away from the access road, and there had been fresh tire tracks through the mud.

She angled her head. "I heard someone say they only use the main access road for visitors. Usually it's gated off. So there must be another way in."

"Perfect. We can walk back to the highway and flag someone down." Before turning, he leaned closer and hugged her. "I was worried about you."

"I was fine, really. I mean, they were *nice*."

"Yeah, well, not to me and Mum." But he was glad to hear it. If they didn't make it out, at least he could hope they'd treat Astarte well. Angling back to his left, he trudged on with renewed effort. "Come on."

Ten minutes later they reached the stream, its waters flowing rapidly as the mountain slowly melted into it. This deep into the woods, the moonlight barely penetrated. Cam could not see their pursuers, but Venus turned periodically and sniffed, sensing a distant presence. He had lost his walking stick, so he broke off a thick branch from a tree to support his balky knee. "Okay, quiet now. Into the stream we go. Careful, it's slippery. And you're going to have some cold toes."

He took her hand. But instead of heading down the hill, he pulled her upward. "Not that way. They'll be waiting for us."

She nodded. "I get it. They'll follow our tracks to the river and think we're going down."

In his pocket he found his compass in a leather carrying case. Using an underhand motion, he tossed it twenty yards downriver, where it landed atop a snow drift near the stream. "They'll think we dropped it on our way down."

Astarte did the same with a pair of goggles, her throw landing even closer to the riverbank. "My point."

"Nice. They can't miss both of them." He unzipped his jacket from the bottom, a cold draft washing over his pelvis. "Here. Take the back of my coat and hold on."

"It's like when I was little and you skied behind me, using that leash." She grinned. "But this is opposite."

"Yeah, and I'm older, so don't pull too hard." He took careful steps, using the stick as a third leg and grabbing whatever overhanging branches he could with his uninjured arm to pull himself along. "We don't need to stay in the stream the whole way," he whispered. "Just until we're out of sight."

Venus joined them in the stream for the first minute or so, but soon scampered to the far bank and followed in the snow. Periodically she looked up and tilted her head, as if asking why they were bothering with such a wet, difficult climb when an easier option clearly existed.

"You're right, girl," Astarte whispered. "Sometimes humans are not very smart."

A few minutes later, they came to a steep ridge. The stream here was more like a waterfall. "No way can we climb that," Cam said. "So I guess we get out." He pointed to the opposite bank from where they had entered. "That way looks a little more passable."

"Good, 'cause my feet are numb."

Cam sloshed across and hoisted himself out of the stream, then turned to help pull Astarte out. Venus rubbed against his leg as he studied the ridge. It looked even more daunting close up, perhaps ten feet in height and sharply angled. He removed from his coat pocket the coil of rope he had purchased. Pointing to a birch tree growing at the top of the ridge, he said, "I'm going to lift you onto my shoulders. Try to loop the rope around the trunk."

They staggered close to the ridge, Astarte's wet feet soaking through Cam's gloves as he braced her and her weight causing his shoulder to bark in pain. She lunged, finally able to toss the rope around the trunk and retrieve it on the far side. Biting back the pain, he dropped her to the ground, glancing back as he did so. "Shit," he whispered.

"What?"

"I think I see someone. They must have figured out our trick."

Grabbing the rope, and using his boots to get a toehold in the steep ridge, Cam hoisted himself upward, the birch tree bending under his heft. As he neared the peak, the tree trembled, vibrating with tension. The vibrating suddenly stopped, replaced by a sharp crack. *Not good.* With a desperate lunge Cam flung himself forward just as the tree snapped near its base. He had the momentary feeling of being in a free fall before he made a frantic grab at the branch of a sister tree. Teetering on the edge, he pulled himself over the ridge and into the snow.

"Nice," Astarte said. "Here's the rope." She tossed it up to him. Venus, meanwhile, had scampered up the ridge. Sensing danger, she barked a warning.

"Venus, shush," Cam ordered.

But the damage had been done. Looking past Astarte, Cam saw two women plodding toward them from a hundred feet away. "Okay, quick." Normally he would have tied off his end of the rope, but there was no time. He tugged as Astarte clawed her way up, the sharp pain in his right shoulder nearly bringing him to tears. As she neared the top, he reached his left hand down to her while holding the rope firmly with his right. As she grabbed at his glove, her foothold gave way.

"Astarte!" he yelled.

"I'm okay," she said as she skidded down a few inches, yanking his glove free as she did so. "Just slipped."

Grunting, she reached again for his hand. But just before grasping it, she froze. Her face changed and she yanked her arm away.

"Astarte, grab hold. Hurry!"

Eyes wide, she slowly shook her head. "No." She let go of the rope. "No," she repeated. After a long, sad sigh, she jumped away from him to the base of the ridge, the thump of her landing and Venus' mournful whimper the only sounds in the forest.

Astarte didn't want to believe it. But she was not a kid anymore, pretending the world was a perfect place and they'd all live happily ever after. She needed to know. She needed the truth.

She turned toward the two women running her way through the snow. Erin with another staff member Astarte didn't know. "Stop right there," she ordered.

The women, taken aback by the harsh command, halted a school bus length's distance away.

Astarte continued. "If you come any closer, I'll pull myself up this ridge and you'll never catch us. But I want to talk for a minute."

"Okay," Erin said, shrugging and smiling. "We don't want you to do anything you don't want to do."

Astarte turned to Cam. "I need to know. I saw a picture, a man's hand on a woman's butt. That was your hand, right?" The scar, the wedding ring, it was too much of a coincidence.

Erin answered for him. "Of course it's his hand. Why do you think he came alone? Don't you think your mom would have wanted to help rescue you? But he couldn't risk her seeing the pictures. So he left her home." Astarte sensed the truth in her argument. No way would Amanda have let him do this without her.

She looked up at Cam. He swallowed. "Yes. It's my hand."

"Is that Mum you're … touching?" It was not, she knew. But she had to ask, had to give him every chance to make this nightmare go away. Maybe the photo had been altered…

Cam paused and swallowed again. His mouth moved but nothing came out.

Erin filled the void. "The girl deserves an answer, *counselor*. Lies are easy. The truth is hard. What's it going to be? You going to lie to her more, like you have been doing for years?"

Cam found his voice. "We haven't been lying to her."

Erin cackled. "Ha. That's all you've been doing, letting her live one big lie. Being the Fortieth Princess is her fate, her destiny, her *true* path. But you've been keeping her from it." She turned to Astarte. "That's why we want you to stay with us, here. To follow your true path."

Astarte swung her head back and forth, torn and almost paralyzed by indecision. As if sensing her dismay, Venus offered a single bark and skidded down the slope to nuzzle her thigh. "Then why did you attack my dad with the bat?" Astarte asked.

Erin guffawed. "How was I supposed to know it was your dad? Some guy sneaks into the dorm and takes one of our girls in the middle of the night. What am I supposed to do?"

Astarte nodded. Erin lowered her voice and continued. "Be honest, Astarte. I bet you've learned more about being the princess here in two days than in the past year at home. Right?"

Astarte swallowed, nodding again. It was true.

Pushing her advantage, Erin continued, "They can't teach you what Jamila can. And it's not like things are so perfect at home." She pointed her chin at Cam. "Go ahead. Answer her question. Tell her whose hand that is, and when the picture was taken."

"It's mine," he whispered. "My hand. And it's not Mum I'm touching. But I can explain—"

"Can you, *counselor*? Go ahead," Erin challenged, holding her phone up as if to record his explanation.

Cam's chin dropped. He swallowed. "Like I said, it's not Mum—"

Erin interrupted. "Damn right it's not. And that's why she's not here. You don't want her to see the picture. You *can't let her* see the picture. Why else wouldn't she be here? Tell Astarte the truth: Has your wife seen it? Does she even know about it?"

Cam shook his head. "No. Not yet."

Astarte cut him off. "Please stop." Enough. "It doesn't matter." She understood how these things worked. The idyllic home life she shared with Amanda and Cam was not real. It was illusory, just like every other family she had known. He was having an affair, Mum would find out, things would get ugly. She knew how this stuff ended. And even beyond all that, it was time she set her own course, not be constrained and manipulated by others. The vernal equinox after her twelfth birthday had passed, and the Messenger of the Goddess had, as prophesized, reached out to her. Like Erin said, it was time to follow her true path.

She looked up at Cam, holding his eyes even as hers pooled. "I love you, Dad. And Mum too." Her stomach felt funny, as if she were about to throw up. She sucked in the cold air and blinked twice, recalling the words in the letter from the Messenger: *Soon you will be faced with a decision. You will know the correct course in your heart, even as you realize the course you choose will be a difficult one.* She breathed again. "But I need to do this." The words sounded hollow to her ears, but she said them anyway. "I need to follow my destiny."

Beginning to shiver as the wind bit at her, she turned slowly away from her old life and began to trudge back down the slope, wondering if she'd ever feel warm again.

Cam sat on the lip of the ridge, paralyzed by remorse. He had watched Astarte march out of their life, powerless to do anything about it. That's not true: He could have sacrificed his career, told her about the sex sting. But he had misjudged her, underestimated how scarred she was from the loss of her past families. Scarred and scared.

And now gone. How could this girl—this confidant, vulnerable, amazing, needy, young lady—whom he had let into his life and had in short time captured his heart, brush him aside like flakes of dandruff on a dark blue blazer. When he had met Amanda, he had reorganized the priorities in his life as he began to understand that being in love meant making room for someone else was not a sacrifice but an investment in a lifelong relationship. But when Astarte had come to live with them, he had come to look forward to those sacrifices, to welcome the opportunity to carve out room in his life for his new daughter. The unselfishness of his devotion to her had surprised him, resulted in him liking himself more than he had in years. But now she had chosen a different path, one that didn't include him. And it hurt like hell. It was one thing to lose something one cherished. It was another entirely to have that thing run away.

He couldn't even bring himself to call Venus back to him, realizing that Astarte would be otherwise completely alone.

He might have sat there all night and perhaps even frozen to death had rage not jarred him back to life. Who were these people, using a twelve-year-old girl as some kind of pawn? They may have won this battle, but the war was not over.

Erin had given him one last haughty wave as she left, but otherwise the ski school soldiers ignored him. They had what they wanted. Astarte had gone with them of her own accord. All that was left was for him to lumber, stiff and numb, through the woods, following the stream back to his SUV. To make matters worse, he realized—too late—that he could have explained everything to Astarte, that once Erin had displayed the picture herself, it was no longer privileged. But he had been in the snowy woods facing an aggressive adversary, not in a law library writing a memo. The subtle point of law had been lost on him.

When he finally arrived back at the hotel, he'd somehow have to figure out how to explain all this to Amanda. His heart, already heavy, clenched even tighter at the thought of Amanda's reaction. She would feel anger and betrayal, he was certain. But worse for her would be the loss of her daughter. She had poured her spirit, her entire essence, into her love for Astarte. Would she ever be able to refill herself?

Standing at a bend in the access road, her flashlight probing the forested area, Nicolette had been shocked to see Erin emerge from the woods with Astarte, a dog trotting alongside. "Where's Thorne?" Nicolette had asked, expecting to see him jump from behind a tree in an effort to free his daughter. Like Nicolette's father would have done.

Erin flashed that haughty smile that had become her signature. Apparently Jamila had been right to give her a second chance. "Astarte told him she wanted to stay with us." She shrugged. "I imagine he's on his way home."

Nicolette had flown home for the funeral Monday evening after the sex sting, then returned in time to meet the middle school bus on Thursday. Her mother, it turned out, had died in Westford, only two days before Nicolette had been there herself. Nicolette guessed she had been on her way to visit the Knight, perhaps in some kind of pilgrimage, though her mother had not told anyone of her plans. Including Nicolette, even though they would have only been a few hours drive apart.

She pushed her melancholy aside and focused on Astarte, who looked nothing like someone who had just gotten what she wanted. Nicolette wrapped a protective arm around the girl's shoulder, feeling oddly maternal in the wake of her own mother's death. If ever she could relate to what Astarte was going through, it was now. "Tough day, huh?"

Astarte nodded slowly, her eyes downcast. "Will I ever get to see them again?"

Nicolette dropped to a knee in order to look up into the girl's eyes. "Listen, Astarte. Nobody wants to take you away from your family. Not me, not Jamila, nobody. This is a school, not a prison. You can have visitors, you can go home for holidays, you can even leave if you want."

"Then why wouldn't you let my parents see me yesterday?"

"That was a mistake. Jamila was afraid … we all were afraid … that they would take you. We wanted you to have time to make your own decision. Like you have." She stood and smiled. "Look, tonight was hard because your parents haven't had a chance to get used to the idea yet. But they will. Especially when they realize how much this school will help you fulfill your destiny. If they truly love you, and I'm sure they do, they will want what is best for you. Okay?"

It wasn't like Astarte broke into a grin, but she did seem to rally a bit. "Okay. Can Venus at least stay with me?"

"Of course. This is the Venus School." Nicolette smiled again. "Who could make a more perfect mascot?"

Wrapped in a blanket by the fire in her chalet. Jamila finished reading the short text message, stood and stretched. They had the girl.

Using the back door, she followed the trestle-covered path to the chapel. She entered and stood in front of the Goddess shrine. She knew that the Goddess did not condone vengeance. But she could not help but take satisfaction in the pain Cameron and Amanda would feel at the loss of their daughter. As the expression went, revenge was a dish best served cold. Jamila shivered. The irony, of course, was that at her age almost everything seemed to be served cold.

"As you know," she whispered, fingering her amulet, "I have been inspired in part by vengeance, a motivation unworthy of someone in your service. I ask your strength that, in going forward, I can act on your behalf rather than continue to pursue my petty quest for retribution."

But in merely taking Astarte, Jamila knew she had not yet extracted her pound of flesh from Cameron and Amanda, had not caused them nearly the pain they had caused her. She thought of Astarte, asleep in the dormitory, her fate in Jamila's hands. She scratched at her sausage-skin scar. There was no denying that the girl had a beautiful face. But Jamila had often believed that a true servant of the Goddess should be one whose beauty shone from within.

Amanda sat on the floor in the dark living room of their hotel suite, her knees at her chest, hugging a pillow as she rocked slowly back and forth. There would be no more tears, no more shouting. All that remained was a cold, heavy, empty sorrow at the thought of Astarte's loss coupled with a hot, sharp, consuming anger at Cameron for lying to her.

Abandoned by Astarte. Betrayed by Cameron. The two foundations upon which she had built her life had dissolved beneath her, leaving her dangling over a void of, well, nothingness. And Venus gone as well. How had her idyllic life turned into such a house of horrors over the course of a single day?

After she had icily uttered the words, "I thought we were a team," Cameron had slunk off, probably to sleep in his car. She tried to find it in her to forgive him, and perhaps someday she might, but for now she was numb to anything but anger and sorrow. Did he really think that going Rambo, that lying to her, was the best way to handle this? He had tried to explain the whole attorney-client privilege thing—even showing her the naked ass photo, which apparently was no longer privileged since the client herself had made it public. But she had no interest in his legalese. Their family had been threatened, Astarte was in danger, and he had chosen to hide behind some silly lawyer rule rather than confide in his wife.

Of course Astarte had reacted the way she did—her entire life had been a series of events in which her family unit disintegrated around her. So when Cameron arrived to rescue her alone, Astarte made the astute and accurate assumption that he was trying to hide the naked ass photo from Amanda. It wasn't a far leap from there to conclude that the incriminating picture would threaten their marriage. That, of all things, had sparked Amanda's fury. "Don't you think it would have been better to have me there, explaining to

Astarte that I believed you about the bloody photo and didn't give a damn?"

Amanda punched the pillow. Cameron was a skilled attorney and brilliant researcher. But sometimes he did the most infuriatingly daft things.

Half-reclining in the passenger seat of his SUV, Cam stared at the stars twinkling above the mountains barely visible on the horizon. The stars and the mountains had been around for millennia, had witnessed pretty much every human folly and foolishness, every idiocy and imprudence. Yet still they shined, still they stood. The thought should have brought him some comfort. It did not.

All along he had assumed the sex sting photo was going to be used to blackmail or extort him, the threat of revealing it to Amanda hanging over him like the proverbial Sword of Damocles. But he had been wrong. It was never intended to be shown to Amanda. It was targeted for Astarte, an ugly weapon used to pry her from her family. Amanda would have understood it might be a setup, but for Astarte, naïve and inexperienced, the sight of Cam with a naked woman could only mean one thing. Well-played, he had to admit. The combination of Astarte's obsession with fulfilling her destiny, and her history of having her loved ones be yanked away from her, left her particularly vulnerable to the fear of Cam and Amanda splitting up. Just another family unit ripped apart on the rocks. Poor kid. And he had never seen it coming. So busy dodging the left hook, he had ducked his head straight into an incoming right uppercut. He was lucky to be still standing, even if just barely.

He had been up all night, not even bothering to try to sleep after Amanda had kicked him out. That was almost two hours ago, at 2:30. He sure had fucked things up. He knew Amanda would do whatever it took, including working with Cam, to get Astarte back safely. Beyond that, Cam worried for their future together. Amanda could forgive many things, but betrayal was not one of them.

But first things first. They needed to get Astarte away from that ski school. He opened up his laptop. At his core, Cam was a researcher. Problem-solving, he had found, was almost always facilitated by the acquisition of knowledge and information. It was time to learn more about this bizarre Venus School.

An hour later, he had some answers. Not that they brought him any comfort.

After turning the car engine on to pump some heat and warm his fingers, he sent Amanda a short text. "I'm so sorry. I truly messed this up. But I also found some info we need to discuss. I think I know what is going on. The ski school is owned by Jamila Bashear."

The revelation explained some things yet left many others still a mystery. Jamila had been part of a cabal of women claiming to be descendants of the lost colony of Atlantis—they called themselves the Crones—who had made a pawn of Amanda while attempting to steal an ancient device which turned base metals into gold. Amanda resisted, things had gotten ugly, and in an explosion Jamila had been disfigured and many of her cohorts killed. Jamila, irrationally but predictably, blamed Amanda and Cam. The fundamental question now was whether this was all a revenge play for Jamila, or whether instead she truly wanted to help Astarte fulfill her unlikely destiny.

Or, Cam supposed, it could be both. Despite the heat pumping into the front seat, he shuddered.

Amanda and Cam met for an early breakfast at a Dunkin Donuts around the corner from their hotel. The tension was as thick as the cream cheese on Cam's bagel, most of which went uneaten. Amanda managed to sip some tea and choke down a bit of bran muffin.

"Jamila, huh?"

Cam nodded. "The good news is that at least we know our enemy."

"That's not good news, Cameron. Jamila Bashear is as deranged as she is resourceful. And she swore revenge on us." She swallowed, her stomach wrenched with anxiety. "If she has Astarte…"

Cam frowned. "We'll get her back."

Amanda grunted noncommittally. There was no way she was going to leave Vermont without Astarte, especially knowing Jamila had her. And it was obvious to Amanda that she and Cam needed some time apart. She sighed. "I know you have the treasure dig at the Knight site this afternoon. Why don't you go back, and I'll remain here? I can hire a car."

"I'm not going anywhere without Astarte."

She didn't even try to swallow her anger. "You know what, you've done quite enough already. On top of all your other ... stupidity, that commando raid of yours is going to make it even less likely that the police will help us. Breaking into the dorm? Really? You'll be lucky if they don't arrest you." She scrunched up her bag. "I'd like to deal with this myself now." Not that she had any real plan.

It was as if he didn't hear her. "I'm staying, Amanda."

She slammed the table, not caring who heard. "Damn it, Cam! You're not listening. I don't *want* you here. You're not helping." She spoke slowly, emphasizing each word. "You. Are. Making. Things. Worse."

He blinked twice, began to reply, and then finally nodded. Not, she sensed, because he agreed. But because he saw how resolute she was. "All right. All right. I'll head back. I want to look into the Katherine Morville death more, now that we know Jamila is involved. That may tell us what Jamila is up to. May help us figure out how to get Astarte back."

Amanda sipped her tea, trying to calm down. She needed to think clearly. They both did. "Morville? You think all this is related? The journals and the death and Jamila and Astarte's prophecy?"

Cam shrugged, a gesture that, along with his sad, bloodshot eyes and hangdog brooding, projected an air of despondency Amanda had never seen in him before. The fact that his sadness touched her was, she realized, a good thing. But the fact she had no interest in taking his hand meant they still had a long way to go.

He replied, his voice little more than a whisper. "Think about the timing. And the Morville death never seemed right to me."

"Okay then." She stood and began to walk away. In their six years together, they had never separated without a kiss. She paused, but only for a second before the memory of his betrayal propelled her toward the door. In a sad voice, she said, "Let me know if you find anything."

Chapter 10

Cam stood next to Madame Segal, trying his best to be upbeat and friendly after the nightmare in Vermont the night before. He sensed that the Sinclair journals and Katherine Morville's death were connected to Astarte's abduction, so learning more about the journals had become his top priority while he was exiled from Vermont. And if that included digging for treasure, well, he supposed it was better than sitting at home moping.

A small crowd had gathered, attracted by the sight of an archeological team amassed on a Sunday afternoon at the Westford Knight site. There was no way to keep the dig a secret on a main thoroughfare in the center of town, so Cam and the homeowner had decided to embrace the attention. But other than Cam and Amanda, nobody knew about the journals. They just assumed Cam was playing a hunch by digging near the Knight.

Again holding her white cat and wearing her pink beret, Madame Segal leaned in and whispered. "We don't have to share the treasure with all these people, do we?" She drew out the word *treasure* in her French accent, as if the longer and more exotic the word, the richer would be their find.

Cam smiled. "There's no *we*, Madame Segal. This is your property. You own whatever we find."

There was no magic in an archeological dig. Just lots of documentation, photographs and painfully slow digging in the semi-frozen soil. Every spoonful of dirt was sifted, every manmade object bagged and saved for further analysis. It was a bit overdone, Cam thought. Either there was a treasure chest at the bottom of the hole or there wasn't. It wasn't like they were likely to find pottery shards. But, in the interest of extreme caution, the team worked slowly and methodically. Finally, just before five o'clock, the dig leader climbed out of a waist-high hole. He went by the single name Salvatore, with disheveled hair and playful blue eyes magnified to almost twice their size by thick eyeglasses.

"So," Cam said, "what's the verdict?"

He rubbed at his beard. "At first, the soil did not look right to me," he said, his Italian heritage evident in his accent. "The, how you say, *texture* is not right. But I think that is because she is frozen still."

"Okay."

"Now, at bottom of hold, there is something hard beneath the dirt. And my metal detector, she is going crazy."

The news gave Cam his first smile of the day. Though it killed him that Amanda was not here to share the find with him. "Gold?"

"No, the resistivity is too high. More like iron."

"So maybe the brackets on some kind of chest?"

Salvatore grinned. "This is what I am thinking also."

With a trowel, Salvatore leaned over the hole and scraped away a few cupfuls of dirt. Ten minutes later he lifted his face from the pit, his oversized eyes widening even further. "I think I am hitting some kind of fabric. Perhaps leather. This make sense to you?" he asked Cam.

Cam nodded, recalling the journal passage, his heart rate accelerating in anticipation. "They wrapped the chest in hides soaked with oil, to protect the wood."

Salvatore winked an oversized eye and bent back over the hole, speaking out of the side of his mouth as he worked. "The good thing about leather is she can be carbon-dated."

"Can't the wood?"

"Yes, but theoretically I could make a chest today using 600-year-old wood, so it does not really prove anything. But I am not so likely to find 600-year-old leather lying around, yes?"

Salvatore worked another hour, widening the hole around what they believed to be the chest. Finally, as darkness was beginning to set in, Salvatore photographed the hole with his phone before lifting his head out again, dirt caking his hair and cheek. "Okay. It is time to pull baby out of womb. We will start with the leather." He grinned and blew on his hands. "Cameron, you might want to make video. I have feeling people are not going to believe this story."

Amanda kicked at a clump of parking lot snow as she trudged toward the local police station on a sunny, temperate Sunday afternoon. Not what she expected to be doing on what was supposed to be a romantic getaway. "Blast it," she murmured. "What was Cam thinking?" She kicked again, this time at a chunk of frozen mud. "Or *not* thinking."

She didn't really expect to make any more progress today than they had yesterday. In fact, she was just hoping that Cam's commando raid had not made matters worse. It didn't take long for even those modest aspirations to be dashed.

The desk clerk, a short, twenty-something woman with a fleshy face, set her jaw when Amanda gave her name. "Someone from the Venus School came in this morning to swear out a complaint against your husband. Breaking and entering, assault, criminal trespass." She leaned forward. "Is he here with you?"

"No, he went back to Massachusetts."

"Well, if he's smart, he'll stay there. We'll arrest him if we see him near the school again."

Amanda raised her chin. "I understand. But they are still holding my daughter against our wishes."

"No, Ma'am. I believe the officer on duty explained this to you yesterday. And it is my understanding the girl chose to stay at the school even after your husband made his scene."

The policewoman's body language—arms crossed and jaw clenched—made it clear how she felt about the situation. More bad luck. An older woman, perhaps a mother herself, might have been more sympathetic. And Amanda might have been able to charm a male cop. Amanda sighed and made one last attempt at reason. "Very well. I can guess how things look from your perspective. But the bottom line is that a minor child is being held without the permission of her parents."

"Well, then I suggest you tell it to a judge."

Amanda trudged back to her rental car and turned the ignition. "Aargh," she yelled. She stared at the mountains in the distance, her eyes pooling with tears. But only for a few seconds. The policewoman was right. She needed to tell her story to a judge and end this insanity.

Cam stared down at the semi-decayed wooden chest, now sitting on a plastic blue tarp covering the cement floor of Madame Segal's garage. They had moved out of the yard, the crowd reluctantly dispersing, because the evening had begun to turn cold and, well, leaving the treasure sitting on the lawn seemed imprudent. The cat must have been jealous of the attention the chest was getting, because he tried to spray it before Salvatore kicked him aside. He hissed at the bug-eyed man, perhaps seeing an oversized goldfish in a tank, before scampering into the corner to watch from the shadows.

Salvatore had carefully preserved what he could of the leather wrapping and sealed it in an oversized Ziploc bag. He and Cam had then lifted the chest from the hole by sliding a mesh fabric to serve as a cradle underneath it. Now Cam, Madame Segal and Salvatore's two cohorts, a middle-aged husband and wife who had just returned from volunteering at an archeological dig in New Mexico, watched Salvatore pace around the garage, as if in a silent debate with himself as to whether they should open the chest. Finally he spoke. "I think we should wait. Maybe get someone from the state to watch. Make things official."

Cam lifted his chin. "You're in charge of the dig. But I want nothing to do with the state."

Salvatore nodded, closing his eyes in a long blink and smiling. "Yes, I know. But, still."

Cam raised a hand. "Hold on. I agree about making this official." He dialed Sergeant Poulos' cell, holding the phone out so everyone could hear. "Any chance you're on duty?"

"Matter of fact, I am."

"I think I just found a possible motive for Katherine Morville's murder." Cam gave the address.

"Be there in ten."

Cam hung up and turned to the group. "Probably not a bad idea to have a police presence." Because, well, treasure.

"So do we wait?" Salvatore asked.

Cam took a deep breath. Would Poulos try to stop them from opening the chest? Cam couldn't think why he would. But who knew what he might come up with. "You know the old saying, it's easier to get forgiveness than permission. I say let's open it now." He smiled. "Before the cat urinates on it." He turned to Madame Segal. "You okay with that?"

"Okay? At my age, there is no guaranty I will be breathing in ten minutes. *Mon Dieu.* Open the damn chest."

Nicolette peered through the grimy garage window, hoping to get a clear view of the treasure chest as they prepared to open it. Instead of being part of the dig team, she was stuck behind an old garage, stomping her feet to keep warm, while a priceless treasure was being revealed only feet away, a treasure that in fact looked to be part of her family history.

She had milled around the front yard during the dig, her dark wig, baseball cap and clunky eyeglasses sufficient to keep Cam from recognizing her. Cam seemed to be a bright guy, but as an operative the best that could be said about him was that he made a hell of a historian, as the treasure chest find confirmed. It had simply not occurred to him that one of Nicolette's cohorts had circled around and attached a tracking device to his SUV during his aborted rescue attempt. But, he might point out in rebuttal, *he* was the one in the garage with the treasure while melting snow dripped from the roof onto her head.

The guy with the thick glasses dropped to one knee, using a small brush to scrub dirt and rust off the metal latch that held the lid of the wooden chest closed. A single bulb, controlled by a pull string, illuminated the room. The wood itself had pitted and become mealy in places, collapsing partly, though the integrity of the chest had not been completely breached. Nicolette leaned forward, her nose touching the window. She wished her father could share this moment with her. *The Templar treasure.* They had discussed it often. Did it exist? If so, what was it? Riches? Religious relics? Historical artifacts? Secret knowledge? In some ways, it didn't really matter. The fact that the chest was *here*, in America, proved that Europeans had been crossing the Atlantic long before Columbus. And that was probably more valuable than any treasure could be.

She rubbed gently at the glass, trying to clean it, smiling as she realized her hypocrisy in doing so—she really *was* curious, it really *did* matter what the treasure was. History and knowledge were great things. But a treasure was a treasure.

Salvatore stood and backed away from the chest. "The latch, she is free. Cameron, it is up to you to open the lid."

Cam smiled. "It belongs to you, Madame Segal. You should do the honors."

She shook her head slowly. "No. You found the treasure, Cameron. You open it."

"Actually, Salvatore found it," Cam replied.

Salvatore took another step back. "I am merely a mole who digs where told."

Cam smiled again. "I get it. Cam opened it, so Cam gets in trouble."

Salvatore's blue eyes danced. "Yes, there is that also."

Cam bent to lift the lid, then caught himself. "Madame Segal, do you have WiFi out here?"

"Yes, it should reach." She gave him the password.

"Okay. Please just give me one minute."

Cam backed to the corner of the garage and phoned Amanda. "Hi," he began, "any update on Astarte?"

"No, other than the police are looking for you."

"Great. Anyway, I know you're pissed at me, but I don't want you to miss this." He described the dig. "If you're at the hotel, we can Skype so you can watch us open the chest."

"Okay. I'm doing research, trying to find the best lawyer for this. The police aren't going to do anything without a court order."

Guilt washed over Cam. This legal stuff should be his job. But he had botched it. "Okay, good idea."

"Anyway," she said, "thanks for thinking to include me."

Cam set his phone up on a sawhorse and made sure one of Salvatore's cohorts was filming. Madame Segal stood just behind him. "Okay, here goes."

He lifted the wooden lid, the metal hinges creaking as six hundred years of detritus combined with gravity to resist his efforts.

"Do not force it," Salvatore breathed. "That wood, she could snap."

Cam nodded, easing it open, his eyes drawn to the interior of the chest. Dust swirled in the light and a dank, musty smell escaped from the trunk. "There's a cloth on top, covering everything," Cam said. "Should I just take it off?"

Salvatore approached with his camera. "Let me take close-up. And I will bag the cloth."

Cam took a deep breath. "Abracadabra." He pulled back the dark cloth, releasing more dust, the particles stinging his eyes. But he could not turn away. A pile of gold-colored ornaments had been stacked two or three deep—candelabras, serving trays, vases, goblets, a crown, bracelets, chains. In the middle of the pile sat a gold jewelry box decorated with jewels. Atop the gold box sat a terra cotta Goddess figurine with oversized hips and breasts. Cam gently moved the Goddess aside, smiling to himself as he realized subconsciously he had been careful not to touch her private parts. He lifted the lid of the jewelry box to find gold coins stacked neatly inside like checkers in their case. Everyone stared.

Amanda finally broke the silence. "Are you still there? My picture froze."

Cam smiled, tearing his eyes away to address her. "*We* froze, not the picture. Can you see? It's filled with gold artifacts and coins."

"Odd," came her odd reply.

"Why?"

"It's just that, why bother? Gold had value in Europe, not America. Recall, your Natives traded it away for glass beads."

"Maybe they were just stashing it here," Cam replied.

"Perhaps," she conceded.

Not that it mattered what they thought. The truth was in the chest in front of them. Gold. And dust. He coughed, turning his face away. "Don't need 21st century DNA on our treasure," he said.

"Can you hold the Goddess figurine closer to the camera?" Amanda asked.

It was the only object in the chest not made of gold. Cam held it for Amanda to examine.

"I've been studying these figures," Amanda said. "She looks like she comes from the Middle East, perhaps 500 or 600 BCE. Originally Sumerian, but adopted by the Israelites."

"Why would she be in medieval chest of treasures?" Salvatore asked.

"I'm guessing the Templars brought her back with them from the Crusades," Amanda replied. "As for what she's doing in the chest, the answer is obvious." Amanda paused. "She's a talisman. She's guarding the treasure."

Amanda appreciated Cam including her electronically in the opening of the treasure chest. And she was fascinated by the inclusion of the Goddess figurine, sitting atop the cache like Cleopatra on her barge. The clay object clearly had no monetary value, which left no doubt that its inclusion had been for religious purposes.

A knock on the garage door interrupted her musings. "Must be Sergeant Poulos," Cam said.

The heavy-set officer strolled into camera view and eyed the open chest. With a wry smile, he looked at Cam. "You better not be jerking my chain, Thorne."

Cam smirked. "Yeah, I bought all this gold and stuck it in an antique chest just to prove I was right all along."

Poulos shined his flashlight into the chest. "Is it real?"

Cam shrugged. "We haven't even touched it yet."

"Any idea what it's worth?"

"Historically, it's priceless." Cam did some quick calculations in his head. The chest, full, had weighed about a hundred pounds. He guessed two-thirds of that was the contents. "A pound of gold is worth about $20,000. So, assuming the artifacts have some impurities, maybe a million bucks, melted down? But nobody's melting anything."

The sergeant nodded. "And you think this is what got Katherine Morville killed."

"The journals are one thing. But a treasure chest full of gold is something else entirely. Maybe something to kill over."

Amanda half-listened, intent instead on studying the figurine. Salvatore had turned it once for her. She was about to ask him to spin it again when a movement in the background, behind the figurine, caught her eye. "Cameron," she called, using his full name. "I need a word, please. Right away."

Cam blinked and picked up his phone, moving to the corner of the garage. "What's wrong?"

"Don't turn, but I think I saw a face in the back window of the garage. Someone's watching."

"Okay, thanks." He set the phone back down and gestured to Poulos. "Someone's watching us through the back window," he said casually, his voice low.

The policeman nodded. "You go one way, I'll go the other."

To cover them, Cam said in a loud voice, "I'm going to show Sergeant Poulos the hole. You guys take more pictures, start documenting all this."

Cam sprinted, hugging the side of the garage along the lot line. Poulos must have been noisier because as he neared the back corner of the structure a human figure, a woman, turned into Cam. Reacting instantly, Cam ducked his shoulder into her midsection and executed a perfect tackle, landing atop the spy.

With a thud they hit the semi-frozen ground, her hat and glasses flying off. Cam lifted his head and peered down. In the moonlight, he recognized her face. *The cold-lipped woman.*

Cam recoiled, loosening his grip on her. But rather than try to fight him off, she swallowed, took a breath, smiled, and arched an eye. "If you get off of me," she rasped, "I promise not to kiss you again."

Nicolette didn't actually mind having Cam Thorne sprawled atop her. He was an attractive man and, well, it had been awhile since she had taken a lover. Life in an all-girls school had its drawbacks.

"So," she teased, puckering, "what will it be?"

He rolled away, the look of revulsion on his face bruising her ego a bit. But she shouldn't take it personally. It just meant he was devoted to his wife. Which in turn meant Astarte had benefited from healthy role models in her life. But, still, he might have lingered a bit longer...

"What, what are you doing here?" he sputtered.

"Believe it or not, I'm here to help. Help Astarte."

He pushed down on her shoulder, hard. "Fuck off."

She grabbed for his arm. "Wait. Just listen. I know you're pissed. And you have every right to be. But if you want to help Astarte, you'll at least listen to me. Five minutes." She saw she was beginning to reach him. "Just five minutes. What do you have to lose?"

He shook his head, still holding her down. "Good point. You've ruined my life already."

"Not totally. Astarte is safe where she is. For now. But I'm worried about her."

These last words finally resonated. "If anything happens to her—"

The sound of heavy footsteps approaching cut off his thought. She hissed quickly, "We need to talk. In private."

He sighed and rolled off. "All right. Get up."

They scrambled to their feet as the burly policeman she had seen in the garage rounded the corner. Cam brushed himself off. "False alarm," he said airily. "She's part of our dig team."

"I was, ah, looking at some of the rocks in the stone wall," Nicolette blustered. "I thought maybe Prince Henry and his gang might have carved other things."

The cop folded his arms across his chest. "Why is it that whenever I'm around you, Thorne, I get the feeling I'm being bullshitted?"

Cam shrugged and smiled sheepishly. "You're right. Can't bullshit a bullshit artist." He glanced at Nicolette. "But who she is doesn't matter. What matters is that the treasure is real. Can we store it at the police station until we figure out what to do with it?"

After the policeman nodded and began traipsing back to the front of the garage, Cam turned to Nicolette, studying her, wondering what her angle might be. "Look," she offered, "I didn't have to come." She pulled off her wig and shook her hair loose, hoping the gesture would convey a lack of duplicity. "We have Astarte already. And if you don't hear me out, and something happens to her…" She held his eyes as she let her words hang. He seemed like a nice guy, and she really did feel bad for him, so it wasn't a lie when she said, "I truly am here to help."

"Okay. Okay." He pulled at his hair. "I need to take care of things here first. Meet me at the Town Common in a half hour. The bench near the bandstand." He gritted his teeth. "But just so you know, if anything happens to Astarte, so help me God I will hunt you down."

Cam normally wouldn't have let the treasure out of his sight. But he knew Sergeant Poulos, an ex-Marine, valued honor and duty over any monetary temptation. If he said he'd guard the treasure, he'd either do so or die trying. And all Cam really cared about now was finding out what the cold-lipped woman could tell him about Astarte.

They hoisted the chest, using the fabric cradle, into the trunk of Poulos' squad car and secured the hood. "You want to ride with me?" Poulos asked, smirking.

"Um, yes, I do," Cam replied. No sense testing Poulos' honor unnecessarily. Cam used to joke during real estate closings, as he accepted and examined the purchase money check: "Nope. Not enough to give up my license over." But one time, during an especially large transaction, the check he held in his hand was for thirteen million dollars. He had resisted making the joke that one time, knowing that a sum that large might just tempt him to try to flee to Tierra del Fuego.

Twenty minutes later, the chest draped under a blanket in the corner of the locked evidence room inside the police station, Cam jogged across the street to the Town Common, the evening wind whipping across the triangle of land in the twilight. The cold-lipped woman—had she given the name Nicolette at the ski school?—sat on a bench, staring at the evening stars. Cam glanced skyward. *Venus*, of course.

He joined her, keeping a body-width between them. "You say you're here to help me. First blackmail, now, what, torture?"

"It was never the plan to show the picture to Amanda. I thought you would have figured that out by now."

He rolled his eyes. "No, you were just going to show it to my daughter. Like that's any better? And now you expect me to believe you're here to help me?"

"Actually, I'm here more to help Astarte. But you are a secondary beneficiary."

That, at least, was easier to believe.

She turned to face him. "You need to go to the hospital. Have a full drug test done."

"Why?" he replied, even as a memory of himself bombing down the highway at eighty-five flashed in his mind.

"The tea," Nicolette replied. "It was laced with an herbal stimulant. Gives users a feeling of invincibility. Just yours, not your wife's." She paused to allow her words to sink in. "It's why you were behaving so aggressively. So irrationally. Jamila is an expert in herbal medicines." She smiled. "You're lucky she didn't turn you into a toad."

Cam felt a surge of hope. If true, it might be a path to reconciliation with Amanda. "Why are you telling me this?"

"Because you're a good guy. And more importantly, because Astarte needs her dad. Needs her family back together. Go get that test. Tonight, before it flushes out of your system."

"That's it? You're not asking for anything in return?"

She stood. "Not yet." She pulled her jacket tight around herself in the cool evening air. "But we will. Consider this a down payment."

Cam watched Nicolette stroll across the Town Common, her lithe form intermittently illuminated by the headlights of passing cars. He didn't trust her. She had, after all, ensnared him in a sex sting and been part of the team that kidnapped Astarte. But that didn't mean she was lying about the tea.

Energized by the arrival of a possible lifeline when he thought himself alone and adrift, he jogged the half-mile back to his car parked at Madame Segal's house and headed straight for Emerson Hospital. Hopefully, on a Sunday night, they'd be able to test him quickly. Before the drugs leeched from his system.

As he drove, he thought about the treasure. On the one hand, as Amanda pointed out, why bring gold to the New World, where it had little or no value? Yet here it was, buried just where the journals said it would be. So the question of why wasn't really relevant. A better question was why nobody had returned to claim it.

An hour after arriving at the outpatient desk, Cam strolled out of the hospital main entrance toward the parking garage, a band-aid on the crook of his left elbow and a spring in his step. The lab tech said drugs like Ecstasy could be detected in blood tests for only about 24 hours after use, but in urine for two to five days. And in hair for many weeks. Thirty hours had passed since his cup of tea. Cam assumed whatever psychoactive drug he had been given would be metabolized at a similar rate and had asked for all three tests, figuring he just needed one positive result to plead his case to Amanda. He actually considered driving into Lowell to purchase a few Molly pills just to ensure the tests came back positive, but in the end rejected the idea. Amanda deserved better than more lies. He'd wait for the results to come back tomorrow, then, hopefully, drive up to Vermont to share the news with her.

A cool wind blew, rustling the trees and moving a few wispy clouds across the moonlit sky. He found Venus again, in its normal evening location in the western sky. When he looked back down, the tall figure of Rene Lapierre stood in front of him, blocking his path. Cam sensed this was not a social visit. He stepped back, digging into his pocket for his keys in case he needed some kind of weapon. "What do you want?"

"I want you to come with me." Unsmiling, his face appeared even less pleasing than normal. "We need to talk."

"What if I don't want to?"

Lapierre's eyes flickered and he dropped his chin slightly. Cam realized too late it was a signal. Two pair of strong arms grabbed Cam on either side and wedged him between them. "Don't be stupid and fight them, Cameron."

From the power in their grip, Cam quickly realized the advice was sound. He would need to outsmart them. "You should know, I'm contagious. Tuberculosis." He coughed. "That's why I'm here."

The grips loosened, but only until Lapierre responded. "Nice try. I know why you're here."

"You may know I came for a drug test. But they diagnosed me when they heard my lungs." He coughed again, this time directly at the face of the thug on his right. This time the man recoiled and Cam took the opportunity to wrench his right arm free. Twisting, he placed his left foot behind the other assailant's leg and shoved, upending him. Lapierre rushed at him. Cam dove to the side and rolled behind a tree, Lapierre's hand clawing at his shoulder. He rolled again, trying to get to his feet, but as he scrambled and clawed and fought, a voice inside his head spoke to him. *The drugs have worn off. You can't really think you can fight off three trained operatives.* As if to push the point home, Cam caught a forearm to the jaw, knocking him sideways back to the ground.

Lapierre's voice came to him from a long way away. "Damn it, Thorne, I said don't be stupid. We can *make* you talk to me, or you can do it voluntarily." He lifted Cam's head up by the hair and put his face close to Cam's. "But there is no third choice."

Cam blinked, the blow to his head reproducing the symptoms he had experienced on the ski slopes a couple of days ago—dizziness and a feeling of nausea. He tried to focus on Lapierre through the stars. "There's always a third choice," he slurred.

"No." Lapierre, who still had a grip of Cam by the hair, shook Cam's head back and forth as if to emphasize the point. "Sometimes we are lucky if there is even a second choice, never mind a third." He let go of Cam's hair and stood as his henchman hoisted Cam to his feet. "And this is one of those times."

Lapierre sat in the back seat while one of his men drove. The other sat opposite Lapierre, Thorne wedged between them in the Buick. Both henchmen worked for a private security firm employed by the Masons when they needed to operate outside the law. Thorne seemed a bit dazed, though Lapierre watched him closely, fearing he might be faking.

After a couple of miles, Thorne spoke. "Where are you taking me?"

"I told you. We need to talk."

"Most people just use a phone."

"Yeah, well, what I have to say can't be said over the phone."

"I know. A society with secrets."

Lapierre snorted. "You don't know the half of it."

"How did you find me?" Thorne asked.

"Easy. My daughter told me where you'd be."

"Your daughter?" Thorne blinked and swallowed. "Wait, what, Nicolette is your daughter?"

Lapierre imagined Thorne's mind racing as he realized what he thought had been two unrelated planets orbiting his universe suddenly collided. He gave him time to process the revelation.

"So, you're working for Jamila." Thorne practically spat as he said her name.

"For? No. *With* is a better word. And even that might be generous. Jamila Bashear has an agenda all her own. But, in this case, it coincides with ours."

"When you say 'ours,' you mean the Freemasons?"

"Yes. Or at least the top Masonic leadership. The rank-and-file members don't really know about what we are doing."

Thorne nodded slowly. "It was like that with the Templars also."

It was a good analogy. Just as the average Templar Knight in the field thought he was fighting for the Church even while Templar leaders conspired against the Vatican, so, too, most Freemasons had no idea what its leadership was planning.

Thorne continued to connect the dots. "But Jamila is promoting Goddess worship."

"Yes. It is rather complicated, I admit."

Lapierre leaned forward to speak to the driver, not wanting to continue this conversation with others listening. "There's a Residence Inn in that office park. Pull in there."

Thorne didn't resist, and ten minutes later Lapierre and the two henchmen had manhandled him into the suite Lapierre had rented for the weekend. "So what now?" Thorne asked. "Sodium pentothal? Water-boarding in the bathtub? Maybe jumper cables to my testicles?"

"Something worse," Lapierre replied as he grabbed a rectangular metal object and held it up. Thorne recoiled, fearing it was some kind of torture device, perhaps a stun gun. "Sit down." Lapierre held the object closer, showing Thorne it was nothing more than a remote controller. "I'm going to make you watch some television commercials."

Had Cam heard correctly? Television commercials? One of the thugs pushed him into a desk chair in the hotel suite.

Lapierre removed his black leather jacket, revealing a muscular physique beneath a white golf shirt. He nodded and his two henchmen retreated to an adjoining room. "Again, don't try anything stupid." His close-set eyes peered at Cam over his hooked nose. "I didn't choose those guys for their conversational abilities."

Every pulse of Cam's heart sent blood throbbing through the veins of his forehead like ice cream through a straw. And his neck had stiffened from the altercation outside the hospital, making it hard to look at Lapierre without turning his whole body. Not to mention his injured shoulder and knee from the rescue attempt. He rotated in the office chair and nodded. He'd keep his eyes out for some kind of weapon or escape opportunity, but it had been a rough few days and he had no burning desire to wrestle with the two gorillas. Besides, he was curious. Had Lapierre wanted to harm Cam, he would have driven to some remote location, not back to his hotel. Apparently he really did want to show Cam something.

Lapierre clicked the remote and a video began to play on a laptop set up in front of Cam. "You might remember this." He dropped into a chair next to Cam. "The old margarine commercial."

A wholesome woman in a long white dress with yellow flowers in her hair sits under a tree reading nursery rhymes to a circle of animals around her. A male voice-over interrupts the scene, saying, "Mother Nature, is it true the current administration wants to disband the Environmental Protection Agency?"

She furrows her brow and responds, "I was told they just want to streamline things."

"No. The man appointed to head the EPA transition team said the president plans to disband the entire agency."

Mother Nature stands, an angry look on her face, and spreads her arms wide. The animals cower. The camera zooms in on her face as her eyes narrow and the skies darken. "Mister President," she says, in the voice of an angry school principal, enunciating every word. "It's not nice to fool ... Mother Nature!" On the last word, she claps her hands together, triggering an explosion of thunder.

Cam blinked, not sure how to respond.

"Well," Lapierre finally asked.

"Well what?"

"What do you think?"

Cam turned the chair. "What I think depends on the context. What's it for?"

Lapierre smiled wryly. "You really don't know?"

Cam wasn't in the mood for games. "You going to run these for the midterm elections?"

Shaking his head, Lapierre replied. "It's part of a campaign all right. But not a political one. We want to pave the way for America to accept the return of the Goddess."

"What? I still don't get it. You told me ... threatened me ... to stop lecturing about the Goddess. Now you're paving the way for her?"

Lapierre leaned back in his chair, hands in front of his chest, fingers linked as if in prayer. "My objection to your lectures was merely one of timing, which, of course is no trivial thing. We were not ready for the Goddess campaign to begin. We would have preferred a delay of a year or two. But Jamila is impatient, knowing her days are numbered. And then you came along, and people started listening, learning, *understanding*." He shrugged. "The congregants were flocking to the new church even before it was finished being built. We figured we should open the doors and accommodate them best we could."

"Church? Congregants? You sound like you're talking about a new religion. When I talk about the Goddess, I'm just talking about history."

"No, you are talking about a universal truism. The Goddess has always been a part of our lives, even if she has often been hidden from us. And we are not talking about a new religion, per se. It is more like a crusade, a crusade to harness what once made America great and redirect it into, as the political slogan goes, making America great once again. America is still good, but it has slipped. It no longer strives for the moral high ground. It no longer fights for its ideals. The words on the Statue of Liberty, once looked upon so proudly, ring hollow now: *Give me your tired, your poor, your huddled masses yearning to breathe free.* Today we only want immigrants with college degrees who speak perfect English. America being merely good is not good enough. Just as Freemasonry takes good men and makes them better, so too can it take America and make it great again."

Cam shook his head. "Nice speech. But just hold on a second." He blinked. "Isn't it disingenuous, or even hypocritical, for a group that doesn't allow women members to be championing the Goddess? I mean, really? There's a Groucho Marx joke in there somewhere."

Lapierre was nodding even before Cam finished. "Yes, true, I get that." He smiled. "Just hold that thought for a few minutes. I have more ads to show you."

"More?"

"The ads are the beginning of our campaign. The first one, the one you just watched, is meant to be tongue-in-cheek, to make people laugh and get them thinking about the Goddess." He eyed Thorne. "So. You never told me. Do you think it's effective?"

Cam blinked again. The man really did want Cam's opinion. He shifted. "Yes. Yes, I think it is. It plays to the Baby Boomer generation. And it's dramatic. I like her tone, as if she is chastising a boy in school."

Lapierre grinned, revealing a pronounced overbite. "That was a late change. I'm glad you like it."

"Is that it? Is there a call for action or anything?"

"No. That's it. Just the message that the current administration is anti-nature. We think that, by not having any call for action, it will make people wonder more about it. Again, this is meant to reintroduce the concept of the Goddess to the people." He pressed a button on the remote. "Here's another ad."

This piece begins with a shot of the night sky, with music beginning to play. As the camera zooms skyward, the form of a human figure takes shape among the pattern of the stars. A female figure, a Zodiacal sign. The music bursts into familiar lyrics:

When the moon is in the Seventh House,
And Jupiter aligns with Mars,

The stars fade, replaced by a cascade of faces of modern women as the song continues: Christa McAuliffe, the astronaut; soccer player Mia Hamm; Princess Diana.

Then peace will guide the planets,
And love will steer the stars.

More female faces. Angela Merkel, German chancellor; Madonna; Melinda Gates; Oprah. The Fifth Dimension continues to sing.

This is the dawning of the Age of Aquarius...

As the song moves to its chorus, the images change. Now we see younger girls, school-aged. An Asian girl peering into a microscope; an African girl holding a political sign; a blond-haired girl reading a book to a hospital patient.

The screen fades to black, and a simple yellow script appears. It sits there in silence for a few seconds before it is read aloud in the iconic, gravelly voice of James Earl Jones: "Relying on half of our population always to be in charge is like asking a bird to fly with one wing. Isn't it time we tried something different?"

Cam took a deep breath. This was the world he wanted Astarte to live in. He felt like clapping. Instead he brushed his sleeve across his eyes. "That's really good. Powerful."

"Do you think people will get it? Get that it's time for a change?"

Part of him resisted helping Lapierre, after all that had happened. But in the end Cam felt like his fate, and Astarte's, would be enhanced if he made himself valuable. "All of them? No. But you don't need everyone. You need, I don't know, ten percent. That's enough to start a movement. Same thing with the other ad, the Mother Nature one. It's hokey, and some people will just roll their eyes, but you'll get the older generation, who grew up with the margarine commercial."

"What about the male narrator?"

"I like it. Especially a deep voice like his. It makes it less 'us versus them' than it would with a female voice."

"Good. Thanks. One more." He hit the play button again.

A tall, bearded man in a tuxedo stands in front of the Masonic Temple in Washington, D.C., next to a marble sphinx statue. The camera zooms in to reveal his Masonic regalia—apron, collar sash, white gloves, top hat. "We Freemasons are not a secret society. But we are a society with secrets." A pause. "I am about to reveal one of them to you now." The camera shifts to an aerial view and begins to pan away, offering a bird's eye view of the capital city, before zooming back in on the Statue of Freedom atop the Capital building dome.

As the Freemason continues to speak, the viewer sees a series of other statues around Washington, all of them Goddess representations. "The secret is this: We are now and always have been a nation dedicated to the values of the ancient Goddess: liberty, justice, equality, compassion, harmony between humankind and nature. But recently we have strayed from this path." The man's voice lowers. "It is time to correct this. Time to find our way again. Time to recognize the importance of balance in our society by turning back to the teachings of the Goddess. Our first Masonic Grand Master, the Biblical King Solomon, was himself a worshiper of the ancient Goddess." A painting of the Biblical king, bearded and regal, appears on screen. "As it is written in the Old Testament, 1 Kings 11:5: 'Solomon worshiped Ashtoreth, the Goddess.'" The bearded Freemason nods, eyes locked on the camera. "That's right. Solomon, renowned for his wisdom, the greatest king of the Bible, venerated the Goddess. As he also venerated Yahweh. Wise King Solomon understood we must look to both the male and the female to provide balance in our lives."

The camera pulls back and refocuses, this time on the Statue of Liberty. The narrator continues. "But how can we venerate the Goddess if we do not embrace the feminine? Simply, we cannot. So, beginning today, and continuing forever into the future, Freemasonry in the United States will begin to open its membership to women. We invite women of high moral character to join us. Join us and help us to help America find its way again."

The spokesman begins to walk away, then stops and turns. "And, by the way, we have no interest in taking over the world or even running the country, despite what some people may say. But we do care very much about who does run things." The camera fades back again, this time revealing a shot of the continental United States from space. The voice concludes: "We care about American ideals, and we want to live by them."

The ad ends.

Cam whistled. "Wow. You're opening up your membership?" He thought about it. Every Mason had a mother or wife or daughter or sister. Unlike racists and homophobes, even the most ardent chauvinist probably had a healthy relationship with at least one woman in his life. So the idea of Goddess worship might not be so repulsive.

Lapierre shrugged. "There's going to be hell to pay. Some of the old geezers will go apoplectic. And some state Lodges will resist; technically we can't force them to do anything." He explained how each state Lodge was sovereign, not subject to any nationwide regulation. "But most Lodges need two things right now: money and members. By taking women, they get bodies. And we're going to offer a bounty, probably a few thousand dollars for every woman they take." He tilted his head and smiled. "Even the old geezers understand cash."

Lapierre paused and rubbed his face, the strain of what he was proposing evident in the circles under his hawkish eyes. "Who knows, maybe the Lodges resist. But, either way, it's been too long. Like you said, it makes us hypocrites. We should have done it decades ago. Astarte gives us the chance now. And, of course, we're not going to sell it as Goddess worship. We're going to sell it as bringing back balance to society. I mean, how many people don't like balance?"

Cam didn't really care about all this, beyond its effect on his family. "But why Astarte? Why her?"

Lapierre seemed surprised by the question. "She's the figurehead. She's what brings everyone together—Christians, Muslims, Jews, Mormons, Native Americans. She has the blood of them all running through her veins." He shrugged. "Anytime there's a movement like this, a transition to a new era, there needs to be a narrative to accompany it. Astarte is the chosen one, the princess of the prophecy." He gestured to the laptop screen. "Without her, this is all just a bunch of white noise."

The vice constricting Cam's chest lessened slightly. If they *needed* Astarte, they would probably protect her. It was something, at least. He refocused and stared at the frozen screen. At his country. "These ads, all together … they are going to make quite an impact."

"That's what we're hoping. Who can argue with King Solomon?"

"I didn't know he was a Goddess worshiper."

Lapierre nodded. "He built temples to her. And it gets better." He smiled. "Or worse, depending on your politics. Solomon was Freemasonry's first Grand Master. But some people think he was actually second, with King Nimrod, who built the Tower of Babel, being first. Nimrod was a pagan, a Goddess worshiper. And," he added with a chuckle, "there's even a third candidate, Hiram Abiff, the guy who actually built Solomon's temple for him. Some people consider him the true first Grand Master. You guessed it: Goddess worshiper." He shrugged. "So, whichever way you slice it, Masonry's first Grand Master was a Goddess worshiper."

Cam smiled. "I'm surprised it took you guys so long to come around." He turned back to the computer screen. "How many of these ads are you going to run?"

"Hundreds. For the next few months. TV, internet, some radio ads." He shrugged again. "We have a huge war chest. Might as well spend it on something important. Ads, and then the bounties."

Cam took a deep breath. Until now the whole Astarte prophecy thing was just a silly legend. Or, if real, something to happen in the distant future. But the 'something important' that the Masons were about to spend their war chest on wasn't a legend and it wasn't in the future. It was real. It was now. It was Astarte.

Now that Cam realized television commercials were going to be the worst of his tortures, he relaxed a bit. He leaned back in the hotel office chair, rubbed his neck and studied Lapierre. The fact that the Masons needed Astarte—that she was, in fact, central to their plans—gave her a level of security and him a level of comfort he hadn't felt an hour ago. And the fact that Nicolette was Lapierre's daughter also helped. Astarte was being held captive, but at least nobody wanted to harm her.

The Mason smiled wryly. "I'm guessing you're wondering if you can trust me."

Cam shook his head. "No. I know I can't. You'll do what is best for your group. I'm just trying to figure out if that is also best for Astarte." Actually, what would be best for her would be to live the life of a normal 12-year-old. But that ship had sailed.

"It is, in fact."

"I sort of see that, but not completely. Jamila is trying to push for a return of the Goddess. You seem to want balance or duality or whatever you call it. They're not really the same thing. Astarte could end up in the middle of a tug-of-war."

Lapierre pushed himself off the bed and began pacing the room. "Actually, they pretty much are the same thing. Jamila ideally may want the world to be ruled by women, but she knows that's not realistic. She just wants, like you said, balance. A recognition that the feminine point of view and feminine values are important. Crucial, even. We agree."

"Odd position for a group that doesn't let women in." Cam shrugged. "Or at least not until now."

"Again, not really. Masonry is all about balance. You answered my question at the Lodge the other night about the Templars and how they understood the need for balance. Like you said, nature requires it."

"But you just said your membership is going to fight you on this." Cam shifted. "Either they believe it, or they don't."

"No." Lapierre stopped. "That's just it. Most of them just go through the motions. They hear, but they don't really listen. They learn, but they don't really acquire wisdom." He reached for a book on the night table, thumbed through until he found the picture he wanted and set it on the desk in front of Cam. This was a different Lapierre than the guarded, reserved man Cam had first met in the Masonic Lodge. "This is a great example. The twin pillars of

Freemasonry, Jachin and Boaz. It is one of the first things new initiates are taught: Pass between these pillars to find wisdom, represented by the all-seeing eye, on the other side." He turned the image so Cam could study it.

Masonic Pillars, Jachin and Boaz

Lapierre continued after giving Cam a few seconds. "Let's just focus for a second on the pillars. The one on the right-hand side of the eye, looking out at us, is Jachin. He represents strength."

Cam interrupted. "He must be the male. That's why he's on the right."

"Yes. And that's why the sun is always shown with Jachin. See the sun, next to him?" Cam knew the sun was traditionally associated with the male. Lapierre continued. "Boaz is on the left-hand side of the eye. With the moon. Boaz is the feminine. But, again, we need both if we are going to achieve wisdom and understanding."

Cam nodded. "That's the all-seeing eye in the middle. Wisdom and understanding."

"Right." Still leaning over Cam, Lapierre jabbed at the page. "Now look at the square and compass."

"Okay."

"What do you see?"

"A 'G' in the middle. Which I'm guessing stands for the deity."

Lapierre rose onto the balls of his feet, his face flushing with enthusiasm. "Right again. But what else?"

Cam tried to look past the tools themselves, to focus on the underlying shapes. Slowly he smiled. "I see what you're getting at. The square is an upside down triangle, the symbol for the womb, the feminine. And the compass is the male, the sword, the phallus."

"Yes!" Lapierre shouted, banging the book with an open hand. "And together they give us balance. Again, we need both, *life* needs both. Duality. Masculine and feminine. Together they hold the deity within, together they bring us to an elevated state. Jamila is correct. Hell, *King Solomon* was correct. We need the feminine, the Goddess, in our lives. Our members know this, but they don't really *know* it. At least not yet." He stood straight. "But they will." He gestured at the laptop screen. "With a little push, they will. And so will others."

Cam nodded. He almost believed him.

It was after ten o'clock when Lapierre walked Cam out to the parking lot of the hotel. The henchmen were gone, barely a memory. Apparently Cam and Lapierre were buddies now. The throbbing inside Cam's head, and his sore neck, reminded him otherwise.

"I'll give you a ride back to your car," the Freemason said.

Cam still had a lot of questions. And who knew when Lapierre might be this chatty again. "Do you really think those three commercials will be enough to convince the country to accept the Goddess, or at least duality?"

"Before I answer, there's another ad I didn't show you because it's not done yet. A mother bear is in a stream, fishing, a pair of cubs nearby watching. A hunter appears on the far river bank; he looks sort of villainous, dirty teeth, leering smile, you know what I mean. He raises his rifle at the mother bear and shoots. He skims her with his first shot, not injuring her enough to stop her from charging, splashing through the stream. He shoots again, but she doesn't stop. She leaps at him, claws out, and takes him down—we don't see the carnage, but we see the water turn red and the hunter's hat float downstream. The bear trots back to her cubs and resumes fishing, ignoring the gunshot injuries. A text scroll appears on the screen: *Dear Islamic State: If you think Americans are weak because we respect our women for being strong, we suggest you stay out of our woods.*

Cam nodded as Lapierre unlocked the door of the Buick. "I like it. Appeals to the NRA types, the hunters."

"Yes. If this is going to work, we need to attract the meat-and-potatoes Americans. Highlighting how radical Islam treats women is a good leverage point. Sort of like, if you don't respect women, you're just like ISIS."

Lapierre started the car and continued. "So, to answer your question, I do think these ads can change the way people think. People are funny. Did anyone really think we'd elect a TV reality show host? Sometimes the message just resonates. As it's been explained to me, you can't convince people to do something they are opposed to. But you can convince them to do something that never occurred to them before, as long as it makes sense to them. You know, that *oh yeah* moment."

Cam thought of the bottled water industry. Nobody dreamt they needed something better than tap water until a sleek advertising campaign made the bottled product seem chic. "And you think you have that? The *oh yeah*?"

Lapierre pulled out of the parking lot. "No, not yet. We need three more things. First, what you saw was just a rough cut. We have the best production teams in the business all in competition to really make the ads pop. Music, graphics, sizzle. We're spending more to produce these ads than anyone ever has before."

Cam nodded. "And the other two things?"

Lapierre turned. "A fifth ad."

"Featuring what?"

He lowered his voice. "Featuring you and Amanda."

"Wait, what?"

"Finding the treasure. The journals. Your research about the Goddess. It's one thing for us to tell people they should turn to the Goddess. It's another entirely to show that it's been done before. Especially since it was done by the Knights Templar."

Cam swallowed. No surprise Nicolette told him about the treasure. And he had a point. The Templars had an aura, a mystique.

Lapierre continued. "We need the macho factor, and the Templars give it to us. Brawling, drunken soldiers who never surrendered and also never bathed. That's what's going to clinch it for us, allow us to reach the meat-and-potatoes guys in the red states." He smiled. "Real men don't shower. But they do venerate the Goddess."

Cam wasn't ready to be chummy with his captor just yet. Who knew what his, and the Freemasons', true motivations were? Cam said, "One more thing you said you need. What is it?"

"Yes." Lapierre hit the gas pedal, the Buick jumping as if to emphasize his point. "This is the most important. As I mentioned, every campaign, every movement, every awakening ... needs a figurehead. Without Astarte, we're just pissing our time and money away." He turned sideways and held Cam's eyes. "We need the girl. We need the Fortieth Princess."

Cam set his jaw. "Well, I don't have her. Your partner Jamila does. She kidnapped her."

Lapierre exhaled. "Yes. I am aware of that. I'm afraid Jamila went a bit off-script. She can be ... mercurial ... in her behavior." He lowered his voice. "Honestly, we don't know what her intentions are."

Chapter 11

Amanda had spent Sunday afternoon compiling a list of the most prominent attorneys in central Vermont. Most of them were congregated in Rutland, Vermont's second largest city, in the downtown area near the county and federal courthouses. Early Monday morning, as a few flurries fell and swirled, she dressed as professionally as she could given the limited clothes in her overnight bag and drove her rental car the half-hour to Rutland. The front door to the first office building she had targeted was still locked at eight o'clock, so she turned the heat on in her rental car and waited in front of the stately brick Colonial.

The phone rang at ten past. Cam. "Hello."

"I'm an hour away. We need to talk."

She exhaled. "No, Cam. I'm handling this. Last thing we need is you arrested."

"I get that. Really." She heard desperation in his voice, but also excitement. "I just need ten minutes. I promise."

"Very well. I'm in Rutland. Text me when you arrive."

Twenty minutes later a medium-height, middle-aged man with a receding hairline parked a Subaru Outback in the reserved spot closest to the front door and exited his car. Amanda recognized him from the firm website. Robert Lachance, apparently regarded as the best litigator in the area. She followed him to the door. "Mr. Lachance?"

He nodded, his eyes kind and unblinking. "That's me. What can I do for you?"

"I need a lawyer. It's sort of an emergency."

He unlocked the door. "Is it the kind of emergency that needs to be dealt with before a morning cup of coffee?" he asked, smiling.

"It's the kind that should have been dealt with over the weekend." She sighed. "But, I suppose it's more of an urgency than an emergency. I'd fancy a cup myself. Black. Thanks."

He showed her into a conference room, left to brew the coffee, and returned ten minutes later with a legal pad, pen and two mugs. He had a nice way about him, unthreatening, the sort of man you'd like your daughter to grow up and marry. She could see why juries would like him.

She explained the situation, not sure how much detail she should go into regarding the whole Fortieth Princess thing. He scribbled notes, only occasionally interrupting her for clarification.

"It seems pretty cut and dry," he said. "Even with the consent form, you're still her legal guardian. If you want to pull her from the school, you have every right."

"There is one small complication." She explained Cam's commando raid. "I'm guessing that won't go over well."

He nodded. "No. It won't. And it'd be best to keep your husband away. But it doesn't change the underlying merits of the case. I can file a request for relief this morning, get it served on the school this afternoon and probably have a hearing tomorrow." He arched his head. "You're not alleging any abuse, are you?"

She shook her head. "No. I don't think so."

"Okay, if so I might have been able to get a judge to hear this today. But if you're okay taking the extra day, I think that is the prudent course." He lifted his mug to her. "As much as this must be killing you, judges don't like it when emergencies are not really emergencies."

Relieved at finally taking steps to resolve the situation, Amanda returned to the office lobby and checked her phone. Cam had just arrived in town. She texted him to meet her at the public library in ten minutes. The flurries had stopped, and the sun broken through the cloud cover. The forecast was for the breeze to shift to a southerly one, ushering in warmer spring temperatures. But she knew better than to count on that. New England weather was notoriously unpredictable. As, she had discovered, were its people.

She walked the three blocks to the library, another red-brick Colonial building in a picturesque downtown dominated by them. Cam had parked his SUV out front. With a deep breath she turned and marched toward the entrance. Cam must have been watching for her, as he emerged and jogged toward her, meeting her along the stone walkway.

She froze. Of all the things she expected, a silly grin was not one of them. "What?" she asked.

He pulled an envelope from his jacket pocket and handed it to her. "This is a lab report. They drugged me."

"Who drugged you?"

"At the ski school. The tea they gave me. Some kind of herbal stimulant, sort of like Ecstasy. It makes you reckless, aggressive. Makes you feel invincible." He smiled. "Makes you feel like Rambo. They wanted me to do something stupid, probably so we would look bad when we went to court. Or maybe even to prove to Astarte we didn't really want what was best for her." He shrugged. "But, whatever. They did it."

With a shaky hand she grasped at the envelope. She pulled a paper from it, but the words barely registered. Could this really be the lifeline she never thought would come, the path back to her marriage? She forced herself to read the report, even as her eyes pooled. Finally she looked up. "Can we sit down please?"

He took her gently by the elbow and escorted her to a bench lit by the morning sun. "I know this doesn't explain everything. But at least it explains some things."

She let out a long sigh. *No, not everything.* There was still his decision not to tell her about the sex sting. But that had been selfless, not selfish. He was trying to protect her, to protect their family. It was, in her mind, the wrong decision made for the right reasons. And now, it turned out, the whole commando raid thing had not been his decision at all. She took his hand, tentatively.

"You know," she said, looking into his sad brown eyes, "It's one thing to get mad at you. It's another thing entirely to *stay* mad."

They found a diner and ordered two stacks of pancakes, both of them barely having eaten in the past day.

"You need to be more careful with your blood sugar," Amanda chided.

Cam finished chewing. He had chosen a booth in the back so they could talk freely. "Between digging for treasure and getting abducted and fighting to get my family back, I've been a little busy."

She took his hand. "Fair point. But you're no good to any of us hooked up to an IV in some hospital."

He nodded and changed the subject. "I haven't even told you about last night." He did so for fifteen minutes, beginning with Nicolette suggesting he get a blood test and ending with Cam watching TV ads in Lapierre's hotel room. "Apparently the Freemasons are all in on this Goddess stuff."

"Are TV ads really going to be enough to bring about a culture change?"

Cam shrugged. "I was skeptical too. But the ads are pretty compelling. And the country really is in a state of flux. The challenge is going to be to present the Goddess in such a way as she is not a betrayal of people's current religion. Millions of people already worship the Virgin Mary. The message needs to be not that we should reject God, but that we need to listen to the Goddess also."

"Even so..." She chewed her lip. "There's something not ... right about this story."

"In what way?"

Amanda stared out the window. "You said Lapierre wanted us to make the fifth ad. And he specifically said he wanted us to talk about the treasure?"

As the waitress cleared their plates, Cam replayed the conversation in his head. "Right. He said he wanted us to talk about finding the journals and finding the treasure."

Amanda sat back. "Well, how would he know about the treasure? You had just pulled it out of the ground a few hours earlier. Nobody should have known about it."

Cam reached across and took her hand again. Astarte was still being held, but at least he was half-complete. "I'm guessing Nicolette told him. She was at the dig, the woman you saw peeking through the window. She's his daughter."

Amanda raised her eyebrows, surprised at this revelation. She tilted her head. "Perhaps. But wouldn't Lapierre need to get this all approved? He's on some council, but he's not the Grand Poobah or whatever they call it. These ads sound like they've been strategized for months. Now, all of a sudden, he adds a fifth ad by himself?" She shook her head. "No. It doesn't feel right. Just like the treasure itself didn't feel right." She repeated her point that it made no sense to bring gold across the Atlantic to a place where it had little value.

He knew better than to ignore Amanda's intuition. But for now it was just another mystery in what had become a series of extraordinarily strange events.

His cell phone rang. The name 'Nicolette Lapierre' popped up. He raised an eyebrow and showed it to Amanda as he answered. "This should be interesting." He pressed the speaker button.

Nicolette didn't waste time on the preliminaries. "My dad says you were impressed with the advertisements."

Cam resented her tone of familiarity, as if they were all on the same team now. "Impressed is the wrong word. Surprised is probably better."

"He's on a flight to Salt Lake City now. Showing the ads to the Mormons."

"Why would they go along with all this? They're not exactly raging feminists."

"No. But think what will happen to their membership if a Mormon girl becomes the figurehead for a new cultural movement. And they had their slowest rate of growth last year since 1937. They need members. It's their membership that gives them power and influence."

Cam nodded. Most Mormon leaders would probably happily swallow some of their chauvinism in exchange for vastly increasing their power and influence. "Speaking of which, where's Astarte?"

"Still at the school. That's why I called. I thought we could talk, try to resolve this. Before it gets to the court."

Cam and Amanda exchanged a glance, neither surprised that Jamila and her team already knew about Amanda's meeting with the lawyer. "There's nothing to talk about. We're her parents. And we want her to come home."

"Yes, that's true. But you're omitting one key fact: Astarte wants to stay at the school. You can drag her home, I suppose. But my sense is that's not the kind of parents you really want to be."

Amanda made a face and leaned in, as if to jump in with a sharp retort. Cam put up his hand to stop her. It wouldn't hurt to listen. He said, "She only wants to stay because you tricked her with that photograph."

"Yes, well, sorry for that. Not our finest moment. But don't kid yourself. She follows Jamila around like a puppy, waiting for morsels of knowledge to fall to the floor." She paused. "I know. I've been there. Being an apprentice to Jamila can be addictive."

"Apprentice?" Amanda burst out.

Nicolette kept her voice even. "Student, apprentice, acolyte, whatever. The point is, there are things Astarte needs to learn that only Jamila can teach. We know that, and Astarte knows that. Even the Freemasons know that, which is why they're working with her. Hell, even the Mormons understand it. Astarte is supposed to be a princess, the prophetess of the Goddess." She paused. "Even you must be able to see that she needs someone to teach her how."

Rene Lapierre stepped out of the Salt Lake City airport terminal and straight into a wall of spring rain. Staying dry under the concourse, and wheeling his overnight bag with one hand, he hailed a taxi. "Downtown, please. The Mormon Temple."

"The Temple itself?"

"No." Lapierre knew that only Latter-day Saint members were allowed in the holy Temple. "The Conference Center."

A half hour later the massive, three-spired Temple rose up through the fog in the distance, facing east toward the ancient Temple of Solomon, the angel Moroni and his trumpet atop the middle spire. Did the Mormon elders know Solomon was himself a Goddess worshiper, Lapierre wondered? If so, it was not one of the Biblical facts trumpeted by Moroni, or any other Mormon spokesperson for that matter.

The cab navigated around the Temple and dropped Lapierre behind it, in front of a sprawling, mostly-windowless, white-granite structure. The building, like others in the Temple Square area, was both massive and immaculate, designed to awe and inspire. As the upstart religion, the Mormons knew they had to try harder. A man more superstitious than Lapierre would have wondered at the rain fortuitously stopping as he stepped from his taxi.

He was escorted immediately into a plush conference room with views of the side of the massive Temple structure. A half-dozen older men in suits and ties, elders of the Mormon church, were already seated. Hardly a Rainbow Coalition, and an unlikely breeding ground for Goddess worship. Still, they had agreed to see him. "Sorry I'm late," he said as he strolled in. "My plane was delayed."

Apostle Bertram, whom he had worked most closely with, stood, greeted him and did the introductions. A bald man with wire-rim glasses seated at the head of the table cleared his throat. "We all have busy schedules," he said, glancing at his watch in apparent annoyance at Lapierre's tardiness, "so let's begin." He didn't waste time on any preliminaries. "We've seen your advertisements. They are impressive. But still, we wonder, can we really expect to sway the American public with slick television ads?"

Lapierre shifted in his chair. He thought the Mormons were already on board, but apparently not completely. "I think the one thing we've learned is that it is impossible to predict what will sway the American public. A year before the 2016 presidential election, it was universally assumed that Jeb Bush would sail through the Republican primaries and Hillary Clinton would run unopposed among the Democrats. And we all know what happened—had the DNC played it straight, it would have been Bernie Sanders versus Donald Trump. This, despite gazillions of dollars in advertising." He shrugged. "So, no, we can't predict anything." He leaned forward, making eye contact with the other men in the room. "But that's what makes this so possible. Sometimes, an idea catches fire and it consumes the nation. Jimmy Carter's presidential run, for example. Nobody knows why or how. But one thing is certain: The raging fire needs some kind of spark. These ads are that spark. Will the fire spread?" He angled his head. "Nobody can say for certain. But the Freemasons are betting hundreds of millions, perhaps even billions, that it will."

He left the point hanging. He had, on purpose, never asked the Mormons for any money. He did not want to give them ownership, and therefore decision-making power, in this venture. And they had been happy to go along for the free ride. Until getting cold feet now.

The bald man pushed back. "You are trying to change thousands of years of religious history. For hundreds of generations God has been a man." He snapped his fingers. "And you expect to change things just like that."

"No. Not just like that. As I said, we are just the spark being touched to an already dry stack of tinder." He held his palms up to the sky. "Listen. The fact you guys, who obviously belong to a very male-oriented church, are willing to even consider supporting this is a testament that the idea in some way resonates with all of us. Fifty years ago you would have laughed me out of the room. But times are changing. People are concerned about the environment. People are more accepting of alternative lifestyles. People are worried about the worldwide rise in violence. Yet despite all that, people are turning away from religion. There is a growing need for some kind of spirituality, yet nothing to fill that void." He shrugged. "We think this might be it." He paused. "*Astarte* might be it."

Apostle Bertram leaned in. "But she is so young. She has so much still to learn."

"Yes. Frankly, we would have preferred to wait a couple of years. But Jamila Bashear is not a patient woman. She has brought things to an early boil. And Cameron Thorne has begun lecturing about things we would have preferred not be publicized yet." He shrugged. "Sometimes the winds of change come early. In any event, we believe that with guidance," he paused nodding to those in the room with him, "young Astarte can learn as the movement takes seed and grows. We, all, can help her."

The bald man continued to push back, perhaps testing Lapierre. "But why her. Why are we convinced people will follow *her*?"

Lapierre smiled. "Well, first of all, it's *your* prophecy we are relying on here. But to answer your question, I think people will respond to her because she truly does have the blood of almost all the great religions—and their leaders—running through her veins. All of us, everyone, has a horse in this race." He smiled. "And fortunately for us, it is the same horse."

Astarte and Maestra Jamila waited as the ski lift attendant guided the chair behind their knees. Ski-less, they sat, the device lurching them upward. Snow covered some of the flatter terrain on either side of the lift, though in most areas spring had begun to assert itself by pushing plants through the snowpack like stubble on an old man's face. The sound of birds singing competed with the whirring of the chairlift, and the sun had snuck between a couple of wispy clouds to warm their ride.

Jamila closed the safety bar. "It'd be a shame to ruin everything by having you fall out," she said, smiling.

Something about the way she said it alarmed Astarte. She pictured herself tumbling, falling, landing with a thud on the exposed, jagged rock ledge below. She scooched back in the chair.

After a few minutes of silence, Jamila poured some hot chocolate from a thermos, a cup for each of them. She leaned in conspiratorially. "My one weakness. Chocolate."

Astarte smiled, beginning to relax again. "Me too."

They ascended for a few seconds, sipping the warm cocoa. "The Freemasons," Jamila declared.

Astarte turned, the headmistress' discolored cheek only inches from hers. She was beginning to learn that sometimes Jamila just said things to see how Astarte would react. She swallowed. "I know who they are. Cameron is friends with some of them. Cameron says they used to be the Templars. Is he right?"

"Astarte, we don't use the word 'right' here to mean correct. It is a direction, or a side, not a value judgment."

She nodded. "I'm sorry, is he *correct*? Did the Freemasons used to be the Templars?"

"He is," Jamila said, "though only the highest ranking Masons are aware of the connection." She sniffed. "Though the clues are everywhere. Roslyn Chapel is full of Masonic imagery, and it was built in the mid 1400s. How could that be if modern Freemasonry—which traces its roots back to Biblical times—was not invented until more than a century later, as the historians tell us? The truth is that the Sinclair family, who built the chapel, were part of the group that took the outlawed Knights Templar and reconstituted them as the Freemasons. That's why the Sinclairs were usually the Grand Masters."

"The Sinclairs are the ones who carved the Westford Knight."

"Yes." Jamila smiled. "Without that carving, you and I would not be sitting on this chairlift right now. That is what ties us all together. You, me, Cameron, Amanda, the Freemasons." She shifted. "But back to the Freemasons. You may not know it, but they are going to be key allies of ours. Of yours. They, too, venerate the Goddess."

Astarte knew the Sinclairs were Goddess worshipers, because they kept saying so in the journal. So it was not all that surprising that the Freemasons, formed by the Sinclairs, would be also. "Are there lots of Freemasons?"

Jamila nodded and drained her cup. "About two million in this country. And there are about six million Mormons. These two groups will be your base, your biggest supporters." She paused. "Hopefully."

Astarte blinked. It wasn't like Jamila to leave anything to chance. "Why hopefully?"

Jamila exhaled. "People are fickle, Astarte. I have made alliances with the Mormon and Masonic leadership. But what if the members don't follow along? The Mormons tend to follow the directives of the church elders, but the idea of Goddess worship is going to be alien to them and will take some time. And the Freemasons, well, they're a men's group that does not allow women to join. So Goddess worship is going to be alien to them as well."

"So why did the leaders agree?"

Jamila brightened. "For the Mormons, the reason is obvious: You yourself are a Mormon. For the Freemasons, most of them don't realize it but they are already right-brain thinkers. Almost everything Freemasonry does is done with the right brain. They have complex rituals using props and imagery, in which they wear elaborate costumes and jewelry. Rather than just read their lessons, they memorize and recite them. And they teach using metaphor and allegory and symbolism." She chuckled. "In fact, I borrowed some of their ideas for this school." The lift reached the summit, as if to emphasize her concluding point. "Like I said, the Freemasons have already been trained in right-brain thinking. They're practically Goddess worshipers already."

Cam got back into his SUV to drive back to their hotel near Okemo Mountain. He had agreed to lay low, but refused to leave Vermont again. "What am I going to do back in Westford?" he had asked.

"Keep from screwing things up here in Vermont?" Amanda had replied, kissing him lightly as she said so.

He drove the speed limit this time, not wanting to risk any kind of encounter with law enforcement. Things were looking up a bit. He had reconciled with Amanda. And Nicolette, though not an ally, was at least someone who could be counted on to act reasonably on Astarte's behalf. Which was more than could be said about Jamila. She was just irrational enough that she might do Astarte harm if for no other reason than as revenge against Cam and Amanda.

Cam's newfound sense of optimism lasted about ten minutes. His cell phone rang as he pulled into the parking lot of their Okemo hotel. Sergeant Poulos' private number. On what Cam recalled had always been the officer's day off. Probably not good news. "This is Cam."

"So it's a good thing I don't trust you."

"How so?"

"That woman the other night outside the garage? The one you said was part of the dig? I watched her leave the town common after meeting with you. I decided to follow her. Pulled her over for running a stop sign."

He paused, as if expecting Cam to know what came next. "And?" Cam had no idea.

"You really don't know who she is?"

"Her name is Nicolette." Cam didn't want to get into the sex sting stuff with Poulos, so he left that out.

"And her last name is Lapierre."

Cam clenched the steering wheel. He didn't like that Poulos was sniffing around this. At some point he might stumble on the journals, which Cam had, to be blunt, lied to him about. Cam tried to redirect the conversation. "Yes. Her father is Rene Lapierre, a leading Freemason. I met him at a Lodge in Nashua last week." Cam could hear Poulos scribbling notes. "I don't think it was a coincidence."

The policeman exhaled. "Neither is this. Rene Lapierre used to be married to Katherine Morville. The dead woman who drove all night to see you was Nicolette's mother."

Nicolette walked into the ski lodge and grabbed some soup and a salad, greeting the students as she ambled to a table in a corner overlooking the mountain. Many of the students had hit the slopes at first light and were now coming in for an early Monday lunch.

She sat alone, using the time to think. She had driven back to Vermont late Sunday night, after her encounter with Cam Thorne, her mind on the Westford treasure. Mom had been correct, it turned out, to be obsessed with her family history. The legends really had been true. Maybe that's why Mom had been in Westford when she died. She should have quizzed Thorne on it; maybe he had met her.

But for now the Templar treasure and even the Sinclair family history were secondary. What was paramount was that somehow the unlikely alliance between Jamila, the Freemasons and the Mormons was holding together, and that Astarte was receiving the training she needed. Even if that training was rushed. The girl wasn't ready yet. It reminded Nicolette what she had read about Princess Diana: When she had first taken the throne, she was young and naïve and unprepared for the spotlight and pressures of being constantly in the public eye. She had grown into the job, becoming a beloved and effective advocate for the misfits and outcasts of British society. But it had taken nearly a decade. Astarte would not have that luxury. Once the ads ran, the movement would either take hold or it would not. And if it did, it would need a leader to coalesce around, likely within the next few years. How old, Nicolette wondered, had Joan of Arc been? She Googled it quickly: Thirteen when her visions began, seventeen when she first led troops into battle.

Nicolette flipped her phone onto the table. Four years. By then Astarte would be sixteen. Not an adult, but no longer still a child. And a very poised one at that. Perhaps Jamila knew what she was doing after all.

After getting off the chairlift, Jamila led Astarte along a snow-covered path to a log cabin-style structure at the peak of the mountain. Attached to one side of the structure was a thirty-foot fire tower with a staircase winding its way up the center. Jamila, bypassing the log cabin, escorted Astarte to the foot of the tower.

"I keep an apartment in the cabin," she said, explaining it was formerly used as an uphill snack bar. "But I wanted to show you the view from atop the fire tower."

Jamila set a surprisingly brisk pace, the amber dress flopping in the midday breeze as Astarte counted the steps. The headmistress paused once at a landing at step 25. From the landing, Astarte could see a short walkway leading to a doorway accessing the top floor of the cabin. "Have you ever heard the story of the resurrection of Ishtar?"

"No."

Nodding, Jamila resumed the climb. At step 54, they reached the top. Jamila pushed open a hatch and they climbed through. Astarte felt dizzy, perhaps from the spiraling of the stairs. Or maybe from the altitude. Silently, they gazed north over the Green Mountains, the hilltops still white-capped even as their flanks sprouted green. A strip of sweat glistening above her upper lip from the climb, Jamila pointed to her right, toward the east. "The tallest one is Mount Washington. In the 1930s they measured wind at 231 miles per hour, the strongest surface wind ever recorded by man." A warm gust buffeted them, causing the tower to creak as if to emphasize the point. "And wind-chills can fall to minus 100 Fahrenheit. Mother Nature is not to be trifled with."

Astarte was not sure if the comment required a response. "No."

"Which brings us back to the story of Ishtar." Jamila reached up and pushed a red button mounted on a beam above their heads; an engine whirred, and below Astarte could see the bottom eight or ten stairs to the fire tower fold up into themselves like a turtle pulling its head into its shell. "Sometimes the bears like to climb up here," the old woman said by way of explanation.

Returning to Ishtar, Jamila continued. "As you may know, Ishtar is her Babylonian name. The Sumerians called her Inanna; the Egyptians, Isis; the Armenians, Astghik; the Greeks, Gaia; the Romans, Venus." She paused. "And, of course, the Canaanites called her *Astarte*. But she is one and the same. The Great Goddess. In any event, many religious historians believe the story of Jesus' resurrection is, in fact, based on the Ishtar resurrection account. The story is that Ishtar descends to the underworld to visit her evil sister. She is arrested by soldiers and put on trial."

Astarte nodded. "Just as Jesus was." She knew the story well from her many hours at the Mormon temple.

"The authorities strip her and hang her on a stake to die in public."

Astarte nodded again, the parallels to Jesus' crucifixion obvious. Though her dizziness was making it harder than usual to remember the details.

"In Ishtar's absence, the earth becomes sterile and fallow; animals do not breed and crops do not grow. After three days, the other gods rally to her defense and descend to the underworld, where they resurrect her."

Three days. Just like Jesus.

"Once Ishtar is resurrected, the earth then comes back to life." The old woman turned and faced Astarte, leaning closer, Astarte's eyes drawn for some reason to the pus-filled scar. "So, what do you think the story means?"

Astarte held on to the rail to steady herself. She had an idea, but she wasn't sure. She decided to trust her intuition. "It's like all this," she said, gesturing toward the mountains. "Every year things die, then they are resurrected the following spring. It's the circle of life."

Jamila clapped her hands together silently. "Yes. That is clearly part of it. But let's go back to the early part of the story, when Ishtar … Astarte … first dies. It seems clear to me that the message is that Ishtar must first die in order for the world to survive."

Astarte swallowed. *Again, just like Jesus.* This was getting weird.

Jamila locked her yellowish-brown eyes on Astarte, one hand on Astarte's elbow. Astarte tried to edge away, but the old woman's bony fingers held fast. "This is a story about *faith*, about *sacrifice*. Recall that I warned you the Goddess sometimes asks much of us, even more than we think we can give. Ishtar must trust that in her death the world will be resurrected. She must not be afraid. She must not resist. Her death will allow the world to be reborn." The old woman's eyes shone as the wind whipped her long gray hair. She dug deeper into Astarte's arm, her voice rising to a fevered pitch. "As you said, the wheel of life. Around it goes. But something must first set the wheel in motion." She now lowered her voice. "There must be death before there can be rebirth, mustn't there be?"

Astarte blinked, her knees feeling wobbly. For some reason her mind returned to the stairs and she wondered if the bear story was true. The sky darkened as the sun slid behind a thick cloud. The old woman was beginning to frighten her.

Nicolette sopped up the last of her chicken barley soup with a wedge of wheat bread and checked her watch. 12:30. The students and staff had been told to gather in the lodge for a 1:00 meeting. What they had not been told, and what Nicolette had just learned via a text from Jamila, was that the meeting had now been moved to the top of the mountain. She sighed. Not that everyone taking the chairlift to the peak was a big deal. But why the change? Sometimes it seemed like Jamila pulled stunts like this, well, just because she could.

Nicolette stood on her chair and made the announcement. "I don't know how long it will take. Feel free to wear your skis or boards. Or you can take the lift back down."

Even before she stepped off her chair, her phone buzzed. A text from Cam Thorne. "We need to talk. Urgent."

"I'm sort of busy."

"Trust me, this is important."

She sighed. "OK. Meet me at front gate in 15?"

The reply came immediately. "Confirmed."

Leaving the herding of the girls onto the high-speed chairlift to Erin, Nicolette jumped into an SUV and drove down the resort access road. Cam and Amanda pulled up in a maroon Highlander a minute later. "I only have a few minutes," she said, leaning against the front hood of her vehicle as she spoke through the steel security gate.

Cam and Amanda had approached the gate, as if every inch closer they could get to their daughter relieved some of their anxiety. Nicolette pushed thoughts of her own mother away. Cam spoke, his words pulling her mother right back in. "Did you know why your mother was in Westford the night she died?"

Nicolette shook her head, surprised that Cam even knew about the death. "No. I assumed it had something to do with the Westford Knight."

Cam nodded. "It did. In fact, she called me that night, just min-utes before she died. Of course, I didn't know she was your mother. She claimed to have the Sinclair family journals." He stood taller. "But it was no accident. Someone had been following her. And that someone ran her off the road."

"Wait, what? The police said it might have been road rage. But you're saying it was more than that?"

Amanda replied. "A lot more. The detective in Westford has been going through your Mum's old emails and phone records. Apparently some distant aunt gave her the journals last May, almost a year ago. Then, a couple of months later, Jamila Bashear reached out to her to discuss your job application."

Nicolette nodded. "Yes, that would have been last July. Jamila wanted to talk to my relatives, bosses, boyfriends, ex-roommates, pretty much everyone who knew me. It was like getting a job with the CIA."

Cam jumped back in. "Well, here's where it gets interesting. The IP address for Jamila matches the one used by the distant aunt."

Nicolette felt a fluttering in her stomach. "So Jamila is the one who gave my mother the journals? That doesn't make any sense."

"It will," Cam said. "Apparently Jamila and your mother became friendly after Jamila first contacted her in July. At one point your mother asked Jamila for advice on what to do with the journals. She wanted to share them with you, to use them to reconnect."

Nicolette merely stared, waiting, numb. *Reconnect.* It might have been nice.

Amanda continued. "Jamila recommended getting the journals authenticated first, before reaching out to you. She suggested it would actually harm your relationship if it turned out the journals were fake." Amanda leaned closer. "She recommended your Mum bring them to Westford and show them to Cam. He would know how to authenticate them."

"So that's what she was doing last week," Cam concluded. "Bringing the journals to me." He looked down. "But she never made it."

Nicolette exhaled. The revelation was bittersweet. It was nice to know her mom had been trying so hard to reconnect. But why had it taken so long? Why now, when Nicolette had essentially moved on with her life?

As if reading her mind, Cam added, "From what the detective read in the emails, your mom saw this as a family legacy you two could share. Something about her, and her family, that you could be proud of. She knew you were interested in this ancient history. She was actually pretty excited to tell you that you were *part* of it."

Nicolette started to smile, and then a sudden realization washed over her like a rogue wave. *Was this just a coincidence?* Jamila had known exactly where her mother would be. And exactly what she would be doing. That was why Cam and Amanda were here, why they said it was urgent...

Her phone shrieked, jarring her from her horrific realization. *Erin.* On the fourth ring, Nicolette answered. "You need to get up here, right away. Jamila is up in the fire tower. With Astarte. She's pulled up the stairs. And she's talking crazy shit."

Nicolette closed her eyes and squeezed the bridge of her nose. She exhaled. In front of her sat the mystery of her dead mother. But behind her stood the safety of a young girl. Her mother would have to wait. "I'll be right there."

She began to jog away. "Sorry, we have an issue."

A voice in Nicolette's head ordered her to stop. *Do you really still trust Jamila?* It struck her suddenly that the mystery of her mother's death might be tied to the fate of the young girl. She turned to Cam and Amanda. "Move back, I'm going to open the gate. You guys need to come with me."

Amanda wasn't sure what kind of game Nicolette was playing. And she wasn't going to fight against being let into the compound. But she sensed something was wrong. "What is it?"

"Get in," Nicolette said, hopping into her SUV. She explained that Jamila had called for a school-wide assembly atop the mountain. "She's up in a fire tower with Astarte." She didn't say more, but the squealing of tires as she sped through a turn spoke volumes. Amanda took Cam's hand.

Three minutes later Nicolette skidded to a stop near the chairlift loading area. A dozen or so students waited to board. "Sorry girls, I need to cut the line." She pushed through, Amanda and Cam in her wake. To the lift attendant, she said, "Maximum speed." And to Cam, "The snowmobiles are out of commission, as you may recall."

They scrambled into the chair, Amanda wedging herself in the middle as the thought of Cam's hand on Nicolette's naked ass popped into her head. The lift jolted them upward. Cam broke the silence. "What are you not telling us?"

Nicolette rubbed her face. "All I know is that they said Jamila is acting weird. And the stuff about Jamila giving the journals to my mother…"

She let the comment hang.

Cam nodded. "So it's possible the journals were bait, used to get your mother out to Westford."

"Or they could even be fake," Amanda added.

Nicolette leaned forward in the chairlift as they approached the mountaintop and pointed. A pair of figures stood against a railing near the top of a wooden fire tower rising above the tree line. Nicolette swallowed. "Yes. With Jamila, anything is possible. That's what I'm afraid of."

A stiff breeze caused the chairlift to sway as Cam, Amanda and Nicolette hopped off at the summit. The same wind, racing eastward from western Canada, buffeted the fire tower. Cam heard the tower creak. He thought he also saw it sway. But that could have been his imagination, his reaction to Astarte being atop it with the fanatical Jamila Bashear.

As if waiting for their arrival, Jamila began to speak just as Amanda, Cam and Nicolette joined the crowd of students and staff gathered around the base of the tower. The old woman's eyes settled on Cam and Amanda, narrowed, and then seemed to dance with delight. Cam's gut clenched, nearly doubling him over as Amanda took an involuntary step back. "Cam, I'm frightened," Amanda whispered.

He swallowed. "Me too."

Jamila's words trumpeted down upon them. "Most of you by now know Astarte," she began, her voice strong and vibrant, cutting easily through the wind. "The name Astarte is the Phoenician name for the Babylonian Goddess, Ishtar." She turned and smiled at Astarte, her right arm around the girl's shoulder. "Today, fittingly, I wish to share with you the story of the resurrection of Ishtar."

Cam and Amanda shared a glance. He edged closer to the tower and froze when he saw the bottom flight of stairs had been hoisted upward like a back alley fire escape. But nobody was looking to steal anything from the fire tower. He clenched his teeth and listened. He knew the story of Ishtar. In the end, she was resurrected. But barely, and only after dying a hideous death. He glanced up. Easily a forty-foot fall from the top. He shook the thought away.

Amanda and Nicolette appeared at his side. He whispered to Nicolette. Somehow, she had become an ally. "Is there another way up there?"

She nodded. "Through the cabin, then across that bridge. But she will have locked the door. It's massive, thick oak, with a new deadbolt." Jamila would have left nothing to chance.

"What about up the side, climbing the frame?"

"Sure." She shrugged. "But how fast could you go? She'd see you coming."

Cam looked up again, focusing. "The tower's not swaying," he said, replaying the earlier scene in his mind. "*Astarte* is." He leaned in to Amanda. "Look at Astarte. I think she's been drugged."

His mind raced. *What was Jamila planning?*

Perhaps it was because she better knew how Jamila's mind worked, or perhaps because Astarte's parents could not bring themselves to consider the unimaginable, or perhaps because she had murder on her mind. Whatever the reason, Nicolette was the first to intuit the head-mistress' intent. *Jamila's plan is that Astarte must die.* Just like her namesake, Ishtar. Death, then resurrection. What better way to prove the power of the Goddess? What better way to usher in a new era?

Jamila's next words drove home the point. "Sometimes, res-urrection is spiritual, not physical. Did Jesus really return to life, or is his story just an allegory, a reference to a *spiritual* revival?" Her words echoed across the valley, seemingly carried by the wind. "Sometimes, in death, we can have rebirth many times as powerful as the single life that is lost."

Nicolette avoided meeting Amanda's and Cam's eyes. They, too, now understood what Jamila was contemplating. Somehow, in the warped mind of the self-proclaimed Messenger of the Goddess, the death of Astarte, of the royal bloodline, would usher in a new age just as the death of Jesus, of the royal bloodline, had done two millennia ago.

"I don't understand," Amanda lamented. "I thought she needed Astarte to usher in the new age?"

Nicolette clenched her fists. Jamila had fooled them. Fooled them all. "To usher in the new age, yes. But not to lead it. I fear Jamila sees herself in that role." She cursed. "I should have seen it coming. No way would she step aside and let someone else be the Messenger of the Goddess."

Cam refocused them back on the present. "So she must have a plan. She can't stay up there forever. And she can't see herself as the Messenger of the Goddess if she's sitting in a jail cell."

Nicolette nodded. "Good point." Her eyes scanned the cabin, built into the slope of the crest of the mountain. "The back entrance," she breathed. "The back of the mountain falls away steeply, almost like a cliff. But there's a narrow trail that runs down to the highway. The only way to get to it is out the basement door of the cabin. That must be Jamila's escape route."

Cam reacted immediately. "What's the easiest way to get there?"

"There is no easy way. Like I said, it's a cliff-face."

"All right then. What's a *hard* way to get there?"

Cam's heartbeat pounded in his ears like a bass drum in a mini-van. But worse than that was the image of Astarte, swaying near the railing of the fire tower, etched in his mind's eye. He took a deep breath. *You need to focus.*

The mountaintop cabin was built up to the very edge of the cliff-face, three sides accessible from the peak of the ski resort but the back side essentially a continuation of the steep slope of the cliff. Cam edged along the side of the cabin, grasping the branch of an evergreen as he leaned out over nothingness and peered around the corner. As Nicolette said, a door perhaps twenty feet below—apparently accessed through the sub-basement of the cabin—opened onto a welcome-mat-sized landing which immediately fell away to a steep, narrow, S-shaped trail. Still snow-covered, the trail made an Olympic luge run look like the bunny hill. Jamila's escape.

Cam had no interest in following the trail. But there was a chance that by going down he might eventually be able to go up. The back door, remote and inaccessible as it was, would likely not be secured by any kind of sophisticated lock. But how to get there? The twenty foot jump—even assuming he was able to arrest his fall on the steep slope once he landed—would probably break an ankle. And there were no handholds or footholds along the cabin exterior.

He was due for a lucky break, and it appeared in the form of a coil of rope stuffed in his jacket pocket, left over from his previous failed rescue attempt of Astarte. Reaching out as far as he dared, he looped the rope over the branch of the evergreen and tied it off. Lifting his feet, he hung from the rope, testing the branch. It bowed, but held. Estimating the ground to be twenty-four feet below the branch, and figuring he would want the rope to catch him with his outstretched arms seven feet above the ground, he measured out seventeen feet of rope by tripling his body height and subtracting a few inches, then tied a thick knot he could use to help his grip.

He exhaled and grabbed the rope knot. There really was no time to plan it out any more elaborately. Astarte was in danger, and his only chance to save her was to swing down like Tarzan on his vine.

Putting his left hand on top of the rope to take weight from his injured right shoulder, Cam stepped back a few steps, took a running start and leapt over the edge of the cliff, angling himself as close as he could to the cliff face itself. A shower of snow, loosened from the tree branches by the force of his leap, enveloped him, momentarily impeding his vision. But he broke through the cloud, focused on the narrow landing pad at the base of the door, kicked out with his feet to carry himself a bit further, and let go just as the rope reached the far arc of its swing.

The fall was steeper than he anticipated, his swing having carried him past the arc's nadir, and by the time he released he was a good six feet in the air. And he did not have the luxury of bracing for impact by bending his knees. Instead, he reached out with his arms and legs like a kid doing a belly-flop, hoping he would splat onto the snow-covered slope and stick, much the way a bug stuck to a car windshield instead of sliding down its face.

As he flew, he realized it may not have been the ideal metaphor. But it was an apt one, the kick in his gut and snow up his nose the unwelcome products of a stuck landing. Moaning, he rolled to his back and fought to fill his lungs. Jamila's voice jolted him to action. "As you know, there is nothing I won't do in the service of the Goddess, no sacrifice I will not make to her."

Amanda had lost sight of Cameron, probably because she couldn't tear her eyes off of Astarte above. She rubbed her face and groaned. *How had things come to this?*

She looked around. There were close to a hundred people milling nervously around the fire tower, sensing danger, all of them fit and, presumably, willing to help rescue Astarte. Was there nothing they could do?

An idea hit her. She ran to the chairlift unloading area, where the lift attendant was attending to a few late arrivals. "Do you have any blankets?" she asked breathlessly.

The middle-aged woman nodded. "Sure. You cold?"

"No. I mean yes. Please give me some."

The woman crinkled her face at the odd request on the mild day, but shrugged. "They're in the hut."

Amanda followed her in and grabbed at one of the folded, orange rectangles. She opened it. Beach-towel-sized. "Damn," she said, seeing how small it was. "Do you have anything larger?"

"No. These are for people on the chairlift when it's cold. Not for sleeping."

Could she make these work? "Can I have four?"

The woman shrugged again. "Sure."

Hugging the blankets close to her chest, she sprinted back toward the fire tower, slowing only to make sure she stayed out of Jamila's sight. She found Nicolette. "I need you to find eight strong girls."

Nicolette glanced at the blankets. "I know what you're thinking, but those blankets aren't big enough to catch Astarte."

"They are if we overlap them. Two blankets, side-by-side, going in one direction. Then two more, underneath, going in the other. That way nothing," she couldn't bring herself to say *nobody*, "can fall through the cracks."

Nicolette nodded. "Like basket-weaving. I get it." She began to move away. "But we'll need to stay hidden. There are three open sides to that tower. We can't run from side to side, hoping to guess which way Jamila will go."

"Bollocks that," Amanda called, running back to the hut. "We won't need to. I'll get more blankets. Make that twenty-four strong girls, not eight."

Jamila had been surprised to see Cameron and Amanda gathered in the crowd below. Surprised, but far from disappointed. They would see that Astarte had been drugged. See the potential of a forty-foot fall. See Jamila's hand on her back. Jamila, in turn, had seen the cold fear in their eyes. And would see more. Sweet revenge.

A text came in, interrupting her sermonizing. Keeping one hand clenched on the back of the unsteady girl's jacket, she glanced down and paused. Lapierre. The Mormons had agreed to go ahead with the plan, the Goddess apparently having thawed their cold feet. She nodded. So be it. The Goddess had spoken. Jamila's path was now clear.

She resumed, from high above. "As you know, I have given my life to the Goddess. I mean that in a figurative sense, and also in a literal one. All I have to give, I give to her. Gladly. We all must." She scanned the crowd. Some of these girls would remember her words, be moved by them years or even decades from now. Others would forget them. But none would forget the day itself.

"We are now in a time of great need. The Goddess herself needs us, needs our sacrifices. Great change requires great sacrifice." She shoved the wobbly-legged Astarte forward, against the low rail, Jamila's right hand clawing the back of her ski jacket." She raised her voice. "Now, here, today, we have our very own Ishtar. Here, today, we will witness death and resurrection." She lifted her chin and spread her arms. "Here, today, the Goddess will be reborn."

Jamila's fanatical rantings from on high assaulted Amanda's ears like a shrieking bat in the night. She turned to Nicolette. "Now. We are running out of time. Get everyone in position."

Nicolette nodded. With the precision of a dance troop the three teams of blanket holders moved out from beneath the fire tower. Amanda exhaled. There was no guarantee the safety measure would work. A blanket might rip, Astarte might miss them entirely, a girl might let go, Astarte might hit her head on the tower itself during her fall, or she might land on her head and break her neck. A hundred things could go wrong. But at least they had a chance now. She turned to Nicolette. "Why? Why are you suddenly helping us?"

"Look, I didn't sign up for murder." The acolyte stared up at her mentor, her jaw set. "But don't kid yourself. I'm not doing this for you. I'm doing this for Astarte and for the Goddess."

Astarte had a vague memory of climbing stairs and now felt the sensation of being high in the air, wind buffeting her face and birds chirping nearby on the upper branches of trees. When she had her tonsils removed over the winter, the doctor told her to count back from 100. At 95 she remembered the room beginning to spin, and at 92 the doctor's face seemed to morph into three separate versions of itself while his voice came to her as if from underwater. That's what this felt like—92, with Jamila's face and words dancing and swirling around her as if Astarte were inside some kind of giant kaleidoscope. Instinctively, she feared what might come after 92.

She tried to focus on Jamila, to concentrate on the middle version of the headmistress' three faces. But when Astarte did so, the scar on the old woman's cheek grew, spreading like snakeskin across her face. And Jamila's tongue flicked like a candle flame when she spoke, the final syllables of words like 'Goddess' and 'witness' hissing from her lips. Astarte tried to blink the illusions away, but every time she closed her eyes the tower seemed to sway, and she to sway with it...

Stumbling, she careened into the tower railing, banging her knee. Even more than the dull pain, a stab of cold realization shot through her. Her stumble had not been due to losing her balance. She had been shoved in the back.

Cam had shouldered his way through the basement door, found a light switch and was now bounding, two steps at a time, up the steep, dank stairwell. The dust of a dozen seasons filled his lungs and eyes, and cobwebs reached out to slow him. He barely noticed.

He ignored a landing where a closed door led, he figured, to the basement above the subbasement. At the next flight he pushed through an unlocked door into an open area laid out as a living room, decorated with antique skis and poles. Through a window he could see the fire tower abutting the cabin, the muffled sound of Jamila's voice telling him he was not too late.

He raced to another staircase across the room, now taking the steps three at a time. The stairs ended at a landing tucked under the peak of the roof. Cam yanked the door inward. Crossing a short bridge, he sprinted up the spiral steps of the fire tower, only to find a hatch blocking his way at the top. Retreating a few steps, he took a running start and launched himself upward, driving his shoulder into the hatch. It lifted an inch but held in place. "She must have latched it," he hissed. And he just lost any element of surprise he might have had.

Cursing, he leapt back down the stairs, his feet barely touching the treads as he let gravity carry him. Across the bridge and through the door, he quickly found what he was looking for hanging on the stairwell wall: an old metal ski pole. He yanked it free, raced back to the spiral stairs, bound up them and wedged the tip of the pole into the gap between the hatch and its frame. Using the pole as a crow bar, he snapped the old metal latch. The hatch flew open. He poked his head through.

Jamila's voice froze him in place. "What a racket you make, Mr. Thorne. And I fear you are too late." The sun slipped from behind a cloud, illuminating the ugly patch of skin on her face. She practically cackled the words. "It is time to make our sacrifice to the Goddess."

The sun slipping from behind the cloud must have been the sign Jamila was looking for. "It is time to make our sacrifice to the Goddess," she said for a second time, as if gathering her courage. Amanda's chest tightened. She glanced around. The three blanket teams were in place, tight to the tower. Astarte was not a large girl, weighing just seventy pounds, but it would be all Jamila could do to hoist her over the railing. No way would the old lady be able to toss her outward.

That, Amanda had concluded, was the main danger: Astarte, drugged and addled, would likely be unable to avoid banging her head on the tower frame as she fell. It might not matter if they caught her or not. Amanda closed her eyes and prayed. *Please, Cam, get there.* She had watched him sprint up, down, and back up again. She imagined him knocking the old woman aside, or perhaps grabbing Astarte by the arm just before she tumbled. He was really their only hope. But the old crone was savvy, sly. She would not likely allow Cam to sneak up on her…

A scream jerked Amanda's eyes upwards even as her heart sank. She knew that voice, knew that scream. *Astarte.*

The image would remain etched in Amanda's mind for a lifetime: A body tumbled downward, pinwheeling, a yellow mass of fabric falling from the sky. But arching at an angle away from the tower, not straight down, as if someone had leapt. *Yellow fabric.* Amanda's heart sang. Astarte was wearing purple. Beautiful, gorgeous, eye-watering purple.

For a split-second Amanda imagined the tumbling, golden mass taking flight, flapping its wings and swooping away like some mythical dragon. But the dull thump of Jamila's body thudding to the ground beyond the blanket teams brought Amanda back to reality. Nobody would be taking flight today.

Amidst the wails and screams of the wide-eyed girls, many scurrying away from the inert body, Amanda didn't even bother to check on the old lady. Instead she waited for Cam to lower the stairs so she could race up to Astarte.

Nicolette leaned over the crumpled body of her mentor.

Somehow, she was still alive. "Did I have you fooled?" Jamila whispered, blood running down the side of her mouth.

Nicolette leaned closer. No way would she be able to survive such a fall. "Yes. I thought you were going to sacrifice Astarte."

Jamila coughed. A shaky hand reached for her Hamsa amulet. "I almost did. Only when ... your father told me ..." She spasmed, her eyes flickering.

"Told you what?"

"Told me ... Mormons ... on board." She exhaled, fighting for breath. "Wasn't sure ... which path Goddess ... had chosen for girl."

"I understand," Nicolette replied. Jamila had been wrestling with the question: How was Astarte to serve the Goddess? As a modern-day Ishtar, sacrificed so that the spirit of the Goddess might be resurrected? Or rather as the young prophetess, as her destiny seemed to proclaim? Apparently Jamila wasn't certain which path the Goddess had chosen until the very end, when she learned the Mormons were on board. Nicolette shook her head. What if the cell coverage had been bad and the text not come in?

Nicolette took her hand, felt the life force ebb from her mentor, surprised to be feeling a bit of sadness at the death of the person who, she no longer doubted, had killed her mother. Such a complex individual. Maniacal, even diabolical. But not, apparently, completely evil. Somehow, in the end, Jamila's devotion to the Goddess exceeded her thirst for vengeance on Cam and Amanda. The Goddess had chosen that Jamila rather than Astarte should be the public sacrifice, should be the death that sparked rebirth. And Jamila had complied. Had flung herself off the tower, an example to her adoring acolytes of true and absolute devotion to the Goddess. Again, not completely evil, even if maniacal.

Jamila convulsed in a final spasm, then her body went limp. Nicolette exhaled. She stood, took a blanket from one of the girls, and covered the body.

Nicolette stared down at the lump, at the once-vibrant life force that was no more. She would have liked to think the best of her mentor, would have liked to believe Jamila in the end would have spared the innocent girl even if the Goddess had asked for Astarte's sacrifice.

But she doubted it.

Chapter 12

"Mum, it's silly for you to sit in the back seat," Astarte said as they pulled out of the Venus School parking lot. Cam drove, with Astarte behind him, Amanda behind the passenger seat and Venus sprawled between them on the back seat.

Amanda took her hand. "I know. But please indulge me. I thought we might have lost you."

Cam sped around an access road curve. Astarte guessed he was anxious to put the school, and this entire weekend, behind them. "Can you slow down?" Astarte asked. "I'm still feeling nauseous." At least her head had cleared. Three hours standing atop a cold mountain answering questions from the police would do that. "What time is it?"

Cam replied, "Almost six."

"I'm hungry."

Amanda smiled. "That's a good sign."

They drove in silence for a few minutes. Astarte had a hundred questions, not the least of which was why Cam's hand was on that woman's bottom. But first she knew she needed to apologize. "I know I put you guys through a lot. I'm really sorry. I just wanted … to learn … how to be the Fortieth Princess." She exhaled, feeling the tears pooling in her eyes. "It's so hard to know what to do."

Amanda lifted her hand to her mouth and kissed it. "It *is* hard, darling. And you had to make some hard choices. We can talk more about it later, okay?"

Cam chimed in. "For now, we're just happy to have you back."

But Astarte wanted to talk now. "I don't remember much about being up on the tower. But when Jamila jumped, I remember screaming. It was like it woke me up."

"Probably a shot of adrenaline," Amanda said. "We're not programmed to witness things like that."

Astarte would probably never forget the site of the old woman vaulting over the tower railing. But she was oddly unbothered by it. Jamila was very old, and she felt like she needed to make the sacrifice to serve the Goddess. Maybe she did it as a lesson to Astarte. But Astarte knew one thing for certain: She wasn't jumping from any tower, no matter who asked. "I feel like having ice cream," Astarte announced.

Amanda turned. "For dinner?"

"That's just what I feel like."

"Fine with me," Cam said. "Assuming we can find one open."

"So what happens next?" Astarte asked. With Jamila dead, she was back to not having a mentor. But at least she could go back to reading as many books as she wanted.

Cam glanced back at her in the mirror. "Turns out Nicolette's father was working with Jamila. He's a high-ranking Freemason. So I'm guessing he, and maybe also Nicolette, will be showing up at our door pretty soon."

"Lovely," Amanda sighed. "We can all have tea." She turned again in her seat. "Do you still want to do this, Astarte? Still want to be the prophetess of the Goddess?"

Astarte nodded. "I learned a lot from my few days with Jamila." She stared out the window. "And it felt, I don't know, *like it fit me*. Like this is what I'm supposed to be doing." She shrugged. "Besides, it's my destiny. I'm the Fortieth Princess. I don't really have a choice."

"Of course you do," Amanda retorted. "We always have a choice. Our destiny is what we make it to be, what we want it to be."

"Well, that is what I want. I want my destiny to be to usher in the age of the Goddess." As they stopped at a traffic light, she pointed to a diner with an ice cream cone poster in the window. "But for now I just want an ice cream sundae."

After dinner and ice cream, they piled back into the SUV for the drive back to Westford, Astarte refusing to allow Amanda to stay in the back with her. "Dad looks like a fool, alone in the front. Maybe we should get him one of those hats." Being called a fool, with his family reunited, was the best thing that had happened to Cam all week.

Astarte fell asleep, Venus's snout on her lap, even before they hit the highway. Amanda reached over and put her hand on Cam's shoulder as he drove. "Not my favorite adventure," she said.

"No. But at least Jamila is out of our lives."

"You know, we may never know the truth about those journals. Or the treasure."

Cam pursed his lips. "As much as I'd like to believe they're legit, I think we have to assume she planted them as a way to prove the Templars were Goddess worshipers. At the very beginning, we asked who would possibly go to the trouble and expense to create such an elaborate hoax. Well, we have our answer. Sorry to sound like a lawyer, but she had motive, means and opportunity."

Amanda nodded. He guessed she had reached the same conclusion, but was leaving the door open a crack because she knew how excited he had been about validating the Sinclair story. She caressed his cheek. "I'm sorry. I know you wanted them to be real."

"Yeah, well, win some lose some."

"I just don't understand why Jamila needed to kill the Morville woman."

"Speaking of which, Nicolette was pretty sure Erin Donovan was driving the car that ran her mother off the road. She plans on calling Poulos."

Amanda sniffed. "Won't break my heart to see her locked up. Nicolette either, for that matter."

"But especially Erin. She almost took my head off with a baseball bat. And she seemed to actually enjoy tormenting us. Nicolette, at least, in the end did the right thing."

Amanda nodded. "And she lost her mother in all this. What a waste."

But it had worked. The Katherine Morville phone call and car crash had set Cam careening down a path directly into the trap Jamila had laid for him. "Jamila killed Nicolette's mom to up the stakes, to make me think this all was really serious. That was the hook she dangled in front of my face. And I bit down hard." He shook his head. "Someone was willing to kill for the journals. Heck, someone *died* for them. What better way to make me think they were real? Nobody would commit murder over a hoax, right? It really was a pretty good plan."

"And she hid the treasure to make it even more real."

"Again, who willingly throws away a million dollars in gold?" He slapped the steering wheel. "She really had me going. Salvatore had said the dirt looked funny, but we ignored it because we were so excited. And you know what else? Madame Segal must have been in on it. Think of the timing: Some French woman buys a house out of the blue in Westford, just in time for a treasure chest to be found on it. She must have been working with Jamila also. She's probably on a plane back to France right now." He paused and took a deep breath. "Not to mention the whole sex sting. Then the attorney-client privilege. Ugh. I really got my ass kicked this time."

"Not just you. She had us all fooled."

He risked the thin ice. "Yeah, well, I don't see any pictures of your hand on some guy's naked butt."

Amanda smiled. "When was the last time you checked your email?"

He took her hand off his shoulder and brought it to his lips. "Thanks. Thanks for being able to laugh all this off. I know this has been hard for you."

"Oh, you'll be paying for this one for quite a while." She smiled. "But for now, I'm just happy to have my family back."

They drove in silence for a few minutes, each drained from their ordeal. But there was much still to discuss. "So," Amanda said, "what happens to the Freemasons and their big ad campaign? The journals and all their references to the Goddess were a key part of that fifth ad, with you and your research."

Cam shrugged. "Well, I'm not going out on that limb. But there's still lots of evidence that the Templars were Goddess worshipers. So they can still do their whole real-men-don't-bathe-but-they-do-worship-the-Goddess thing. They just can't use the journals."

"Well, they could," she countered. "I know you think Jamila planted them, and I agree. But that doesn't necessarily mean they're fake. What if she somehow got hold of authentic Sinclair journals? Then used them to send Katherine Morville on her fatal road trip to Westford, where we picked them up and ran with them?"

"Why would she need to do that if they were real? Why not just show them to the world?"

"Because she wanted to ensnare you in all this, Cam. She wanted *you* to show them to the world. A respected researcher, a college professor. And not just you. Us. Including Astarte."

He nodded. "Okay, it's possible. But where would she get real journals?"

Amanda shrugged. "The woman had more money than God, and seemed to know all about these ancient sites. If the Sinclairs and the Templars really *were* Goddess worshipers, it stands to reason Jamila would know the families and maybe even their secrets."

Chuckling, Cam replied, "I suppose it's possible. As always, there's just enough here to keep us in the gray area." He shook his head. "I thought the treasure was the smoking gun. Complete with the Goddess figurine guarding the chest."

"If the journals are real, it still is."

"We're just going in circles. The only one who knows if it's all real or not is dead."

Amanda gazed out the window, chewing her lip. "That's not necessarily true. If we can find one thing in the journals, one thing that nobody could have known about in modern times, and then prove it is true, that would authenticate them, right?"

Cam nodded. "Yeah, I suppose it would."

She punched him playfully on the shoulder. "Okay then, we still have some work to do."

"But until then, no way can the Freemasons use the journals as proof the Templars were Goddess worshippers. It could blow up in their faces. This is too important to put the blinders on. If someone is going to go on record that the Sinclair journals are authentic, there has to be no doubt. Otherwise it's just wishful thinking." He shrugged. "Like I said, we're going in circles.

But for now, it's all an open question. The journals, the treasure, everything."

"Not everything." She smiled.

"What do you mean?"

Her face lit up. "The stone sanctum. Think about it. That's been here too long. Jamila could have planted the journals and the treasure chest in the past year as part of some elaborate plan, but those stones have been here for decades at least. You said so yourself."

He blinked. "Holy shit. You're right."

"I wager she somehow knew about the site and included it in the journals. But the site itself is authentic. And it clearly is some kind of Goddess worship shrine. Could be Native American, could be European, probably a combination of both. It resembles sites on both sides of the Atlantic. But either way, the location can't be denied."

Cam's excitement rose. "Yes. It's *exactly* where we know Sinclair and his group disembarked to climb Prospect Hill. That can't be a coincidence."

"So, there's your Goddess evidence. A Goddess shrine connected to the Sinclair expedition, connected to the Templars." She squeezed his thigh. "Maybe you can do that ad campaign after all."

Cam pulled off the highway in Westford under a bright, near-full moon. "So, we wake up tomorrow, and what do we do?" he asked.

"Wait for Lapierre, I suppose," Amanda replied. "It's going to take him a few months to get these ads going. In the meantime, we can paint the guest room."

Cam gave her a funny look. "Why? It's fine."

"No, it's just plain white. That won't do." She smiled and took his hand as he waited for a traffic light to turn. "So, in all the commotion, I haven't had a chance to tell you the news."

His eyes widened. "What news?"

She patted her stomach. "I'm pregnant."

"Wait, really?" He whooped, ignoring the green light. A car honked behind him. "Really?" he repeated.

"Yes. And please drive before we get rear-ended." She grinned. "I wasn't feeling great up in Vermont, but I figured it was because, well, because my life as I knew it was ending. But it turns out it was because a life was *beginning*."

Suddenly Cam's face darkened. He pulled his hand from hers. "Hold on. Today is April 1st. This isn't another of your April Fool's jokes is it?"

She raised her eyebrows. "Really? Is today the first?" Last year she had made arrangements with the sandwich shop Cam frequented to give out free scratch tickets to customers as a thank you. Cam had scratched a $20,000 winner. After buying lunch for everyone in line, he had breathlessly called Amanda with the news. She had, with equal breathlessness, informed him the ticket was a fake.

"You know it is, Amanda."

"And do you really think I'd be that cruel?" She smiled. "Though it'd serve you right after what you've put me through."

He nodded his head violently. "Given your track record, yes. I do. Come on, tell me the truth, Amanda. You can't joke about this."

"Okay," she laughed. "Even I am not that bloody cruel." She re-grasped his hand and lowered her voice. "Goddess willing, we are going to have a baby. Middle of December." She smiled. "Maybe even the winter solstice."

He took a deep breath. "I'm thrilled. But, honestly, the thought also scares the shit out of me. What kind of world will our baby be born into?"

Amanda glanced back at Astarte, still asleep in the back seat, but also still intent on fulfilling her destiny, on changing the world. Amanda slid her seat back, licked her thumb and rubbed away a dab of chocolate sauce from the cheek of the young prophetess. "Hopefully, into a world on its way to recovery."

The End

Author's Note

On a warm Sunday in June of 2016, a visitor arrived at the Westford Museum, thirty miles northwest of Boston. The visitor, an Illinois resident named Dianna Muir, claimed to be a descendant of Scottish Prince Henry Sinclair, purported to have journeyed across the Atlantic to Westford in 1399. Ms. Muir claimed further to be in possession of Sinclair family journals dating back to the mid-14th century, detailing this journey. The Museum docent, knowing of my interest in the Sinclair saga, phoned me immediately. Alas, I was out of town.

A few weeks later, the journals found their way into the hands of friend, fellow researcher and History Channel television personality, Scott Wolter (star of *America Unearthed*), in Minnesota. Scott shared photos of the journals with me, and together we read through them with breathless, though sometimes skeptical, amazement. We agreed the journals should be tested to determine their authenticity. But before Scott could make final arrangements to conduct these tests, Ms. Muir reported that the original journals had been stolen, leaving her with only photocopies and digital files.

Scott and his wife Janet have spent much of the past year investigating and examining these journal reproductions, attempting to determine their validity. In fact, these journals will likely be the subject of a new television series featuring Scott, tentatively entitled, *Hoax or History.*

I will allow Scott, and his viewing audience, to make the final determination as to the journals' authenticity. For me, the fascinating possibility that the journals of Prince Henry Sinclair exist triggers this, the seventh book in my "Templars in America" series, and allows me to revisit the Westford Knight legend. Perhaps the most intriguing aspect of the journals is the frequent reference in them to the ancient Goddess, worshiped throughout Europe and the Middle

East before the advent of Christianity. Is it possible that the medieval Sinclairs, builders of Roslyn Chapel and long associated with both the Knights Templar and Freemasonry, were actually secret Goddess worshipers?

Adding credence to this possibility is a discovery made shortly after Ms. Muir's visit to Westford. Over the course of 2016, a severe drought hit New England. This drought caused a local kettle pond to go dry, revealing a long-hidden and enigmatic arrangement of white stones laid out along the pond's bottom. The arrangement, which I refer to as the Grassy Pond "stone sanctum," is clearly ceremonial in nature, resembling ancient Goddess-worship sites on both sides of the Atlantic. To add to the mystery, the pond is only a short walk from the Westford Knight site. Credit goes to Cori Ryan and her husband Bill for discovering the "stone sanctum." Cori immediately sensed the site was ceremonial in nature and contacted me through my friend, Wayne Wagner. We continue to research this fascinating site.

As is the case with all the books in this series, if an artifact, site or object of art is pictured, it is real (except as specifically noted below). And If I claim it is of a certain age or of a certain provenance or features certain characteristics, that information is correct. Likewise, the historical and literary references are accurate. When, for example, I quote from the Old Testament or Masonic ritual, those quotes are accurate. How I use these artifacts and references to weave a story is, of course, where the fiction takes root. For inquisitive readers, perhaps curious about some of the specific historical assertions made and evidence presented in this story, more information is available here (in order of appearance in the story):

* The journal entries throughout this novel were written by me, and are not necessarily reflective of what is written in the journals discovered by Ms. Muir.

* As referenced on page 29, I relied heavily on the book, *The Alphabet Versus the Goddess,* by Leonard Shlain (Penguin, 1998), for the

premise that worship of the Goddess was negatively affected by cultures adopting a written alphabet. I recommend this book to interested readers.

* The owners of the America's Stonehenge site have graciously named the triangular wall stone featured on page 65 as the Brody Stone, as I was the first to identify this particular alignment.

* For information on, and a fascinating discussion of, the In Camera Stone and the Catskill Mountain discoveries discussed at pages 74-75, see *The Templar Mission to Oak Island and Beyond,* by Zena Halpern (2017).

* For more information on the three-lettered Tetragrammaton at Montreal's Basilica of Notre Dame, discussed on pages 77-78, see *The Templars' Legacy in Montreal, the New Jerusalem,* by Francine Bernier (Frontier, 2001).

* The poem on page 88 is from *The Golden Ass,* by Roman author Apuleius, written in the 2nd century AD.

* The discussion of the attorney-client privilege on page 107 is an accurate summary of the state of the law.

* The book discussed on page 153, *In Plain Sight,* by Gloria Farley (Isac Pr, 1993) is an excellent overview of the many American petroglyphs believed to evidence exploration of the continent prior to Columbus.

* For Zena Halpern's discussion of Tanit and the metal trade, referenced on pages 153-155, see remarks made at the 2009 Atlantic Conference, found here: https://www.migration-diffusion.info/article.php?id=169 .

* The information regarding the Egyptian marriage contract discussed at page 163-164 is derived from *When God Was a Woman,* by Merlin Stone (Barnes & Noble, 1976), which is an excellent resource for information on the ancient Goddess.

I have thoroughly enjoyed exploring the history of Goddess worship from ancient times down to today. Hopefully this novel has provided you with some entertainment and intellectual stimulation as well. Thanks for reading.

David S. Brody, August, 2017
Westford, Massachusetts

Dear Reader

I love to get reader feedback, both to help me continue to write in a way and about things that you (hopefully) enjoy and also to improve on the things you don't. Please feel free to reach out to me at dsbrody@comcast.net, and/or also to leave a review at Amazon or Goodreads. Thanks!

If you enjoyed *The Cult of Venus,* you may want to read the other books featuring Cameron and Amanda in my **"Templars in America"** series, all of which have been Kindle Top 10 Bestsellers in their categories:

Cabal of the Westford Knight
Templars at the Newport Tower (2009)
https://www.amazon.com/dp/B00GWTZYLS

Set in Boston and Newport, RI, inspired by artifacts evidencing that Scottish explorers and Templar Knights traveled to New England in 1398.

Thief on the Cross
Templar Secrets in America (2011)
https://www.amazon.com/dp/B006OQIXCG

Set in the Catskill Mountains of New York, sparked by an ancient Templar codex calling into question fundamental teachings of the Catholic Church.

Powdered Gold
Templars and the American Ark of the Covenant (2013)
https://www.amazon.com/dp/B00GWTYJ5K

Set in Arizona, exploring the secrets and mysteries of both the Ark of the Covenant and a manna-like powdered substance.

The Oath of Nimrod
Giants, MK-Ultra and the Smithsonian Coverup (2014)
https://www.amazon.com/dp/B00NW13QTG

Set in Massachusetts and Washington, DC, triggered by the mystery of hundreds of giant human skeletons found buried across North America.

The Isaac Question
Templars and the Secret of the Old Testament (2015)
https://www.amazon.com/dp/B016E3X2QK

Set in Massachusetts and Scotland, focusing on ancient stone chambers, the mysterious Druids and a stunning reinterpretation of the Biblical Isaac story.

Echoes of Atlantis
Crones, Templars and the Lost Continent (2016)
https://www.amazon.com/dp/B01MXJ0BNX

Set in New England, focusing on artifacts and other evidence indicating that the lost colony of Atlantis, featuring an advanced civilization, did exist 12,000 years ago.

Available at Amazon and as Kindle eBooks

Photo/Drawing Credits

Images used in this book are the property of the author, in the public domain, and/or provided courtesy of the following individuals (images listed in order of appearance in the story):

Page 48: America's Stonehenge Spring Equinox Sunset, Credit Matthew Cilento.

Pages 44-46: Alignment Maps, Credit Google.

Page 51: America's Stonehenge Serpent Wall, Credit Bethany Spreadborough.

Page 65: America's Stonehenge Equinox Sunrise Alignment, Credit Dennis Stone.

Page 88: "Venus Tree" Goddess Sculpture, Sculpture and Photo by Kimberly Scott.

Page 95: Grassy Pond Stone Sanctum, Credit Cori Ryan.

Page 155: Tanit Figures (New Mexico and North Carolina), Credit Gloria Farley.

Page 156: Tanit Figure (Vermont), Credit Zena Halpern.

Page 156: Tanit Figure (Tal Dor): Credit Ephraim Stern.

Page 187: Minoan Snake Goddess: Credit C Messier.

Acknowledgements

Readers may not realize that the finished version of a novel is often the fifth or sixth draft of the story, each draft becoming iteratively improved (hopefully) over the prior version. Those tasked with reading these early versions, armed only with red pens and caffeine, perform an invaluable task. I want to offer heartfelt thanks to my team of early readers (listed alphabetically): Jeffrey Brody, Renee Brody, Spencer Brody, Michael Carr, Jeanne Scott, Richard Scott, Mary Yannetti and Michael Yannetti.

For assistance and guidance in researching the ancient Goddess and her symbolism, I owe a huge debt of gratitude to my dear friend, Zena Halpern. Other experts in their fields who assisted and guided me include (alphabetically): Richard Lynch, Dennis Stone, Janet Wolter, Scott Wolter and Michael Yannetti. The inclusion of their names in this paragraph list does not necessarily indicate these experts agree with my research conclusions, but it does mean they were invaluable to me in my efforts to write this book.

For other authors out there looking to navigate their way through the publishing process, I can't speak highly enough about Amy Collins and her team at New Shelves Books—real pros who know the business and are a pleasure to work with.

Lastly, to my wife, Kim: This is my tenth novel, and none of them would have been possible without you. It is no easy manner criticizing a spouse's creative work. To paraphrase Theodore Roosevelt, you have become adept at editing softly while carrying a big red pen. Thanks for your patience, your insight, your candor, your support, your guidance and, most of all, your love.

Made in the USA
Middletown, DE
03 March 2024

50748866R00179